Abou

Christine Rimmer ca
around. She tried every
telephone sales. Now sl
her perfectly. She insists
a job—she was merely gaining "life experience" for her future as a novelist. Christine lives with her family in Oregon. Visit her at christinerimmer.com

New Zealand born, to Dutch immigrant parents, **Yvonne Lindsay** became an avid romance reader at the age of thirteen. Now, married to her "blind date" and with two fabulous children, she remains a firm believer in the power of romance. Yvonne feels privileged to be able to bring to her readers the stories of her heart. In her spare time, when not writing, she can be found with her nose firmly in a book, reliving the power of love in all walks of life. She can be contacted via her website, www.yvonnelindsay.com

After years of living in a small inland city in New South Wales, Australia, **Jennie Adams** re-embraced the country lifestyle of her childhood. When she isn't writing Jennie dedicates her time to promoting the natural wonders of her new area and encouraging others to visit and enjoy what now constitutes her backyard—large tracts of native bushland, flora and fauna reserves, and wetlands. Jennie's family has grown to embrace in-laws (and outlaws, as she always jokes), sisters, daughters and brothers of the heart. Find Jennie at joybyjennie.com

The Single Dads
COLLECTION

July 2019

August 2019

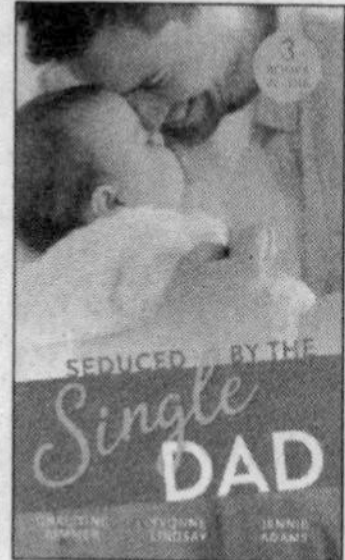

September 2019

October 2019

November 2019

December 2019

Seduced by the Single Dad

CHRISTINE RIMMER

YVONNE LINDSAY

JENNIE ADAMS

MILLS & BOON

First Published in Great Britain 2019
By Mills & Boon, an imprint of HarperCollins*Publishers*
1 London Bridge Street, London, SE1 9GF

ISBN: 978-0-263-27616-9

0919

MIX
Paper from responsible sources
FSC™ C007454

This book is produced from independently certified FSC™ paper to ensure responsible forest management.

For more information visit: www.harpercollins.co.uk/green

Printed and bound in Spain
by CPI, Barcelona

THE GOOD GIRL'S SECOND CHANCE

CHRISTINE RIMMER

For Kimberly Fletcher, AKA Kimalicious,
Kimalovely, Kimhilarious--and more.
You warm my heart and make me smile.
I'm so happy to call you my friend.
And this one's for you!

Chapter One

Chloe Winchester woke with a startled cry.

She popped straight up in bed as her heart trip-hammered against her ribs. Splaying a hand to her heaving chest, she sent a frantic, frightened glance around the darkened room.

No threat. None.

Just her shadowed bedroom in the middle of the night, silvery moonlight streaming in the high, narrow window over the curtained sliding glass door.

"Nothing, it's nothing," she whispered aloud between gasps for air. "A nightmare." More specifically, it was *the* nightmare, the one starring her ultrasuccessful, über-controlling, bad-tempered ex-husband, Ted.

Not real, she reminded herself. Not anymore.

Ted Davies was the past. He held no threat for her now.

Chloe smoothed a shaking hand over her hair, pressed her cool fingers to her flushed cheek and took long, deep breaths until her racing heart slowed. Finally, when her pulse had settled to a normal rhythm and the dew of fear-sweat had dried on her skin, she plumped her pillow, settled back under the covers and closed her eyes.

Sleep didn't come.

She tossed and turned for a while, and then tried to make herself lie still as she stared up at the ceiling and willed herself to feel drowsy again.

Not happening.

Finally, with a weary sigh, she shoved back the covers and went to the kitchen. She heated milk and sweetened it with honey. Then she carried her mug to the living area, where she turned a single lamp on low. Gazing out the two stories of windows that faced her back deck, she sipped slowly and tried to clear her mind of everything but the beauty of the Colorado night.

She could see a light on in the big house down the hill from her. Quinn Bravo lived there with his little daughter, Annabelle, and that funny old guy, Manny. They'd moved in a few months before.

Chloe smiled to herself. So. Somebody down there couldn't sleep, either. Maybe Quinn? Could the tough martial arts star suffer from bad dreams, too?

Unlikely. Quinn "the Crusher" Bravo was world-famous for taking down the most unbeatable opponents. No mere nightmare would dare keep him awake. She wished she could be more like him, impervious and strong. He seemed so very self-confident in his quiet, watchful way.

And so different, really, from the boy he'd once been, the one she remembered from when they were children, the wild, angry boy with a chip the size of Denver on his shoulder who was always getting in fights.

Different also from the boy he'd become by high school, still rough-edged, but quieter, with a seething intensity about him. She'd avoided him then, the same as she had when they were children. All the nice girls avoided dangerous and unpredictable Quinn Bravo.

Even if, secretly, he made their hearts beat faster…

Quinn Bravo stood in his living room wearing an old pair of sweats, worn mocs and a Prime Sports and Fitness T-shirt. He stared blankly out the window at the faint gleam of light from the house up the hill. Beyond that house, the almost-full face of the moon hung suspended above the peaks of the Colorado mountains.

He should go back to bed. But he knew he wouldn't sleep. He couldn't stop thinking about what his four-year-old daughter had asked him when he tucked her in that night.

A faint movement beyond the wall of windows up the hill caught his eye. Must be Chloe. She lived there alone. Beautiful, smart Chloe Winchester, who'd gone off to college at Stanford and married some big-shot lawyer as everyone always knew she would. The big shot had carried her off to live the high life down in Southern California.

Quinn didn't know the whole story. He just knew that the marriage hadn't lasted. When he moved back to town several months ago, there was Chloe, minus the rich husband, with no kids, on her own in her old hometown, living in the shadow of the Rockies on the street up the hill from him.

Maybe a little fresh air would clear his head, relax him.

Quinn pulled open the French doors that led onto the back deck. It was a clear July night, almost balmy, the moon very close to full. He stepped outside and quietly shut the doors behind him. Crossing to the deck railing, he folded his arms across his chest, braced his legs wide and stared up at the light in Chloe's house. He indulged himself, allowing his mind to dwell on her a little, to wonder about her, about what might have messed up the smooth trajectory of her life and brought her back to Justice Creek alone.

True, it was none of his business, whatever had happened to bring Chloe back where she'd started. But focusing on what might have gone wrong for a woman he didn't really know took his mind off his little girl and her questions that he had no clue how to answer.

He noted movement again up there on the hill, a glass door sliding open.

And out she came, the one and only Chloe Winchester. Damn, she was gorgeous, even from a hundred yards away. Gorgeous, even in a baggy pink shirt. That long golden hair shone silvery in the moonlight and her fine, bare legs gleamed.

Quinn had no time for chasing women. He had a daughter to raise and a new business to build. But hot damn. Any man with a pulse would want to cut himself off a nice big slice of that.

Chloe went to the railing and rested her hands on it. For a long count of ten, she stared down at him as he looked up at her. She wasn't inviting him up exactly. But he definitely felt the pull.

And how could he help enjoying the moment? Hell. Chloe Winchester giving him the look? Never in a million years would he have guessed that would happen.

And the more they stared at each other, the more certain he became that a hundred yards was too much distance between them. He would much rather look at her up close. Manny was home if Annabelle woke up.

So he went back to the doors, pushed one open and engaged the lock, drawing it shut and hearing the click that meant his daughter was safe inside. When he turned again toward the woman up the hill, she hadn't moved. She remained at the railing, her head tipped slightly down and aimed in his direction, almost certainly watching him.

Fair enough, then.

He descended the back stairs, glancing up when he reached the bottom. She hadn't moved.

So he crossed his small patch of landscaped ground and began ascending the hill between their houses, skirting rocky outcroppings and ponderosa pines, the native grasses whispering beneath the leather soles of his mocs. He took it slow, glancing up at her now and then, expecting any moment that she would turn and retreat inside—at which point he would calmly wheel around and go home where he belonged.

But Chloe stood her ground.

When he reached the base of the stairs leading up to her deck, he paused, giving her a chance to…what?

Run away? Order him off her property?

When she only continued to gaze directly down at him, her eyes steady, her expression composed, he mounted the steps.

And she did move then. She came toward him, meeting him at the top where the steps opened wide. "Quinn," she said.

He nodded. "Chloe."

"Pretty night."

"Yeah, it is."

"How have you been?"

"Doing okay. You?"

A tiny smile flickered at the corner of her lush mouth. "Getting by." With that, she turned and led the way to a pair of cedar armchairs positioned close together in front of her great room windows. She dropped into one of those chairs, a move so graceful it stole his breath, and then gestured with a small, regal sweep of her hand for him to sit beside her.

He sat. And for several minutes, neither of them spoke. They stared up at the clear night sky and the milky smear of the faraway stars. The slight breeze brought her scent to him—like some exotic flower. Jasmine, maybe. And not only that, something…a little bit musky and a whole lot womanly.

Finally, she spoke again. "What keeps *you* awake, Quinn?" Her voice was low for a woman, low and calm and pleasing.

He turned and looked at her. Her eyes were a pale, glowing shade of blue, her face a smooth oval, that tempting mouth so soft and full. She really was a prize, every red-blooded man's fantasy of the perfect woman, a woman who would make a man a beautiful home and provide him with handsome, smart, upwardly mobile children.

And as to her question? He didn't plan to answer her. But then he opened his mouth and the truth fell out. "My daughter asked about her mother for the first time tonight. I'm trying to decide what to tell her."

Chloe hummed, a thoughtful sort of sound. "Her name is Annabelle, right?"

"That's right."

"So I'm assuming Annabelle doesn't know her mother?"

"No, she doesn't. I doubt she ever will."

"Ah." Chloe waited, her head tipped to the side, her eyes alert, giving him a chance to say more. When he remained silent, she suggested, "Tell her only the truth, but tell it carefully. She's how old?"

"Four."

"She wants to know that you love her. She wants to know she's safe and that her mother loves her, too—or would, if she knew her. She wants to know it's not her fault, whatever happened that you and her mother aren't together and her mother isn't in her life." Chloe smiled. God. What he wouldn't give to taste that mouth. "But don't load it on her all at once. Well-meaning parents have a tendency to overexplain. Try to get a sense of what she's ready for and just answer the questions she actually asks."

He faced front again and stared out at the night. She was so tasty to look at, with full breasts, the points of her nipples visible under that pink shirt. She had endless legs, slender arms and that perfect angel's face. He needed to take all that beauty in careful doses. He said, "I thought you didn't have kids."

"I don't. But I like kids." The beautiful voice was weighted with sadness. "Before I moved back home, I did volunteer day care with a San Diego family shelter. I helped out with special-needs children, too. And in college, I took just about every child development class available. I had big plans in college. I was going to be the perfect wife to a very important man—and the mother of at least three healthy, bright, happy children."

Strange. Looking away wasn't working for him. Why deprive himself of the sight of her? He turned his head and faced her once more, something down inside him going tight and hot when he met her eyes. "I remember you always seemed like you knew exactly where you were going."

"Yes, I did. I used to think I knew everything, used to be so sure of how my life would be." A husky chuckle escaped her. The sound rubbed along his nerve endings, stirring up sparks. "And that's what keeps *me* up nights, Quinn. All my big plans that came to dust…"

Somewhere in the distance, a coyote howled. Quinn

considered what, exactly, he ought to say next, if anything. He was still trying to find the right words when she stood.

He let his gaze track upward over those fine legs and her little pink terry-cloth shorts, over the womanly curves under the oversize shirt. The view was amazing. And he needed to thank her for the advice, say good-night and hustle his ass back down the hill.

But then she offered him her delicate, ladylike hand. He eyed it warily, glancing up again to meet those ice-blue eyes. No mistaking what he saw in those eyes: invitation.

It was the middle of the night and he didn't have time for this. He should be home in his own damn bed.

So, was he going to turn such beauty down?

Not. A. Chance.

He took the hand she offered. Her skin was cool and silky. Heat shot up his arm, down through the center of him and straight to his groin. Stifling a groan, he rose to stand with her.

She turned quickly, pulling him along behind her, pushing open the slider, leading him inside, across her two-story great room and down a short hall to her bedroom, which was as beautiful and tasteful as the woman herself, so feminine and orderly—except for the tangled covers on the unmade bed.

She bent and turned on the nightstand lamp, then stood tall to meet his eyes once more. "Somehow I feel…safe with you," she said in that fine alto voice that turned him on almost as much as her face and her body did. "I've noticed…" Her voice trailed away. She glanced down, swallowed and then, finally, raised her head to meet his gaze again.

He couldn't resist. He lifted a hand, nice and slow so

as not to spook her, and ran the back of his index finger along the silky skin of her throat. She trembled and sucked in a sharp little gasp of breath, but didn't duck away. And he asked, "You've noticed what?"

Her mouth twisted, as though the words were hard to come by. "Since you, uh, came back to town, you seem… I don't know. So calm. Kind of thoughtful. I admire that, I really do."

What could he say to that? Thanks? That seemed kind of lame, so he didn't say anything, just ran the back of his finger down the outside of her arm, enjoying the satiny feel of her skin, loving the way her mouth formed a soft O and her eyes went hazy in response to his touch.

She said, "I've been with one man in my life—my husband, who was supposed to be loving and tender and protective, but turned out to be one rotten, abusive, cheating SOB." She moved slightly away from him again, reaching over to pull open the bedside drawer. "I've been out a few times with nice men, in the year since I came home. I keep thinking I need to take the plunge again, take a chance again and be with someone new. So I bought these." She raised her hand and he saw that she held a strip of condoms. They unrolled from her palm with a snap. "To be prepared, you know?" A soft, rueful smile. "I haven't used a single one. I didn't want to. It never felt right. But tonight, with you… Quinn, I…" Her fine voice gone breathless, she said, "Back in high school, sometimes, I used to think about what it might be like, to be with you…"

Those words hit him right where he lived. "I used to think about you, too, Chloe."

Her amazing face glowed up at him. "You did?"

"Oh, yeah." Not that she ever would have gone out with him if he asked her. She'd had her plans for her life and they didn't include a wannabe cage fighter who could barely read. Plus, her snotty parents would've disowned her if she started in with one of Willow Mooney's boys, the ones they called the *bastard Bravos* because his mother hadn't married his father, Frank Bravo, until after Frank's rich first wife, Sondra, died.

Uh-uh. No way Linda Winchester would have let her precious only daughter get near him, one of Willow's boys—and the "slow" one, at that. And Chloe was always a good girl who did what her mama expected of her.

Chloe scanned his face, her expression suddenly anxious. "I have this feeling that somehow I should explain myself, give you a better reason to stay with me tonight..."

"Uh-uh." He stepped even closer—close enough that her body touched his. Her soft breasts brushed his chest, and the dizzying scent of her swam around him. Slowly, carefully, he lifted his hand and speared his fingers into that glorious mane of yellow hair. Like a curtain of silk, that hair. He loved the feel of it so much that he balled his fist and wrapped the thick strands around his wrist, pulling her even closer, right up against him, nice and tight.

"Oh!" she said on a shaky breath, baby blue eyes saucer-wide staring up into his.

All that softness and beauty, his for the night. He bent enough to suck in a deep breath through his nose. God, the scent of her. She smelled of everything womanly, everything most wanted—everything he'd never thought to hold, not even for a single night. He buried his face against her long, silky throat. "You don't need to explain anything, angel." He nuzzled her neck and then scraped his teeth across her tender skin. She gasped. He muttered, "Not a damn thing."

"I'm not an angel."

"Yeah, you are."

"Just for tonight, yeah?" She wrapped those slim arms around him, clutching him to her, tipping her head back, offering him more, offering him everything. "Just this one time…"

"However you want it."

"Just kiss me. Just…hold me. Just make me forget."

Chapter Two

Quinn took her by the shoulders and gently set her at arm's length. She swayed a little on her bare feet, gazing up at him, breathless, eyes starry with need.

He said, "First, I want to see you."

A soft gasp. "Okay."

"All of you."

"Okay."

He took her big pink shirt by the hem. "Raise your arms."

She obeyed without hesitation. He lifted the shirt up over her head, past the pink-painted tips of her fingers and tossed it away. Her hair settled, so shiny and thick, spilling past her shoulders, down her back, over her breasts. She let her arms fall back to her sides and gazed up at him expectantly.

Impossible. Chloe Winchester, naked to the waist, standing right in front of him.

He cupped one fine, full breast in his hand and flicked

the pretty nipple. His breath clogged in his throat, and the ache in his groin intensified. "You're so damn beautiful, Chloe."

"I..." She didn't seem to know what to say next. Which was fine. He was getting one night with her. And it wasn't going to be about what either of them might have to say.

He leaned close again, because he couldn't stop himself. He stuck out his tongue and licked her temple. She moaned. He blew on the place he'd just moistened, guiding her hair out of the way and whispering into the perfect pink shell of her ear "Take off those little shorts."

She whipped them down and off in an instant, so fast that he couldn't help smiling. And then she stood tall again, completely naked in front of him, an answering smile trembling its way across her mouth. "Quinn?"

"Shh. Let me look."

She widened her eyes—and then she shut them. And then she just stood there, eyes closed tight, and let him gaze his fill.

Touching followed. How could he help reaching for her? She was smooth and round and firm and soft. And she was standing right in front of him, Chloe Winchester, who had starred in more than one of his wild and impossible sexual fantasies when he was growing up.

He pulled her close again, wrapped his arms around the slim, yet curvy shape of her and pressed his lips into her hair. "Beautiful."

She lifted her face and gazed up at him. "You, too, please." He must have looked confused, because she added, "I want to see you, too."

He chuckled and stepped back. "Yes, ma'am." It took about ten seconds. He kicked off the mocs, reached back over his shoulders and pulled his shirt up and off. He eased the sweats over his erection and pushed them down, dropping them to the floor and stepping free of them.

"Oh," she said. "Oh, Quinn…" She reached out and ran her palm over his belly and then over the series of tats that covered his left arm. And then she touched the one for Annabelle, the angel's wings and the green vines, the trumpet flowers and his little girl's name, written right where it should be written, over his heart. "I never thought…you and me. Like this…?"

"Hey. Me, neither."

"Life can be so awful."

"Yeah."

"But then there are surprising, magical moments—like this one, huh?"

He nodded. "Yeah." He turned and shoved the tangled sheets and blankets out of the way. And then he took her by the waist, lifted her and set her on the bed. "Lie down."

She obeyed, stretching out on her side with a sigh. He went down to the mattress with her. He kissed her, tasting her mouth for the first time, finding it as sweet as the rest of her. Her tongue came out to play and for a while, they just lay there, on their sides, kissing and kissing, as if nothing else mattered in the whole damn world, nothing but his mouth and her mouth, the scrape of white teeth, the tangle of tongues.

One night they had together. He wanted to stretch every second just short of the breaking point, enjoy every touch, every sigh, every soft, tempting curve. He wanted to share her breath and the tender, urgent beat of her heart.

After he kissed her mouth, he kissed her everywhere else, too, taking forever about it, getting carried away, using his teeth as well as his tongue. He knew he left marks, marks he soothed with softer, gentler kisses. She never once objected when he used his teeth.

Far from it. She gasped and cried out her pleasure, clutching him close, telling him "Yes" and "More" and "Again, Quinn. Oh, again…"

He gave her more. More strokes, more kisses, trailing his mouth down the center of her, biting a little, trying not to be too rough, opening her, dipping his tongue in. He pushed her legs wide and settled between them for a long time.

She came twice then, as he played her with his mouth and his hands. She had his name on her lips, over and over. He loved that most of all: Chloe Winchester, calling his name as she came.

After that second time, when she was boneless and open for him, he rose to his knees between her spread thighs. Ripping the first condom off the strip, he took off the wrapper and rolled it down over his length, easing it into place nice and tight. She stared up at him, dazed and flushed and softly smiling.

"Quinn." She reached for him. "Please…"

And he went down to her, taking most of his weight on his arms. She slipped her hand between them, closing those slim fingers around him. He was the one groaning then, the one calling *her* name.

She guided him in. He sank into her slowly, carefully, little by little, stretching her and the moment, making it last. She felt so good—better than anything he'd ever known, soft and welcoming, and a little bit tight.

He varied the rhythm, watching her face, matching his strokes to her pleasured moans, her hungry cries. Somehow he stayed with her, until she went over for the third time. After that, there was no holding back. He was rough and fast, and she clung to him, nice and tight, all the way to the peak and over the edge.

She cradled him close then, stroking his shoulders and his arms, whispering "So good. Just right," laughing a little. "Who knew, really? Whoever would have thought…?"

"Beautiful," he said. "Never would have guessed."

They must have dozed for a while.

He woke to find her sleeping peacefully, one arm across his chest. He'd been hoping that maybe they would have time to play some more.

But it was later than he'd thought. The clock by the bed said 5:05 in the morning. The first glow of daylight would be bleeding the night from the sky all too soon. The houses in their neighborhood were spaced far apart, built to conform to the shape of the land, with plenty of big trees between them. He might make it down the hill in broad daylight with no one the wiser.

But why take that chance? It was nobody's business, this one unforgettable night they'd shared.

With care, he eased out from under her arm. She sighed and rolled to her back, but didn't wake. He slid from the bed. Before settling the covers over her, he stole another long glance at her and got struck by a last hot bolt of pure lust at the sight of the faint marks he'd left on her perfect breasts, her pretty belly.

They would fade soon, those marks. He tried not to wish…

Uh-uh. Never mind. One night. That was the deal.

He pulled on his clothes and went out the way he'd come in, noting that she hadn't rearmed the alarm on the wall by the slider when she led him inside.

Good. That meant he didn't have to wake her to go. He locked the slider and then went out through the front door, which he could also lock behind him, thus securing her inside.

He ran around the side of the house and then on down the hill.

At home, he got the spare key from its hiding place under the stairs and let himself in. The house was just as he'd left it. Silent and dark.

He stepped inside and shut the doors with barely a sound—and found Manny, his former trainer and long-time business partner, sitting in one of the big chairs by the moss rock fireplace. The old fighter switched on the lamp beside him. He wore a knowing grin on that road-map of a face. "Hey, Crush. Where you been?"

Quinn locked the doors. "Since when are you my mother?"

Manny rumbled out a low laugh. "You and that gorgeous uptown blonde up the hill? I never had a clue."

"I don't know what you're talkin' about." Quinn headed for the stairs.

Manny watched him go. "She's a fine one. I find I am lookin' at you with new respect."

"Night, Manny."

"Got news for you, Crush. It's tomorrow already."

Quinn just kept walking. Manny's knowing cackle followed him up the stairs.

Chloe was sound asleep when her alarm went off at seven.

She woke with a smile, feeling thoroughly rested and a little bit sore. If it weren't for that soreness and the small, already-fading red marks and bruises on her breasts and stomach, she almost might have been able to tell herself that the night before was all a dream.

Not that she wanted to deny what had happened. It had been glorious. She'd loved every minute of it.

As she sat up and stretched, yawning with gusto, she couldn't help wishing she hadn't told Quinn that she only wanted one night. Because he was remarkable. He'd given her hope that love and passion and tenderness weren't all just some fantasy, some bright, naive dream that could never come true.

She would love to spend more time with him.

But she let her arms drop and her shoulders droop with a sigh.

No. They had a deal and she would stick by it. He'd been great and the sex had been mind-blowing. Now she knew for certain that there were better lovers out there than Ted. She would be grateful for that and eventually, maybe, she'd find someone who made her want to take another chance on forever.

She got ready for work and then had breakfast. The house phone rang just as she was heading out the door. Probably her mother. She'd check her messages later and call her back then.

As she was pulling out of the driveway, her cell rang. She slipped the SUV into Park and checked the display. With a sigh, she gave in and answered. "Hi, Mom. Just on my way over to the showroom."

"But it's not even nine yet," Linda Winchester complained. "You have time to stop by the house. Let me fix you some breakfast."

"I've already eaten. And I have to get the shop opened."

"Sweetheart, it's your shop. You're the boss. No need to rush over there at the crack of dawn."

"Come on, Mom. A successful business doesn't run itself." Not that Your Way Interior Design was all that successful. Yet.

"I hardly see you lately. We need to chat."

Chatting with her mother was the *last* thing she needed. They hadn't been getting along all that well since Chloe's divorce. And it had only gotten worse after she returned to Justice Creek. Linda knew what was right for her only child and she never missed an opportunity to lecture Chloe on all she'd done wrong. And somehow, whenever they "chatted," her mother always managed to bring up Ted and the perfect life Chloe had thrown away.

"Mom, I'll have to call you later. I need to get to work."

"But, sweetheart, I want to—"

"Call you tonight, Mom."

Her mother was still protesting as Chloe disconnected the call.

She drove to her showroom and unlocked the doors at nine, an hour before most of the businesses on Central Street opened. She had a good location and an attractive shop, with neutral walls and sleek, modern cabinetry and red and yellow accents to give it energy and interest. Her motto was Your Space, Your Way. She had attractive displays, and plenty of them, lots of table space for spreading out samples. And she was trained in every aspect of home design, from blueprints up.

Her website looked great and she stayed active on Facebook, Pinterest, Twitter and Tumblr. She kept a blog where she gave free tips on great ways to spiff up your living space. During the school year, she ran a workshop right there in her showroom for high school students interested in interior design. She contributed her expertise to local churches, helping them spruce up their Sunday school rooms and social halls. And she worked right along with the other shop owners in Justice Creek on various chamber of commerce projects.

Still, it took time to build a business. Chloe had found

a real shark of a divorce lawyer who'd put the screws to Ted and got her a nice lump settlement, which Chloe had asked for. The onetime payout was less than monthly alimony would have been in total, but the last thing she wanted was to be getting regular checks from Ted. With the settlement, she'd been able to cut ties with him completely.

She'd tried to spend her money wisely. She loved her house, which she'd redone herself, and she was proud of her business. But the past couple of months, she had more to worry about than putting Ted behind her and whether or not there might someday be love in her future.

Chloe's nest egg was shrinking. Your Way needed to start paying *its* way.

That day, as it turned out, was better than most. She had steady walk-in traffic. A new couple in town came in and hired her to do all the window treatments in the house they'd just bought. She scheduled three appointments to give estimates: two living room redesigns and a kitchen upgrade. When her assistant, Tai Stockard, a design student home from CU for the summer, came in at one, Chloe sent her to the Library Café for takeout paninis. It was turning into a profitable day and they might as well enjoy a nice lunch.

Chloe went home smiling—until she remembered she owed her mother a call.

"Come on over for dinner," her mother coaxed. "I've got lamb chops and twice-baked potatoes just the way you love them. We're leaving for Maui tomorrow." Chloe's mom and dad would be gone for two weeks, staying at a luxury resort where her mother could enjoy the spa and the lavish meals and her father could play golf. "I want to see you before we go."

Chloe went to dinner at the house where she'd grown

up. It wasn't that bad. Linda managed not to say a single word about Ted. And it was good to see her dad. An orthodontist with a successful practice, Doug Winchester had a dry sense of humor and never tried to tell his only daughter how to live her life.

By nine, Chloe was back at home. She got ready for bed, settled under the covers with the latest bestseller and tried not to let her mind wander to the question of what Quinn Bravo might be doing that night.

Quinn heard the soft whisper of small feet across the tiled floor as he stared out the window at the single light shining from inside Chloe's house. "Go back to bed, Annabanana," he said softly without turning.

"I can't."

"Why not?"

"The monsters are very noisy. And I'm not a banana. You know that, Daddy."

"Yes, you are." He turned and dropped to a crouch. "You're my favorite banana."

Dragging her ancient pink blanket and her one-eyed teddy bear, Annabelle marched right up to him and put one of her little hands on his shoulder. "No, I'm not. I'm a *girl*."

He leaned closer and whispered, "Ah. Gotta remember that."

"Pick me up, Daddy," she instructed. "Get the flashlight."

He wrapped his arms around her and stood. She giggled and hugged his neck, shoving her musty old teddy bear into the side of his face. He detoured to the kitchen, where he got the flashlight from a drawer. Then he returned to the living room and mounted the stairs.

She didn't object as he carried her up to her room, set

her down on the bed, flicked on the lamp and then pulled the covers up over her and the stuffed bear, smoothing the ancient blanket atop her butterfly-printed bedspread.

"Closet," she said, when he bent to kiss her plump cheek.

He went to the closet, pushed the door open and shone the light around inside. "Nothing in here."

"You have to tell them," she said patiently. "You know that."

He ran the light over her neatly hung-up dresses and the row of little shoes and said in his deepest, gruffest voice, "Monsters, get lost." He rolled the door shut. "That should do it."

But Annabelle didn't agree. "Now under the bed."

So he knelt by the bed and lifted up the frilly bed skirt and shone the light around underneath. "Holiday Barbie's down here. With her dress over her head."

The bed skirt on the other side rustled as small hands lifted it and Annabelle appeared, upside down. "Oops." She snatched up the doll and let the bed skirt drop. "Okay, tell them."

"Monsters, get lost." He gave a long, threatening growl for good measure. On the bed, his daughter laughed, a delighted peal of sound that had him smiling to himself. "So, all right," he said. "They're gone." And then he got up and sat on the bed and tucked her in again, bending close to press a kiss on her cheek and breathe in the little-girl smell of her. Toothpaste and baby shampoo, so familiar. So sweet. "Anything else?" he asked, suddenly worried about how she might answer, recalling Chloe's wise advice of the night before. *She wants to know it's not her fault, whatever happened that you and her mother aren't together and her mother isn't in her life…*

Annabelle shook her head. “That’s all.”

He felt equal parts guilt and relief. Guilt that he wasn’t as good a father as Annabelle deserved. Relief that he wouldn’t have to tackle the tough questions tonight, after all. “You know there are really no monsters in your room, right?”

She nodded slowly. “But I like it when you scare them away.”

He got up. “Sleep now, princess.”

She beamed at him. “Princess is good. Not banana.”

“Close your eyes…”

“I want a princess room. All the princesses. Snow White and Cinderella and Mulan and Elsa and Belle and Merida and—”

“Time for sleep. Close your eyes…” He heard Chloe’s rich alto again, as though she whispered in his ear. *She wants to know that you love her.* “I love you, princess.”

“Love you, Daddy.” With a little sigh, Annabelle closed her eyes. He turned off the light and shut the door silently behind him on the way out.

Back downstairs, all was quiet. Manny had gone to Boulder for the night to visit his current lady friend. Quinn took up his vigil at the wall of windows in the living room. Up at Chloe’s the light remained on. He could see it glowing through the pale curtains that covered the slider in her bedroom. He pictured her, wearing that big pink shirt, propped up against the pillows in her bed, with her laptop or maybe a good book, which she would read effortlessly, turning the pages fast to find out what would happen next.

And then, well, after last night, he couldn’t help picturing her other ways—like, say, naked beneath him, moaning his name in that low, sexy voice that drove him crazy. He told himself it was a good thing that Manny wasn't there to watch over Annabelle if he stepped out.

Because climbing that hill again?

Way too much on his mind.

"Crush, I gotta say it," Manny grumbled. "I'm disappointed in you."

It was Friday night, five nights since the one Quinn had spent with Chloe. Annabelle had been tucked safely in bed, the monsters chased away. Quinn and Manny sat out on the deck having a beer under the clear, starry sky. Quinn took a long, cool swallow and said nothing.

Manny wiggled his white eyebrows. They grew every which way and he never bothered to trim them. "Aren't you gonna ask me why?"

Quinn gave a low chuckle. "We both know you'll tell me anyway."

Manny snorted. "Yes, I will. I've spent over a decade makin' sure you learn what you need to know. No reason to change now."

Quinn only looked at him, waiting.

Manny announced, "Romance is like everything else worth doin' in life. You gotta follow up, put some energy into it, or it goes nowhere."

"I don't know why you're telling *me* this."

"I'll give you a hint. Chloe Winchester. Only a fool would pass up his chance with a woman like that."

"That's given that he *had* a chance in the first place."

"See there? That's defeat talkin'. Quinn the Crusher, he spits in the face of defeat."

"Quinn the Crusher retired, remember?"

"From the Octagon, sure. But not from life. Last time I checked, you still got a pulse."

"Leave it alone, Manny."

Manny did no such thing. "A woman like that, she lets you in her house in the middle of the night, you got a chance. You got more than a chance."

"You need to stop sticking your nose in where it doesn't belong. Somebody's likely to break it."

"Won't be the first time." A raspy cackle. "Or the second or the third." Manny swiped a gnarled, big-knuckled hand back over his buzz cut and then took a pull off the longneck in his other fist. "I will repeat. Momentum is everything."

Quinn got up from his deck chair and headed for the French doors. "Night, Manny."

"Where you going?"

"I'm halfway through *A Tale of Two Cities*." He had it in audio book, and tried to get in a few chapters a night. Little by little, he was working his way through the great books of Western literature.

Manny wasn't impressed with Quinn's highbrow reading. "It's just dandy, you improving your mind and all, but a man needs more than a book to keep him warm at night."

There was no winning an argument with Manny. Quinn knew that from years of experience. "Lock up when you come in." He stepped inside and shut the doors before the old fighter could get going again.

The following Monday, Chloe was selling new carpet to Agnes Oldfield, a pillar of the Justice Creek community and a longtime friend of her mother's, when who should walk in the door but Manny Aldovino? Quinn's little girl was with him, looking like a pint-size princess in an ankle-length dress with a hot pink top, a wide white sash at the waist and a gathered cotton skirt decorated with rickrack in a rainbow of bright colors.

Chloe ignored the fluttering sensation beneath her breastbone that came with being reminded of Quinn, and greeted the newcomers with a cheery "Hi, Manny. Annabelle. Have a look around. I'll be right with you. Crayons and paper in the hutch by the window treatment display, in case Annabelle would like to color. And there's coffee, too." She gestured at the table not far from the door.

"Sounds good," said Manny. He winked at Agnes. "How you doin' there, Agnes?"

"Mr. Aldovino." Agnes gave Manny an icy, dismissive nod. She'd always been a terrible snob and she looked down on anyone she didn't consider of her social standing. Also, Quinn's father's first wife, Sondra, had been Agnes's beloved niece. Agnes thoroughly disapproved of Quinn's mother, Willow, and of all of Willow's children. Now Agnes pointedly turned her back on Manny and said to Chloe, "Please continue, dear."

Agnes's attitude could use adjusting. But Chloe reminded herself that she needed the business and she couldn't afford to offend a customer. She sent Manny an apologetic smile and waited on the old woman, who wanted new carpet for three rooms. She'd already settled on a quality plush in a pretty dove gray. Chloe accepted her deposit and gave her the number to call to arrange a time to have the spaces measured.

In her eighties, Agnes always dressed as though she'd been invited to tea with the Queen of England. She adjusted the giant, jeweled lizard brooch on her pink silk Chanel suit and said, "Thank you, my dear."

"Have a great day, Agnes."

The old lady sailed out the door.

"Wound a little tight, that one," Manny remarked drily once Agnes was gone.

With a sigh and a shrug, Chloe joined the old man

and the little girl at one of the worktables. "Now. What can I do for you?"

Annabelle glanced up from coloring an enormous, smiling yellow sun. Chloe saw Quinn in the shape of his daughter's eyes and the directness of her gaze. Really, the little girl was downright enchanting, with that heart-shaped face and those chipmunk cheeks. Chloe felt a bittersweet tug at her heartstrings. Annabelle reminded her of the children she should have had.

But after that first time Ted punched her, having kids had never felt right. And Ted hadn't really cared about children anyway. He wanted his wife focused on him.

"I want a princess room," the little girl announced. Chloe gladly put away her grim thoughts of Ted to focus on the sprite in the darling dress. "Manny says you can make me one."

"Yes, I can."

"I want *all* the princesses. Belle and Merida and—" Manny chuckled and tapped the little girl on the arm. She glanced up at him. "But, Manny—"

"I know, I know. You want all the princesses and you're gonna get 'em, but what did we talk about?"

Annabelle huffed. "To wait my turn and not be rude."

The old man beamed. "That's right."

Annabelle leaned close to him, batted those big eyes and whispered, "But I want my princess room."

"It's yours. Promise. But the grown-ups have to talk now."

"Okay." Annabelle bent to her smiling sun again.

Manny spoke to Chloe then. "Quinn's pretty busy getting the business off the ground." His gym, Prime Sports and Fitness, was just down the street from Chloe's showroom, at the intersection of West Central and Marmot Drive. "You know Quinn, don't you?"

"Of course. We…went to school together."

"Right. So Quinn takes care of the business. I look after Annabelle and run the house. You ever seen the inside of our house?"

Chloe blinked away a mental image of Quinn, up on his knees between her legs. Quinn, gloriously naked, his beautiful blue-green eyes burning down at her. "Erm, your house? No, I haven't been inside."

"It's a good house, big rooms, great light, four thousand square feet. But built in the eighties, and looks like it. Too much ceramic tile and ugly carpet."

"So it needs a little loving care?" she asked, trying to sound cool and professional and fearing the old man could see right inside her head to the X-rated images of Annabelle's dad.

"What it needs is a boatload of cash and a good decorator. Starting on the ground floor and moving on up."

"You want to redo every room?" That would be good for her. Very good. Not only for the money, but for Your Way's reputation. She could put up a whole new website area, if Quinn and Manny agreed, showing the before and after of at least the main rooms. Their housing development was an upscale one. However, like Quinn's house, most of the homes were more than twenty years old. Doing a full-on interior redesign always got the neighbors' attention, got them thinking that their houses could stand a little sprucing up, too. She could end up with a lot of new business from the job Manny described. She asked, "What about the bathrooms and the kitchen?"

"Like I said, all of it. Every room."

She couldn't help wondering if Quinn was behind this? "What will you need from me? I'll be happy to show you examples of my work—my portfolio? We can take a look at the website so you'll have a better feel of what I can do. As for references, I—"

"Naw. I already looked at the website and I liked what I saw."

Was she blushing? Manny had a gruff way about him, but he also knew how to turn on the charm. She really liked him. She liked his way with Annabelle, liked that teasing twinkle in his watery eyes. "Well, thank you."

"I got a good feeling about you, Chloe. A real good feeling." The old guy smiled, deepening the network of wrinkles on his craggy face. She really did wonder exactly how much he knew about her and Quinn and what had happened between them eight nights ago. He went on. "I'm thinking you should come over to the house. I'll show you around, show you what I want done and then you can come up with some drawings and blueprints and all that. We can start right away, as soon as you're ready to go..."

"Do you have an architect or any contractors you want to use?"

"Bravo Construction, if they give you a decent bid on the job—and if you're okay with them. You'll be running this, so you gotta be happy with the people you're working with."

Chloe nodded. "I know them, of course." Quinn's older brother, Garrett, ran the company, from what Chloe had heard. And his youngest sister, Nell, worked there, too. Garrett had been three years or so ahead of Chloe in school, so she didn't remember all that much about him. And Nell was four years younger than Chloe. Still, Chloe vaguely remembered her. Gorgeous, and something of a wild child, wasn't she? Never one to back down from a fight. She told Manny brightly, "They have a great reputation. I'll ask them for a bid, absolutely."

Manny winked at her. "Might as well try and keep it in the family."

Chloe got the message. Manny did want her to use the Bravos. "Sounds good to me." She made a mental note to go with them if at all possible.

Half an hour later, when Manny and Annabelle left, Chloe had an appointment at Quinn's house for two in the afternoon the next day.

She was thrilled.

But then again, come on. It was too much of a coincidence. She suspected rough-edged old Manny of matchmaking, because it just didn't seem like something Quinn would engineer. Quinn Bravo was more direct than that. If he wanted to see her again, he would just say so.

Wouldn't he?

She had to admit she couldn't be sure. Maybe Quinn hesitated to ask her out now, after she'd made such a point of that one night being the *only* night the two of them would ever share.

Maybe he knew nothing about Manny's plans to tear their house apart and redo it, top to bottom.

Maybe, come to think of it, Quinn had no desire at all to ask her out. What if he ended up hating the idea that his daughter's caregiver planned to hire the woman up the hill, with whom he'd had a one-night stand? What if he wanted nothing to do with her now? If she took the job, she would be in and out of his house for weeks.

That would be awful, if it turned out that Quinn really didn't want her around. Here she was, gloating over this plum job that had magically fallen in her lap, when Quinn might know nothing about it—and not be the least bit happy when he found out.

By the time Tai arrived at one, Chloe had made up her mind.

Before she went to Quinn's house tomorrow and consulted with Manny on the changes he wanted made, she needed to know for sure what Quinn really thought of her being there.

And the only way to know for sure was to ask the man himself.

Chapter Three

Chloe sent Tai to get takeout again. They shared lunch. And then she left Tai in charge and walked the two blocks to Prime Sports and Fitness, her heart hammering at her ribs all the way.

Quinn's gym filled a three-story brick building directly across the street from the popular Irish-style pub, McKellan's. Chloe hesitated outside on the sidewalk, ordering her pulse to slow down a little, noting the good location and the clean, modern lines of the building itself. There were lots of windows and various athletic activities visible from the street. In one room, some kind of martial arts class was in progress. Another room took up most of the second floor and held rows of cardio equipment, with people in exercise gear working out on stationary bikes, treadmills and elliptical trainers.

She stood there staring up for a couple of minutes at least. Until she finally had to accept that her nervousness hadn't faded at all. In fact, it was worse. So she smoothed the front of her narrow white pants, tugged on the hem of the light, short blazer she wore over a featherweight black tank, squared her shoulders and went in.

The gorgeous, hardbody brunette at the front desk said that Quinn was just finishing up leading a boxing conditioning class. Chloe could wait in his office. It shouldn't be long.

So Chloe sat in his office, where the walls were lined with pictures of Quinn in his fighting days and more than one big, shiny trophy stood on display. She had become absolutely certain that she'd made a horrible mistake in coming here and was just about to rise and bolt from the building, when the door swung open and there he was, looking sweaty and spectacular in gray boxing shorts and a muscle-hugging T.

"Hello, Chloe." Quinn thought he'd never seen anyone so smooth and beautiful, in those perfect white pants and pointy little shoes, not a single golden hair out of place.

"Quinn." She sounded breathless. He liked that. And she bounced to her feet. "I… How are you?" She held out her hand.

"Good. Real good." He stepped forward and took it, already regretting he hadn't run to the locker room and grabbed a quick shower after class. Her slim fingers were cool and dry in his sweaty paw.

But she didn't seem to mind. She held on and he held on and they stood and stared at each other. She looked a little stunned, but in a good way. And he had no doubt his expression mirrored hers.

Finally, she said in a breathless rush, "I need… Well, there's something I really have to discuss with you."

"Sure." He made himself release her hand and went

back to shut the door as she returned to the chair. "Something to drink? Juice? Tea?" When she shook her head, he slid in behind his desk and gestured for her to sit back down. "Okay. What's going on?"

"I, uh, had a visit from Manny and Annabelle today, at my design showroom. Manny offered me a really good project, redoing all the rooms in your house." She paused to swallow and smooth her already perfect hair. "I agreed to meet him at your house tomorrow in the afternoon to go over the changes he wants. If he still wants to hire me, I'll work out the numbers and put together a contract."

This was all news to Quinn. But not bad news. He asked cautiously, "And this is a problem somehow?"

"Well, after Manny and Annabelle left, I started wondering if you even knew that he was planning to hire me. I thought I should, you know, check with you, make certain you're on board with Manny's plan…" Her voice trailed off.

He watched her try not to fidget. And the longer he sat there looking at her, the more he came to grips with the fact that the one night he'd had with her wasn't enough. Luckily for him, her signal came through loud and clear: she felt the same way.

No, he had no time for romance.

But for a woman like Chloe, he might just have to make time.

Should he be pissed off at Manny for taking the situation into his battered old hands? Probably. Manny had no business butting in.

But Quinn had just spent a week keeping himself from climbing the hill to get to her. Manny's bold move had brought her right to him. Pissed off? Hardly. Downright grateful was more like it.

Not that he'd ever admit that to Manny.

A small, embarrassed sound escaped her. "Oh, God. You *didn't* know, did you?"

"Doesn't matter. Manny's in charge of the house and we agreed when we bought the place that it would need major upgrades. It's his call who he hires to make that happen."

"So you're okay with it—with me, working in your house?"

He was more than just okay with it. "Sounds like a good idea to me—I mean, if you're willing."

She gave him one of those glowing smiles that could light up the blackest night. "Well, then. Yes. I'm willing, definitely." She got up. "So, then, I guess I should be…"

He couldn't let her go. Not yet. He pushed back his chair. "Now that you're here, how 'bout I show you around?"

"The gym, you mean?"

"That's right."

"Yes. Yes, I would like that."

"Well, okay, then. This way…"

Chloe followed Quinn past the reception area, into a series of wood-floored classrooms with mirrored walls and different kinds of equipment stacked in the corners. In one, a fitness ball class was in progress. In another, the participants were paired up for intense stretching. They went upstairs to the second floor and the giant cardio room as well as a room with all kinds of weight machines and one with boxing equipment and two rings.

He explained that Prime Fitness tried to offer something for everyone. "We have martial arts for all ages, boxing, kickboxing, general fitness and yoga classes…"

She listened and nodded, just glad to be walking along

beside him, glad that he seemed to want to keep her there longer, to be drawing the moments out before she left.

On the top floor there was a beginning women's self-defense class in progress. They watched through the observation window as a big guy in a padded suit tried to take down a woman about Chloe's size. The woman shouted and fought him off violently, kicking and slugging at him, spinning away and sprinting off as soon as she got the guy to let go of her.

Watching that made Chloe's mouth go dry and her palms feel clammy. It made her think of Ted and how she ought to be better prepared if anyone ever hit her or threatened her again.

"What do you think?" Quinn asked.

She turned to him, met those wonderful, watchful eyes. "I think I might want to take a class like this."

There was a bench a few feet away. He backed up and sat down. She left the viewing window and sat beside him.

He said, "This class is wrapping up. A new one will start next week, and there's an evening class, too. Starts in two weeks. It's an eight-week course, one two-hour class per week."

"I'll be fighting off guys in padded suits for eight weeks?"

He shook his head. "No. Initially there are sessions on staying out of violent confrontations in the first place."

"How?"

He chuckled. "What? You want an outline of the course?"

"Can you give me one?"

"You're serious?"

"I am, yes."

He watched her for a long moment. And then he shrugged. "Well, all right. The class starts with a section on the nature of predators. Basically there are two types. Resource and process. Resource predators want your stuff. Process predators are in it for the power and the thrill. They want to mess you over. They actually enjoy committing crimes. The class shows you how to identify what kind of scumbag you're faced with and how to deal with him. Next comes a study of avoidance, because the best option is always steering clear of any situation where you could get hurt. After avoidance, there's a section on deescalating conflict. If you can't escape trouble before it happens, the second-best option is to diffuse it. And finally you'll learn how to fight off an attack."

"Wow," she said, and wondered if any guy ever looked as good in shorts and a T-shirt as Quinn did. And he smelled so good, too. Clean. Just sweaty enough to be exciting…

He grunted. "See? More information than you needed or wanted."

She shook her head. "That was exactly what I wanted to know. And how do *you* know all that? Do you teach this kind of class yourself?"

"No. But I've been through every class that we offer here. I run the place. It's my job to know what I'm selling. I want to franchise this operation. This location will be the model for Prime Sports and Fitness gyms all over the country."

"You dream big."

"Hey. Balls to the wall. It's the only way to go."

She made a decision. "I'm taking the next evening class."

"Am I a salesman, or what?" He got up. "Come on." He put his big hand at the small of her back. Such a light touch to wreak such total havoc through every quivering cell in her body. "We'll sign you up."

At the front desk, Quinn tried to comp her the class. She shook her head and whipped out her checkbook. Once she'd paid for the course, he walked her out the door.

He caught her arm as the door eased shut behind them. "So, Chloe…"

She was achingly aware of him, so close, his big, warm fingers wrapped lightly around her upper arm. He walked her forward several feet along the sidewalk and then pulled her gently around to face him.

"Yeah?" she asked low, her voice barely a whisper.

He stepped in closer and spoke for her ears alone. "The other night…?"

Her breath tangled in her throat. "Yeah?"

"You said just for that night, just that once. But you're here and I'm looking in those fine blue eyes and I'm wondering, did you really mean that?"

Her stupid throat had clutched up tight. She swallowed convulsively, and then shook her head hard.

His brow rumpled in a frown, but the hint of a smile seemed to tug on his mouth. "I'm still not sure what you're telling me here."

And somehow she found her voice again. "Sorry…"

"Nothing to be sorry for. You just say it right out loud, whatever your answer is. I can take it, I promise you."

She cleared her throat to get her going. "Ahem. That night, I needed to find a way to give myself permission to do something I wanted to do but had never done before. That night, I needed to think of it as just that one time and never again. But since then…"

"Yeah?"

"Oh, Quinn. I wish I hadn't said what I said. Because I've been thinking about you a lot. And it's really good to see you again."

Those fine eyes were gleaming. “Yeah?”

And she was eagerly nodding, her head bouncing up and down like a bobblehead doll’s.

“So, then…” He started walking backward toward the doors.

She resisted the urge to reach out and stop him—and also the one that demanded she follow him. Instead, she held her ground and asked hopefully, “So, then, what?”

He stopped at the doors. “How ’bout Friday night? You and me. Dinner.”

“Dinner…” How could one simple word hold so much promise?

“Yeah.” He was definitely smiling now. “You know, like people do.”

“I would like that.” She knew she wore a giant, silly grin. And somehow she had gone on tiptoe. Her body felt lighter than air.

“Pick you up at seven?”

She settled back onto her heels and nodded. “Seven is great.”

A trim, fortyish woman in workout clothes approached the doors. Quinn opened one and ushered her in. Then, with a final nod in Chloe’s direction, he went in, too.

That lighter-than-air feeling? It stayed with her. Her feet barely touched the ground the whole way back to the showroom.

Strange how everything could change for the better in the course of one afternoon.

All at once, the world, so cruel to her in recent years, was a good and hopeful place again. Suddenly everything looked brighter.

Yeah, okay. It was just a date. But it was a date with a man who thrilled her—and made her feel safe and protected and cherished and capable, all at the same time.

* * *

That night, Chloe made chocolate chip cookies. Once they'd cooled, she packed them up into two bright decorator tins. She took them to the showroom the next morning. One she offered at the coffee table.

The other she carried with her when she went to meet with Manny at Quinn's house after lunch.

"Cookies!" Annabelle nodded her approval. "I *like* cookies." She sent Manny a regretful glance. "Manny's cookies are not very good."

Manny told Chloe, "Never was a baker—or that much of a cook, when you come right down to it. I enjoy cooking, though. Too bad nobody appreciates my efforts." He wiggled his bushy eyebrows at Annabelle. "And what do you say when someone brings you really good cookies?"

"Thank you, Chloe."

"You're welcome."

She turned those sweet brown eyes on Manny again. "Can I have one now?"

"That could be arranged." Manny led them to the kitchen, which had appliances that had been state-of-the-art back in the late eighties, a fruit-patterned wallpaper border up near the ceiling and acres of white ceramic tile. Annabelle made short work of two cookies and a glass of milk, after which she wanted to take Chloe up to her room.

Chloe looked to Manny. The old guy shrugged. "Don't keep her up there all day," he said to the little girl.

"Manny, I want *all* the princesses, but it won't take *that* long." She reached right up and grabbed Chloe's hand, at which point Chloe's heart pretty much melted. "Okay, Chloe. Let's go."

After half an hour with Quinn's daughter, Chloe knew exactly which princesses Annabelle wanted represented in her new room, as well as her favorite colors. They went back downstairs, and Chloe spent a couple of hours with Manny, going through the house, bottom to top, talking hard and soft surfaces, color choices, style preferences and the benefits of knocking out a wall or two. Chloe jotted notes and took pictures of existing furniture and fixtures that would be included in the new design.

Before she left at four-thirty, she promised to crunch the numbers. The contract would be ready for his and Quinn's approval early next week.

"Give me a call," said Manny. "We can decide then whether to meet here or at your showroom."

"That'll work."

Annabelle urged her to "Come back and see me soon, Chloe. And bring cookies."

Chloe promised that she would. She drove to the showroom, let Tai go home and got to work on the contract, planning out the estimated costs, room by room. At six, she closed up and headed for her house, a big, fat smile on her face and a thousand ideas for the redesign swirling in her brain.

She parked in her detached garage and was halfway along the short breezeway to the front door when she caught sight of the gorgeous bouquet of orchids and roses waiting in a clear, square vase on the porch. It must be from Quinn. The arrangement was so simple and lovely and the gesture so thoughtful, she let out a happy cry just at the sight of it.

Okay, it was a little silly to be so giddy at his thoughtfulness. But she hadn't had flowers in so long. Ted used to buy them for her, and since the divorce, well, she had no desire to buy them for herself. To her, a gorgeous bouquet of flowers just reminded her of Ted and all the ways she'd messed up her life. But if Quinn gave her flowers, she could start to see a beautiful arrangement in a whole new light.

She disarmed her alarm and unlocked the door—and then scooped up the vase and carried it in.

Dropping her purse on the entry bench, she took the vase straight to the kitchen peninsula, where she set it carefully down. The card had a red amaryllis on the front and the single word, Bloom. Bloom was the shop that belonged to Quinn's sister, Jody.

Whipping the little card off its plastic holder, she flipped it open and read *Beautiful flowers always remind me of you. I hate that it went so wrong for us. I miss you.*

Ted

Chapter Four

"No!" Chloe shouted right out loud, not even caring that she sounded like some crazy person, yelling at thin air. "No, you do not get to do that. You do not." She tore the note in half and then in half again and she dropped it on the floor and stomped on it for good measure. They were *divorced*, for God's sake. He had a new wife. And all she wanted from him for now and forever was never to see or hear from him again.

Her heart racing with a sick kind of fury that he'd dared to encroach on her new life where he had no business being, Chloe whipped the beautiful flowers from the vase. Dripping water across the counter and onto the floor, too, she dropped them in the trash compactor, shoved it shut and turned the motor on. The compactor rumbled. She felt way too much satisfaction as the machine crushed the bright blooms to a pulp.

Once the flowers were toast, she poured the water

from the vase into the sink, whipped the compactor open again and dropped the vase on top of the mashed flowers. She ran the motor a second time, grinning like a mad-woman when she heard that loud, scary pop that meant the vase was nothing but shards of broken glass. After that, she picked up the little bits of card, every one, threw them in with the shattered vase and the pulped flowers, took the plastic bag out of the compactor, lugged it out to the trash bin and threw it in.

Good riddance to bad trash.

She spent a while stewing, considering calling Ted and giving him a large piece of her mind.

But no. She wanted nothing to do with him and she certainly didn't want to make contact with him again. That might just encourage him.

She wondered if the flowers and the creepy note could be considered the act of a stalker.

But then she reminded herself that Ted and his bride, Larissa, lived more than a thousand miles away in San Diego. It was one thing for Ted to have his assistant send her flowers just to freak her out, but something else again for him to show up on her doorstep in person.

Wasn't going to happen. He was just being a jerk, an activity at which he excelled.

God. She had married him. How could she have been such an utter, complete fool?

Back in the house, she changed into jeans and a tank top. Then she took her time cooking an excellent dinner of fresh broiled trout with lemon butter, green beans and slivered almonds and her favorite salad of field greens, blueberries, Gorgonzola cheese and toasted walnuts, with a balsamic vinaigrette.

When it was ready, she set the table with her best dishes, lit a candle, poured herself a glass of really nice sauvignon blanc and sat down. She ate slowly, savoring every delicious bite.

A little later, she took a long scented bath and put on a comfy sleep shirt and shorts. Even after the bath, she was still buzzing with anger at the loser she'd once had the bad judgment to marry. Streaming a movie or reading a book was not going to settle her down. She needed a serious distraction.

So she went to the cozy room on the lower floor that she used as a home office and lost herself in the plans for Quinn's house. Within a few minutes of sitting down at her desk, the only thing on her mind was the rooms taking shape in her imagination—and on her sketch pad. And the numbers coming together for each room, for the project as a whole. She worked for hours and hardly noticed the time passing.

When she finally went back upstairs to the main floor, it was almost midnight. Time for bed.

But she didn't go to bed. It was cool out that evening. So she put on a big sweater over her sleep shirt, pulled on a pair of fluffy pink booties and went out onto her deck. It was something she had not done after dark since the night Quinn spent in her bed.

But she was doing it tonight.

She padded to the deck railing and stared down at Quinn's house.

Was she actually expecting him to be watching, waiting for the moment when she wandered out under the stars?

Not really. It just felt…reassuring somehow. To gaze down at his house, to know that she would see him again, would share dinner with him on Friday night.

When the French doors opened and he emerged, she let out a laugh of pure delight and waved to signal him up.

He didn't even hesitate, just went on down the steps at the side of his deck and forged up the hill. She went to meet him at the top of her stairs, feeling breathless and wonderful.

Tonight, he wore ripped old jeans, a white T-shirt that seemed to glow in the dark and the same moccasins he'd been wearing that other night. He said, "Love those furry boots." When she laughed, he added, "I was getting worried you might never come outside."

"And I was absolutely certain there was no way you might be glancing up to see if I was looking down for you." She held out her hand. He took it. His skin was warm, his palm callous. Just his touch made her body sing. "Come sit with me?"

He looked at her as though she were the only other person in the world. "Whatever you want, Chloe."

She tugged him over to the two chairs they'd sat in that other night and pulled him down beside her.

Silence.

But it was a good silence. They just sat there, staring out at the clear night and the distant mountains. A slight wind came up, rustling the nearby pines. And an owl hooted off in the shadows somewhere between his house and hers.

Finally, she said, "I met with Manny. I think it went well."

"He says so, too."

"And I'm in love with your daughter."

He chuckled, a rough and tempting sound. "She has that effect on people. Manny's tough, but Annabelle still manages to wrap him around her little finger. Truth is she rules the house. We just try to keep up with her."

She looked over at him. "Has she asked you about her mother again?"

"Not yet." He met her eyes through the shadows. "I

know, I know. Wait until she asks. And then don't load her up with more information than she's ready for."

"That's the way." She thought of the flowers she'd crushed in the compactor—and then pushed them out of her mind. Why ruin a lovely moment by bringing Ted into it?

Instead, she asked him how he had met Manny. He explained that the old ex-fighter had been his first professional trainer. "I met him at the first gym I walked into after leaving home. Downtown Gym, it was called, in Albuquerque. Manny ran the place and worked with the fighters who trained there. We got along. When I moved on, he went with me. I had a lot of trainers. And over time, Manny became more like my manager, I guess you could say. And kind of a cross between a best friend and a dad." He shot her a warning look. "But don't tell him I said that."

She grinned. "Why not?"

"He already thinks he knows what's best for me. If he ever heard I said I thought of him as a father, he'd never shut up with the advice and instructions."

She softly advised, "But I'll bet it would mean the world to him to know how you really feel."

"He knows. Hearing it out loud would only make him more impossible to live with." Quinn faked a dangerous scowl. "So keep your mouth shut."

She laughed and held up both hands. "I swear I'll never say a word."

"Good."

"So, how did he end up back here in Justice Creek with you and Annabelle?"

"I don't think either of us really considered a different option. He moved in with me when Annabelle was a baby, to help out."

When Annabelle was a baby…

So the little girl had been with her dad from the first? What had happened to the mother, the one Quinn said Annabelle would most likely never meet?

So many questions.

But Chloe had such a good feeling about the man beside her. She trusted him to tell her everything in his own good time.

He said, "When I decided to retire from the Octagon last year, Manny was already taking care of Annabelle full-time." Chloe knew what the Octagon was: the eight-sided ring in which Ultimate Fighting Championship mixed-martial-arts fighters competed. During the rough years when she was still married to Ted, she'd watched more than one of Quinn's televised UFC fights. It had lifted her spirits to see how far the wild, angry boy from her hometown had come. He continued, "I asked Manny to stick with me when I moved back home. He agreed right off, said he supposed it was about time he settled down. Annabelle's a handful, but so far he's managing."

"From what I've seen, he's great with her. He's patient, encourages her to express herself and make some of her own decisions—but he stays in charge, too."

"Yeah. He's a champ with her, all right…" Quinn's voice kind of trailed off and there was another silence, one somehow not as comfortable as the first.

She glanced over at him again and found him watching her. "Whatever it is, you might as well just say it."

"I got a question, but I don't want to freak you out."

An unpleasant shiver traveled down the backs of her arms and she thought of Ted again. Because if her freaking out could be involved, it probably had to do with Ted.

Then again, how would Quinn know that? She'd mentioned her ex once, on the night that Quinn came to her bed. What she'd told him had been far from flattering to Ted, but she'd said nothing about how thinking of him made her want to crush flowers and break expensive vases.

"Ask me," she said. "I can take it." The words came out sounding so confident. She was proud of them.

"All right, then. Does your mama know you're going out to dinner with me?"

Her mother. Of course. "No."

"It's Justice Creek, Chloe."

"Meaning she *will* know?"

"I'd say the odds are better than fifty-fifty, wouldn't you?"

Chloe kept her gaze steady on his. It was no hardship. Looking at him made her think of hot sex. And safety. And that combination really worked for her. "That girl—the mama's girl I was in high school?"

"Yeah?"

She slanted him a teasing glance. "You're not even going to argue that I was never a mama's girl?"

"Hey. You called it, not me."

And she made a low, rueful noise in her throat. "Yes, I did. And I was. But I'm not anymore. I tried living my life my mother's way. It didn't work for me. I'm all grown up now and my mother doesn't get to tell me what to do or whom to spend my time with."

One side of his beautiful mouth curved up then. It was a smirk, heavy on the irony, more like the old, dangerous, edgy Quinn from back in high school than the one she'd been getting to know lately. "*Whom*. Always so ladylike."

"Don't tease me. I'm serious."

His smirk vanished. "So you're admitting that your mother's not gonna like it, you and me spending time together?"

"What I'm telling you is that she doesn't have a say, so it doesn't matter whether she likes it or not."

He reached out his hand between their chairs. She put hers in it, and he lifted it to that wonderful mouth of his. Hot shivers cascaded down her arm and straight to the core of her, just at the feel of his soft lips against her skin. Then he rubbed his chin where his lips had been, teasing her with the rough brush of beard stubble, reminding her of their one night together, making her long to jump up and drag him inside.

But she didn't.

A moment later, he let go of her hand. He started talking again—about his plans for Prime Sports. She told him how much she appreciated the chance to rework the interiors at his house and then she shared with him some of the ideas she and Manny had discussed for upgrading the kitchen and opening up the living-room space.

A couple of hours passed as they sat there talking quietly under the waning moon. She even told him a little about her failed marriage—no, not about the flowers, and not about the times Ted had struck her. This thing with Quinn was so new and sweet and heady. Sharing ugly stories about her ex would definitely dim the romantic glow. Instead, she tried to explain how disappointed she was in the way things had turned out.

"It hurts so much," she confessed, "when something that should have been so right somehow goes all wrong. And I feel… I don't know, *less*, I guess. Shamed, that I didn't make better choices."

He regarded her for several seconds in that steady way he had. "You said the other night that the guy was abusive…"

She held his gaze as she shook her head.

He frowned. "I'll need more than a head shake to get what you're trying to tell me."

She let out a hard sigh. "Oh, Quinn. It's a beautiful night. And you're here beside me. It's good, you and me, talking like this."

"Yeah, it is."

"I probably shouldn't even have brought up my divorce."

"Yeah, you should. Whatever you want to tell me, that's what I want to hear."

"That's just it. I really don't want to go into any of that old garbage right now."

He gave her another of those long, thoughtful looks. And then, "All right."

And just like that, he let it go.

How amazing. He let it go. She'd grown up with a mother who never let anything go. And Ted? He would hound a person to hell and back to find out something he wanted to know.

But not Quinn. She said she didn't want to talk about it—and he just let it go. He said, "Whatever that story is, whatever happened in the past, you're going to be fine."

She made a low, rueful sound. "You're sure about that, huh?"

And he nodded. "You're brave and beautiful, Chloe—and not only on the outside. You're beautiful in your heart, where it matters. I admire the hell out of you."

Tears burned in her eyes at such praise. She blinked them away and whispered a soft, sincere "Thank you..."

By then, she really wanted to take him inside and spend a few more thrilling hours in his arms. But she felt somehow shyer now than that other night—shy and tentative.

And other than kissing her hand that one time, he'd made no move on her.

It was two in the morning when he said good-night.

She stood at the railing watching him jog down the hill to his house, and felt disappointed in herself that she'd let him go without so much as a single shared kiss.

But then, he *had* asked her out. She would see him again on Friday night…

Friday evening, Quinn arrived five minutes early. "Better grab a scarf," he warned.

She ran and got one, then followed him out across the breezeway and around the garage to the side parking space, where a gorgeous old convertible Buick coupe waited—top down, of course. With sidewalls so white they were blinding even in the shade.

"Wow." She couldn't resist gliding her palm over the glossy maroon paint. "It looks brand-new." The bright chrome gleamed in the fading early-evening light. It had round vents on the front fenders and an enormous, toothy grille.

"It's one of Carter's rebuilds. A '49 Buick Roadmaster." Carter, Quinn's oldest brother, designed and built custom cars. "I saw it at his shop a couple of weeks ago. Don't know what came over me, but I wanted it. So I bought it." He opened the door for her. She slid in onto the snow-white, tuck-and-roll bench seat. "Had him put seat belts in it, along with a decent sound system and power windows." He was leaning on the open door, bending close to her, his gray suit jacket already off and slung over his shoulder, hanging by a finger.

She got a hint of his aftershave, which was manly and fresh. He looked so good, in a white shirt and gray slacks, with a dark blue tie. She thought about kissing him, and turned away to run her hand over the leather seat in an effort to distract herself from a sudden, vivid memory of how pliant and hot his lips felt pressed to hers. "It's gorgeous," she said, altogether too breathlessly.

"Yeah." The single word seemed to dance along her nerve endings. She looked back up at him, and he grinned at her. And she just knew that *he* knew what she'd been thinking. "You look beautiful," he said, his gaze taking in her little black dress and her double strand of pearls that her dad had given her when she graduated from high school. "So smooth."

"Um, what?"

"You, Chloe. You're smooth."

"That's good, I hope?"

"That is excellent. Buckle up now." He shut the door as she tied her scarf over her hair.

He took her to the Sylvan Inn, which was a few miles southeast of town nestled in among the pines. The inn had a quiet atmosphere and great food.

"We used to come here when I was little," she said, once they were settled with their tall goblets of ice water, hot bread and giant menus in the traditional Sylvan Inn blue leather cover with the fancy gold lettering on the front. "For special occasions. My dad loves their hammer steaks. So do I, as a matter of fact."

"Good memories, then?"

"Very good." She glanced up at him—and spotted a familiar face across the dining room. Chloe smiled. The tall, thin blonde smiled right back. She gave Chloe a jaunty wave and disappeared behind a potted plant.

"What's up?" Quinn asked.

Chloe brushed a hand over the crisp white cuff of Quinn's shirt. "Don't look now, but we've been spotted by Monique Hightower. Did you know she works here?" They'd gone to school with Monique. The woman never met a secret she wouldn't share with the whole town.

"Uh-oh." He pretended to look worried. "Like I said the other night, it's Justice Creek. You go out with me, everyone in town is bound to know."

Now she brushed the back of his hand, which was warm and tan and dusted lightly with brown hair. It felt so good to touch him. She had to watch herself or she'd be all over the poor guy. "I hope you don't mind that the gossip mill will be churning."

"Me?" He gave a low chuckle. "I think I can deal with it."

"Such a brave man…"

They shared one of those looks. Long. Intimate. Wonderful. Finally, he said, "Read your menu, Chloe."

She closed the blue folder. "I did."

"You know what you want?"

"Oh, yes, I do." She said it slowly, with a lazy smile.

He warned low, "Keep looking at me like that and we won't make it through the appetizer."

But they did. They had it all. Appetizers, a nice bottle of cabernet, salad, hammer steaks with cheesy potatoes and a decadent chocolate dessert. And they took their sweet time about it.

Monique dropped by their table around nine, just after they'd been served their coffee and dessert. "Chloe. Quinn. What a surprise."

Quinn asked, "So, how's life treating you, Monique?"

"I'm getting by." Monique tossed her topknot of curly blond hair and stuck her hands in the pockets of her black service apron. "When did you two start spending time together?"

Chloe sipped her coffee. "This is our first date. I'm having a fabulous time."

Quinn said, "Chloe always had a thing for me, since way back in high school."

Monique blinked three times in rapid succession. "Really?"

Chloe stifled a silly giggle and said with great seriousness. "I finally got up the nerve to tell him." *And to show him, as a matter of fact.* "And then he asked me out. The rest could be history. I mean, if I play my cards right." She lowered her voice to a whisper. "But, Monique…"

Monique leaned a little closer. "What?"

"Don't say a word to anyone."

"Oh. Never. I would never tell a soul…" Translation: she couldn't wait to tell the world. Monique asked about Prime Sports, and Quinn gave her a card good for a free visit and one class of her choice. And then she turned to Chloe again, her dark eyes sharply gleaming. "I was so surprised when you moved back to town. I mean, we all knew you were headed for great things. No one ever would have guessed you'd end up running back home to Justice Creek. I'm just so *sorry* that things didn't work out for you."

Six months ago, Chloe would have been shamed and infuriated by Monique's barbed words and pretended concern. Or at the very least, embarrassed. At the moment, though, all she felt was amused. "Thanks, Monique. You're all heart."

Monique sighed heavily. Across the room, the manager who'd greeted them when they arrived had his eye on her. "Well, good to see you two. Gotta go." She scuttled off.

Chloe took a bite of her delicious dessert. "Everything we told her will be all over town. Twenty-four hours—thirty-six, max."

Quinn leaned closer and spoke low. "Maybe I shouldn't have said that you had a thing for me in high school."

She met his eyes directly and she couldn't keep from

grinning. "Are you kidding? I loved it. Not to mention it was the truth. If Monique Hightower's going to be spreading rumors about us, they might as well be true."

After their slow, wonderful meal, they returned to Chloe's house.

Quinn eased the gorgeous old car into the space beside the garage and turned off the engine. "Are you up for a walk around the block?"

"Sure." It was a nice night. "A walk would be great. We'll work off some of that amazing dessert."

He followed her inside and waited while she changed into flats. Then off they went, down the front steps and out to the street, where they strolled beneath the silver crescent of the moon.

Their development, Haltersham Heights, had no sidewalks. The houses were set back from the street, among the trees. Quinn stopped at a lot three doors down and across the street from Chloe's. It had a For Sale sign at the curb with a big SOLD plate stuck on it. The large contemporary log and natural stone house could be seen, windows gleaming, through the trees.

"The sold sign went up a few weeks ago," she said. "About time. This one's been on the market for months."

"I know. I bought it. Got a great price, too."

She laughed—and then she realized he wasn't kidding. "Wait a minute. You're serious?"

"I am." He put his hand over her fingers, where they curled around his arm. She'd barely had time to enjoy the flare of pleasure at how good his touch felt, when he said, "I bought it before I knew you would be fixing up my house. But it should work out great. We're closing on this one Monday, so we can move in here next week. We'll stay here while you renovate the other one—and not to get ahead of myself or anything, but once we move back to our house, you can start on this one. It's the same story as the other one. Solid construction, but it's begging to be brought into the twenty-first century. When you're finished, I'll sell it."

She only stared.

"Chloe, your mouth's hanging open."

"And why wouldn't it be? You're too much."

"Too much of what, exactly?"

"Well, let's see. Quinn Bravo, world-champion cage fighter, fitness empire builder, real estate mogul…"

"That all sounds pretty good to me."

"You must have made a fortune as a fighter, huh?"

"I did all right. The payout for winning a championship fight is a hefty one. And I landed some big-time endorsements, too."

"I think I'm speechless, Quinn."

He gave her his high school bad-boy smirk. "You'll get over it. And the truth is, Prime Sports will never make much money unless my franchise plan pays off. The housing market's rebounding nicely, though. I *can* make money in real estate."

She admitted softly, "Start-ups aren't easy, and I say that from experience. If you hire me for both of your houses, it will make a big difference for me. I really do need the business."

"So you've got it. Everybody wins."

She made a low, disbelieving sound. "As simple as that?"

His eyebrows drew together. "Why not?"

"I don't know. I wouldn't want to take advantage of you just because you, um, like me…"

He framed her face in his big, calloused hands. "Look at me."

"Oh, I am." She stared straight up into those soft aquamarine eyes and never wanted to look away. "I really am."

"Are you telling me you can't do the job?"

She stiffened and answered with heat, "Of course I can do the job."

He chuckled then. "See? We got no problem here."

Standing there in the darkness of her quiet street with his warm, rough hands cradling her cheeks, she decided he was right. "No, I guess we don't."

He lowered his head, until his sexy, plump lips were a hairbreadth from hers. He had lips like a girl's, but the rest of him was all man. "I got a request, though."

She longed for his kiss. Her heart was beating slow and deep. Sparks flared across her skin. And low in her belly, she seemed to be melting. "Oh, God. Anything."

"Work with my brother's company, Bravo Construction?"

She made herself focus on what he'd just asked of her—and it wasn't easy, with those lips of his so close.

Use his brother's company…

She'd left that possibility open-ended when she talked to Manny. But really, why not? Bravo Construction had a great reputation. She felt confident she could develop a solid working relationship with them. It could be good for everyone. "All right."

His warm breath touched her lips. The guy was driving her crazy. "I already talked to my sister Nell—just paving the way. Nell says she'll fit the project in the schedule and they can start work a week from Monday."

"That's quick."

"Yeah. And I like to keep it in the family if I can."

"I get that." She tried really hard not to sound as breathless as she felt. "No problem. Bravo Construction it is."

"Good, then."

"Quinn…"

"Hmm?" A teasing light shone in his eyes. She realized he knew exactly what he was doing to her.

And *she* knew that she couldn't take it anymore. She only had to lift herself up a fraction higher to get what she wanted. So she did. And it worked.

At last, he was kissing her.

"Chloe…" Quinn whispered her name right into her pretty mouth.

And then he let go of her arms—in order to pull her up nice and close. She tasted so good. Hot and wet.

And all of her, every graceful, sweetly scented inch of her, was so, so smooth.

Worth the endless, twelve-day wait since the last time he'd had his mouth on hers.

He lifted his head an inch. She let out a tiny moan, as though she couldn't bear not to have their mouths fused together. He slanted his head the other way and drank that moan right off her sweet, sweet lips.

Those slender arms glided up his chest and then her soft hands were stroking his collar, caressing his neck, her slim fingers threading up into the close-trimmed hair at the nape of his neck. He scraped his tongue along the smooth edges of her teeth, pushing deeper, into all that wet sweetness.

Coffee. Wine. Chocolate.

Chloe.

There had been women in his life, maybe too many. Especially when he was first making his name in the Octagon. Women liked fighters. And they particularly liked fighters who won. For a while there he'd gotten carried away with all the attention. Beautiful women everywhere he turned, his for the taking.

But even an endless chain of gorgeous women got old after a while. He started to see that to most of them, he was just a cheap thrill. And he wanted to be more than that to someone.

He found he wanted heart in a woman. He wanted someone he could talk to. He wanted real, gut-deep integrity. He wanted truth. He wanted a powerful connection.

Oh, and yeah. Brains and a sense of humor, too.

It wasn't that there weren't women out there with all that. It was just that most of them had no interest in a guy who still couldn't read past about fourth-grade level, a guy who got bloodied and battered for a living. Plus, when he was fighting, it ate up his life. He didn't have time to go looking for the one for him.

And then along came Annabelle. Her life, her happiness, her chance to grow up and take on the world—suddenly that was what mattered to him. To raise his little girl up right was more than enough. He didn't need that special woman, after all.

Or so he'd believed until twelve nights ago.

Until Chloe led him into her house and straight to her bed.

Chloe.

She had it all—everything he'd already accepted he wasn't going to find. And no one had ever tasted so good.

Reluctantly, he broke the kiss.

She stared up at him, eyes full of stars. "Come back to my house? Be with me tonight?"

"Damn, Chloe. I was afraid you'd never ask."

Her belly all aflutter with anticipation, her pulse a rushing sound in her ears and her cheeks feeling way hotter than they should, Chloe ushered Quinn in her front door and then turned to engage the lock and reset the alarm. "You can hang your jacket there." She gestured at the coatrack. He hung up his jacket, and she grabbed his hand. "This way…"

But he held back, tugging her close, into the hard, hot circle of his arms. He kissed her, a slow one that had her knees going weak and a meltdown happening in her core.

However, when he lifted his head that time, his eyes were way too serious.

She frowned, suddenly struck with concern for whatever might be bothering him. "What is it? What's wrong?"

He pulled her close again. And he whispered in her ear, "I want to take all your clothes off and see you naked. I want to kiss every inch of you."

She sighed. "We are definitely on the same page about that."

"But…"

She pushed him away enough that she could see his eyes. "Oh, no. There *is* something. What?"

"Don't look so worried." With his big thumb, he smoothed the scrunched place between her eyebrows. "It's nothing bad. I just have some things I want to say first."

Would she rather be kissing him? Absolutely. But then again, whatever he wanted to say, she wanted to hear. "So…coffee or something?"

"Sure."

She led him into the kitchen and whipped him up a quick cup, pouring cream in a little pitcher because she'd watched him at dinner and knew he took cream.

"Aren't you having any?" he asked.

Her tummy was all fluttery, what with wondering what kind of thing he just *had* to say to her. Coffee would only make it worse. "Maybe later. How about the living area? It's more comfortable there."

"Good enough." He poured in the cream, picked up his cup and followed her to the sofa.

They sat down together, and he set his cup on the coffee table. She folded her hands tightly in her lap. He'd said it was nothing awful, but he seemed so intense suddenly…

Was there going to be drama? Oh, she hoped not. She'd had enough drama to last her a lifetime, and then some.

He said, "There are things about me I want you to know."

Uh-oh. She gulped down the giant lump in her throat and gave him a nod to continue.

"First, about Annabelle's mother."

Chloe realized she'd been holding her breath. She let it out slowly. Annabelle's mother. Actually, she really wanted to know about Annabelle's mother…

"Her name is Sandrine Cox. She's an actress and model. We went out a few times. She got pregnant. She came to me, told me she was fairly certain it was my baby and she felt I had a right to know."

Chloe studied his wonderful face. He seemed… relaxed when he talked about his little girl's mother. Relaxed and accepting. "You believed her."

"Yeah. Sandrine was always straight ahead about things. I believed that *she* believed the baby was mine. Then later, right after Annabelle was born, a paternity test proved Sandrine was right. Annabelle's mine. And I knew from the moment Sandrine told me she was pregnant that I wanted the baby. Sandrine didn't. She didn't want to be a mom. She liked her single life and she had a lot of ambition, a heavy focus on her career. I made her an offer. I would pay her a large lump sum to have the baby and then she would sign over all rights to me."

"And that's what happened?"

He nodded. "She kept her end of the bargain. I kept mine."

"You haven't heard from her since Annabelle was born?"

"No. I doubt I ever will."

"But with something as important as a child, Quinn, you never know. Someday Annabelle's mother might regret her choice, change her mind."

"Anything's possible."

"And if she did come to you, if she wanted to meet Annabelle?"

"Can't say for certain. If she was as honest and upfront as before, we would work something out so that she could know Annabelle and Annabelle could know her."

Chloe liked his answer. It could be difficult for him to make room for his daughter's mother in their lives. But it was the right thing. "That sounds good. For Annabelle, most of all. It's very likely, as she grows to adulthood, that she's going to want to know about her birth mother and meet her, if possible."

"Maybe. But it's like you told me that first night. I'm not going to borrow trouble. I'll answer Annabelle's questions and pay attention to the signals she gives me. And then take it from there." He loosened his tie. "I didn't want you to wonder anymore about how I ended up with sole custody of my little girl and no mother in sight."

Tenderness washed through her—for him, for the kind of man he was. A good man. Honest. True-hearted. A man who would do what was right even if it wasn't the best or easiest thing for him, personally.

She reached out and brushed his hand. "Let me..."

He sat so still, so watchful, as she undid the tie completely. It made a soft, slithering sound as she slipped it from around his neck. She laid it carefully over the arm of the sofa. Then she turned to him again and unbuttoned the top two buttons of his snowy dress shirt, smoothing the collar open, revealing the powerful column of his neck and the sharp black point of one of those intricate tattoos that covered his shoulder and twined halfway down his arm.

"Better?" she asked.

They shared a smile as he nodded. He said, "There's more."

She took his right hand and turned it over, revealing his cuff buttons. One by one, she undid them. "Tell me."

"I'm dyslexic," he said, his voice rougher than usual, freighted with something wary, something wounded. "You know what dyslexia is?"

"I think I do. I think I remember reading that it's when a person has difficulty in learning to read or interpret words, letters and other symbols?"

"That's pretty close to the generally accepted definition."

She took his left hand and unbuttoned that cuff, too.

He spoke again. "Most people think dyslexia is what you just said. A learning disorder, period. It's more. It's a challenge, a tough one. But it's a gift, too." She sat with his hand in her lap, the buttons undone, drinking in every word, as he explained, "You remember how I was as a kid. Trouble. Always getting in fights. Everyone thought I was stupid because I couldn't get the hang of reading. I hated school, hated being the slow kid. I acted out constantly. Only later did I figure out that my problem was I couldn't learn the way most kids learn. A traditional school environment did nothing for me. I don't get phonics, don't get learning things in rote sequence. It completely overloads me. So I would lash out."

She did remember that troubled boy so well. "You always seemed so angry."

"You bet I was. By the time I was eleven, my mother was at the end of her rope with me. As a last-ditch effort to find something I could do well, she enrolled me in a karate class—and everything changed for me. For once, I got something, really *got* it. Yeah, I have to work my ass off to try and get the meaning out of a line of letters across a page. But I'd always been damn good at fighting. The way my brain is wired makes me more capable than most people of visualizing the moves of my opponents in advance. I see the whole picture, I guess you could say. And that makes me more willing to follow my instincts. So I was good at karate, and finally being good at something was damn motivating. It got me going, gave me hope. I was driven to excel." He took her hand then and wove his fingers with hers.

It felt so good, her hand in his. She held on tight. "Answer me a question…"

"Name it."

"You seemed nervous about telling me this. Were you?"

He squeezed her fingers. "Yeah, I was."

"But I can't see why you would be, not after the way your life's worked out."

"There's more. And you need to hear it."

She *needed* to hear it? She almost asked him why, but then decided that the whys could wait. "All right…"

"Dyslexia is often genetic."

She frowned. "So you're telling me that Annabelle is dyslexic?"

"No. So far, Annabelle shows none of the signs. Already, she can recognize her alphabet and sound out simple words. But you should know that any child of mine could possibly be dyslexic."

She should know? It was an odd way to phrase it.

And he still had more to say. "I plan to be proactive. If a kid of mine showed signs of dyslexia, I would be on it, arranging for early testing, providing alternative learning systems and support, working with the school so everyone's on the same page about what needs to be done. If one of my kids was dyslexic, I would see to it that he didn't have to go through the crap I went through. I would make sure any kid of mine never had to feel stupid and incompetent and lag way behind the learning curve." He tipped his head then and asked with wry good humor, "You still with me, Chloe?"

"Absolutely. Yes. And I'm so sorry, Quinn. That you felt stupid and incompetent when you were little. No child should have to feel that way."

"I got past it."

"That doesn't make it right." At his chuckle, she chided, "It's nothing to joke about, Quinn."

He shrugged. "Tell me something."

She had that odd feeling again; there was more going on here than she was picking up. "Of course."

He let go of her hand, reached for his coffee—and said just what she'd been thinking. "Do you have any clue why I'm laying all this on you?"

She watched him take a sip. "Whatever your reasons, I have to say it's really nice to have a guy just sit right down and talk to me about the toughest things. It's rare."

"Right." He set the cup down again and rolled one of his unbuttoned cuffs to the elbow. "It's what women love. A guy who won't shut up…"

"I don't know about 'women.' But I know what *I* like.

And you telling me about what matters to you, about what made you who you are? I do like that. A lot."

"Well, all right." He rolled the other cuff. She watched him, admiring the hard shape of his arms, thick with muscle, roped with tendons, dusted with light brown hair, nicked here and there with small white ridges of scar tissue. He went on, "But I do have a reason for loading you up with way more info than you asked for."

"And I keep trying to make you see that you don't *need* a reason."

He slanted her a teasing look. "Got that."

A low laugh escaped her. "Well, okay, then. I get it. You're trying to tell me the reason—so go ahead. I'm ready for it."

"You sure?"

She groaned and executed a major eye roll. "Will you *please* stop teasing me?"

Now he looked at her so steadily, a look that made her warm all over, especially down in the center of her. "All right." And then, just like that, he said, "I want to marry you, Chloe."

Chapter Five

Quinn wasn't finished. "I want to build a life with you, have kids with you. Like I said, I'm a guy who follows my intuition, a guy who has trouble sounding out a word—but also a guy who gets the big picture. And once I know what I want, I go for it. I want you, Chloe, for my wife. I want you for my little girl, too, because I know you'll be the mother Annabelle needs."

Chloe just stared at him. Words? They'd completely deserted her.

He put up a hand. "It's okay. You don't have to say anything now. All you have to do is take your time. Think it over. And you should know the kids aren't a deal breaker for me. I want more. But if you don't, I can live with that. Annabelle will be enough."

"I, um…" She had no idea what to say next.

That didn't seem to bother him. He simply waited.

And she found that she couldn't sit still. She got up,

eased from behind the coffee table and then kept going to the sliding door, the one she'd slipped out that first night, when he came up the hill and she took him to her bed.

He didn't try to stop her. He didn't say a word, only sat there, patiently waiting for her to process all he'd just said.

She appreciated his silence and stillness now, appreciated it every bit as much as she did all that he'd told her moments before. She flipped on the deck lights and stared out at the two empty cedar chairs.

Was this really happening? Just like that, out of nowhere, he wanted to marry her?

But then again, no. Not out of nowhere, not really. He was such a focused sort of man. Of course, he would decide what he wanted and lay it all out for her so honestly and directly.

She fiddled with the pearls her dad had given her years ago, when she thought she knew everything and saw so clearly how her life would go.

What about love? Quinn hadn't mentioned love.

Should that bother her?

Well, it didn't. She'd had enough declarations of love from her rotten-hearted ex-husband to last her into the next century. And where had all that love talk gotten her but wounded, divorced and bitterly disappointed?

This, what Quinn offered, was better.

It wasn't a fantasy, not perfect. But it was honest. It felt real.

Quinn spoke then. "One more thing. About Manny..." He waited for her to look at him, and then for acknowledgement that she'd heard what he said. When she gulped and nodded, he went on. "Manny's part of the family. So you would not only be getting me and Annabelle. There's Manny, too. He can be a pain in the ass, I know. But he's not going anywhere. If you said yes, you would need to deal with him, work with him."

She felt a soft smile tremble across her mouth. "I would never for a second expect it to be any other way."

He didn't smile. But his eyes were so bright. "Well, all right, then."

The part about Manny had been so easy to answer. But the rest of it… She really didn't know what to say. She stared out the sliding door again.

He asked into the heavy silence, "Want me to go?"

Turning from her study of the empty deck chairs, she faced him once more. "No way. I want you to stay."

He stood. "Will you think about it, consider my offer?"

"I will."

He came for her then. She waited, her whole body humming with sweet anticipation as he approached.

And when he was close enough that the heat he generated seemed to reach out and touch her, she canted her chin higher and gazed straight into those beautiful eyes. "You are like no one I've ever known."

"That's good, I hope?"

"Oh, yes. It's very good."

"Angel." He lifted a big hand and brushed a finger down the curve of her cheek, stirring up goose bumps, making her sigh. And then he lowered that wonderful mouth of his and brushed those lips, so gently, back and forth across her own.

She smiled into his kiss, brought her hands up between them and went to work undoing the rest of the buttons down the front of his shirt. It didn't take long. She spread the shirt wide and pressed her palms to his broad chest, to that beautiful tattoo with his little girl's name in the middle of it. His skin was hot, wonderfully so. Sandy hair formed a tempting T across.

And down.

Best of all, she could count the strong beats of his big heart. She whispered against those velvety lips of his, "I should have made a move on you back in high school."

He chuckled, the low rumble sending a thrill shivering straight to the core of her. "That wasn't your style—and I wasn't your type."

"Oh, but Quinn. You *were* my type. What a fool I was then. I took what I thought was the safe way—and it wasn't safe in the least. It turned out all wrong."

"Hey." His voice was heaven, the perfect blend of rough and tender. He kissed the tip of her nose. "No regrets, huh?"

"But I do have regrets." She slid her hands up over his thick, hard shoulders, and clasped them around his neck. "And I can't just wish them away."

He shrugged out of his shirt and let it fall. Then he bent his head lower, smoothed her hair aside and pressed his hot mouth to the crook of her neck. "Forget 'em, then." His breath so hot across her skin, branding her, burning her. "For now, at least?"

She threaded her eager fingers up into his hair. "Help me with that?"

"Happy to." He breathed in through his nose. "You smell so good..." And then he scraped his teeth where his lips had been.

She shivered and moaned as he kissed his way back up over the curve of her jaw to claim her lips again. She opened for him. Heat speared through her as his tongue swept her mouth.

He lifted her hair off her neck with one hand. With the other, he took down the long zipper at the back of her dress and guided the dress off her shoulders. It dropped to the floor. She broke the lovely kiss in order to step out of it. He bent, picked it up and tossed it on the nearest chair.

Unbuttoning and unzipping, flinging articles of clothing toward the chair as soon as they had them off, they undressed each other.

Finally, when the only thing left was her pearls, he ordered gruffly, "Turn around."

She showed him her back. He unhooked the diamond clasp and took the necklace away. She faced him again in time to watch him reach over and lay the double strand on the nearby side table.

That was it. They were naked. Completely naked. And it seemed such a very long way to the bedroom.

Good thing she'd planned ahead.

He asked roughly, "What are you smiling about?"

And she pulled open the little drawer in the side table and took out the condom she'd tucked in there. Just in case.

"God. Chloe." He hauled her close, licked her ear and whispered in it, "You think of everything."

She whispered back, "A design teacher I had once told me that what I lack in imagination, I make up for in efficiency and good planning. I was really insulted at the time."

He took her earlobe between his teeth and tugged on it, biting down just a little harder than he needed to.

It felt so good it made her moan.

He whispered, "Put it on me."

She pulled back a little, far enough to meet his eyes. They were the color of some tropical sea right then, so deep, going down and down to deeper blue. Focused so completely on her. "Right now?"

For that she got a slow, deliberate nod from him.

She started to tear the top off the pouch.

"On second thought..." He caught her hand. "Wait..." And he pulled her close and kissed her some more. She gave herself up to that, to the taste of his mouth and the heat of his breath, to the feel of him, fully erect against her belly, making her burn for him.

Making her moan. She eased her free hand between them and wrapped her fingers around him, stroking. Oh, he felt so good—his powerful body pressed close, his mouth covering hers, the long, hard length of him held tight in her grip.

He kissed her endlessly, kissed her and caressed her, his fingers tracing magical patterns over her skin, teasing her breasts, first cradling them so gently, then catching the nipples, rolling them, so that she moaned some more. He seemed to really like it when she moaned.

He made a wonderful growling sound low in his throat. "Yeah," he said. "Like that?"

She couldn't say "Yes" fast enough. So she said it again, moving her hand up and down the thick length of him. "Yes..." And again, "Oh, yes, Quinn. Like that..."

And then his hand went lower, all the way to the feminine heart of her.

She cried out as he stroked her, opening her. She felt her own wetness, her readiness for him. She didn't want to wait a second longer. She couldn't wait...

"I..." She got that word out, and then couldn't for the life of her remember what she'd meant to say next.

"Yeah?" He was kissing his way along the line of her jaw, biting a little, licking some, too. Below, his fingers kept up their clever, thrilling play on her wet, secret flesh.

Oh, she was lost in the best way, totally gone. She kept her left hand wrapped around him, holding on for dear life. In her right, she still clutched the unused condom. She kind of waved it at him. "I..." Just that word. Nothing more. It was the only word she seemed to have at her disposal at the moment.

And apparently it was enough. He took the condom from her. She opened her eyes and stared up at him, dazed. Transported.

He lifted the small pouch, caught the corner between his teeth and tore the top off, all the while staring directly into her eyes, his other hand continuing to do amazing things to her below.

"Here," she whispered, holding out her free hand. He gave it back. She let go of him to use both hands, removing the wrapper and dropping it on the little table next to her pearls. And then she rolled the protection down over him. He moaned. And she granted him a small, triumphant smile. "There."

He reached for her, clasping her waist. She gasped in surprise. His right hand was slick and wet. It was *her* wetness, her desire. She was shocked at herself, at her own complete abandon.

Shocked. Amazed.

And gratified.

It was the same as that other night. Only better. He took her, claimed her, carried her right out of herself. He just swept her away—at the same time as he made her feel that she'd somehow come home, that nothing and no one would ever hurt her again.

And then he was lifting her. He did it so effortlessly, as though she weighed nothing. She grabbed for him, hungry for the feel of him, for her flesh pressed to his flesh, hot and tight and hard. She wrapped her arms and legs around him.

He whispered her name.

"Quinn," she whispered in return. "Oh, yes." She sank her teeth into his neck and when he growled at her, a dark, hot laugh escaped her. He bent to nuzzle her and she turned her face to his and claimed his mouth.

The kiss went deeper, wetter, hotter. And he was moving, with her all twined around him like a vine. He went to the short section of bare wall beside the entry closet, just walked her right up to it.

And then he lifted her, positioning her just so…

She felt him there, nudging her, right where she wanted him. And she pressed down.

He made the deepest, hottest, hungriest sound then, as she lowered herself onto him. He was wonderfully thick and large. Still, her body took him easily, gliding down around him until he filled her all the way.

They froze. She let her head fall back and her eyes drift shut. He had her perfectly braced, with the wall to give them stability. He canted his upper body slightly away from her, while below, he held her so close, just right, big hands cradling her open thighs. She clutched his shoulders, fingers gripping tight, her legs locked securely behind his waist.

She was…gone, lost in wonder, swept up in the connection, her breathing harsh and hungry, just like his.

"Chloe…"

And she opened her eyes and looked at him. His blue-green gaze was right there, waiting for her. He gripped her thighs tighter, pushing them wider, pressing his lower body closer, sliding into her that fraction deeper.

That did it. She felt the gathering, the build—and the lovely, hot sensation, as though all of her was blooming.

She asked, "Quinn?" For permission? Acknowledgment?

She had no idea which.

But he seemed to understand, even if she didn't. "Yeah,"

he answered, one corner of that soft, bad boy's mouth of his curling upward. "Go for it, angel."

And she did. She let go, let it happen, let it roll out from her in a hot, endless wave. Pleasure cascaded from the core of her, sizzling along every nerve, hitting the tips of her toes and the top of her head, spilling all through her in a flood of light and glory. He stayed with her, pressing up into her hard and tight, as the fire flamed so bright and then slowly faded down to a lovely, glowing ember.

And right then, when she thought it was over, when she was more than ready to ease her shaking legs to the floor, he started to move again.

She groaned in sexual overload and shoved fitfully at his rocklike shoulders. But he didn't release her.

And, well, could she blame him? After all, it *was* his turn. He'd swept her right off her feet and straight to paradise. The least she could do was stick with him now.

With a sigh of surrender, she stopped pushing him away and held on instead, bracing to ride it out.

But then, out of nowhere, all at once, it became more than just sticking with it for his sake. So much more.

In a split second, she was catching fire again.

"Oh… Oh, my!" She yanked him tight against her.

He let out a laugh, deep and knowing. Full of heat and joy.

She moaned his name as she pressed her open mouth to his, her body moving in time with his, picking up speed, finding the hard, insistent rhythm he set—and matching it, giving it back to him.

Time whirled away. The edge of the world was waiting for her. Waiting for both of them. She spun toward it, dizzy with the thrill of it. She hovered on the brink—and went over.

And he was right there with her, hitting the peak a moment after she did, pulsing hard and hot within her.

And then following her down.

Chapter Six

It was three-fifteen on Saturday morning when he left her.

Chloe put on a robe and walked him out to his beautiful old car. She kissed him goodbye—a long, slow, lovely kiss.

When he would have let her go, she grabbed him back and kissed him some more.

He laughed when he finally lifted his head. "Hey. I'm only going around the block."

"I know." She sighed, wrapped her arms around his waist, and beamed up at him. "But I want to make sure you don't forget me."

"No chance of that." He took a curl of her hair and wrapped it around his hand. "We got a special thing going, you and me."

"Oh, yes, we do."

He touched her chin with his thumb, brushed one last kiss across her upturned lips. "Get some rest."

She promised she would and reluctantly stepped back so he could open the car door and slide in behind the wheel. Then she waited, her arms wrapped around herself against the predawn chill, as he backed from the driveway and drove off down the street.

As soon as his taillights disappeared, she missed him. She wanted to run inside, grab the phone and call him back.

Which was totally silly. He'd asked her to marry him. And she was redecorating his house—*both* of his houses, as a matter of fact.

One way or another, she would be seeing him very soon.

She saw him the next day. He called and invited her out for ice cream with him and Annabelle. Chloe spent two lovely hours with father and daughter. Annabelle enchanted her. It might be too soon to talk about falling in love with Quinn. But she had no problem admitting she was head over heels for his little girl.

And then, that night, Quinn came up the hill to join her. He stayed for two hours. They talked about Annabelle and about Chloe's plans for his houses—and then they made love. He left at a little past midnight.

Same thing on Sunday night.

Monday at nine in the morning, Quinn closed on the house across the street from Chloe. Then, at eleven, he brought Manny and Annabelle to Chloe's showroom to see the plans and sign the contract for the redesign of the house down the hill. Chloe had cookies on offer at the coffee table, which Annabelle spotted immediately. Manny said she could have one.

Annabelle chose a cookie, thanked Chloe sweetly—

and asked if she knew how to make a fairy princess dress. "I want one, Chloe. Will you *please* make me one?"

Before Chloe could reply that she absolutely could and would, Quinn said, "Anniefannie, you are pushing it."

"Daddy!" The little girl tipped her cute nose high in a perfect imitation of disdain. "I'm not a fannie."

"But will you stop pushing it?"

Annabelle dimpled adorably. "But Chloe can make a *room*. I know she can make me a fairy princess dress." She turned pleading eyes on Chloe, who longed only to give her whatever she wanted. "Pleeeaaase, Chloe."

Manny spoke up then. He said one word. "Annabelle." After which he pushed back his chair and held out his hand.

Annabelle's lower lip started quivering. "Oh, no. Not the *car*. I don't want to sit in the *car*. Pleeaaassse, Manny."

Manny let out a heavy sigh. "Are you gonna stop pestering Chloe and sit quietly at the table while we finish our business here?"

Annabelle announced loudly, "Yes, I am!"

Manny mimed locking his lips with a key.

Annabelle straightened her small shoulders and folded her hands on the table, all the while pressing her lips together and pointedly glancing from one adult to the next.

Finally, Manny nodded. "All right. We'll give it a try."

Annabelle nodded wildly but kept her little mouth tightly shut.

"Eat your cookie," Quinn said in his gentlest voice.

Annabelle made short work of the treat. And then Manny gave her a cup of crayons and some paper. She was a perfect little angel, happily coloring away as the grown-ups finished their meeting.

That afternoon, Chloe visited Bravo Construction, which consisted of three trailers and a warehouse on the southwest edge of town. She met with Nell Bravo, who was in her late twenties and stunningly beautiful, with long auburn hair and a vivid half-sleeve tattoo down her shapely left arm. The baby of the Bravo family, Nell had always been outspoken and tough-minded. Everyone knew you didn't mess with Nell.

Chloe had the plans with her for Quinn's redesign. She spent two hours in Nell's office trailer, going over everything in detail, coming to agreement on the budget and the schedule.

Nell would personally run the job. Tomorrow, Chloe would get busy ordering cabinets and appliances, counters and flooring. Nell would put in for the permits they would need. Demo would begin first thing next Monday morning. If all went as planned—which it rarely did—the project would take nine to ten weeks.

At four o'clock, when they had everything pretty well hammered out, Chloe got up to leave.

And Nell hoisted her heavy black biker boots up onto her battered desk. "Before you head out, we need to talk. Hey, Ruby?"

The plump, motherly looking clerk at the desk near the door glanced around. "What do you need?"

"Take fifteen?"

"Sure." Ruby got up from her laptop and left the trailer.

Chloe had a sinking feeling in her stomach.

Nell proved the feeling right as soon as the door closed behind the clerk. "So, I hear you've had a thing for Quinn ever since high school. Is that true?"

Chloe dropped back into her chair. "Monique Hightower's been talking."

"Did you think she wouldn't?"

Chloe suppressed a sigh. "No. I knew she would." It had all seemed so amusing Friday night. But looking in

Nell's narrowed eyes right now, she didn't think it was funny at all.

Quinn's sister demanded, "Answer my first question."

Chloe drew herself up. "Yeah. I had certain…fantasies about Quinn way back when. Is that somehow a crime?"

"He's not just a piece of tasty meat. He's a good man."

Tasty meat? Chloe took care to keep her voice even. "I know he's a good man, Nell."

"You slumming?"

Chloe didn't let her gaze waver. "I absolutely am not—and why would you think that? Quinn's a brilliant man with a whole lot going for him. The word *slumming* just doesn't apply."

"Oh, come on, Chloe. Your mother was practically best friends with my father's first wife. No way Linda Winchester's going to approve of you seeing one of the bastard Bravos—especially not the 'stupid' one who barely managed to finish high school."

Chloe felt the angry color flooding upward on her cheeks. When would people stop assuming that her mother made her choices for her? "Nell." She made a show of clucking her tongue. "Where do I even start with you? Not fair. Not to Quinn. And not to me. He's far from stupid and he's done just fine for himself. We both know that. As for me, yes, it's true. I *used* to let my mother have way too much influence over me. But that was then. Right this minute, I'm thirty-one, divorced, fully self-supporting and on my own. My mother has zero say about whom I go out with."

Nell's lush mouth twisted. "Does your mother know that?"

Busted. "I'll say it again. *I* decide whom I spend time with."

Nell dropped her heavy boots to the floor, braced both

elbows on the desk and folded her hands between them. "Am I pissing you off, Chloe?"

The perennial good girl in Chloe pushed for denial, for smoothing things over after neatly sweeping them under the carpet. But no. The truth was better. "Yes, Nell. You are pissing me off."

"Good." Nell tipped her head to the side. The overhead fluorescents made her fabulous hair shimmer like a red waterfall. "Don't you hurt him, or you'll be answering to me."

Chloe sat tall. "I don't know for sure what's going to happen. But Quinn's an amazing man who means a lot to me. The last thing I would ever want to do is hurt him."

Nell's swivel chair squeaked as she flopped back in it and folded her arms across her spectacular breasts. She stared at Chloe, unblinking, for a grim count of ten. Then: "Look. I like your plans for the house. You know your job. I like the way you carry yourself. And I hardly knew you, back in the day. You were four years ahead of me in school. I only knew your reputation as the perfect one, the one headed for a good marriage to a rich husband, two-point-two children, a soccer-mom-and-country-club life—and some chichi career that you could fit in between social engagements."

"Something like interior design, you mean?"

"Hey. If the glass slipper fits…"

"As it turned out, it didn't. Not by a long shot. And that was then, Nell. I'm not that girl anymore."

Another long, measuring stare from Nell. Finally, she shrugged. "You know, I think I believe you." She got up and held down her hand. Chloe did want peace with Quinn's sister—with all of his family. After a moment's hesitation, she took Nell's offered hand and rose. Nell said, "Looking forward to working with you."

"I'm sure it will be interesting."

"Right. And listen. When you tell Quinn about this little talk we had—"

Chloe didn't even let her finish. "Why would I tell him? The way I see it, what just happened is between you and me."

Nell arched an auburn eyebrow. "Fair enough." And then she grumbled, "I'm really starting to like you. How 'bout that?"

"I'm glad. I'm going to do my best not to disappoint you—though you did go a little overboard just now."

Always a fighter, Nell stuck out her chin. "You think so?"

"Yes, I do. Then again, it's nice to know how much you love your brother and that you have his back."

That evening, Chloe spent a pleasant hour with a sketch pad, drawing a series of small figures that looked a lot like Annabelle. The figures all wore different versions of a magical, multilayered, brightly colored fairy princess costume, complete with wings—because what's a fairy princess costume unless there are wings?

A little later, when Quinn showed up, she took him downstairs to her home office and showed him the drawings.

"She would love it," he admitted with some reluctance. And then he shook his head. "You know she wants a puppy, too? There's no end to what Annabelle wants."

Chloe laughed. "The puppy's your problem."

"So far, we're holding the line on that."

"I just want to make this costume for her."

He took the sketch pad from her, dropped it to her desk, then wrapped his arms around her and kissed the end of her nose. "You're a pushover."

She grinned up at him. "I promise to get myself under

control soon when it comes to dealing with her. But I want to do this for her. I want her to have her dream room and I want her to have her fairy princess dress."

He chuckled. "You're giving me the big eyes. You're as bad as she is."

She traced the crew neck of his Prime Sports T-shirt with her index finger and then she pressed her lips against the hot skin of his powerful neck. "I would need to take her measurements, and probably let her see the sketches, to make sure I've got it right, got it just as she imagines it. So she would have to know ahead of time that she was getting what she wanted…"

"Yep. The big eyes," he muttered gruffly. "I know what you're doing." He kissed her then, a lovely, deep, slow one, after which she sighed and gazed up at him hopefully. Finally, he grumbled, "Wait a week or two before you bring it up to her. At least she won't think all she has to do is bat her eyes and beg a little and everything she wants will just drop in her lap."

"I'll check with Manny, too, to make sure he's okay with it. And if he gives the go-ahead, I'll wait two weeks to show her the drawings. How's that?" she asked, batting her eyes for all she was worth.

He gave in. "Fine."

"Thanks." She sighed and turned in his embrace so she could lean back against him.

He put his arms around her waist, and she felt his warm lips in her hair. "How'd your meeting with Nell go?"

Chloe thought of his little sister's biker boots hitting the desk, of the hot, protective gleam in Nell's emerald-green eyes. "Great. I like her. I think we'll work well together."

"She can be a hard ass. Don't let her intimidate you."

Chloe smiled to herself. "Not a chance."

And then she caught his hand and led him back upstairs to her bedroom, where they made slow, delicious love.

He put his clothes back on at a little after midnight. She hated to see him go and she told him so. And then she kind of waited for him to point out that, if they were married, he wouldn't have to go.

But then he just kissed her again and said he'd see her tomorrow.

She put on her robe and walked him to the sliding door in the great room. Once he was gone, she stood looking out at the stars, thinking about saying yes to him.

Wanting to.

Because she wanted *him*. She *liked* him—and she liked his daughter and Manny, too. He wanted a wife and a mother for Annabelle. And all her life, she'd longed to be an excellent wife to a good and decent man, to be a loving mother. The idea of having Annabelle as her own made her heart feel too big for her chest. And the part about having Quinn's babies?

That hollowed her out and made her burn.

But speaking of burning...she'd been burned before, and badly. And it hadn't even been three weeks since that first night Quinn came up the hill and joined her in her bed.

How could she be sure of him in such a short time? With her track record, how could she be sure of anyone?

The stars outside were silent. They had no answers for her.

Tuesday flew by. She had several customers at the showroom. And she had shopping to do, an endless list of goodies that would be needed for Quinn's remodel.

When Chloe got home that evening, she saw a moving van at the house across the street. She went on over. Manny was there, directing the movers. He greeted her with a grin and a hug and said that Quinn was down at the other house feeding Annabelle her dinner on the last night they would spend at home until after the remodeling.

Chloe explained about the fairy princess dress.

Manny said, “She’s gonna love that.”

“So it’s okay with you? You don’t think I’m a complete pushover?”

“I think we got a little girl who loves her princesses. And you want to help her with that. Sounds about right to me.”

She thanked him and then glanced around, admiring the soaring stone fireplace and the thick log walls. “Give me a tour?”

“Getting ideas for this one already?”

She nodded. “I’m happy that I’ll have a chance to get to know this house ahead of time, get familiar with it, you know? I’ll have an opportunity to mull over what changes will work best for it. Redoing a log home presents a special set of challenges.”

Manny seemed to be studying her. “You’re all right, Chloe.”

“I’m glad you think so, Manny. I’m growing quite fond of you, as well.”

“Quinn pop the question yet?”

Chloe fell back a step. “He told you he was going to?”

“Hell, no. He told me zip. But we been together more than a decade. I got a good idea what’s going on with him, whether he lays it out for me or not.” The two burly moving guys came in with the dining-room table. Manny said, “Through there, boys.” And on they went. Manny lowered his voice for Chloe alone and said, "You haven't said yes yet, have you?"

Chloe pretended to ponder. "Hmm. Let me see. Would Quinn really want me to answer that?"

Manny chortled out a rough laugh. "Come on. Let me show you the house..."

The landline was ringing when Chloe got back to her place. It clicked over to her old-school answering machine before she could pick up.

It was her mother. "Sweetheart, we're home. Walked in the door five minutes ago. Maui was heaven, as always. But it's nice to be back and I can't want to see you, find out how you've been doing and tell you all about our trip. Call me the minute you get this. Love you..."

Chloe stood by the phone and considered getting it over with, calling her mother back right away. Years of conditioning had her feeling she really *ought* to call now, that a good daughter could be counted on to keep in contact with the ones she loved.

But as soon as her mother asked her what she'd been up to in the past two weeks, Chloe would be confronted with the question of how much to say.

Ha. As if there was a choice. Monique Hightower was spreading the news about her and Quinn far and wide. One way or another, it wouldn't be long before her mother got an earful. And it would probably be better if her mother heard it from Chloe.

Better being a relative term, knowing her mother.

Chloe picked up the phone.

And then set it back down again.

Her hand was shaking slightly, and that made her mad.

Why should she live in fear of her own mother? She'd faced Nell Bravo right down and told her that Linda Winchester did not run her life. She'd told Quinn the same thing. She needed to live by her own words.

Chloe turned the ringer off on the kitchen and bedroom phones and turned the volume on the message machine all the way down. Then she switched the sound off on her cell, as well. She'd check to see who'd called her at *her* convenience, thank you very much.

And she would get in touch with her mother later, after she'd had a little time to decide exactly what she wanted to say to her.

The evening went by—a goodly portion of it spent joyfully in Quinn's strong arms. After he left, she had trouble falling asleep. She couldn't stop stewing over what to tell her mom.

Somehow, in the morning, she slept through her alarm. That left her rushing to get ready and out the door in time to get the showroom opened by nine.

Her mother called the showroom number at ten. "Sweetheart, there you are!"

Chloe still wasn't ready to deal with her. "Mom. Glad you're home safe. Can't talk now. You know that. I'm at work."

"But how am I supposed to get hold of you if you won't answer your—?"

"Mom, I have another call," she outright lied. "I'll call you this evening, I promise."

"But—"

"Gotta go. I'll call. Promise."

Her mother was still protesting as Chloe hung up the phone. She knew time was running out. She was going to have to stop being such a coward. All day long, in the back of her mind, she rehearsed the things she would say when she called back that night.

I've been seeing Quinn Bravo. I care for him, Mom. Deeply. He's asked me to marry him and I am seriously considering telling him yes.

It all sounded so simple. It was…what people did. They found each other and they fell for each other and realized they didn't want to be apart. So they got married and raised a family.

Why shouldn't she have that—and with the right man this time? With a good man, a strong man. A man who cared about more than money and power and *things*. A man who considered her a whole person, with a heart and mind of her own, not just his most prized possession who looked good on his arm and had great taste and could work a room with the best of them.

Short answer: she absolutely *should* have that. And she *would* have it. With Quinn.

By the time she locked up the showroom and went home, she was all fired up to get it over with. To call her mother and tell her simply and proudly that she and Quinn were together.

But as it turned out, no call was necessary. When she pulled into her driveway, her mother's Mercedes SUV was parked in the side space next to the garage.

Chloe's stomach lurched at the sight, which was so pitiful it made her want to throw her head back and scream. But she didn't scream. She drew in a slow breath and told herself to man up. It was her life and she was going to live it for herself, not her mother. She would tell her mom the simple truth about her and Quinn and that would be that.

But then, as she left the garage by the breezeway door and caught sight of her mother waiting on the front step, it became crystal clear from the tight, furious expression on Linda Winchester's face that she already knew about Quinn.

Chloe's steps faltered. Only for a second, though. She quickly caught herself, straightened her shoulders and kept right on walking. "Mom. I don't remember you mentioning that you would be dropping by."

"Oh, please." Her mother gave her a truly withering glance. "Let me in. I have a few things to say to you and I'm not going to say them on your front step."

Chloe froze with her key raised to unlock the door. "Look, Mother. I don't want to—"

"Open the door. Now, please."

The temptation was so powerful to tell her mother right then and there that this was *her* house and *she* would decide who did or didn't enter it.

But then again, well, Linda Winchester wasn't the only one who had a few things to say. And she wasn't the only one who preferred to have this out in private.

So she unlocked the door. Her mother brushed past her as she disarmed the alarm.

Carefully, quietly, Chloe shut the door. Her mother stood beside the formal dining table, her blond head high, bright spots of color flaming on her cheeks, her lips bloodless with tension.

Chloe almost felt sorry for her. "Look, Mom. Why don't you sit down?"

Linda whipped out the chair at the end of the table and sat in it. She put her hand to her mouth and shut her eyes.

Chloe took the nearest chair. She waited until her mother dropped her hand away from her mouth and opened her eyes again before she said gently, "You're obviously very upset. Please tell me why."

Her mother sucked in a gasp and snapped, "Don't you play coy with me, Chloe."

"I'm not playing coy," Chloe said with a calm that surprised her. "What I'm doing is trying my best not to jump to conclusions."

"All right." With two sharp tugs, Linda straightened the sides of the linen jacket she wore. "Agnes Oldfield dropped by to see me an hour ago. She says it's all over town that you've been seeing Quinn Bravo. She says you went to the Sylvan Inn with him last Friday night, where you told Monique Hightower right to her face that you were…*attracted* to that man ever since high school. Agnes also says that you've been seen having ice cream with him and that child of his. She says that everyone says how…intimate you seem together, that it's obvious something serious is going on between you." Linda pressed her hand flat to her chest, and shook her head fiercely. "I do not believe this. Tell me that none of it is true."

Chloe just stared. God. She'd known this would be bad. But somehow, now that it was actually happening, all she could think was *What are we doing here? How could I have let it get his far? Why didn't I back her down years ago*?

The questions were all too familiar to her. They were the same ones she'd asked herself over and over about her ex-husband.

"Well?" her mother demanded. "What do you have to say for yourself?"

"You know, Mom. I don't think I have to say anything. But I would like to know what happened to *you*? I just don't understand how you got so messed up."

Another indignant gasp. "Excuse me?"

"It's not going to work on me, Mother. Not anymore. All your trumped-up outrage, your sad, small-minded ideas about who's okay and who's not. Your judgments about the right kind of people and the ones who just don't measure up."

"Wait just a minute, now—"

"No. No, I'm not going to wait for you to try and fill my head with more of your small-minded garbage and your snobbish, silly lies."

"Well, I have never—"

"Stop. I mean it. I don't want to hear it, never again. Quinn Bravo is a fine man and I'm not listening to one more word of this ridiculous crap you're dishing out against him. Yes, I am seeing him. And I am *proud* to be seeing him. Also, you should know that I am redoing his house and I'm gratified that he and Manny Aldovino have confidence in my ability to do the job well. In fact, Quinn has asked me to marry him and I am seriously considering saying yes."

"Dear, sweet Lord. Have you lost your mind?"

"No, I have not. I am perfectly sane, saner than I've ever been in my life before. And all that old stuff about Quinn's mother and his father and his father's first wife, all those ancient, ridiculous distinctions between the *real* Bravos and the *bastard* Bravos… Nobody cares about that anymore. Nobody but you—and maybe Monique Hightower and Agnes Oldfield, who both ought to get a life and stay out of mine."

"But you surely can't—"

"Wake up, Mother. Smell the Starbucks. I mean, look at it this way. Haven't you heard? Quinn Bravo's rich now. He's made a big success of his life. You know how much you love a big success."

Linda Winchester paled. "How dare you imply that I care how much money a man makes?"

Chloe knew she had lost it completely when she shouted, "I'm not implying it, I'm saying it straight out!"

Her mother cringed and jerked back in her chair, as though terrified—which Chloe knew very well she was not. "There's no need to shout," Linda said with a wounded sniff. "And I would hardly consider beating other men to a pulp a 'successful' way to make a living. And what about that motherless child of his being raised by that strange old man?"

"Manny is a wonderful person and he's doing a terrific job with Annabelle."

"Oh, please. It doesn't matter how much money he has. Quinn Bravo will never measure up and I raised you to know that."

"Enough." Chloe stood. "What I know, Mother, is that I'm done. I'm finished. I've had enough of your narrow-minded, holier-than-thou, manipulative behavior to last me a lifetime."

Another hot gasp from her mother. "What's happened to you? What's the *matter* with you? You're acting like a crazy person. I brought you up to be better than this."

"Stop. Quit. There's just no point. I want you to leave now. I want you to leave my house and not come back until you've had a serious change in your attitude."

Something happened then. Linda's gaze shifted away. When she looked back at Chloe, she actually seemed worried. Was it possible she'd finally realized she'd gone too far? She said, more softly than before, with a hint of appeasement, "It's only that I don't want you to throw your life away. It's only that you're special. You deserve the best life has to offer. I want that for you. I want *everything* for you."

"I really do want you to go now." Chloe gentled her tone, but didn't waver. "Please."

Linda didn't get up. She only talked faster. "Oh, sweetheart. I know. I understand. You had it all. And you threw it away. But the good news is, if you'll only make a little effort, you and Ted can work through this rough patch and—"

Chloe put up a hand. "Get back with Ted? You can't be serious. I don't believe you, Mother. How many times have I told you I never want to hear his name? How many times have I told you that he hit me and he cheated on me and there is no going back from that? I don't *want* to go back. All I want is never to have to look in his evil, lying face again."

"You're overwrought."

"Oh, you bet I am." She stepped back and pointed at the door. "Please leave my house. Now."

Finally, her mother stood—and kept on talking. "Can't you see? That new wife of his? She's a pale imitation. She can't hold a candle to you. Ted realizes that now. And you know that you're exaggerating about his behavior, making a big drama out of a little marital spat or two."

"Wait." Chloe really, truly could not believe her ears. "What did you say?"

"I said, you're making a big drama of—"

"'He *realizes* that now'? How could you know what Ted Davies realizes?"

"Well, sweetheart, now listen. You really need to settle down, so that we can speak of this reasonably."

"Reasonably?" Chloe echoed in a near whisper. The awful truth had hit her like a boot to the head. Her ears were ringing. "You've been in touch with him, haven't you? You've been *encouraging* him."

Linda got right to work blowing her off. "Well, I... You know I only want what's best for you and I—"

"You've given him my address, haven't you?"

"Oh, don't be foolish. It's not as if you're in hiding."

"So you did give him my address."

Linda just wouldn't give it up and answer the question. She let out a low sound of complete disdain. "Don't make such an issue of it. Anyone could find out where you live with a minimum of effort."

"But Ted didn't have to make *any* effort, right? Because you'll tell him whatever he wants to know." She grabbed her mother's arm. "That does it. You're leaving."

Linda squealed. "What are you doing?" She slapped at Chloe. "Let go of me. You're *hurting* me..." The tears started then.

Chloe ignored them. She pulled her mother to the door, yanked it open and shoved her over the threshold.

Linda sobbed, "How can you do this to me? You're breaking my heart."

Chloe's answer was to firmly shut the door in her face.

Chapter Seven

That night, it took Quinn an extra half hour to chase off all the monsters and get Annabelle settled in bed. He performed his monster-removing duties happily. Partly because he was a total pushover for his little girl. And partly because he knew she needed the extra attention on her first night in her temporary bedroom in the log house across the street from Chloe.

After Annabelle finally went to sleep, he and Manny took beers out to the back deck, where they touched base on the usual household stuff, finances and the move.

They were just wrapping up when his cell chimed. A text. From Chloe. The first, he realized, that he'd ever gotten from her.

That made him smile—initially. And then he had to deal with the words in the little conversation bubble. At least it was only one sentence: Can you come over now?

Unease curled through him. Something in the starkness of the question didn't sit right. Chloe was generally so gracious and well mannered, the kind of woman to offer a drink and ask a man how his day had been before ever getting down to what she needed from him.

Manny asked, "Chloe?"

"Yeah." Texting was not his best event. He debated the option of turning up the sound on his text-to-speech app and voice-texting her back. Or he could just call her. But she was only across the street and he felt an urgency to get to her. He rose.

"Something wrong, Crush?"

Quinn clasped Manny's shoulder. "Probably nothing."

Manny reached up, patted his hand and let him go without a single wiseass remark.

Chloe must have been standing at the door, peering through the peephole, because she whipped it open before Quinn could raise his hand to knock. One look at her too-pale face and shadowed, red-rimmed eyes and Quinn knew his instincts had been right. Something had gone way wrong.

"Quinn." She grabbed for him.

He stepped inside, gathered her close and shoved the door shut with his heel.

"Quinn…" She curled against him, tucking her golden head under his chin, her slim arms clutching tight around him, as though she wanted to crawl right inside skin.

It freaked him out a little to see her so out of control. That only happened when he had her naked in bed. The rest of the time, she was the queen of smooth, hard to ruffle. Something had really spooked her. He stroked her hair and rubbed her back and reassured her with low, soothing words. "I'm here. It's okay now, all right? You just hold on tight…"

She burrowed even closer against him and confessed in a torn whisper, "I never, ever had the guts to stand up to her and now it's come down to this. Oh, I hate myself. I'm such a wuss. It shouldn't have gotten to this, I should have stopped her a long time ago. I—"

"Shh," he soothed. "Shh, now. Take a breath, a long, slow one…"

Obedient as a cowed and frightened child, she took a long, deep one and let it out nice and slow. "Oh, Quinn…" A sob escaped her.

He caught her beautiful face between his hands, tipped it up so he could see her haunted eyes again and took an educated guess. "This is about your mother?"

She hitched in a ragged breath and nodded. "After tonight, she's out of my life. I never want to see her again."

"Whoa," he said gently. "Come on, now, angel. Whatever she did, she *is* your mother."

Chloe pursed up her lips and stuck out her chin. "Don't even remind me."

"I'm only saying, whatever happened with her, give her a little time. She'll come around."

"Oh, you don't know her, Quinn," she insisted. "You don't know her at all." She sounded downright pissed off.

Which wasn't so bad, he decided. He'd take pissed off over brokenhearted and out of control any day of the week. "Hey." He stroked her hair some more, brushed a quick kiss across her sweet, trembling mouth. "You gonna talk to me? *Really* talk to me? Because I need a better idea of what happened before I can do much more than hold you and tell you it'll be okay."

"It was awful. We went at each other. She was like one of those crazed, jealous girlfriends on *The Jerry Springer Show.*" Chloe shut her eyes and sucked in another slow, careful breath. "And I wasn't much better."

Now, there was an image. Chloe and Linda Winchester going at it on *The Jerry Springer Show*. "Come on. Make some coffee or something. You can tell me what happened."

A few minutes later, they sat on the sofa. Chloe sipped the hot tea she'd made for herself. "She was waiting on the front step when I got home from work, and she was furious."

It didn't take a genius to figure out why. "Someone told her about you and me."

"That's right. She..." Chloe met his eyes then. "I don't even know how to tell you how awful she was."

"It's okay. You don't have to give me a blow-by-blow. She's never thought much of me or of my family and we knew that from the first."

"I, well, I want you to know that I didn't back down, Quinn. I didn't evade, either. For the first time in my life I stood right up to her. I told her I was seeing you and I intended to *keep* seeing you and that she'd better accept that."

"But she wouldn't accept it."

"No. We yelled at each other. I realized it was going nowhere and I asked her to leave. That was when she let it slip that she's been in touch with my ex-husband." Chloe's gaze slid away. "I hit the ceiling and threw her out." She fell silent, and she still wasn't looking at him.

He waited. When she didn't volunteer any more, he said, "It's probably about now that you should tell me whatever it is you're *not* telling me about your ex-husband."

She did face him then. And she looked stricken. In a small voice, she said, "I don't even know where to begin." He took her mug from her and set it on the low table. Then he hooked an arm around her shoulders and pulled her close to his side. She crumpled against him. "Oh, God..."

He pressed a kiss into her sweet-smelling hair. "It doesn't matter where you start. I'm not going anywhere until you've told me everything I need to know."

She let out a small, sad little sound. "All my life, all I wanted was to be my mother's good little girl. And look where that's gotten me..."

Quinn said nothing. He held her close.

Finally, hesitantly, she told him the story. "I met Ted Davies at Stanford in my sophomore year. He was four years older than me, in law school. And he was everything my mother raised me to want. Handsome and charming, already rich, from a powerful California family, bound for a successful career as a corporate lawyer. I saw him as perfect husband material, and he saw me as exactly the right wife to stand by him as he climbed to the top. We got married in a gorgeous wine country wedding at the end of my senior year and I went to work being his wife, which both of us considered a full-time job. It was all going so well until Ted lost his temper. He'd decided I'd been too friendly to one of the partners at his office Christmas party. We had a fight. We'd been married for a little more than two years. That was the first time he hit me." She tipped her head up and looked at Quinn then.

He knew that look. She was checking to see how he was taking it. He met her eyes and stroked her hair and didn't let her see what was going on inside him. He was a simple man, really, especially when it came to stuff like this. A simple man who wanted to track down that jackass she'd married and beat his face in for him.

Chloe lowered her head again and tucked herself against his chest. "I left him."

"Good."

She glanced up again. He was ready for that. Playing it easy and accepting for all he was worth, he kissed the tip of her elegant nose. With a sigh, she settled again. "Ted…wooed me back. He went into counseling for anger management to prove to me that he was a changed man."

"But he wasn't."

"I'll say this. He didn't hit me again for a long time, though his scary temper was increasingly in evidence as the next four years went by. Three years ago, I found out he was having an affair with a college student, an intern at his firm. I confronted him. When he couldn't convince me that he was totally innocent and that I was only being a small-minded, jealous wife, he lost it. He punched me in the face hard enough to bloody my nose and blacken both eyes. I left him. And after that, I was done. No cajoling or high-powered charm offensive or promises that he'd get more counseling could sway me. I sued for divorce. As it happened, he was still seeing the other woman—and she wanted to be his wife. So I got my divorce and a nice settlement. And Ted got a new, younger wife. And except for how I still feel guilty that I didn't press assault charges against him, that should have been the end of it, right?"

He rubbed a soothing hand up and down her arm. "But it wasn't."

"I tried to keep going in Southern California. But then Ted started coming around again, talking reconciliation, as if I would even let him near me, as if he didn't have a wife waiting at home. I decided I needed to make a new start—or rather, I realized what I really wanted was to come back where I began and try to get it right this time."

He tipped her chin up then and kissed her.

She said shyly, "I do feel like I'm finally getting it right, Quinn. Getting it right with you."

Those fine words dampened his carefully masked fury against the abusive loser she'd married, enough that he kissed her again. And then he asked, "So you're sure that your mother's been in contact with this guy?"

"She wouldn't admit it straight out, but yes. I'm sure she has. She told me how he wants to get back together with me—and my mother's all for that. That was when I finally threw her out. I'm done with her, Quinn. Finished."

Quinn blew out a slow breath. He was no more a fan of Linda Winchester than Linda was of him. And it turned his stomach that the woman would go behind Chloe's back and encourage the man who'd hurt her.

But there had been deep and painful rifts in his own family, especially back in the day when his father refused to choose between Sondra Oldfield Bravo and Quinn's mother. It wasn't all roses now, but it was better. Since returning to Justice Creek, he'd discovered he actually *liked* his half siblings. That couldn't have happened if they'd refused to give each other a chance.

"Still," he said. "There's a bond there, a strong one, between you and your mother."

"It's broken. Broken beyond repair."

"Chloe, she's family. You gotta keep that in mind, you know? I'm not saying just forgive her and act like nothing happened. But try to be open, okay? Give it time and see if she comes around, makes amends."

"I wish I could be as accepting and patient as you are."

Quinn had to stifle a grunt of disbelief when she said that. Yeah, he might be willing to be patient with her mother. But Chloe's ex? He'd like to meet good old Ted in a dark alley some night. Only one of them would come out, and it wouldn't be Davies.

Chloe snuggled in close again. "Can we just…leave the subject of my mother alone for now?"

"Sure. But I got a question."

She must have picked up something not all that accepting in his tone, because she pushed free of his arms and scooted back to the other couch cushion. "What?"

"You heard from this Ted character since you moved back to Justice Creek?"

Chloe cleared her throat. A definite tell. "No. He, um, hasn't called."

Quinn knew then that the guy *had* been in contact with her. He reminded her, "You and me, we got something special. And I know when you're not being straight with me."

She wrapped her arms around herself and pleaded with those pretty blue eyes. "You have to promise me you won't do anything, won't…go after him or anything."

Quinn's pulse leaped. He couldn't keep a promise like that. "You just gotta tell me what he did, Chloe. You know that you do, you know that's how we need to be with each other. We need to tell the truth to each other—and *then* we can decide what to do about it."

She swallowed. Hard. "All right. One time."

"You've heard from him one time?"

"Yes. He sent me flowers. With a short note that said how flowers remind him of me and he was sorry it didn't work out…"

There was more, he was certain. He pushed for it. "And?"

"The note also said that he, um…missed me. I threw everything—the vase, the flowers, that damn note, too—in the trash compactor and ground it all to bits."

"When was that?"

"A week ago. Last Wednesday night."

He wanted to pick up her tea mug from the table and hurl it at the far wall. But he kept it together and said levelly, "That was the night we sat out on your deck and talked for two hours."

She gazed at him warily now. "What are you getting at?"

"I wish you had told me then—or any day or night since then."

"That's not fair and you know it. It's been happening pretty fast with us. Think about it. I just couldn't tell you, didn't even know *how* to tell you—not the night it happened or the next day, or the day after that. I can barely talk about it now."

She had a point. He knew it. And really, he only wanted to neutralize any threat to her. "I don't blame you, angel." He said it softly, without heat. Because it was true. "No way do I blame you."

Her sweet face crumpled. "You mean that?"

"You know I do." He reached for her. She let out a small cry and allowed him to wrap his arms around her again. He held her tight, loving the way she felt, so soft in all the right places. "That's it, then? That's the only move he's made on you since you came back home?"

"Yes. That's it."

"Did you call him and tell him to leave you alone?"

"Uh-uh. You have no idea how many times in the past I told him to leave me alone. That only seemed to encourage him."

"I hear that. So, then, don't engage him." He lifted her hand and pressed his lips to the back of it. "Did you go to the police?"

"And tell them what? That my ex-husband sent me flowers out of the blue and a nice little note?"

"Don't get defensive. I agree that you don't have anything to charge the creep with. I just want to be sure, to know everything that happened, to know exactly where we stand with this piece of crap."

"We?" She pushed away from him again, smoothed the yellow skirt of her pretty summer dress over her knees and then looked him straight in the eye. "Quinn. Ted is in no way your problem. This thing with him is for me to solve. I will not drag you into my mess. I don't want you going after him, or approaching him, or contacting him or getting near him, ever. I need your word on that."

He would give her anything—the world on a gold platter. But not this. "That guy needs to know you're not alone anymore. He needs to know someone's got your back."

"I couldn't care less what *he* needs, Quinn. I'm talking about what *I* need. And that is to know I can tell you my hardest secrets and trust that you won't go racing off to solve all my problems for me in your own way. Because they are *my* problems and I'm the one who gets the final say when it comes to dealing with them. It's about respect, and you know it. You have to respect me and let *me* figure out how to mop up the mess I created. Please."

He really hated that what she said made sense. "You *will* tell me, if he does *anything*, if you hear so much as a word from him again?"

"I will, yes." She folded her hands on her knees. "And you will honor my wishes and let me handle this in my own way?"

He scraped both hands down his face. "You got me up against the ropes here."

"Because you *do* respect me. I know you only want

to protect me and you have no idea how much I love that about you."

Love. It was a big word. And it was also the first time she'd used it in reference to him. Quinn liked the way it sounded coming out of that fine mouth of hers. He liked it a lot.

What he didn't like was not being allowed to teach Ted Davies an important life lesson. Then again, guys like that always managed to get what was coming to them eventually. Quinn fervently hoped he'd have the honor of taking Ted to church when the time came.

"Quinn?" she asked, all breathless and hopeful. "I need your word that you'll leave Ted alone."

Damn it to hell. He gave it up. "All right. For now, for as long as he never tries to get in touch with you again, you got my word."

Chloe was no fool.

She fully understood what it cost Quinn to make her that promise. He'd done a really good job of hiding his anger at Ted. But already, in the short time they'd been together, she'd learned to read him. He wanted to go after Ted, he *needed* to do that, needed to step forward and be her protector.

What woman wouldn't appreciate that in a man?

But he'd done protectiveness one better. He'd agreed to go against what he needed to do and leave Ted alone. Because she'd asked him to. And if she hadn't already been halfway in love with him, well, that he *had* made that promise kind of sealed the deal as far as she was concerned.

"Thank you," she whispered, taking his big hand, turning it over and smoothing his beefy fingers open.

"Thank you…" She bent close and pressed a kiss in the center of his rough, hot palm.

"Let's just hope we've seen the last of him," Quinn muttered gruffly.

She couldn't agree more. And not only because she wanted nothing to do with her ex. Now there was Quinn to worry about. If Ted made another move on her, convincing Quinn to stay out of it was going to be exponentially tougher.

But they'd spent altogether too much of their evening on unhappy subjects. She forced a brighter tone. "First my mother, then Ted. Let's forget about both of them for now, huh?" She reached up and smoothed the thick brown hair off his forehead. "Now I want it to be just you and me, here on the sofa, doing whatever comes naturally."

He studied her face for a moment, his head tipped to the side. And then he kicked off his shoes. She followed suit, sliding off her sandals and pushing them under the coffee table.

"Come here." He took her by the shoulders, turned her and settled her with her head in his lap.

Chloe stared up at him, feeling better already. The hard things had been said. And now it was just her and Quinn, alone for the evening. He traced the curves of her eyebrows with a slow finger and then caught a lock of her hair and wrapped it around his hand the way he liked to do.

She said, "I hope I didn't drag you away from anything important at home…"

He shook his head. "Annabelle's all tucked in bed. Manny and I were just having a beer on the deck."

"Do you still want to marry me?" The words kind of popped out. She'd hardly known she would say them—until she did.

He gave her his bad-boy half smile. "Oh, yeah. But I'm not pushing. You decide what you want and you do it in your own time."

"Even after all the grim stuff I told you tonight? I'm not sure I'm such a good bet, Quinn."

He unwrapped her hair from around his fingers—and then twined it right back again. "You're not your mother and it's not your fault that your ex is a psycho dog. You *are* a good bet, angel. You're a fine woman with a big heart, the best there is."

His generous words warmed her, made a glow down inside her that all the trials of the afternoon and evening couldn't dim.

I think I'm falling in love with you, Quinn.

It sounded so right inside her head. But she wasn't quite ready to say it out loud yet. Talk of love still had some taint for her. It still held ugly echoes of the past.

She shut her eyes and drifted, cradled, safe, with her head in Quinn's lap.

Marriage. To Quinn.

Was she ready for that? They'd been together such a short time and she'd messed up so badly before. How could she be certain?

She opened her eyes.

And he was gazing down at her, steady. Sure. Not having to say anything, just being there with her.

When she looked in his eyes, her doubts about herself and her future and her iffy judgment just melted away. When she looked in Quinn's eyes, she *was* sure.

And come on. She'd dated Ted for a year before she said yes to him. And then it was another year until their lavish wedding. She'd given herself plenty of time to really *know* Ted. She'd done everything right.

And still, it all went wrong. Ted was the man her mother wanted for her.

And Quinn?

It was so simple. Quinn was the one *she* wanted for herself. He was *her* choice, her second chance to get it right. She trusted him. She knew he would be good to her, that she would be good for him—and for Annabelle and Manny, too.

Together, they could make a full, rich life, the life she'd always wanted. The life she'd given up hope that she would ever find.

Until now. Until Quinn.

He unwound her hair again. And she sat up and took his arm and wrapped it across her shoulders. He gathered her closer. She drew her legs up onto the sofa and folded them to the side so she was facing him. Looking right into those wonderful eyes, she said, "Well, I've decided, then. And my decision is…" She stretched up enough to nip his scruffy jaw with her teeth. "Yes."

For once, he actually looked taken completely off guard. "What did you say?"

"I said yes, Quinn. I will marry you. I want it to be a small, simple wedding, just family and close friends. And I want it to be soon."

"Chloe." He took her face between those big hands. "Seriously? You're sure?" He looked so vulnerable right then, as if he couldn't quite believe she really meant it.

She did mean it. "Yes, I am very sure."

"Damn," he whispered prayerfully.

He kissed her, a kiss that curled her bare toes and created that incomparable heavy, hot yearning down in the core of her. And then he scooped her up in those big arms of his and carried her to her bedroom.

Late into the night, he showed her exactly how happy her decision had made him.

Dawn was breaking when he left her. She stood out on her front porch in a robe and slippers, watching him walk across the street to his temporary home, knowing her hair needed combing and her eyes were low and lazy. She was fully aware that she had the look of a woman thoroughly and repeatedly satisfied—and she didn't care in the least who saw her.

She'd made her decision. She was marrying Quinn and finally getting the life she'd always dreamed of.

Chapter Eight

At the showroom a few hours later, Chloe called Tai and asked her to come in early.

At ten, Quinn picked her up. They drove to Denver, where they had lunch and he bought her a beautiful engagement ring and a platinum wedding ring to match. She bought him a ring, too, a thick platinum band that she couldn't wait to slip on his finger when the big day came. She was back at her showroom by four.

That evening, just as she was letting herself in the front door, the house phone rang. She saw it was her parents' number and let it go to the machine.

A few minutes later, she checked to see what her mother had said. But it turned out it was her dad. He'd left a two-sentence message: "Chloe, this is your dad. Please call me."

She did, right then.

He asked her if she was all right and Chloe told him that she would be fine.

Doug Winchester said, "Your mother's just brokenhearted over what happened last night."

Chloe refused to let him play the guilt card on her. "We don't see eye-to-eye, Mom and me. And I don't think that either of us will be changing our positions anytime soon."

"She loves you. You know that. *I* love you."

"Thanks, Daddy. I love you, too. But sometimes love really can't make everything right. Not with Mom, anyway. With Mom, it's her way or nothing. And I'm through doing things her way. In fact, Quinn's asked me to marry him and I've said yes."

The line went dead silent. Then her father asked cautiously, "Isn't this a little sudden?"

She resisted the urge to say something snappish. "I care for him deeply, Dad. It's what I want."

"You're sure?"

"I am."

Another silence. And then her father had the good grace to say that he hoped she would be happy. "I think I'll wait a few days to tell your mother about your engagement, though."

"Right now, Dad, I don't care if you tell her or not."

"Chloe. You don't mean that."

She didn't argue. What was the point? "I'll call and let you know about the wedding. It's going to be small and simple." Nothing like the three-ring circus in Sonoma when she'd married Ted. "I hope you can come. Quinn wants me to be patient with Mom, so I'm going to give it a little time before I decide whether I'm willing to have her at the wedding."

Another deep silence from her dad. Then, "Let's just see how things go, shall we?"

Chloe agreed that would be wise. They said goodbye.

A few hours later, when Quinn came over, she cried

a little for her fractured family. He held her and told her it would all turn out all right. Somehow, when he said it, she almost believed it.

Friday morning first thing, Nell Bravo dropped by Chloe's showroom. Chloe broke the big news and showed off her gorgeous ring.

Nell said, "So, then. This makes it official. You're gonna be my sister. And that means we'll have to bury the hatchet permanently, you and me."

"You know, you really scare me when you talk about hatchets."

Nell laughed and grabbed Chloe in a hug and waltzed her in and out of the various carpet and flooring displays. Then Quinn's sister confessed, "I already knew. Quinn told me this morning. And I'm here to find out when you're breaking for lunch so I can get a table at the Sylvan Inn for you and me and my sisters."

Chloe met the Bravo sisters at the Sylvan Inn at one. There were four of them. Clara and Elise were the daughters of Franklin Bravo's first wife, Sondra. Jody's and Nell's mother was the notorious Willow Mooney Bravo, who'd been Frank's mistress during most of his marriage to Sondra. The day after Sondra Bravo's funeral, Willow married Frank. He moved her right into the mansion he'd built for Sondra. Frank Bravo's refusal to observe even a minimal period of mourning after Sondra's passing caused no end of shock and outrage in the angry hearts of the judgmental types in town, Chloe's mother first among them.

Tracy Winham, Elise's best friend and business partner, joined them, too. And so did Rory Bravo-Calabretti, a cousin to the Bravo sisters. Rory was an actual princess from a tiny country called Montedoro. But Rory didn't act like a princess. She loved Justice Creek and she was down-to-earth and lots of fun. Recently she'd decided to make her home in America. She lived with her fiancé, Walker McKellan, at Walker's guest ranch not far from town.

As a matter of fact, all the Bravo women were lots of fun. Even more so after a couple of glasses of the champagne Nell had ordered to toast Chloe and Quinn and their future happiness together. Chloe never drank alcohol at lunch. After all, she still had half a day of work ahead and she preferred to be alert and clearheaded on the job.

But today, she drank the champagne—more than she should have. And she had a fabulous time sharing stories about the old days with Quinn's sisters.

"Quinn was always so moody," said Jody, and everyone nodded. "He was mad at everything and just about everybody."

"But even then there was a certain sweetness about him," said Clara, who was Sondra's oldest daughter and considered the family peacemaker.

Back in the day, when the two sides of Frank's family were constantly at odds, Clara was the one who kept trying to get them to make peace and come together. She and Quinn and Chloe were the same age.

"I remember," Clara said, "when we were in Miss Oakleaf's class, first grade. Remember, Chloe?"

"Yes, I do. Miss Oakleaf was so pretty. I wanted to be just like her when I grew up."

"Oh, me, too," Clara agreed.

"She pinned her hair up in a twist and she always looked so elegant. And she wore high heels and pencil skirts." Chloe frowned. "Were they even called pencil skirts back then?"

Clara considered. "Straight skirts, I think. And yeah. Miss Oakleaf was a beauty. Quinn had a big crush on her."

"She was patient with him," Chloe said softly, remembering how he struggled to keep up with the rest of the class.

Clara remembered, too. "He would get mad and act up and she would talk to him so gently."

"And then," said Chloe, "the Hershey's Kisses started appearing on her desk every morning…"

Clara took up the story. "Just a few of them, lined up in their shiny silver foil wrappers, waiting there for Miss Oakleaf on her desk pad at the beginning of every day."

"No one knew who was leaving them," said Chloe.

And Clara said, "Until Freddy Harmon spotted Quinn in the act. Freddy spied on Quinn through the window, didn't he, and saw him sneak in and put three Kisses on Miss Oakleaf's desk?"

"That's right," Chloe replied softly. "Quinn was so humiliated…" She shook her head, aching for the troubled little boy he'd once been.

Jody said, "The way I heard it, he went ballistic."

Clara nodded. "He chased Freddy around the playground till he caught him, and then he beat the crap out of him. For that, Quinn was suspended for two weeks. Looking back on our elementary school years, it seems like he spent more time suspended or in detention than he ever spent in class."

They all laughed. They could afford to laugh about it now that Quinn was a grown man who'd built himself a fine, productive life.

Nell asked, "Remember that time he and Jamie and Dare got into it on the playground?" James and Darius were Clara's and Elise's full brothers, Sondra's sons.

Elise nodded. "It was two against one. Plus, Jamie and Dare were older and bigger. But Quinn just wouldn't give up and go down."

Rory shook her head. "It's so strange, knowing him now, to hear what a troublemaker he used to be."

"By the time he was twelve or so," Clara said, "no one would fight with him. By then, they all knew that he would never quit. If you took on Quinn Bravo, it was going to be long and ugly and there would be way too much blood."

"But look how he turned out," Tracy piped up. "Rich and successful, with a beautiful daughter, about to marry the one and only Chloe Winchester." Tracy raised her glass and everyone followed suit. "To Chloe. You go, girl."

Chloe blushed a little. "Aww."

Nell shook her gorgeous head of auburn hair. "Chloe. Seriously. You and Quinn? Never woulda seen that coming."

Chloe beamed at her future sister-in-law, her heart full of fondness, her brain pleasantly hazy with the champagne and the good family feelings. She really was starting to feel seriously bondy with Nell. Was it only five days ago that they'd squared off in the trailer at Bravo Construction?

"Heads up, my sisters," Elise whispered out of the side of her mouth. "Don't look now, but here comes trouble."

Trouble in the tall, thin form of Monique Hightower. Wearing jeans, a silk top and giant sunglasses, Monique had just breezed in the door. She said something to the hostess and then spotted the Bravo women at the round table in the center of the dining room. Slowly, she eased the big sunglasses up to rest on her head. And then she smiled.

And then she came striding on over. "Hey, Clara, Elise, everyone. Looks like a party..."

Nell said, "It is. We are celebrating."

About then, Monique zeroed in on Chloe. "Chloe. Well. How's every little thing?"

Chloe raised her champagne glass—with her left hand, so that her engagement diamond caught the light and sparkled. "Remember how I told you if I played my cards right, I might have a chance with Quinn?"

Somebody snickered. Chloe thought it was Elise, but it could have been Tracy.

Monique's eyes got wider. "Wow. That's, uh..." For once, she actually seemed at a loss for words. Chloe savored the moment.

Then Nell instructed, "Pull yourself together, Monique. Quinn and Chloe are getting married. You need to wish my future sister-in-law a life of love and happiness."

Monique sent Nell a quelling glance that had zero effect on Quinn's baby sister. Nell just rolled her eyes and drank more champagne as Monique trotted out another big, fake smile and a too-perky "Best wishes, Chloe. Quinn's a lucky man."

"Thank you, Monique."

Clara, ever the peacemaker, offered, "Monique, why don't you join us for a glass of champagne?"

Everyone went dead quiet then. They'd been having such a great time and Monique would have them trying to remember to watch what they said, because anything Monique heard was fair game for her gossip mill.

Then Monique sighed. "Wish I could. But I got called in early. I need to change and get to work."

"That's too bad." Somehow Nell kept a straight face when she said it.

By then, Monique had recovered her equilibrium.

"Chloe. That ring is spectacular. And truly, I'm so happy for you."

"Monique. What can I say? Thank you again. That's so nice to hear." And strangely enough, it kind of was. Chloe had the definite warm fuzzies at the moment. She was crazy about the Bravo women, crazy about Quinn. Crazy about *everyone*. She was even crazy about Monique, who couldn't keep a confidence if her life depended on it.

Champagne at lunchtime? She should try it more often.

Nobody said a word until Monique disappeared into the kitchen. And then Nell tapped her water glass with her spoon. "So. Engagement party. We need to throw one."

Chloe started to protest that they didn't have to.

But then again, that could be fun, right?

How much fun had she had in her life, really?

Not enough. She'd always been mama's good girl, a busy little bee, working so hard to do everything right, to get straight As and get into a great college and find the perfect husband to make a perfect life.

There'd been no time for fun, not when she was so laser-focused on chasing the life her mother wanted for her.

And after her marriage to Ted? Well, it only went downhill from there. Hard to have fun when your life that looked so perfect on the outside was empty at the core, when you lived with a man you couldn't trust not to hurt you.

But now she had Quinn and anything seemed possible. All the good things: passion and tenderness and lots of laughter. And sisters to call her own.

And, for the first time, champagne at lunch.

Chloe let Quinn's sisters plan the party. She smiled and nodded and giggled a lot.

Nell leaned close to her. "Better cut back on the bubbly, baby."

And Chloe giggled some more. But she took Nell's advice and started drinking ice water. By three-thirty, when they left the restaurant, she was almost sober.

They filed out to the parking lot. There were hugs and cheek kisses. Chloe thanked them all profusely.

Nell tapped her shoulder. "You still look a little high. Ride with me. You can get your car later."

So just to be on the safe side, she let Nell take her back to the showroom. When Nell pulled in at the curb, Chloe leaned across the seats and hugged her good and hard. "I'm so glad you're going to be my sister. I never had a sister before."

Nell hugged her back. "Well, now you've got four—five, including Tracy, who always gets insulted if we don't include her."

That evening, Manny went to Boulder to visit his girlfriend. Quinn and Annabelle picked Chloe up at the showroom and took her back to the restaurant to get her car.

Then she joined them at the log house. They had pizza. And after Annabelle was all ready for bed, they watched *Frozen*, which Annabelle seemed to know by heart.

She kept popping in with "Look out!" or "Watch this!" just before something surprising would happen.

Quinn finally had to pause the movie and remind her that it was no fun to watch a movie when little girls were shouting.

Annabelle was sweetly contrite. She turned to Chloe.

"I'm sorry, Chloe. I'm not s'posed to do that. But I get so 'cited!"

Chloe said, "Well, maybe if you don't do it again, your dad will let us watch the rest."

Annabelle turned those big brown eyes on Quinn. "Daddy, I promise I will be quiet."

She managed to get through the rest of the movie without a single exclamation. And by the end, she had edged up close to Chloe on the sofa and rested her head against Chloe's arm. Chloe treasured that small, perfect moment: the first time Annabelle had leaned on her.

It took a while to get the little girl to bed for the night. Quinn spent twenty minutes or so tucking her in. Then, half an hour later, she came out carrying a ratty blanket and an ancient-looking one-eyed teddy bear and demanded that he chase the monsters away. Quinn scooped her up in his arms, blanket, bear and all. He sent Chloe a sheepish look before heading upstairs to Annabelle's bedroom.

"I think she'll stay in bed now," he said when he returned a few minutes later. He confessed that he enjoyed chasing monsters. "It's more of a game with us than anything."

"Don't even think you need to explain," Chloe reassured him. "It looked like you were both having fun and she didn't seem scared in the least."

"Manny says I'm a sucker for Annabelle's monster act."

Chloe chuckled. "Sometimes being a sucker is a good thing."

"I'm going to tell Manny you said that."

They sat on the sofa in the living room in front of the unlit fireplace, with the lights on low. He reached over and ran a finger along the curve of her cheek.

She shivered a little in pleasure, remembering that first night, when he'd come up the hill to her. His daughter had been on his mind that night. "Did she ever have more questions for you about her mom?"

He idly smoothed a curl of her hair back over her shoulder. "Not yet. Just about every night, I think she's going to bring it up. But then she doesn't."

"Give her time."

"I just hope when she does that I don't blow it."

"No way can you blow it, Quinn. You love her and she loves you. She feels safe and protected. And you give her space, you really do. She's allowed to be a little girl, to let her imagination run a little wild…" Chloe felt kind of wistful suddenly.

And Quinn picked up on that. "Hey…" He touched her mouth, traced the bow of her upper lip. "Why the sad face?"

"I don't know. I had a great time with your sisters today at lunch. And it kind of got me thinking that I never had much fun growing up."

"Too busy trying to please your mom?"

"That's right." She made the edges of her mouth turn up. "But I think I'll look on the bright side. Your sisters will be my sisters. Did I tell you they're throwing us an engagement party? Probably at McKellan's, in the party room upstairs." The popular pub was owned by Ryan McKellan, lifetime best friend of Clara Bravo. Ryan's brother, Walker, was engaged to the family princess, Rory.

"And when is this big event?"

"Tentatively, Saturday night two weeks from tomorrow. Clara said she'd get with Ryan and call me this weekend to firm up the date, location and time."

He hooked an arm around her and drew her close

against his side. His warm lips brushed her hair. "Did you know that Clara and Dalton are getting married in three weeks?"

"I did, yes." Clara had a baby daughter, Kiera Anne, with Dalton Ames, president of Ames Bank and Trust. From what Chloe had heard, Clara had taken her time saying yes to her baby's father. But anyone who saw them together could see how much in love they were.

Quinn added, "It'll be a small wedding, Clara said. Food and drinks at her house afterward."

"I heard. Nell said she thought Clara had too much on her plate. So, as soon as Clara sets up our engagement party with Ryan, Nell's taking over to pull the party together."

"You should know we're going to Clara's wedding." He gave her shoulder a squeeze. "You, me, Manny and Annabelle."

"I would love to." She snuggled in, rubbing her cheek against the soft knit fabric of his shirt.

He traced the line of her jaw with his thumb, and then tipped up her chin so she looked in his eyes. "Hey."

"What?"

"The other night, when you said yes?"

"Um?" Oh, those beautiful eyes of his. She could just fall down inside them and never come out.

"You said you wanted it small—and soon. So…" He lowered his wonderful bad-boy lips and brushed a hint of a kiss across her upturned mouth. "What do you say we set the date?"

Set the date. Her heart contracted. Worse, she was suddenly thinking of her mother, and of Ted. Problems. Unresolved problems. *Her* problems that she'd yet to deal with effectively…

But then again, how resolved were things ever going to

get with those two? She might never speak to her mother again. And Ted? The best that could happen with him would be nothing. Ever. For the rest of her life.

So it wasn't about resolving anything; it wasn't about closure…

"Chloe?" Quinn looked at her so tenderly, reminding her suddenly of the little boy who never fit in at school and used to sneak inside before class to leave chocolate candy Kisses for the teacher who'd been kind to him. "So when you said soon, you didn't mean *that* soon?" He asked the question gently.

She let out the breath she hadn't realized she'd been holding. "I'm thinking if we could at least wait until after the engagement party to start planning the wedding?"

His chuckled, the sound low and lovely. "I just don't get it. Why are you dragging your feet? We've been engaged for two whole days now."

She echoed his teasing tone. "People will start thinking we have trouble making commitments."

But then his expression turned serious. "Is it all going too fast for you?"

"I didn't say that." She hated the edge of defensiveness in her tone.

"Hey. I mean it. We can have a long engagement if you want it that way. It's okay with me."

"But I don't *want* a long engagement." It came out as a whine. Dear God, what was the matter with her? Her emotions were bouncing all over the place. She made it worse by grumbling, "And I meant it about a small, simple wedding, too. I really did."

"Easy." He bent close, nipped a kiss against her throat.

"Sorry," she murmured, honestly contrite, not really understanding herself at that moment.

He nuzzled her cheek. "We got no problem here."

Oh, yes, we do. I'm the problem. My mother's a hopeless bitch and I married a psychopath-in-training.

Why would a great guy like Quinn, with everything going for him now, with a good life he'd worked so hard to earn, want to marry someone with her history and track record, anyway?

People always used to treat her like some kind of prize. She was no prize. Not anymore, anyway. In her case, the bloom was seriously off the rose. Perfect Chloe Winchester? What a joke.

And wait a minute.

Really, she needed to snap out of it.

Where had all these grim thoughts come from?

It was dangerous to start running herself down. Half the battle for sanity and a good life was in keeping her spirits up, fostering a positive attitude.

She'd worked hard to face the tough challenges life had thrown in her path. She'd survived the disaster of her own choice, her own making: her marriage to Ted. She'd fought and fought hard to get free, to make a new life. To hold her head up and move on.

And she'd honestly begun to believe that she'd done it, that she'd put the past behind her.

Until Ted sent her flowers and made her fear deep in her soul that she hadn't seen the last of him, after all. Until her mother showed up on her doorstep spouting such ugliness and rage, revealing such an unforgiveable betrayal, that she'd had no choice but to sever ties with her.

Maybe it wasn't the wedding she was putting off. Maybe she'd had no right to tell Quinn that she'd marry him in the first place.

Maybe she needed to face the fact that he deserved better than her.

"Chloe?"

"Um?"

"We got no problem at all," he said again, more softly, but more firmly, too.

She met his eyes. They were so steady. So knowing and wise. She asked in a tiny, weak, disgusting little voice, "We don't?"

"Uh-uh. We got each other, Chloe. We got it all."

And somehow, when he looked at her like that, when he spoke with such affection and total confidence, she believed him.

She absolutely believed him.

I love you, Quinn. She thought the words and knew that they were true.

If only she felt she had the right to say them out loud.

Chapter Nine

Clara called Saturday afternoon. The engagement party was on for two weeks from that day. Nell called an hour later to go over the guest list.

Monday, the demo began at Quinn's house.

Chloe let Tai run things at the showroom. She put on old jeans and one of Quinn's Prime Sports and Fitness T-shirts and helped Nell and her crew of burly guys bust out some walls. The one between the kitchen and dining area had to go down. And the one between a bonus room and Manny's room needed knocking out, to give him a larger private area. Same thing with the master suite. They were combining it with the smaller bedroom next door. With all the extra space, they would enlarge the master bath and walk-in closet, too.

The men went upstairs. Nell and Chloe took the kitchen. Chloe got right to work attacking that wall. After just one blow, Nell teased her that she was dangerous with a sledgehammer.

Chloe raised the hammer again and sent it crashing through the Sheetrock, making a nice, big raggedy hole that showed light on the other side. "There's something about a demo that makes the whole world seem brighter."

"Whack it down, baby!" Nell made her own big hole.

Upstairs, they heard other hammers demolishing other walls.

"Music to my ears," said Chloe, and gave that wall another serious blow. It was very therapeutic, she decided, to get to beat a wall down.

Since Friday, when she'd realized she wasn't ready to set a wedding date and didn't feel worthy to tell Quinn she loved him, she'd been feeling a little down.

But wielding the hammer helped, made her feel useful and powerful, as though she was getting stuff done. Just what the doctor ordered, without a doubt.

That evening she attended her first Self-Defense for Women class. She got some great tips on how to spot predators and avoid situations where she might be attacked. She almost raised her hand and asked what you did when someone you trusted hauled off and hit you.

But really, she didn't need to ask.

She already knew the answer: you left and you never went back. You started again and rebuilt your life.

And she *was* rebuilding, she reminded herself. Rebuilding in her hometown with a great guy and his sweet little girl. With more family than she'd ever had before, including cool, smart old Manny and a bunch of new sisters, Nell best of all.

A week later, she presented her fairy princess ideas to Annabelle, whose eyes lit up so bright you would have thought Chloe had offered her the moon. "Chloe! I need to hug you." And she reached out and threw her arms around Chloe's legs.

Laughing, Chloe grabbed her up. Annabelle wrapped her legs around Chloe's waist and Chloe spun in a circle, both of them giggling.

When Chloe finally let her go, Annabelle chose the design in lilac, hot pink and purple. The next day, Chloe visited her favorite fabric store and came out with plenty of satin, velvet, bridal tulle, organza, organdy and purple brocade. After the fabric store, she stopped in at the craft store, where she bought special paint and twelve-gauge wire to frame the wings. After lunch, in the studio behind her showroom, she started to work on the costume, taking a break before Tai went home to drive over to Quinn's house down the hill from hers, where the electrician was busy rerouting some of the wiring and Nell's crew was almost finished ripping out the old floors.

She went home that evening feeling good about the remodeling, about Annabelle's fairy princess dress, about pretty much everything. With so much to do and her soon-to-be new family around her, the dark mood brought on by Ted's unwanted flowers and her mother's betrayal had faded. Life seemed bright and full of promise once again.

That Saturday was the engagement party at McKellan's. Quinn hired a babysitter for Annabelle so that Manny could come with them to celebrate. Manny brought his girlfriend, Doris Remy, who was in her midseventies, a widow with fifteen grandchildren and five great-grandsons. Doris had an infectious laugh and loved to dance. She'd once been a Rockette at Radio City Music Hall and she remained slim and spry. McKellan's upstairs party room had a small dance floor, and the Bravos had hired a DJ. Manny and Doris spent most of the evening out on that little square of floor.

Quinn and Chloe danced, too. Chloe also danced with his brothers and with charming Ryan McKellan, who told her she looked happier than he'd ever seen her before. Ryan, like Clara and Quinn, had been in the same grade as Chloe back in school.

Ryan, whom they all called Rye, said, "You always seemed so serious and distant back then."

And she agreed. "Because I was. I had places to go and things to do. Enjoying myself was never on the agenda."

"All that's changed now, though, huh?" Rye asked.

They danced past Quinn, who stood at the upstairs bar with his brother Carter and Clara's fiancé, Dalton Ames. Quinn glanced over as they passed, almost as though he could feel her eyes on him. They shared a smile and a nod and a lovely, sparkly feeling shimmered through her.

And Rye said, "No need to answer. You look at Quinn and your face says it all."

Because I love him, she thought. But she didn't say it. That wouldn't be right, to tell Rye McKellan that she loved Quinn when she'd yet to tell the man himself.

At a little after midnight, with the party in full swing, Quinn's mother, Willow Mooney Bravo, arrived. Chloe, Quinn, Nell and some guy named Ned were sitting at a table not far from the stairs when Willow appeared, looking more beautiful than ever in a white silk blouse with a prim little collar and a black satin skirt, her short blond hair softly curling around her luminous face.

She came straight for their table.

Nell rose. "Mom." Nell and her mother exchanged air kisses. "Big surprise. I thought you were in Miami."

Since her husband's death, Willow traveled a lot. "And miss the party? Never."

Quinn got up and hugged her. She smiled at him so fondly, laying her hand against his cheek, staring up into his eyes. "Congratulations, honey."

"Thanks, Mom."

Chloe rose.

Before she could say a word, Quinn's mom said, "Chloe. So good to see you. You must call me Willow." She took Chloe's hand and laced their fingers together, as though the two of them were BFFs. "Tell you what. Let's steal a few minutes alone and catch up a little."

Catch up? How could she catch up with someone she hardly knew? In her lifetime prior to that moment, she'd exchanged maybe three or four words total with Quinn's mom.

"Mom," Quinn said cautiously. "Are you up to something?"

Willow let out a bright trill of laughter. "What in the world could I be up to?"

Nell made a snorting sound. "Anything's possible. Be nice."

"Of course. I'm *always* nice."

Even Chloe was reasonably certain that was a lie, but she wanted to get off to a good start with Willow. "I'd love to, er, catch up."

"Great." Willow gestured at a hallway across the room. "There's a balcony in back. Let's try that."

Willow led her through the crowd, pausing only for the occasional wave of greeting in the direction of someone she knew.

Accessed through double glass doors, the balcony spanned the back of McKellan's. It had a view of the pub's full parking lot below and the dark humps of the Front Range in the distance.

Willow pulled Chloe to an empty corner. Only then did she release Chloe's hand. She didn't waste time getting right to the point. "So, how are things with your mother?"

Chloe went for honesty. It seemed the only course. "My mother and I aren't speaking. That may be permanent."

Willow gave an elegant shrug. She'd been born in a double-wide southeast of town, but somehow everything she did was elegant. "I can't say I'm sorry. Your mother doesn't speak to me, either, never has. And I like it that way." Chloe had no idea what to say to that, so she said nothing. Willow asked, "Are you saying you and your mother aren't speaking because you're with Quinn?"

"That's part of it, yes. But there are other problems, bigger issues." Chloe shook her head. "And really, that's all I'm going to say about my mother."

Willow rested her slim hands on the railing and stared off toward the mountains. "Quinn has…a tender soul."

"Yes. It's one of the many things I love about him—and Nell's already warned me not to hurt him, so you don't have to go there."

"I didn't think he would ever get married." Willow glanced at Chloe then. "And never to someone like you."

Chloe felt annoyance rising and pointedly did not ask, *What do you mean, someone like me?* Instead, she offered pleasantly, "I think we'll be happy together. We're already happy."

Willow looked toward the mountains again and remarked in a weary tone, "You are a cool one."

"I…" Really, what was she supposed to say to this woman? "What, exactly, do you want from me, Willow?"

Quinn's mother continued her extended study of the distant peaks. "You know, I'm not sure. Except that you never struck me as a person who knew her own mind."

Ouch. That hit a little too close to home. How bad was this conversation going to get? As Chloe asked herself that question, Willow made it worse. "And you were born and raised to marry up, now, weren't you? I just wonder, is Quinn 'up' enough for you? Do you think you're better than he is?"

"Absolutely not." Chloe's voice was hard and final, just as she'd intended it to be.

"You say that as though you mean it."

"I do mean it."

"Wonderful. Then all I need to be sure of is that you can stand up to Linda. You need to be honest with yourself about that. Because if you can't, there will be trouble ahead. Quinn's had enough trouble, enough struggle in his life."

Before Chloe could decide how best to respond to that, Quinn spoke from behind her. "She's doing fine bracing Linda, Mom—not that it's any of your business in the first place."

Quinn to the rescue. Chloe could have hugged him. She turned and slipped her arm through his, finding great comfort in the hard strength of his forearm under her hand, in the solid warmth of him so close to her side.

He slanted her a look both rueful and tender. "How you doing?"

"Just fine. Now."

Willow sighed. "Quinn, you need to stop sneaking up on people."

"I'm in plain sight. You're the one who was looking the other way."

"And it *is* my business," Willow insisted. "You're marrying Linda Winchester's daughter, and Linda and I do not get along. I'm sorry about that, but it's a fact. Chloe needs to be aware of the problem."

"I'm aware," Chloe said. "Painfully so. And I've made it crystal clear to my mother that I run my own life and make my own decisions."

Quinn asked Willow, "Happy now?"

"I only want *you* to be happy."

He put his big hand over Chloe's, a touch of reassurance and support. Really, how did she get so lucky to finally find a man like him? "And I am happy, Mom. Very happy—now, come on. Let's go back inside. It's our party and we want to enjoy it." He offered his mother his other arm.

Willow took it and went in with them. Quinn got her a glass of white wine and she made the rounds, hugging her children, saying hello to various acquaintances. Within half an hour, she was leaving.

"Back to Miami, no doubt," said Nell as Willow slipped away down the stairs. "Or maybe Paris. Or New York. Since Dad died, she never stays here at home for long. I think she's lonely in that big house all by herself."

"She does seem lonely," Chloe agreed. Some of the things Willow had said to her still stung. But the woman *was* alone, and not in a good way. "She seems sad, too."

"Dad was her life. For decades, she battled Sondra to get him for her own. She was always kicking him out in big, dramatic scenes, telling him not to come back until he planned to stay. He would go home to Sondra. But he'd always come around again. And Mom would always take him back, even though he was still wearing his wedding band. Finally, when Sondra died, Mom got what she wanted most of all. For a while, Dad was hers and hers alone. And then he died, too. Now that he's gone, she hardly knows what to do with herself."

"She should sell that house," said Quinn. "It's too big and it's full of stuff that belonged to Sondra."

Nell made a scoffing sound. "Which is why she'll never sell it. In the end, she won out over Sondra. She got Sondra's house and a whole bunch of Sondra's treasures—including her husband." Nell hooked an arm around Chloe and dipped her bright head to rest on Chloe's shoulder. It was a sisterly gesture that warmed Chloe's heart. Nell whispered, "I hope she didn't give you too much crap."

Chloe whispered back, "Look who's talking about giving me crap."

Nell laughed and let her go.

Quinn grumbled, "What are you two whispering about?"

Chloe leaned the other way and kissed him. "Nothing that concerns you."

The following Saturday was Clara and Dalton's wedding.

Quinn sat in the second-row pew with Chloe on one side and Annabelle on the other as Clara and Dalton exchanged their vows. Whenever Quinn glanced at Chloe, she gave him one of those glowing smiles of hers. Annabelle, in a little pink dress with a wide satin bow at the waist and a bell-like skirt, sat up straight with her plump hands folded in her lap, a perfect little lady. Chloe had taken her to Boulder to choose the dress and then made her the cute beaded headband with the big pink silk flower for her hair.

Life was good, Quinn thought. He and Chloe were together every chance they got. Every night last week, they'd shared dinner, the four of them, like the family they were becoming. Chloe did a lot of the cooking, which made everyone happy. Manny had a boatload of great qualities, including a love of cooking. Too bad his cooking sucked.

Yeah. Life was good. Didn't get any better. Though he did feel a twinge of envy as Dalton Ames, his eyes only for Clara, announced proudly, *I do.*

Quinn wanted that, what Dalton and Clara had. He'd never thought it would happen for him. And now that it *had* happened, now that he had Chloe, he wanted it settled, wanted to seal the deal.

Okay, yeah. It had happened pretty fast with them. Some would say too fast.

But he didn't see it that way. They'd known each other since kindergarten. And besides, the way he looked at it, a thing either worked or it didn't. And what he and Chloe had together worked just fine. He wanted her at his side at the end of the workday—and in his bed every night.

She'd said yes. The decision was made. Why not take that walk down the aisle?

Chloe needed time, though. And he knew he had to give her that, had to keep a rein on his growing impatience to set the date and make her his bride, to blend their lives together in the fullest way, be husband and wife for the whole world to see.

Three and a half weeks had passed since the night she kicked her mother out of her house, the night she'd said she wanted to wait to set the date until after their engagement party—but then turned right around and insisted that she still wanted to get married soon.

Well, the engagement party had been and gone. She hadn't said word one since then about when they could stand up in front of a judge.

If she didn't bring it up soon, he would do it. And he had a strange intuition that it wouldn't go well.

Beside him, Chloe shifted slightly. Her fingers brushed

the back of his hand. Heat and longing shivered across his skin. He caught her hand and laced their fingers together, turning his gaze to her.

God, she was beautiful. She stared straight ahead at the altar, where Dalton Ames had just been told he could kiss his bride. A soft smile curved her mouth, a smile Quinn knew was just for him.

When she smiled like that, his worries vanished. What they had was so damn good. And it would only get better. He just had to choose the right moment to remind her that if she wanted the wedding to be soon, they needed to set the damn date.

The next day, Sunday, Chloe gave Annabelle her fairy princess costume, complete with featherweight, glittery lavender wings. Annabelle clapped her hands and jumped up and down with glee. Then she put on the costume and danced around the house, waving the matching wand in the air, tapping the chairs and tables, the sofa and the lampshades. Manny asked her, what, exactly, she was doing.

"Magic," she said, and whirled on to the kitchen.

"I think she's sprinkling fairy dust," Chloe explained. "You know, like Tinker Bell in *Peter Pan*?"

Manny, who was on his way out the door to spend the afternoon in Boulder with Doris, caught the fairy princess as she was dancing by and scooped her up into his arms. "Give me a hug and I'm outta here."

Annabelle tapped him lightly on the head with her wand. "There, Manny. Magic for you. Here's some for Granny Doris, too." She tapped him again. And then she wrapped her arms around his neck and squeezed good and tight.

"How 'bout some sugar?" He pointed at his grizzled cheek.

She planted a big smacker on him. "Now put me down. I'm very busy."

He let her go and she danced off up the stairs, spreading fairy dust as she went.

After Manny left, Chloe packed a picnic for the three of them. Annabelle begged to wear her fairy costume and neither Quinn nor Chloe could see why she shouldn't. Her rubber rain boots had purple flowers on them, and Annabelle decided they were perfect for a fairy princess, so she wore them with the dress. Chloe helped her remove the wings for the ride in the car.

They drove out to the national forest and parked a mile or so from a spot Chloe knew that had picnic tables. Annabelle put her wings back on—and off they went. As they strolled beneath the tall trees, Quinn and Chloe held hands, and Annabelle danced along beside them in her rubber boots and fairy princess dress, waving her magic wand, spreading fairy dust far and wide.

It was a great day. By eight that evening, when Chloe had kissed Annabelle good-night and gone back across the street to her house, Quinn was thinking that this was the night to bring up the wedding date. Manny should be home by ten to look after Annabelle. And Chloe would be expecting Quinn at her place. He would bring up the wedding first thing, before he took off all her clothes and buried himself in her softness.

So yeah, he was maybe a little preoccupied when he tucked Annabelle into bed. She chattered away about her fairy princess dress and how she planned to wear it in her princess bedroom as soon as Chloe finished "dec'rating" down the hill at the other house.

"I will be a fairy princess in my princess room, Daddy."

He smiled and nodded, tucking the covers in around

her and her teddy bear, thinking how she was bound to get princess overload soon and also half rehearsing how best to coax Chloe into settling on a wedding date.

"Daddy?"

"What, Annie-mo-manny?"

"Daddy." She caught his face between her little hands. "I'm not Manny. Look at me. Stop being silly."

He opened his mouth to tease her some more—and something in those big brown eyes stopped him. "Okay."

"I need to ask you…"

"Yeah? What?"

"Well, Daddy. Do you think my mommy would like my fairy princess dress?" She gazed up at him, so sweet and hopeful, her shining brown hair spread across her butterfly-printed pillow.

"I, uh…" His voice had a cracked sound to it and the spit seemed to have dried right up in his mouth. He swallowed hard to get the damn saliva going again and managed, "I think your mommy would love it."

"Can she come to see me, please? I need to show her my fairy princess dress and my wings and my magic wand."

His mind went dead blank, the way it used to do way back in elementary school when he would open a schoolbook and stare down at the incomprehensible chains of letters jittering across the page.

Yeah. Just like being a kid again, his brain refusing to function, his heart like a damn wrecking ball, swinging hard, battering the cage of his chest.

He wanted to leap up and run downstairs and across the street, to drag Chloe back over here, have her handle this. Please God, he really didn't want to blow it.

Annabelle continued to gaze up at him, trusting, serious—and waiting for his answer.

Suddenly he could almost hear Chloe's voice in his mind. *Answer her question as simply as possible.* "No, baby. Your mommy can't come."

"Why?"

His throat locked up tight. But he didn't give up. He squeezed the words right through the tightness. "Because when you were born, she gave you to me. She trusted me to love you and take care of you."

"And then she went away?"

"Yeah. Then she went away."

"Why?"

He realized he hated that question. "She…had a lot of things to do."

"What things?"

"Baby, I don't really know. I only know that she gave you to me to take care of and I am so glad that she did."

"She won't come back, ever?"

"No, I don't think she will. And that's why you have Manny and me, because we love you so much."

"And you like to take care of me?"

"Oh, yeah. We love to take care of you."

Annabelle fingered her old blanket. She had her scruffy teddy bear in a headlock. "Does Chloe like to take care of me?"

He tried a smile, though it probably looked more like a grimace, he was so freaked that he might be royally screwing this up. "Yes, she does."

"Well, then, Daddy. I think it's very good that we have Chloe now."

It damn well was good. And having his first real talk with his daughter about her missing mother had slammed it forcefully home to him: he wasn't the only one who would suffer if this thing with Chloe went south.

Not that it would. They were solid, him and Chloe…

"Daddy?"

"Yeah, baby."

"I love you, Daddy."

His heart seemed to blow up like a hot air balloon, filling his chest, rising into his throat so he had to gulp hard before he could answer her. "And I love you. So much."

She gave him her most beautiful, glowing smile—and hit him up. "So…can I have a puppy, then? Please?"

For once, he felt only relief that she was working him. Because if she was working him, that meant she was okay. It meant that the talk about her mother had gone pretty well. He leaned closer, until their noses touched. And then he whispered, "Nice try."

Damned if she didn't bat her eyelashes at him. "Puhleeeaasse, Daddy?"

He was seriously tempted to just tell her no. But he and Manny were still considering the puppy issue. If he told her no and changed his mind later, she'd only become more adorably impossible, more certain that the word *no* only meant *Keep pushing and the grown-ups will give in.*

She kept after him. "Please, Daddy. A puppy would be so good. Or maybe a little bitty kitten."

He finally spoke up. "Do you want me to say no?"

"Daddy." The big eyes reproached him now. "You know what I want. I want you to say yes, and then I can have a puppy."

"Well, I'm not going to say yes. I'm going to say goodnight. Or no. You get to choose."

"But—"

He put his finger to her lips. "Choose."

"Daddy," she scolded, as though *he* was trying to put one over on *her*. And then she blew out a big sigh that smelled of Bubble Mint toothpaste. "You can say good-night."

He kissed her forehead and gave the covers one more good tuck nice and tight around her and the old bear. "Good night, baby."

She murmured, "Night, Daddy," as he stepped into the hall and shut the door.

At her house, Chloe got to work updating Your Way's website and adding and scheduling posts to the Your Way Facebook page.

It was about time. She'd been seriously neglecting Your Way's online presence. Given a choice between posting decorating tips and picnicking with Quinn and fairy princess Annabelle… Well, what kind of choice was that?

Quinn and Annabelle won, hands down.

Once she had the website spruced up a bit with new content, as well as seven new posts written and scheduled to pop up on the Facebook page daily for the next week, she got to work plowing through email for both email accounts, the one for the website and the one she used for Facebook.

She did the website mail first. There were twenty emails left after purging junk and spam. She tackled them by date, oldest first. The fifth one down was no address she recognized, flwrs4yoo@gotmail.com. The subject line read Question for you.

Should that have alerted her?

It didn't. She assumed it was just someone wanting decorating advice or information about her services.

She so didn't pick up the meaning. She had no clue, just blithely pointed the mouse at the thing and started reading.

Did you like the flowers? I've been waiting to hear from you. We had so much, we had it all. I know you remember. Nothing's right anymore. I can't stop thinking about you.
Ted

Chapter Ten

For a moment, Chloe just stared at the monitor, unblinking and unbelieving. Then she shoved back her chair, ran to the downstairs bath and stood there before the mirror, staring at her too-pale stricken face, not quite sure if she might be about to throw up or not.

Finally, when she felt reasonably certain her dinner wasn't coming up, she went upstairs, poured herself a tall glass of water and drank it down. After that, still shaking, feeling hollow and powerless, vibrating with anger, she went back down to her office and tried to decide what to do next.

Twenty minutes later, she'd trashed and retrieved that damn email five times. She'd composed several replies, all along the lines of *I want nothing to do with you. Do not contact me again.*

In the end, she didn't reply. Any response would only encourage him. How many times had she told him to leave her alone? Too many. It did zero good. She considered blocking the address, but decided against that. If he sent more, she wanted to know about it, wanted to know if he was escalating.

She saved the email itself to a folder that she named TD. Then she wrote a brief description of the flowers and the note he'd sent all those weeks ago. She wrote that she'd thrown the flowers, vase and note in the trash and she marked the date that the incident had occurred. She added that information to the folder, as well.

Okay, it wasn't much. Not enough to get the police interested. But if he kept it up, so would she. From now on, she would have a record of every move he made.

By then, at least, she wasn't shaking. Tomorrow night was the third meeting of her self-defense class. She was on this case, taking responsibility to deal with whatever went down. If she had to confront Ted again, she would be better prepared than she'd been in the past.

She scanned the rest of the website emails and then the messages to Your Way's Facebook page and her own personal timeline page. As far as she could tell, he hadn't tried to contact her again. She decided to consider that reassuring.

She thought about Quinn, pictured his beloved face, the heat of him, the strength and goodness. Instantly, the tears were pressing at the back of her throat. She wanted to feel his arms around her, wanted to tell him everything, about the email, about her decision to keep a record of any and every move her ex made on her.

But then she remembered that look in his eyes the night she'd told him about the flowers. She'd barely been able to get his word then that he would stay out of it.

If she told him about the email, would she manage to get his agreement to stay out of it now?

She knew the answer. Because she knew him.

Really, it was only an email. Only one tiny step along a possible road to another ugly confrontation with the awful man she'd had the bad judgment to marry.

Eventually, if Ted kept it up, she would have to tell Quinn, have to somehow convince him again that this was *her* problem to solve in her own way. When that happened, Quinn would not be happy with her that she'd kept the truth from him now.

But Ted hadn't tried again in the past two weeks. She didn't *have* to tell Quinn now. And she wouldn't. It wasn't his problem and she could deal with this herself.

Downstairs after tucking Annabelle in, Quinn had stretched out on the couch and started *The Great Gatsby* on audio book, expecting his daughter to reappear any minute for their nightly exercise in monster removal. She never came. Bouncing around all day in rubber boots and fairy wings must have worn her out.

When Manny got home, Quinn took five minutes to run down his bedtime conversation with Annabelle, just to keep the old man in the loop on the mommy questions and the ongoing puppy issue. Then he said good-night and headed across the street to Chloe's.

They'd traded keys weeks ago, so he let himself in and dealt with the alarm. She'd left a lamp on by the sofa, as she always did. He could hear the low drone of a television, and light glowed from the short hallway that led to the master suite. Then the TV went silent. She must have heard him come in.

A second later, wearing the same big pink shirt she'd worn the first night he came to her, she appeared in the door to the short hall that led to the bedroom. "Hey." Her sweet mouth trembled slightly. And there was something in her eyes, something that looked a lot like fear.

"What's wrong?"

"Nothing," she said too fast. "I just…heard the door, you know? Came to check…"

"Check what?"

She shivered, though the house wasn't cold. "Nothing. Really." She tipped her head toward the bedroom. "Come on." And then she turned and disappeared back the way she'd come.

Something here was very far from right.

He followed her to the bedroom and found her already in the bed, propped against the pillows. She patted the space beside her.

But he hesitated in the doorway as he tried to figure out what the hell was going on with her. "What's happened?"

"Nothing." Breathless. And lying.

He left the doorway. Her eyes were anxious as she watched him come to her.

Instead of going around to what had pretty much become his side of the bed, he went straight for her. She scooted aside a little to make room. He sat on the edge of the mattress.

She stared at him. He watched her satiny throat move as she swallowed. "What?" she asked finally. "Honestly there's…" She faltered and then seemed not to have the heart to go on.

"See?" he said gently. "You don't want to lie to me, not really." He reached out and speared his fingers in her long, shining hair. He wrapped a thick golden hank of the stuff around his hand and pulled her face right up to his. "I know you, angel," he whispered against her satiny lips. "Know you better every day, every hour, every minute we're together. You're getting inside me, like I'm in you. It's getting so that it only takes me one look in your beautiful face, and I know if things aren't right with you. So I'll say it again. Something is wrong and I want you to tell me what it is."

Her glance shifted away. "Would you let go of me, please?"

He did what she asked instantly, unwinding her sweet-smelling hair from around his fist, sliding his fingers free. "Done." He stood.

She gazed up at him, her eyes like a stormy sea. "You're angry."

He shook his head. And then he turned for the door, more afraid with every step that she was going to let him go.

But she was better than that. "Please, Quinn. Don't go."

He stopped in the doorway and faced her again. "*Is* something wrong?"

She had her arms wrapped around herself, her shoulders curved in protectively. For a moment, she mangled her lower lip between her pretty white teeth. And then, at last, she confessed, "Yes." Once the single word escaped her, she yanked her shoulders back and glared at him. "And if I tell you, you have to respect my wishes. You can't go taking matters into your own hands. I need your word on that, Quinn."

Not her mother, then. The douche canoe ex. Had to be. "Just tell me."

Her delicate jaw was set. "Not until you promise."

He could see it so clearly and it would be beautiful. Just him, the ex and maybe a fat length of steel pipe, up close and personal—and hold on a minute. No. Scratch the pipe. Much more satisfying to deliver the message with his bare fists.

"I mean it, Quinn. You have to promise me."

He studied her unforgettable face for several really

long seconds. No doubt about it. She meant what she said. Plus, a man had to respect the wishes of his woman. He made himself release the pleasant fantasy of teaching Ted Davies a lesson in pain he would never forget. "All right. You have my word. Anything I do, you'll agree to it first."

She watched him narrow-eyed. "Is that a trick answer?"

"Come on. You know me. If I give my word, you can count on it."

Her slim shoulders sagged again. She shut her eyes, drew in a slow breath and when she looked at him once more, she held out her hand. "Please come back."

He couldn't get to her fast enough. He took the hand she offered and dropped down beside her. "I'm here. I'm listening."

She let out a small, sad little sound low in her throat.

That got to him, made an ache in him, the deep-down kind. He hated it when she was sad. He slid his other hand along her soft cheek and then wrapped it around the nape of her neck, beneath the heavy fall of her hair. He pulled her close.

She settled against him, feeling like heaven in his arms, smelling of French soap and fancy flowers he didn't even know the names of. He caught her face between his hands and tipped it up to brush a kiss across those lips he never tired of tasting. "It's okay," he promised, stroking a hand down her hair. "It's going to be okay…" Because he would damn well make it so. He kissed her again.

She clung to him for a minute and then pulled back and settled against the pillows. "I was checking the emails for the Your Way website," she began. And she went on to tell him about the message Davies had sent her and the file she'd started on him. When she was done, she added hopefully, "It was only one email and he sent it two weeks ago. I hadn't gotten around to checking the website in a while. Nothing since then. I really don't think it's that big a deal."

He disagreed, though he didn't say so. It *was* a big deal. The dirtbag refused to leave her alone—after all this time, after she'd pulled up stakes and moved home to get away from him. He said, "You need to write back to him."

She was shaking her head before he could finish the sentence. "That never works. You have no idea how many times I've told him I want nothing to do with him ever again."

"But you're keeping a record now, remember? It's been more than a year since you left San Diego. Unless you have a restraining order on him or some formal proof somewhere that he's harassed you in the past…?"

"No," she admitted unhappily. "God. I was such a big coward."

He took her by the shoulders. "Look at me."

"Oh, Quinn…"

"Listen. This is not your fault. You are not to blame here. This guy is a major scumball and *he's* the one who's causing the trouble. Guys like that, they love to make you think it's all somehow your fault. Don't you fall for that garbage. Don't you let him do that to you."

She pressed her lips together and nodded. "You're right. I know you're right."

"Good." He gave her shoulders a last squeeze and let her go. "So you write a two-sentence email. 'Never contact me again. I am blocking this email address.' And you send it to him. You forward his email and your reply to me and then you block him."

She stiffened against the pillows. "Wait a minute. Why am I forwarding it on to you?"

"I'm going to write to Ted and introduce myself."

"Oh, no. No, now, that is a bad idea..."

"Don't give me that look. There's nothing to get freaked out about. There'll be no dirty words and I won't be making any threats. Just a simple, straight-up little note. I'm going to tell him that I'm your fiancé and I know you've blocked him and told him you don't want to hear from him again. Ever. I'll say that I expect him to respect your wishes and if he has questions, he should write back to me, that I'll be happy to deal with anything he has to say." Her eyes were mutinous. He could see her quick brain working, ticking off objections. He went on. "You can read it before I send it—in fact, emails aren't really my strong suit. Takes me forever to write one. So I'll bring my tablet over tomorrow night. I'll dictate the email to you and you can type it in for me, so you'll know exactly what I'm sending. Then that can go in your file, too."

"But...what if he writes back to you?"

"Oh, angel. I hope he does."

"Quinn. I don't like this. The whole point is that I don't want you involved."

"How can I not be involved? We're getting married, remember?" *If I can ever get you to set the damn date.*

"It's not that. It's not about us. It's my old...*stuff*, you know? My big, ugly mess. I should be the one dealing with it."

He reached for her then and pulled her close. She resisted at first, but then she sagged against him with a long sigh. He wrapped his arms good and tight around her and reminded her, "You *are* dealing with it. You can't get away from it. Look at you. It's tearing you up inside. I'm only backup, that's all. I only want this jerk to know that you're not alone, that you got family and we got your back."

She cuddled in closer. "When you say it that way, I almost feel justified in dragging you into this."

He pressed his lips into her hair. "You're not dragging me. I'm a gung-ho volunteer."

She gave a weary little laugh and then grew serious again as she tipped her head back to meet his eyes. "Any communication you get from him, I have to read, Quinn. You don't get to protect me from anything he says. And I want to read it right away. No putting off sharing it with me while you decide on your own what to do next. You bring it to me. We decide together."

A few bad words scrolled through his head. He'd hoped to have a little more leeway. But at least she'd agreed to the basic plan. "All right. He writes back, I bring it to you, we decide together what to do next."

She lifted herself up and kissed him. "Agreed." She breathed the words against his mouth. Her soft breasts pressed into his chest.

He wanted to kiss her some more, to take off that pink shirt, to see if she had anything else on under it and get rid of that, too. But they weren't finished with the subject of Ted. "There's more."

She moaned. "Oh, God. What else?"

"Do you remember what florist those flowers came from?"

"Bloom. Why?"

He'd figured as much. There were only two florists in town. His sister Jody owned Bloom. Jody had a real flair. Tilly's Flowers, at the other end of Central from Bloom, was kind of boring by comparison. "You call Jody tomorrow and you get her to look up the order for the flowers he sent you. Then you ask her not to accept any more orders from Ted."

"What if the order came from some big online company and Jody only filled it?"

He bent close, nibbled on her ear and whispered, "Jody will know how to refuse any more orders from him, believe me."

"So, then, if he does it again, he'll just use Tilly's."

"And then you'll block him from Tilly's. After that, he'd have to get them delivered from Boulder. All I'm saying is, why make it easy for him? Not to mention, Jody can send you a copy of the original order and of the note that came with the flowers, meaning you'll have proof that he sent them."

"Hmm. Well, proof would be good…"

He studied her worried face. "You're still not on board with this. Why?"

She reached up and pressed her soft hand to his cheek. "I'm ashamed to admit it…"

"You got nothing—*nothing*—to be ashamed of."

"Yes, I do. In the end, I'm my mother's daughter through and through. I don't want to call Jody because I'm worried about what your sister's going to think of me." He probably shouldn't have grinned at that, but he did. And she shoved at his shoulder. "Don't you laugh at me."

"I'm not laughing, and you're worried about nothing. I can tell you what my sister's gonna think."

"Oh, really?" She kind of looked a little like her mother right then, one eyebrow raised, all superior and cool—not that he was fool enough to tell her that. "Now you read minds?"

He shrugged. "Jody will think that you're engaged to me and you don't want flowers from other guys."

She blinked. "Oh. Well. That's a good point. She probably will think that. *I* would think that."

"Damn straight." He bent close and nuzzled her throat. God, she always smelled so good.

She wrapped her hand around the back of his head, threading her soft fingers into his hair. "Come to bed now," she whispered.

He kissed her once, hard and fast. "We're not done here."

She groaned. "I can tell by the look in your eyes. I'm not going to like whatever it is you're going to say next."

"Probably not. You need to call your mother. We need to have a talk with her."

"Quinn! How can you say that? I'm not speaking to my mother."

"Yeah, you are. At least long enough to get what we can out of her. You said she's been in touch with Davies."

"Which is why I don't want to talk to her. She betrayed me."

"Chloe. Think about it. We need to know exactly what she's told him—and what *he's* said to *her*."

"That's assuming she'll answer a single question we ask her."

"We need to try."

"No. Really, I don't want anything to do with her. Everything else will be plenty, *more* than plenty."

He ran a finger down the side of her throat. Smooth as satin, every inch of her skin—and he needed to keep on task here. He explained, "So far, Ted's the aggressor. Always has been. So far, the way it's always been, *he* chases *you*. You see that, right? You see that has to change."

"But I don't want to chase him or *aggress* on him. I just want to be finished with him, to have him completely out of my life."

"Yeah, well, Chloe, sometimes the only way to get rid of a problem is to make yourself ready to stand up against it. So if the time ever comes when you have to go toe-to-toe, you're in the light."

"What does that mean, the light?"

"It means that whatever you can learn about your opponent, you learn. You don't hide from the facts. You don't lie to yourself. You don't go brushing things under carpets and worrying about what other people are gonna think. You admit your own weaknesses and work to get stronger. You never deny his strengths or refuse to admit how far he might go. You bring everything out in the open. Into the light."

She dipped her head close and rested against his shoulder. In a small voice, she asked, "My mother? Really?"

He tipped up her chin to him. "You can call her in the morning."

"Ugh."

"You watch. It's going to be fine."

"Keep telling me that."

He gathered the fabric of her big shirt in his two fists. "Right now I got other things on my mind. Lift up your arms."

Grateful that they were finally through discussing what to do about Ted, Chloe lifted her arms. Quinn took her pink shirt up and away.

"Come here." She tried to reach for him again.

"Wait." He got up, but only to pull back the covers. "What's this?" His eyes had that gleam in them. And the look on his face sent heat surging through her.

"Tap pants."

"Pretty." He bent close and ran a slow finger along the lace band that crossed her stomach just below her navel. Goose bumps chased themselves across her skin, and longing pounded in her veins with every hungry beat of her heart. He eased the tap pants down and tossed them over his shoulder.

By the time he rose to his height and yanked his T-shirt over his head, she'd all but forgotten about her mother, about Ted, about the unpleasant things she needed to do in the morning to bring the situation "into the light," as he called it.

For now, for the rest of the night, there was only Quinn. Only this beauty they had between them, only the feel of his hands on her yearning flesh, the deep rumble of his voice filling her head. Only her need to be with him, held by him, filled so full of him that there was only her love for him and the hope and joy he brought her, day by day.

Naked, he came down to her. She wrapped her arms around him, breathing in the clean, male scent of him, loving the feel of him under her hands. He rolled them until he was on his side of the bed, on his back, with her on top. With a gasp and a short burst of laughter at the suddenness of the move, she gazed down at him. Such a beautiful man, inside and out.

"What?" he asked, gathering her hair and lifting it, wrapping it around his arm the way he loved to do. "You don't want to be on top?"

Any way he wanted it was fine with her. "I'll be on top." She bent and pressed her mouth to his. "On top is perfect." Even better because they didn't have to fumble for condoms anymore, not since the talk they'd had a couple of weeks before. She'd been on the pill for months, long before the first time he came up the hill to her. As for safety, well, there'd been no one for her since her divorce. For him, it had been over a year. And since that slipup that became Annabelle, he'd never gone without protection.

More kisses, deep and wet and never-ending. He unwound her hair and smoothed it back over her shoulder. It only fell forward again, curling between them, tangling around them.

He caressed her with long, lovely strokes. She rose up to her knees above him as he touched her, his big hands moving down her body, cupping her breasts, rolling her nipples between his thumbs and forefingers. When he found the heart of her, she cried out. He answered with a low groan of satisfaction as he dipped inside and, oh, she was so wet and so ready.

She couldn't wait any longer. She reached down and wrapped her eager fingers around the thick, hard length of him. The sound that escaped him then was like a groan of pain.

But it wasn't pain. It was pure pleasure. She guided him into her and sank slowly down, taking him deep and then deeper still. He surged up, meeting her, filling her all the way, until she let her head drop back and gave herself up to him.

The only word in her mouth was his name, the only thought in her head was of him, of the two of them, together, with nothing between them but heat and wonder and the slow, thick pulse of their shared pleasure, their mutual desire.

He came first, his big hands at either side of her waist, holding her down, tight to him, hard. She felt him pulsing and that sent her over, too.

In the end, she collapsed on top of him. He wrapped her up close in those muscled, inked arms of his. And he brushed kisses against her cheek. He breathed them into her tangled hair, laid them in a sweet, hot line along the curve of her shoulder.

A little while later, before they went to sleep, he told her about his bedtime conversation with Annabelle.

When he finished, his sea-green eyes full of fatherly doubt, he asked, "You think I did okay?"

"You did beautifully. Just right."

He grunted. "But I'm not out of the woods on the subject of Annabelle's mom yet, am I?"

"Truth?" she asked.

"Yeah."

"The good news is you've told Annabelle what she needs to hear for now. She probably won't bring it up again for months, maybe years."

"But she *will* bring it up again. That's what you're tellin' me, right?"

"Almost certainly, yes."

"Crap."

"Lighten up, Quinn. It's human nature to want to understand where we came from."

"Yeah. Okay. I know you're right."

"I *am* right—about this, anyway. And you really are a good dad."

"Yeah?"

"Absolutely. You love her. She knows it. She's a happy little girl. That's what matters. The rest, you'll work out as you go along." She turned to glance at the bedside clock. After midnight. "Let's get some sleep." She sat up and turned to reach for the switch.

He touched her shoulder. "Chloe…" His voice was hesitant now. Careful.

She dropped her arm and focused on him. "Now what?" She said it teasingly, with a silly eye roll and a breathy laugh.

But he wasn't laughing. Far from it. He stared at her, a burning kind of look, his eyes gone dark as night. "I want to set the date. I want us to be married. And soon, like you said when you told me yes. I want you living in my house. Or we can buy another house that you like better. Anything you want. It doesn't matter where we live. It matters that we belong to each other and that the whole world knows that we do."

Chapter Eleven

"I..." Chloe had nothing.

It was getting to be a habit with her. Quinn brought up setting the date, and instantly her mind was a muddy swirl of all the stuff she hadn't worked through yet, of Ted and her mother, all the leftover threads of her old, screwed-up life that kept popping back up to remind her of her mistakes, her questionable choices, her longtime fear of facing hard truths.

Quinn's gaze burned right through her. And then he echoed her. "'I...'? One little word. That's it? That's all you got?"

It wasn't all. Not by a long shot. There was so much. Starting with *I love you.* She desperately needed to tell him that. But she just didn't feel she had the right yet. She wanted to be good for him, someone who made his life better, not someone who dragged him down. "There's so much going on."

His full mouth became a hard line. He wasn't falling for her excuses. "Lame, Chloe. You're better than this."

"But that's just the thing…"

"What's the thing?"

What if I'm not better? What if I'm not all you think I am, Quinn?

What if she never really got beyond the stupid choices she'd made in the past? What if he married her and ended up wishing he hadn't?

She had all these horrible doubts about herself. But *he* didn't doubt her. He believed in her, so completely. In a way that no one else ever had.

Somehow she needed to prove herself, needed to be certain that she wouldn't end up letting him down. But how to do that? She didn't have a clue.

"Nothin', huh?" His voice betrayed his disappointment, but his expression had softened. "Go ahead. Turn off the light." He said the words so gently, giving in for now, letting her off the hook once again.

She knew she should do better, say something meaningful and true. But what? He was right. Right now she had nothing more to offer him on this subject, and they both knew it.

So she switched off the lamp—and then didn't have the nerve to cuddle back against him. Instead, she rolled onto her side, facing away from him. Wrapping the covers close again, she clung miserably to her edge of the bed.

His wonderful voice came out of the dark, all rough and low and grumbly. "Come here." He reached out and hauled her back against him.

Shamelessly, she snuggled in tight. She felt his warm breath stir her hair. Safe in his strong arms, she closed her eyes.

* * *

When she woke in the morning, Quinn had already left. She turned off her alarm before it could start chiming and lay back on her pillow and pictured him across the street, sharing breakfast with Annabelle and Manny. She wished she were there with them.

And she *could* be there, living in his house with him, never again having to wake up and slide her hand across the sheet to the cool, empty space on his side of the bed. Even if she wasn't ready to say "I do" yet, he would agree to her moving in if she asked him.

But somehow that didn't feel right, either. When she moved in, it really should be forever, for everyone's sake. And she wasn't ready for forever.

Chloe showered and dressed for work. Before she ate breakfast, she called her mother. No way could she eat anything with that call ahead of her.

Her mother answered on the second ring. "Chloe? This *is* a surprise." Linda's tone was etched in acid.

Chloe ignored the sudden knot in her stomach and got right to the point. "Will you come here, to my house, tomorrow night at seven? I have a few things I'd like to clear up with you."

"What things?"

"We'll talk about them when you get here."

"I don't like your tone, Chloe. I don't like any of this. I don't understand what's *happened* to you. Your father told me that you're engaged to Quinn Bravo—not that he *had* to tell me. Everyone in town knows. Everyone is talking." She started firing off angry questions, not even bothering to pause for Chloe to answer. "Have you lost your mind? What's the matter with you? This insanity is not like you. Are you going through some kind of life crisis?" She stopped for a breath at last.

And Chloe spoke up before she could get rolling again. "Seven tomorrow night. Yes or no?"

A long, nerve-racking silence and then, more softly, almost hopefully: "Yes. All right. I'll be there."

"Good. I'll see you then." Chloe hung up.

She had two cups of coffee and some toast and then went to work. Tai came in at ten that day. It was her first day as a full-time Your Way employee. She'd decided to go to a few online classes for at least a semester and then reevaluate whether to return to CU or not. It was a stretch budgetwise for Chloe, but Tai was willing to take minimum wage for a while, and her presence would free Chloe up to spend more time designing and working with clients. As soon as Tai arrived, Chloe let her handle the showroom and went to the small office room in back to call Bloom.

"Chloe!" Jody Bravo seemed happy to hear from her. "Hey. What can I do for you?"

"I..." Great. She was at it again. Doling out one-word sentences consisting of *I*.

"Chloe? You there? Everything all right?"

She started to lie, to chirp out a cheerful *Oh, yes. Everything's fine.*

But then she thought of all the years she'd told people things were fine when they were anything but. She thought of Quinn last night, telling her she needed to be "in the light."

"Chloe...?"

"Oh, Jody. I'm sorry. This is difficult for me."

"It's okay." Jody really seemed to mean it. "Honestly. Whatever it is, whatever I can do, I'm happy to help."

Chloe forged on. "A month ago you got an order for me. You sent me a beautiful arrangement. Orchids and roses in a gorgeous square vase?"

"Okay, yeah. I remember that. Do you recall the date?"

It was burned in Chloe's brain. She repeated it. Jody said, "Let me look… Got it. Came through FloraDora dot net. From a Ted Davies in San Diego."

"That's it." The truth was right there caught in her throat, pushing to get out. So she let it. "Ted Davies is my ex-husband and I don't want any more flowers from him."

"Whoa. I hear you." Computer keys clicked on the other end of the line. "Okay. That's handled. If I get another order from him, I'll refuse it."

"Thanks. Thanks so much. And one more thing…"

"Just ask."

"Do you have a copy of that order and maybe the text of the card that came with it?"

"I do."

"Could you email that to me?"

"The text of the card, absolutely. I can't send the actual order form. But I can send you a confirmation that I received and filled the order. A confirmation would include the date of the transaction and that Ted Davies in San Diego had the flowers sent to you."

"That would be perfect." Chloe rattled off her personal email address.

Jody said, "Great." More keys clacked. "I've sent what you asked for. And if he tries again, I'll let you know."

"That would really help."

"And, Chloe, just so you know…"

"Please."

"If he starts sending them anonymously from Tilly's or elsewhere, you'll probably get resistance from the florist when you ask for information about who sent them." Jody lowered her voice. "The customer is king and all that…"

"I understand. And I can't tell you how much I appreciate your help."

"Anytime. And, Chloe...?"

"Um?"

"Maybe it's none of my business, but..." Jody hesitated again.

Chloe felt a curl of dread that the conversation was about to veer way out of her comfort zone. But then again, Jody *was* Quinn's sister. And Chloe had already all but said that her ex was a stalker. Comfort zone? Forget about it. Chloe reminded Jody, "We're family, remember?" Or they would be, if Chloe ever agreed to choose a date. "Ask me anything."

"Does Quinn know about this?"

"Yes." It did feel good to be able to reassure his sister that she hadn't kept him in the dark. "Quinn's the one who suggested that I call you."

"Perfect." Jody's relief was clear in her voice. "Exactly what I wanted to hear. You need anything else—anything—you just let me know."

Chloe thanked her again and they said goodbye. She disconnected the call—and the phone rang in her hand.

It was Quinn. "Thought I'd check and see how you're doing."

Just the sound of his voice made her feel better about everything. She reported on her call to her mother and told him that everything was handled with Jody.

"Look at you," he said in that low rumble that turned her insides to mush. "Right on the case."

She chuckled. Okay, it was a slightly manic sound, but a laugh was better than a cry of misery and frustration anytime. "I'm in the light, big guy. Stalker Ted doesn't stand a chance against me."

"Get 'em, killer."

"You'd better be smiling when you call me that."

They talked for a little about mundane things.

She had her self-defense class that night and she was looking forward to more tips on eluding an attacker. Also, for the second half of that evening's class, the guys would finally get into their padded suits. She would have a chance to put some of what she'd learned into practice.

Quinn said that he and Annabelle would miss her at dinner. "Manny's making lasagna," he muttered bleakly.

She teased, "I'm so sorry about that."

Tai appeared in the open doorway to the showroom. A customer wanted an estimate for both a bath and a kitchen remodeling.

Quinn said, "I heard that. See you tonight. I'll be over as soon as I finish with monster removal."

Chloe left her self-defense class that night feeling exhilarated. At first, it was scary, shouting at her "attacker," kicking and flailing, punching and pushing to get out of his clutches, trying to remember the few fighting tricks she'd been taught in earlier classes, like how to behave counter to your natural reaction to jerk away when an attacker grabbed you. Instead, you leaned in, catching him off balance, and then, using that split second when the bad guy wasn't braced, you jerked back and started kicking and screaming for all you were worth.

Bottom line: it didn't pay to be a lady when some scuzzball grabbed you. Once things moved past avoidance and any chance to defuse the situation, a woman needed to be willing to make plenty of noise and fight tooth and nail for all she was worth. She had to accept that she would probably be injured. The battle by then was to survive.

When she got home, she took a long shower and put on cropped jeans and a silk tank top and fixed a light dinner. By then, it was nine and Quinn would be over sometime in the next hour. She went downstairs and checked email, her pulse ratcheting up a notch at the thought that Ted might have tried to contact her again.

But there was nothing from him. Jody had sent her a copy of the note that had come with the flowers, along with the confirmation she'd promised. Chloe copied all that to her TD file. Then she dealt with the few new emails and messages the website and the Facebook page had received.

Finally, she brought up the message Ted had sent her two weeks ago. She and Quinn had agreed that she would answer with a demand that Ted leave her alone and then block the address. She went ahead and composed her reply. It was only two sentences: Never contact me again. I am blocking this address. She zipped it right off, blacklisted flwrs4yoo@gotmail.com and updated the information in her TD file.

Not two seconds later, she heard the door open upstairs.

"Angel?" Quinn called.

"Coming!" She ran up to meet him.

"So, how was the lasagna?" she asked when they met in the middle of the stairs.

He had his tablet in one hand. With the other, he reached out, slid his warm fingers around the back of her neck and pulled her up close. "About as expected."

"That's too bad."

"Yeah." He leaned in even closer, rubbed his rough cheek to her soft one. "You shoulda been there to suffer with us."

"So sorry to miss it."

"I'll just bet you are."

She rubbed her nose against his and then kissed him. When he lifted his head, she stared up at him, feeling distinctly starry-eyed. "How 'bout a beer?" she suggested. "We can sit out on the deck and I'll tell you all about how spectacular the master bath tile work at your house is going to be and what I learned in self-defense class this evening."

He held up his tablet. "First, you're writing me an email to Ted, remember?"

She hadn't forgotten. Far from it. "Actually, I've been rethinking that."

He guided a hank of her hair behind her ear and chided, "We got this all worked out. It's only going to take a few minutes."

Dear Lord, he was a wonderful man. "I've done everything you suggested last night. I'm even going to deal with my mother tomorrow. And I want you to be here when she arrives. But this…" She gestured weakly at the tablet.

"What about it?" He didn't sound happy.

Well, neither was she. "I don't like it, Quinn."

"We've been all through this last night and you agreed—"

She cut him off—but gently. "Yes, I did. And since then, I've had time to think it over a little more and I just…"

"You just what?"

"I just don't want you contacting him. You are not getting directly involved in this—not with Ted. Uh-uh. That is not going to happen."

His eyes had darkened and now his jaw was solid as rock. "You better tell me right now. You think you need to protect that guy from me?"

She gaped in hurt surprise. "No. No, of course I don't. This is about you, not him. This is about—"

"So you're protecting *me*? You think I need protecting from a slimeball like that?"

How had this gotten so out of hand so fast? She drew in a slow breath and told her racing heart to settle the heck down. "Please. Can we dial this back? Can we *not* have this argument right here in the middle of the stairs?"

He answered much too quietly, "Sure, Chloe. Where, then?"

"How about if we just don't have this argument at all?"

He was not about to let it go. "*Where*, Chloe?"

Fair enough. She gestured toward the top of the stairs. "The great room, then."

He turned around and marched back up. Reluctantly, she followed.

In the sitting area, he took an easy chair and she took the sofa. They faced off across the coffee table.

He asked, oh so reasonably, "Did you write that sucker an email and tell him to leave you alone?"

"Yes, I did. And then I blocked the address he used."

"Good." He dropped his tablet on the coffee table and leaned toward her, powerful forearms braced on his spread knees. "So, what's the sudden issue with letting him know that you're with me now and I know what he's up to?"

"It's an overreaction."

"The hell it is."

"Flowers, Quinn. He sent flowers once, a month ago. And he emailed me two weeks ago. That's all he's done."

He made a low, angry sound deep in his throat. "All he's done? He hit you, more than once. He cheated on you. And then when you divorced him, he wouldn't leave you alone. It got so bad you moved back home. And now he's started in again."

"I'm talking about recently."

"You're lying to yourself."

"Two times," she repeated. "Two times he's contacted me in more than a year. Flowers and one email. And now I'm keeping a record of every move he makes on me. I've blocked his email address and he won't be sending me flowers from Bloom again. I've told him, in no uncertain terms, to get lost. That's enough for now. That's... appropriate to the situation."

"Appropriate." He said it as if it tasted really bad in his mouth. "Tell you what. Forget it. Let's drop this right now. Have it your way. Let it go."

"Great. All I need is your word that you won't be looking him up online or calling some private investigator to find him. Promise me you won't go off on your own and contact him."

"I'm not agreeing to that."

"Then we're not done here. I mean it, Quinn. You have to stay out of this. Ted is not your problem."

"You keep saying that." He sat back, then forward again. She saw the born fighter in him so clearly right then. Testosterone seemed to come off him in waves. "Ted *is* my problem." He growled the words. "Anything that ties you in knots and keeps you awake nights and drives a wedge between us..." He jerked his thumb toward his broad chest. "My problem."

She folded her arms protectively across her middle, realized she was doing it, and unfolded them again. "Ted is... He can be a real snake, Quinn." Across the low table from her, he shifted again, furious, coiled, ready for action. She went on before he could interrupt. "He's a really good lawyer. Clever. Ruthless. You get in touch with him, you could end up slapped with a restraining order, or even a lawsuit."

Quinn shot to his feet, the move lightning-fast. He was sitting across from her—and all at once, he was looming above her. But when he spoke his voice was careful and even. "You think I give a good damn about his dirty tricks?"

She answered truthfully, "No, I don't. But *I* do. I care

if he makes trouble for you. I will not be the cause of that. I just won't."

"You won't be the cause of anything. Your ex, *he's* the cause. And I'm responsible for my own actions. It's not on you if I communicate with Ted. So whatever he tries on me, fine. He can bring it."

Where to even start? "Will you please just...sit down?"

He surprised her by doing what she asked, dropping back into the chair and leaning forward on his spread knees again. "I told you last night that I'm not going to be anything but polite and respectful to that piece of crap."

"You're missing the point. I'll say it again. This is *my* problem and you don't get to solve it. I don't want you to solve it. That wouldn't be right."

"Yeah, it *is* right. You're with me and I stand up for what's mine."

"No, Quinn."

"Wait." His eyes burned into hers. "Now you're telling me you're not mine?"

So strange. Such fury in him right now—and yet she wasn't in the least afraid of him. She knew he would never hurt her, never lay a finger on her in anger, that all he wanted was to protect her.

But in this particular situation, she couldn't let him do that.

"Are you mine or not?" he demanded again.

And she gave him a slow, very definite nod. "I am yours, Quinn. Yes. Absolutely."

Heat flared in his eyes and he said, low and evenly, "Give me that email address."

"No."

"Damn it, Chloe."

"Don't swear at me. Listen. I don't feel I have to protect you from Ted and I certainly don't feel I have to protect him from anything. I am with you and only you. You're the one for me. I want your help. I want your strength and your support and I'm grateful for your advice. What I don't want is you standing up *for* me. The whole point here is that I have to learn how to stand up for myself."

He seemed unable to stay in the chair then. Shooting upright again, he glared down at her. "I don't like it. That guy needs to know you got backup, that you're not alone and the man you're with now will fight for you."

"It's my choice, Quinn. Tell me that you will respect my choice. Please."

"Angel, you ask too much."

"Please."

He turned from her, went to the wall of windows and stood staring out, feet apart, hands linked behind him. She resisted the powerful need to plead with him some more. Finally, he said, "I don't like it."

"I get that. It's painfully clear."

He faced her again. "Do I still have your word that you'll tell me if he sends you more flowers or tries in any way to get in touch with you again?"

"Yes."

"Then all right. I won't contact him. Until he makes some other jackass move, I'll stand down."

Chapter Twelve

After Quinn agreed not to contact Ted, the night went on pretty much as usual. They sat out on the deck under the clear night sky. They made beautiful, passionate love.

But it wasn't the same, not really. Except for their lovemaking, which was as intense and ardent as ever, something was missing. There was a certain edge between them. A certain distance.

Chloe hated that distance. But what could she do? No way would she give him her blessing to get into it with Ted.

The next evening, he came over at six-thirty. In the half hour before her mother's arrival, Chloe reminded him that she was running this little talk. He was there to lend support.

He didn't even argue. "I get that. No problem."

His immediate acceptance of her terms surprised her a little after how hard he'd fought her on the issue of his contacting Ted.

And he knew it, too.

He said wryly, "No worries. I don't want to give your mom a bad time. She's going to be my mother-in-law, remember? Eventually I'm hoping she and I can get along together."

"Have you *met* my mother?"

He chuckled then, an easy sound. She dared to hope that maybe they were getting past their disagreement of the night before.

The doorbell rang right at seven.

Chloe opened the door. Her mother stood there in tan trousers, a cream-colored silk blouse and the triple strand of Mikimoto pearls Chloe's dad had bought her for their thirtieth anniversary four years ago.

"Chloe," Linda said with a cool nod.

"Mom." She stepped back. "Come in."

Linda spotted Quinn as she crossed the threshold. She put her hand to her pearls and arched an eyebrow at Chloe. "I didn't realize *he* would be here."

Quinn moved closer. He didn't seem the least offended by her mother's snotty tone. "Good to see you, Mrs. Winchester."

Her mother blinked at his outstretched hand as though she feared it would bite. But then she gave in and took it. "Hello, Quinn."

Quinn might not be upset by Linda's attitude, but Chloe had to resist the urge to boot her mother right back out the door. "Tell him to call you Linda, Mother."

Her mother sent her a barbed look—then caught herself and said in a tight voice, "Yes. Please call me Linda."

"Will do."

Chloe gestured toward the sitting area, and they filed over there. Chloe and Quinn took the couch. Linda perched on one of the chairs.

"I thought maybe you would bring Dad with you," Chloe said.

Linda carefully placed her folded hands on her pressed-together knees. "He wanted to come. But I was under the impression it would be just the two of us, just... between us." She sent a disapproving glance in Quinn's direction and then swung her reproachful gaze right back to Chloe. "So I insisted that I would come alone." She cleared her throat, an officious little sound. "That's a beautiful ring. I hope...you'll be very happy." The words seemed to stick in her throat. Still, they were a definite improvement over the awful things she'd said about Quinn a few weeks ago and yesterday on the phone.

"Thank you, Linda," said Quinn.

Chloe put in, "Give Dad my love, will you?"

A grudging nod. And apparently, Linda had decided she'd had quite enough of making polite noises. "Now, what's this about?"

"It's about Ted, Mother."

Linda stiffened. "What more can possibly be said about Ted?"

"Well, Mom. In the past month, Ted has sent me flowers and then contacted me by email. I want nothing to do with him and I have told him that repeatedly. I've told *you* that often. But I got the impression from what you said at the first of the month that you and Ted have been in touch."

Her mother sniffed. "Oh. I see. Now it's my fault if Ted sent you flowers."

Quinn shifted beside Chloe. She reached over and touched his arm, reminding him of the agreement they'd made half an hour before—that he was there for support.

She said, "I'm going to ask you a direct question, Mom. I want a simple yes-or-no answer."

Linda wore her I-am-gravely-wounded face. "What is this, an interrogation?"

"Have you been in contact with Ted since I moved back to town? Yes or no?"

"I don't see what—"

Quinn spoke up then, his voice coaxing and gentle, "We just want your help, Linda. I realize that you know already, but I think it can't hurt to say again that Ted Davies wasn't a good husband to Chloe. He punched her more than once and he betrayed her with another woman."

"Well, I… Ahem. Yes, I'm aware. Chloe has told me all that."

Chloe took the lead again. She tried really hard to keep the antagonism out of her voice. "So, have you been in touch with him since I moved back to Justice Creek?"

"I don't…" Linda patted her hair, straightened her shoulders. And then, finally, she confessed, "He called me."

"How many times?"

"Once."

"When was that?"

"The middle of July. A week before we left for Maui. He was, well, you know how kind and flattering he's always been toward me. He just said he was thinking of me and hoping I was all right. At first, when he started talking, I reminded myself I needed to tell him that I didn't approve of the way he had treated you and I was going to say goodbye now and I didn't want him to contact me again. But then he just kept on talking and telling me how horrible he felt about how it had gone with the two of you. He said you were the best thing that had ever happened to him and he missed you every hour of every day. He said that things weren't going well with him and that new wife of his, that he deeply regretted letting you go. He just…seemed so sincere." She let out a small sound of honest distress and brought both her hands up. Pressing her fingers to her mouth, she looked at Chloe through pleading eyes.

Chloe made herself speak gently. "Ted is very good at seeming sincere."

Linda drew in a steadying breath and put her hands in her lap again. "Yes. Yes, he is. Before he hung up, he asked me not to tell you that he had called. He said that he…didn't want to cause any trouble."

Not cause any trouble? Ted? Now, that was a good one. "What did you tell him about me, Mother?"

"Nothing. I promise you. He did all the talking. At the end, he said he would like to send you a little card or something, just to say he was thinking of you. He asked for your address. But I told him I wasn't at liberty to give him any of your personal information. And he said of course, that was all right. He completely understood. He said if he decided to reach out to you, he would get your address some other way. He said it wouldn't be a problem. He seemed…very confident about that."

"I'll bet."

Linda's face crumpled, all her earlier bravado cracking to nothing, falling away. She cried, "All right. I just have to say this. I just have to tell you that I *have* been thinking, I truly have, since that horrible evening four weeks ago when you and I fought so bitterly about this. I need you to know that I… Chloe, oh, Chloe… I *know* I was wrong. I was wrong to listen to him at all, wrong not to tell him immediately to leave us alone and then hang up the phone, wrong not to tell you right away that he'd called me. He…well, he charmed me. He fed my ego. And I fell for his lies. But I did *not* tell him anything about you. I gave him no information. I swear it. I didn't!"

Quinn reached over and brushed the back of Chloe's hand. She glanced at him. His eyes spoke of forgiveness.

But Chloe wasn't to the point of forgiving her mother—not yet anyway. She said, "All right, Mom. I believe you. And the truth is if he's determined to reach me, I'm not that hard to find."

"That's what I *told* you, remember, four weeks ago, right before you…threw me out?"

"I remember. Did Ted say anything else?"

"Not that I can think of. Really, that was it. That was all. I haven't heard a word from him before or since."

"Did you tell Dad about that call?"

Linda shook her head. "Not until last night."

A little wave of relief washed through Chloe that her dad hadn't known, hadn't kept that secret from her, too.

Her mother went on. "After you called to say you wanted to speak with me tonight, I just got so upset about everything. I stewed over what you would say to me, knowing that I really did need to admit to you that Ted had called me, to tell you what he said. I just…well, I started crying and I couldn't stop. Your father was so worried. He had no idea what was the matter with me. I realized I couldn't keep the truth from him a minute longer. So I ended up telling him everything, beginning with the call from Ted and ending with exactly what happened when you and I fought four weeks ago."

"So he knows the whole story now?"

Her mother bobbed her head and fingered her pearls. "Your father's not very happy with me at the moment. I know I can't blame him for that. I only want you to know, Chloe, that I have been thinking about what I've done.

Not only thinking about how I've kept a secret of the fact that Ted called me. More than that. So much more. I've been thinking of the past, too."

"Mother, I—"

But Linda wouldn't quit. "No. Please. Don't stop me. I need to say this. I need you to know that I see now, I do. So many ways that I have been wrong. I've been thinking how very proud I was at your beautiful wine-country wedding. How sure I was that you had everything then—and that *I* deserved a lot of credit for how well you'd done, how I had worked so hard to make you the kind of woman you are, an accomplished woman who marries just the right man. I've done a lot of bragging, about you and your 'great' life down in San Diego."

"Mother, I just don't…" Her objections trailed off as Quinn's big hand covered hers. She drew strength from that simple touch, strength enough to let her mother continue. "Never mind. Go on."

"Thank you," Linda said. "Because there are so many ways I know that I've failed you. That first time you left Ted, when you came home to us and said you weren't happy with him? You said you were finished with him, you never wanted to go back. And what did I do? I pushed you to try again, to work it out, even though you told me he'd hit you, even though you said that sometimes he frightened you. I was so very proud of the fine life I thought you had, the life I had insisted you make for yourself—so proud, that I refused to see your desperate unhappiness. If I had listened to what you were telling me then, you might never have gone back to him. He wouldn't have hit you again. But you did go back. And he did hit you. And he betrayed you, too. And I see that I have to face all that now. I have to admit that it happened, to own my part in it. I have not been the mother that you deserve. But I want you to know, at least, that I do finally see how wrong I've been. I hope that someday you will find it in yourself to forgive me. I love you so much, Chloe Janine. You're the bright, shining star of my heart. I hate having to count all the ways I've let you down, all the—"

Chloe couldn't take any more. "Please stop."

Her mother shut her mouth and stared at her, stricken.

Chloe stood. "I would like you to leave now. I need a little time, you know? To process all this."

Linda gazed up at her, eyes brimming, mouth trembling, looking suddenly every one of her fifty-nine years. "Yes. Of course." She got up. "I understand. I'll just..." She waved her hand, a weak little gesture, as though she couldn't recall what she'd started to say. And then she turned to go.

Chloe followed her and pulled open the door.

Linda said in a small voice, "Please believe me. I am so sorry. And I hope that someday you'll give me another chance."

Chloe only nodded. She knew that if she said another word, she would lose it.

Quinn was right there, at her side. He said, "Linda, do you need me to drive you home?"

A single tear tracked down her cheek. She refused to wipe it away and she kept her chin high. "Thank you, Quinn. But I'll manage."

And then she went out into the fading light. Chloe stood in the open door and watched her walk along the breezeway to her car. As soon as she disappeared around the far corner of the garage, Chloe shut the door.

So gently, Quinn took her by the shoulders and turned her to face him. She didn't want to look at him. He always saw too damn much. But he put a finger under her chin and made her meet his waiting eyes.

That did it. With a hard sob, she threw herself against him.

His big arms closed around her. “Hey, now. Hey…”

Chloe held on tight to him and surrendered to her tears. She didn’t even know for certain why she was crying.

Maybe it was the shock of seeing her mother like that—so broken and sad. Or maybe it was relief that for the first time in her memory, her mother had actually admitted that she’d been wrong.

Chapter Thirteen

Two weeks passed. They were good weeks, overall.

Monday through Saturday, Chloe's days were filled with work. When she got home, she went to the log house and had dinner with Quinn and family. At night, Quinn came to her. And most mornings by the time she woke up, he was gone.

He didn't mention setting a wedding date again. But she knew it was on his mind. It was on *her* mind, too. She wanted to move forward with their lives together. But she couldn't, not yet. Not until…

She wasn't sure what. She just felt she was waiting. It was like that old saying about the other shoe dropping. She wasn't really sure what the first shoe had been, but it had already fallen. And now she was just waiting for the other one to drop.

On the first Monday in September, Jody called her at Your Way to tell her she'd just refused a second order from Ted. Chloe felt no surprise. None. In her mind, she pictured one of those classic Christian Louboutin black patent pumps, the dagger-heeled ones with the signature red-lacquered soles. She pictured that beautiful shoe dangling from an unknown hand.

Not dropped. Not yet.

But soon, yes. Very soon.

Jody said she would email her the proof that Bloom had refused an order from Ted at Chloe's request. "But aside from that, I just wanted to give you a heads-up," she said.

"You're the best," Chloe said. "Quinn has such amazing sisters."

"Call me. Remember. If I can do anything…"

"You know I will."

Chloe had her self-defense class that evening. Her trainer in his padded suit didn't stand a chance. She went absolutely postal on the guy, screaming and kicking, punching and gouging. The instructor had to shout at her to stop fighting and run. Later, he reminded the class that the point of the exercise was to incapacitate the attacker long enough to get away, not to keep pounding on him once he'd let you go.

She went home that evening and put another entry in her TD file. She didn't tell Quinn about Jody's call. He knew there was something bothering her, but she insisted it was nothing. And she wasn't nearly as upset as she'd been the night she found the email from Ted. Quinn let it go, but he was watchful and edgy the rest of the night.

Yes, she knew she should tell him. She'd *promised* to tell him if Ted tried to get in touch in any way. And she would tell him. She wasn't actually keeping anything from him, she reasoned—not for long, anyway. Ted would find another way to get the flowers to her. And it would be soon. And she would tell Quinn about

Jody's call and the latest bouquet then. Two birds with one stone, you might say.

As long as Jody didn't let it slip to Quinn about refusing Ted's order before Ted sent more flowers, Chloe figured it would work out all right—not that there was anything right about any of this.

And actually, Chloe dreaded telling Quinn more than she did the inevitable appearance of the next floral masterpiece. Every time she told him about some move Ted had made on her, he got harder to convince that this was her problem to solve.

She truly did fear that the time would come when she wouldn't be able to hold Quinn back. He would go after Ted, do physical damage to Ted. And then what? If Quinn ended up in jail because of her…

Well, she just didn't know how she would bear that.

So, for the time being, she was breaking her promise to him, lying about Ted by omission. The issue of Ted was a wedge between them, a wedge that created an emotional gap, a gap that widened incrementally as the days passed and the problem remained unresolved. Her love for Quinn got stronger and stronger as time went by. And she knew the bond Quinn felt with her was equally as powerful.

But sometimes love and a soul-deep connection just weren't enough, not when he needed to protect her and she wouldn't let him do that. Not when he wanted to marry her and she kept putting him off.

She didn't have to wait long for that second bouquet of flowers.

It arrived the next day, Tuesday.

Like the other arrangement two months before, the flowers were waiting on her doorstep. She found them at a little after eight in the evening, when she came home from dinner across the street. She hadn't expected to be that upset when they came—after all, she knew they would be coming. But the sight hit her hard nonetheless.

Her blood roaring in her ears and her knees gone to jelly, she sank to the front step next to the cobalt-blue vase filled with bloodred roses. The little card in the plastic holder had Tilly's logo on it. But she could have guessed that without the card. The vase wasn't anywhere near as nice as the one from Bloom that she'd smashed in the compactor. And roses were always beautiful. But the whole presentation just came off as ordinary.

"Ordinary," she heard herself mutter under her breath. "No offense to Tilly's, but you're slipping a little, aren't you, Ted?" And then she laughed.

It was a slightly manic-sounding laugh, not altogether a sane laugh. But somehow, it helped. The laugh made her pulse slow, soothed the roaring of her blood in her ears and strengthened the odd weakness in her knees. She was able to grab the blue vase and rise to her feet.

Inside, she put the vase on the counter and read the card. *You're not marrying that guy. You know you're not. My darling, we need to talk.*

Ted

"Look on the bright side," she said to Quinn when he arrived an hour later and saw the roses in their blue vase right there on the counter where she had left them.

"Bright side?" He looked at her as though she'd said something in a language he didn't understand.

"Ted signed his name. I called Tilly's and they've agreed not to send me any more flowers from him. So next time he'll have to pay to have them sent from Boulder."

Quinn took a long time reading the card. Finally, he

said flatly, "There is no bright side. We both know that. Something's got to be done about this guy."

This was not going well. She'd known that it wouldn't. She really, really wished she hadn't told him. But lies didn't work; keeping the truth from him was no way to carry on a relationship.

She made herself tell him the rest, "Also, you should know that Jody called me yesterday to tell me he tried to send flowers through her."

His eyes flashed dark fire. "And last night when I asked you what was wrong, you lied and said there was nothing."

"I…" There she went with the one-word responses again. She made herself give him a few whole sentences by way of explanation. "I knew he would go through Tilly's next and that I was going to have to tell you soon. I didn't see any reason we had to fight twice over this. So I decided to tell you about both the call from Jody and the flowers, when they came, together."

His expression was set as a slab of granite. "You lied."

She threw up both hands. "Fine. All right. I lied. And I'm sorry."

"Are we in this together?" he demanded.

"Of course. Where are you leading me with that question?"

"I'm leading to the fact that 'together' means when something happens, you tell me *now.* And by now I mean, if Jody calls you with information, you call me as soon as you get off the phone with her. You don't store up the bad news to deliver in batches."

She really hated that he was right. "Yes. I get that. I won't do that again."

"And who says we're fighting?"

She felt so…tired suddenly. Just tired to her bones. "Look at you. You're furious at me."

"No. Not with you, angel. Never with you." He held up the little white card in his big, rough, wonderful hand. "This. Him. I need to deal with him."

"No. No, you do not need to deal with Ted. And you will *not* deal with Ted."

He shook the card at her. "He knows about me, knows you're with me." His voice was the low, focused rumble of some powerful predator, crouched and gathering to strike.

"Quinn, come on. That we're engaged wouldn't be all that difficult to find out."

"Not the point, Chloe. This card says I'm in this now. This card says—"

"That card says nothing of the kind. You know it doesn't." She dared to approach him. He watched her come with a stillness so total it raised the goose bumps on her skin. The need to take action seemed to radiate right out of his pores. When she stood in front of him, she said, "Put down the card."

"Chloe." Wary. Vigilant. And so very unwilling.

"Put down the card and put your arms around me."

He didn't. Not for several seconds. But then, finally, with a low oath, he dropped the card to the counter and hauled her close.

She wrapped her arms around him, too, as tight as she could. His big heart pounded, hard and insistent, under her ear. She lifted her head and looked up into his eyes. "If you play his game, you weaken us. You know you do."

He scanned her face, as though seeking the right point of entry. "I got demands. I need you to agree to them."

"This doesn't sound good."

"Hear me out."

She sighed. "Of course."

"Tomorrow, we take what little we've got in that file of yours and we go to the police station. They're gonna tell us that no crime has been committed and there's nothing they can do."

She got that. "But they'll write it up and then if he does make trouble, there's at least a record that we complained."

Quinn nodded. "And I don't like to think of you alone here. You move in with me."

She stepped back from the shelter of his arms. "Not yet. Uh-uh. Look, I really don't think he's that dangerous."

"The guy's a whack job, Chloe. You don't know what he's gonna do next."

She took a slow, calming breath. "As I was saying, if he did try anything, I'm not having that happen in the house where Annabelle lives."

"Annabelle." Quinn said his daughter's name thoughtfully.

"You know I'm right, Quinn. We don't want her traumatized by any of this. We just need to go on as we are for a little longer. That note says 'We have to talk.' I get the feeling he means soon." She was actually starting to hope that it *would* be soon, whatever it was. She wanted that other shoe to finally drop. "I'll be extra careful, I promise. I've got Mace and I know how to use it. Plus, you should see me in self-defense class. I'm outta control, I'm so bloodthirsty."

He grabbed her close again. "Don't make jokes about it."

"Sorry. Not funny, I know. The stress is kind of getting to me."

* * *

Chloe had Tai open the showroom for her the next morning, and Quinn took her to the Justice Creek Town Hall. They talked to Riley Grimes, a patrol officer who had been two years behind them at Justice Creek High. Riley went through Chloe's TD file and said he'd write a brief report of their visit for possible future reference. He suggested that they might try for an order of protection, known in some states as a restraining order. But that would be iffy, as Chloe had reported no incidents of abuse during her marriage and the evidence she'd gathered so far didn't indicate she was in any immediate danger.

Quinn was all for calling his half brother James, the lawyer in the family, and seeing if James thought they had a chance of getting a protection order.

Chloe vetoed that for now. "You heard what Riley said. Ted hasn't come near me. He hasn't broken into my house or even shown up in Justice Creek to have that 'talk' he mentioned. He hasn't threatened me in any way."

"Every move he makes is a threat. He's stalking you, Chloe. Aren't you clear on that yet?"

They were standing on the town hall steps. Chloe reached out and took his big, hard arm. "Can we talk about this in private, please—tonight, when we're alone?"

"Sure." He muttered the word out of the side of his mouth. "Whatever you say."

He drove her back to her house to get her car. When she headed up the front walk rather than straight to the garage, he got out and followed her.

"What now?" She stopped to face him on the front step.

He had that look. Grim. Uncompromising. "I thought you were going to the showroom."

"I will. In a little while. I've got some samples I brought home last night I want to take back with me. And then I'm stopping at your house down the hill to touch base with Nell on the remodeling."

"Lock the door behind you when you go in, and reset the alarm while you're in there—on second thought, I'll just wait here until you're ready to get in your car."

"Quinn." She reached out and put her hand against his bleak-looking face. Tenderness flooded her. Oh, she did love him. And one of these days, she really needed to gather the courage to tell him so. "Please stop worrying and go to work. You can't watch over me every hour of every day."

His eyes had a strange gleam to them, bright and dark, both at once. "I don't like this."

She tried for humor. "I think you might have mentioned that once or twice already."

The corners of his mouth failed to twitch even the slightest bit. "I know more than one good man in personal security—"

"No. I mean it. Don't you even start talking bodyguards. You're overreacting. I do not need a bodyguard."

He hooked a big arm around her and hauled her up close against him. As always, she reveled in the heat, the sheer power of him. "You watch yourself. Promise me. Stay aware."

"I will."

He swooped down and kissed her hard and quick. "We're talking more about this tonight."

A resigned sigh escaped her. "Yes, I'm quite clear on that."

He kissed her once more, as swift and sweetly punishing as the time before, and then, finally, he let her go and returned to his car. She waited until he started up the engine and backed from the space beside the garage before letting herself in the house. After locking herself in and rearming the alarm, she ran downstairs to collect her samples and hurried right back up.

The blinking red light on the answering machine caught her attention as she was about to go out the door. She almost left it for later. But it could be something important.

Turned out it was a hang-up call. A swift ripple of unease slithered down her spine, followed by a burst of anger. *Thank you so much, Ted. Now even a hang-up call freaks me out.*

She considered trying *69. But what for? Whoever was on the other end, she didn't want to talk to them.

Enough. She made herself a promise to banish her jerk of an ex-husband from her mind for the rest of the day.

And she kept that promise.

Until she got home from dinner at Quinn's and found two more hang-up calls on her phone. When she went ahead and tried to call back, she learned that both calls were from blocked numbers. That thoroughly creeped her out. Though she had no proof of who had made the calls, she added them to her TD file and tried not to stew over them.

Then Quinn showed up.

Of course, he knew right away that something had happened. "What?" he said when he was barely in the door. "Just tell me."

So she told him about the hang up calls.

His expression grew even bleaker. "You put it in the file?"

"I did, yes. I noted the date and the times that the calls came in and that whoever made them did it from a blocked number. In case it somehow turns out to matter in some way."

"We need to talk about you trying for that order of protection."

She went over, dropped to the sofa and put her head in her hands. "Can we just…not? Please?" She looked up. He was standing over her, eyes stormy with equal parts anger and concern. She got up. "He's running our lives, Quinn. We can't let him do that."

He clasped her shoulders in his big hands and pressed his forehead to hers. "I've been thinking."

"Thinking about…?" She tipped her face back enough to look at him—and then she lifted enough to touch his lips with hers.

He made that low, lovely growling sound in his throat and settled his mouth more firmly on hers. They shared a slow, delicious kiss. He gathered her in. She slid her hands up over his chest and linked them behind his neck.

"Now, that's what I'm talking about," she said softly, when he finally lifted his head.

"Vegas." He bent and kissed the word onto her upturned mouth. And then, soft as a breath, back and forth, he brushed his lips against hers and whispered, "This weekend. We'll fly to Vegas and get married."

"Married?" She jerked back so that their lips no longer touched. "Quinn, we've talked about that."

He scowled. "I know that tone of voice. Here come all the damn objections."

"I meant what I said before. I just need a little more time, that's all."

"Uh-uh. You need to be my wife and live with me and Annabelle and Manny. I don't want you living alone here. Not anymore."

"I'm perfectly safe. You're here half the time and a

lot of the time I'm at your house. And what about Annabelle? I don't want to put her in danger, I really don't."

"So you do admit you're in danger."

Sometimes the man was too quick by half. "No, no, of course I'm not in danger."

"Listen to yourself, angel. You're 'perfectly safe,' but you're afraid that if you move in with us, you'll put my little girl in danger. You're all over the map about this."

"No, that's not so. I really don't think anything is going to happen. But if something did, I couldn't stand it if Annabelle ended up in the middle of it."

He took her by the shoulders—carefully, but firmly, too. "A few minutes ago, you said that we couldn't let that guy run our lives."

"And I meant it!"

"Then stop."

She searched his face, not following. "Stop…?"

"You're letting him keep you from living your life. You're putting everything on hold for him."

"No."

"Yeah, Chloe. Yeah, you are. How long you gonna do that to yourself, huh? How long you gonna do that to *us*?"

She stared up at him, her heart like a stone, so heavy in her chest. She knew he was right.

And yet she just couldn't do it. Not now. She could not say her love out loud. And she couldn't agree to get married. Not right now. Not until she'd somehow dealt with the problem that was Ted.

Quinn didn't know what to do about Chloe.

She tied his hands at every turn. She wouldn't let him make a move on her ex. She wouldn't marry him and live with him in his house where he could better protect her. She wouldn't let him hire someone to watch over her. She wouldn't let his half brother James check into slapping good old Ted with an order of protection.

She had dark circles under her ice-blue eyes and much of the time she seemed distant and distracted. He only had her full attention when he took her to bed.

Something had to give.

And it had damn well better give soon. She seemed so fragile to him lately and he feared some kind of... breakage. He feared the destruction of what they had together—no, worse. He feared the ruin of her tender heart, her strength, her spirit.

That night, he held her as she slept and wondered what the hell to do.

When Chloe woke in the morning, Quinn was still there. Already dressed in the jeans and knit shirt he'd worn the night before, he sat in the bedside chair, just looking at her.

She pushed up on an elbow and raked her sleep-tangled hair back off her forehead. "Shouldn't you be having breakfast with Annabelle?"

He rose. "I'm going now. I was just waiting for you to wake up."

She saw the shadows in his eyes and felt remorse drag at her—for giving him nothing but trouble lately, for being a source of constant concern. "I'm perfectly safe here. All the locks are sturdy and the alarm system is state-of-the-art. And I promise to keep the system armed when you're not here and to stay alert whenever I'm outside on my own."

He bent close, brushed a kiss on her forehead and said mildly, "I just wanted to wait until you were awake."

She started to accuse him of lying. He'd stayed to watch over her and they both knew that.

But she came to her senses before she could light into

him. He only wanted to take care of her. Had she sunk to snapping at him for trying to keep her safe?

She ended up asking sheepishly, "Give Annabelle a kiss for me?"

He promised that he would and then he was gone.

Wearily, she got up and went about the beginnings of another day.

At a little after eight, as she was eating breakfast, the phone rang. She let out a cry at the sound and splashed hot coffee across the back of her hand. Wanting to slap her own face for being such a nervous twit, she mopped up the spill with a paper napkin and picked up the phone.

It was only Tai calling in sick. "It's just a cold," she said. "I'm thinking if I take it easy today, I'll be ready to go again by tomorrow." Chloe told her to get plenty of rest and drink lots of liquids, and Tai laughed and said, "Yes, Dr. Winchester. I'll take good care of myself."

Chloe left the house at eight-thirty, arming the alarm and locking things up tight. She kept her eyes open and her head up as she crossed the breezeway to the garage. She was careful in the garage, standing in the open doorway to the breezeway, pushing the button on the wall that sent the main door rattling up and then having a quick look around the space before shutting and relocking the breezeway door behind her. Locking herself in the car, she backed from the garage and then sat there until the door was all the way down, just to be certain Ted didn't dart in there when she wasn't looking, to lie in wait for her later.

At Your Way, she exercised the same watchfulness, scanning the little lot behind the building for any lurkers before she got out of the car. And then getting out quickly, locking the doors and hustling toward the back entrance, her right hand in a fist and her keys poking out between her fingers, a makeshift weapon ready to gouge a few nasty holes in anybody foolish enough to jump her.

She didn't fiddle or linger, but quickly unlocked the back door, disarmed the alarm and locked the door behind her. Then she went through the rooms—the office, the restroom, the studio in back and the showroom in front.

Ted was not waiting there. Everything was right where she'd left it the evening before.

And did she feel foolish and overcautious and strangely let down?

Yes, a little bit. But she'd kept her word to Quinn, kept her head up and all her senses on alert, just as they'd taught her in self-defense class, all the way from her front door to the showroom.

Truthfully being vigilant was nerve-racking. And her nerves lately had been racked quite enough, thank you.

She spruced up the showroom and got the coffee going. At nine, she unlocked the front door and turned the sign around. Then she went behind the register counter and called Nell over at Bravo Construction to say she was stuck at the store until closing time but would stop by the remodeling site on the way home.

Nell was her usual bold, funny self. One of the new guys on the crew had asked her to dinner. "Big muscles," Nell said, "gorgeous ink. Too bad the brain is practically nonexistent. I like a big brain. It matters to me."

"So he's only a piece of tasty meat and you're not going out with him?"

"Tasty meat." Nell groaned. "I said that, didn't I, when I was busting your chops about Quinn?"

"You most definitely did."

Call-ump. Call-ump. Chloe recognized the sound of

Nell's boots landing on her scarred desktop. Nell said, "So you think I'm objectifying this guy?"

"Well, maybe just a little."

"You know, he *is* really sweet. Is it his fault he's no Einstein? Dumb guys need love, too. And he's so pretty to look at."

Chloe thought of Quinn, who was not only wonderful to look at with a heart of pure gold, he was brilliant, as well. She felt an ache down inside her, just thinking of him. Because she loved him so, because she kept pushing him away when she knew she ought to be grabbing him closer, holding on tight, promising never, ever, to let him go.

She reminded Nell, "People used to think Quinn was slow, remember? And you *can* be pretty intimidating."

"Me? You're kidding."

"You're a force to be reckoned with, Nellie."

"Keep talkin'. I'm startin' to like where this is going."

"Did you ever stop to think that maybe the guy is shy?"

"Oh, and I freak him out because I'm so awesome?"

"Nell, you are a giant bowl of awesome—with extra whipped cream and cherries on top. So yeah, it's more than possible he's intimidated by you."

"A giant bowl of awesome. I like the sound of that a lot. And so you're saying I should give this guy a chance?"

"Yeah. I think you should. He might turn out to be smarter than you think."

Nell said she'd give it more thought. And then, out of nowhere, she asked, "Baby, are you okay?"

Chloe's throat instantly clutched and tears burned behind her eyes. "Ahem." She turned around and faced the hallway to the back door. Swiping at her eyes, she spoke more softly. "Fine. I'm fine."

"Stop lyin' to me, Chloe. It's so not working."

Chloe gulped down a fresh spurt of tears. "Really, I don't even know where to start…"

"Is it Quinn? If he's causing you grief—"

Chloe let out a laugh that caught on a sob. "Wait a minute. Aren't you the one who asked me if I was slumming with your brother and promised to hurt me if I wasn't good to him?"

"That was before I knew you. I was wrong, all wrong. You and Quinn are a great match, a true love match. And I love you both."

Chloe's throat clutched all over again. "Oh, Nellie. Thank you."

"No need for thanks. We're family."

"And that makes me so glad."

"But the problem is…?"

"Well, I can say this much. Quinn is *not* the problem. He's the best thing that ever happened to me and I love him so much and somehow I don't know how to tell him so. Things are scary right now and—"

"Scary, how?"

"Long story. I'll only say that sometimes I think I'm just too damaged, you know? I think that there's really something very wrong with me and I'm afraid that's never going to change."

"Not a damn thing is wrong with you. And we need some sister time."

Chloe started to object. But then she realized she *did* want some sister time with Nell. "You know, that sounds really good."

"Instead of the remodel, let's meet at McKellan's. Best cosmos in Colorado." The entry chime sounded. Chloe swiped at her cheeks again and tried to compose herself before turning to greet her first customer of the day.

Nell said, "Five-fifteen. Be there. Call Quinn and tell him that there will be drinking and he might have to pick us up later."

"I will. See you. McKellan's. Five-fifteen." Chloe sniffed and smoothed her hair. Then she turned around and carefully set the receiver in its cradle.

When she finally glanced up with a bright smile for whoever had come in, Ted was standing not twenty feet away in front of the showroom door.

Chapter Fourteen

Chloe's heart beat a sick rhythm under her ribs and her throat felt like some invisible hand was squeezing it tight.

She'd done it to herself. It was all her own fault. She'd let down her guard. She'd turned around and forgotten all about how she needed to keep her head up and her eyes front.

She'd let her concentration slip to cry on Nellie's shoulder—and her nightmare had found her.

Somehow he'd not only slipped in the door when she was talking to Nell, but he'd whipped the open sign around, too. It was just a regular glass door with a knob lock you could turn from the inside.

She had zero doubt he'd locked it, as well.

Her nightmare had not only found her, he'd locked himself in her showroom with her.

Beautifully turned out as always in a perfectly tailored designer suit and a Seven Fold Robert Talbott tie, not a single dark blond hair out of place, he gave her a slow, charming smile. And then he said in that smooth, cool voice that had slowly turned all her dreams into nightmares, "Hello, Chloe."

Her purse was under the counter. She needed to reach in there and pull out the Mace. Carefully, trying not to move the upper part of her body and give herself away, she felt for the purse, found it…

Oh, God, she'd zipped it shut. He would know if she tried to get it open now.

Run! She needed to get the hell out of there. She started to whirl for the back door.

Ted said, so very mildly, "Please don't do that."

And her mind went to mush as her legs started shaking. She was rooted to the spot.

It was pitiful, really. Such a sad case, she was. He had trained her so well over all those awful, endless years with him. He only had to look at her, only had to speak to her in that smooth, mild voice of his and she couldn't fall all over herself fast enough to do whatever he demanded of her.

She had dared, in the past year, to believe herself free of him—well, except for the nightmares. She had *made* herself free of him. She'd divorced him and moved on, found Quinn. *Her* Quinn, so fine and true, everything she'd always wanted—only better. Only *more…*

She shut her eyes. No. She couldn't think of Quinn now. She needed to focus, needed to remember her self-defense training, to start acting like the independent, self-possessed, self-directed woman she actually was.

And yet, somehow, she stood there, just *stood* there, and did nothing as Ted came for her.

With his fine Italian shoes light and quick on the showroom's wood floor, he walked right up to the counter, stepped around it, and wrapped his perfectly manicured hand around her upper arm. "You're beautiful, my darling, as always. But you look tired."

The faint smell of the signature cologne he always had specially made just for him came to her. She knew she would gag on that smell. But she swallowed, hard, and glanced down at his fingers encircling her arm. "Where's your wedding ring, Ted?"

He actually chuckled. "Larissa and I are through."

"I'm so sorry to hear that."

"No, you're not. You knew all along she wouldn't last. A diversion, that's all she was supposed to be. I work very hard, and you know that I do, to make a fine life for us. I deserve a diversion now and then. But then you left me and I tried to distract myself, tried to convince myself that any beautiful, reasonably intelligent woman would do. I thought I could forget you. I was wrong. You are mine, and you are perfect for me and I'm ready now to give you another chance."

She simply could not let that pass. "But I'm not yours."

"Yes, you are."

"We're divorced, Ted, in case you've forgotten. And the last thing I want is another chance with you."

His eyes shifted, away—and then back. Other than that, he pretended he hadn't heard her. "Let's sit down, shall we?"

"I don't want to sit down with you. Let go of my arm, Ted. Leave. Now. Please."

Again, he ignored her. "This way." He started walking, pulling her with him, into the hallway that led to the back door, pausing at the open arch on the left. "This will do." He led her into her studio and over to her worktable, where he pulled out a chair and pushed her down in it. Then he grabbed another chair a few feet away and yanked it over next her. He sat down, too. And then he said, "I love you, my darling. And I've come to take you home. I know that I hurt you and I swear to you that I will never do that again." He reached out. She steeled herself not to cringe away as he traced the line of her hair along her cheek and down her neck.

Chloe's skin crawled. She swallowed bile again and stared at her worktable, taking a strange kind of comfort from the tools she used every day: the stacks of thick fabric sample books, the color wheels, the sketch tablets, the loose swatches of fabric, the scissors, drafting compass, tape measure, shape templates, colored pencils and fine-point pens…

Ted kept on talking. "I called you three times yesterday. You never picked up. And then I thought, well, that's all right. It's better that we talk face-to-face anyway. Better that we cut to the chase and you can just come home with me. And it *is* better. It's wonderful to see you, my darling. And now I just want you to look at me. I want you to tell me the truth, that you've missed me and you're so glad to see me. I want to work this out with you—and yes, I know. My temper has been a problem. But I'll return to counseling. Everyone needs a little extra help getting things right now and then."

She tried again. "Ted. I'm in love with my fiancé and I don't want anything to do with you."

"You don't mean that."

"Yes, Ted, I do."

"Look at me." He grabbed her chin in a punishing grip and yanked her head around to face him.

"That's going to leave a bruise." She glared at him.

"Darling, I'm so sorry."

"I don't believe you." She realized she was getting

less numb and more angry. Angry was good. At least her knees weren't shaking anymore.

"You know, Chloe. You really shouldn't bait me. If you would only treat me with the love and respect I deserve, our lives would go so smoothly, everything just so, moving along without a hitch."

She shot to her feet.

But before she could dodge around him and make for the door, he grabbed her hand. "Sit *down*." And he yanked her back into the chair so hard that her teeth clacked together. "What's this?" He still had her hand. Her left hand.

"It's my engagement ring. Remember? I'm engaged." She tried to pull away.

He held on. His face was getting that look, his eyes distant, his skin flushing mottled red. "Take it off."

"You'll have to let go for me to do that."

But he didn't let go. "Already, you are out of hand. You are pushing me too far. You know that you are."

"Let go of me, Ted."

"Don't you ever try to tell me what to do."

"Let me go," she said softly. And then she said it again, a little louder, "Let me go." And then she couldn't *stop* saying it, louder and louder, "Let me go, let me go, let me go, let me go…"

And right then, as she repeated that same phrase like a mantra, for the seventh time, he drew back his fist and he punched her in the jaw.

Chloe saw stars as blood filled her mouth. It hurt—and more than just the fist to the face. She'd bitten her own tongue, bitten it good and hard.

Everything got very clear then. Crystal clear.

She needed to defend herself and she needed to do it now.

Chloe let out a scream. It was a wild cry, feral. Furious. Ted stared at her, bug-eyed in surprise. His perfect darling Chloe would never let out such an animal sound—a tasteful little whimper, maybe. But a full-out, full-throated scream of rage? No way.

However, she was no longer his perfect Chloe. She belonged to herself now—to herself, and to Quinn. She needed to end all of Ted's false assumptions and she needed to end them forever and always.

So she reached over, grabbed one of the heavy sample books in both hands, drew it back and whacked that sucker right across the side of his big, fat head. His chair scraped the floor as the sample book connected. He let out a grunt of surprise.

And that was all he got a chance to do.

Because she went kind of crazy. She lifted that sample book and she hit him again. His chair went over and he was on the floor. She jumped on top of him and hit him some more.

By then he was making these ridiculous little whining sounds, his arms drawn up in front of his face. He was calling her name, "Chloe, stop! Chloe, don't!" as she flailed at him with the sample book.

From out in the showroom came pounding and shouts, followed by the sound of glass shattering. And then, wonder of wonders, Quinn's voice: "Chloe!"

"Back here!" She climbed off Ted and stood, panting, above him, still holding the sample book threateningly over her head, as Quinn came flying into the room.

"Angel, my God..."

About then, she noticed there was blood all down the front of her white silk shirt. She explained mildly, her tongue already swelling in her mouth, "He hit me and I bit my tongue."

On the floor, Ted was curled in the fetal position. "Help me," he groaned. "Get that crazy bitch away from me!"

Quinn said, "This must be Ted." Chloe dropped the sample book on the table, pressed her suddenly quivering lips together and nodded. He asked, "How bad are you hurt?"

"I'm okay, really. It lookth worth than it ith."

Ted rolled and started to get up.

Quinn said flatly, "Stay on the floor, Ted."

With a moan, Ted went over on his side and curled up in a ball. He whined, "You people are insane."

"Just shut up and don't move."

Surprisingly, Ted took Quinn's advice.

Chloe zipped past Ted and got to Quinn. He hooked his big arm around her, pressed his warm lips to her forehead and whispered, "I think he's got your message now. You did good, angel. Real good."

She snuggled in close to him. "How did you know to come here?"

"Nell called me. Told me you'd been cryin' on the phone and I'd better get the hell over here and not leave until all your doubts were dealt with and all your tears were dried."

"I love Nell."

"Yeah, well, for once I guess I won't be pissed at her for sticking her nose in." He kissed her forehead again. "You're okay, you're sure?"

"I am. I really am."

"Good, then. Go call 911. Use the phone in the showroom."

It occurred to Chloe that it might not be such a great idea to leave Ted alone with Quinn. "Pleathe don't hit Ted," she whispered. "He'th not worth it."

"I'm not going to hit him. I'm only going to do what I've always wanted to do and that is to have a little talk with him."

"Quinn, I really don't think—"

"Angel."

"What?"

"Go on. Make that call."

What Quinn said to Ted, only Ted ever knew.

Whatever it was, when Chloe reentered the back studio room after calling the police station, Ted was sitting in the chair again. He had nicks and scratches all over his face, and his right eye was swiftly turning a deep magenta. His tie was askew, his fine suit wrinkled and his hair a mess. He told her quietly that he'd been way out of line and he was very sorry and he would not be bothering her anymore.

She believed him. Now that he knew she would fight him, he wouldn't get near her again. She really was tempted to leave it at that. Pressing charges could be messy. He'd probably string the process out forever. Who knew what tricks he might try?

But she kind of wondered if he'd ever hit Larissa. And if, for the third time, she just let it go, would he only find another woman to bully and hurt?

So when Riley Grimes showed up, she told him and his partner exactly what had happened. By then, she had a doozey of a bruise swelling at her jaw. The blood down the front of her made its own statement about what Ted had done to her. Her tongue thick and slow and very painful, she told them exactly what had happened and said that yes, she did intend to press charges. So Riley and the other officer took Ted away in handcuffs. They'd called an ambulance for her. Quinn had smashed the glass in the front door, so he got hold of his brother Carter to come over and secure the showroom entrance. Then he went with Chloe in the ambulance to the hospital southeast of town.

At Justice Creek General, they took pictures of her injuries and an X-ray of her jaw. Nothing was broken. Her tongue was a mess. They advised saltwater rinses, ice packs and aloe vera gel. The good news? The bleeding had stopped on its own. The doctor said that if she still had pain in a week, she should see her family practitioner.

Quinn hovered close, and Chloe loved that he did. She knew she was going to be fine now. Yes, her face ached, her tongue throbbed and she was talking with a lisp. But all of that was temporary. Down inside, in her heart and soul, she'd never felt better.

She'd never felt so free.

Quinn couldn't wait to get her home to Annabelle and Manny, though he did kind of worry that she might give him grief about it, might demand that he take her to her house.

But no. She just smiled with that beautiful, battered face of hers and said, "Yeth. Take me home to Annabelle and Manny. Thath where I want to be."

At home, Quinn told Manny what had happened. Manny settled Chloe on the sofa with a mountain of pillows at her back and a light blanket over her knees. He brought her an ice pack and a saltwater rinse for her poor, aching tongue.

When Annabelle came bouncing down the stairs, they told her that Chloe had been hurt and she needed them to take care of her. Annabelle demanded to be allowed to kiss the boo-boo on Chloe's jaw and make it all better. She insisted that Chloe have her one-eyed teddy bear. "Hug him real hard, Chloe. Then you will feel much better."

Quinn called Nell to let her know what had gone down. Nell turned right around and called everybody. Within half an hour, family members started arriving. By late afternoon, Chloe had had visits from all of Quinn's sisters and three of his brothers.

Nell even called Chloe's parents. Linda and Doug Winchester rushed right over. Chloe took it well, Quinn thought. She let her dad hug her and then her mom, too. Linda cried. She pulled Quinn aside and said she needed to tell him personally how very wrong she'd been. She hoped, she said, that someday, somehow, she would find a way to make things right with her daughter and with him.

He gave her a hug and told her there was nothing to make right. "We're family now, Linda. Everything's going to be just fine."

That caused Linda to cry even harder.

Then Doug clapped him on the back. "I know I don't have to say it. But I'm a father and that means I'll say it anyway. Take good care of my little girl. She hasn't had it easy."

"I will, sir," Quinn promised. "You can count on me."

Then Doug took Linda home.

Chloe made a list of what she needed from her house. Quinn went over there and gathered everything up.

And that night, for the first time, he had her in his bed where he'd always wanted her. He brought her aspirin for the pain and he wrapped himself around her and he held her all night long.

Chloe never went back to the house across the street. Slowly, she and Quinn and Manny moved everything she needed to the log house.

Within a week, her tongue was fully functional again. On a Thursday night late, she and Quinn sat out under the stars and said the things they'd never managed to say before.

She told him what was in her heart. "I love you, Quinn. So, so much."

And he said, "I love you, angel. I've been wanting to tell you forever. But somehow the time never seemed right."

"I think maybe you sensed that I wasn't ready yet. To say it. To hear it. But I'm ready *now*."

"Yeah," he said gruffly. "I see that. I feel that. I love you, Chloe Winchester." He stared deep in her eyes.

She gazed back at him and knew she'd gotten it exactly right the second time around. "I went all wrong there, for so many years."

"No."

"Yes. I went wrong, took the wrong path. But I'm back where I belong now. I think deep down I always knew you were the one for me, from way back when we were little, from when you used to put those Hershey's Kisses on Miss Oakleaf's desk."

He groaned. "You remember that? Nobody remembers that."

"Well, yeah. We all kind of do." She got up from her deck chair—but only so that she could sit on his lap. Wrapping her arms around his neck, she whispered in his ear, "It was so sweet and so romantic, you leaving chocolate for Miss Oakleaf. Everybody said so."

"You think so, huh?"

"I do, yes."

"I love you, Chloe." He nuzzled her hair. "I love you. Now that I'm finally saying it, I just can't say it enough."

"Good. Because I love you, too."

"Vegas?" he asked, his mouth so warm and soft against her cheek.

She turned her head—just enough so that their lips could meet. They shared a long, sweet kiss. And then she answered him, "Vegas. Definitely. Name the day."

Five weeks later, they moved back to the fully renovated house down the hill. Annabelle put on her fairy princess costume and danced around her new princess bedroom, scattering fairy dust as she went. That same day, Manny presented her with a tiny, long-haired, big-eared Chihuahua puppy, which she promptly named Mouse.

And a week after that, Quinn and Chloe were married in the wedding chapel at High Sierra Resort and Casino in Las Vegas on the Sunset Strip. Annabelle was the flower girl. Manny stood up as best man. Quinn's sisters and Tracy Winham and Rory Bravo-Calabretti were all bridesmaids, with Nell the maid of honor.

Doug Winchester proudly gave his only daughter away for the second time. "This is the one that counts," he whispered to Chloe as he walked her down the aisle to Quinn. Linda Winchester cried all through the ceremony—tears of joy, she said.

For Chloe, it was the happiest day of her life.

So far.

* * * * *

WANTING WHAT SHE CAN'T HAVE

YVONNE LINDSAY

This book is for you, Soraya Lane—the most awesome sprint buddy a writer could ever want. Without you this story would have been so much harder to write. Thank you!

One

Alexis watched him from the doorway to the winery. Late afternoon sun slanted through the windows at the end of the room, illuminating tiny dust motes that floated on air redolent with the scent of fermented grapes. But she was oblivious to the artistic beauty of the setting—her focus solely on the man who worked on, unaware of her presence.

He'd changed. God, how he'd changed. He was thinner, gaunt even, and his signature well-groomed appearance had given way to a self-executed haircut, a stretched and faded T-shirt and torn jeans. His face obviously hadn't seen a razor in several days. But then grief was bound to do that to a man—to diminish the importance of the everyday tasks he'd done automatically and replace them with indifference.

How could she help a man who was clearly long past any interest in helping himself?

The weight of what she'd agreed to do felt heavy and uncomfortable on her shoulders. She, the one who always willingly stepped up to the plate when everything went pear-shaped, was now thinking that perhaps this time she'd bitten off more than she could chew.

Straightening her shoulders, she shook off her doubts. Bree had turned to her in her time of need—had written a letter that begged Alexis to take care of her husband and the child she'd been on the verge of delivering should something happen to her, as if she'd known what lay ahead. While her best friend had died before Alexis could give her that promise, in her heart she knew she couldn't refuse—couldn't walk away. Even if keeping that promise meant putting her heart back in firing range from the man she'd been magnetically drawn to from the moment she'd first met him.

Raoul stilled in his actions. His attention shifted from the table of wine samples before him, his pen dropping from his hand to the clipboard covered in hand-scrawled notes that lay on the stark white tablecloth. He lifted his head and turned toward her, his face registering a brief flash of surprise together with something else she couldn't quite put her finger on. It was gone in an instant, replaced by a tight mask of aloofness.

"Alexis," he said, accompanied by a tight nod.

"I came as soon as I heard. I'm sorry it took so long. I…" Her voice trailed away. How did you tell a man that it had taken almost a year to hear about the birth of his daughter and the death of the love of his life because you'd severed ties with his wife, your best friend since kindergarten, when it became too painful to see her happiness with him? That you'd "forgotten" to give her your new email address or the number to the cell phone you bought when your work started requiring more international travel because you couldn't bear to hear any more about how perfect they were together? Because you had coveted him for yourself?

Because you still did.

She took a deep breath and swallowed against the lump of raw grief that swelled in her throat.

"I've been traveling for a while, ever since my business..." The words died at the expression on his face. Clearly Raoul could not care less about the success she'd been enjoying ever since her clothing line finally started taking off. "Bree's letter caught up with me at my father's house. It must have been following me around the world for the past year."

"Bree's letter?"

"To tell me about her pregnancy."

Should she tell him also that Bree had begged her to watch out for her husband and her, at that time, as yet unborn child? That she'd somehow known that the aortic aneurysm she'd kept secret from her family would take her life in childbirth? One look at his face confirmed he hadn't known of his wife's correspondence to her.

"So, you're back."

Finally. The unspoken word hung on the air between them, both an accusation and an acknowledgment at the same time.

"My mother was ill. I made it back a few weeks before she died at Christmas."

"I'm sorry."

The platitude fell automatically from his lips but she sensed his shields go up even stronger. He didn't want to know, not really. Not when he was still locked tight in his own sorrow, his own grief.

"I only got Bree's letter last week and rang her mom straightaway. I'm here to help with Ruby."

"The child already has a carer, her grandmother."

"Yes, but Catherine needs surgery, Raoul. She can't keep putting her knee replacement off, especially now that Ruby is getting more active."

"I told her to find a nanny if she needed to."

"And I understand you rejected every résumé she presented to you. That you wouldn't even agree to interview any of the applicants."

He shrugged. "They weren't good enough."

Alexis felt her temper begin to rise. Catherine had been beside herself with worry over what to do. The osteoarthritis in her knee caused constant pain and made looking after a small child more difficult every day. She needed the surgery as soon as possible, but that meant Ruby absolutely had to have a new caretaker. By refusing to look at the résumés, Raoul was ignoring his responsibilities—to his daughter, to her grandmother and to Bree's memory. He looked at her again, harder this time. What on earth was going on behind those hazel eyes of his?

"And what about me? Am I good enough?"

"No," he answered emphatically. "Definitely not."

She pushed aside the hurt his blunt refusal triggered.

"Why? You know I'm qualified—I have experience caring for little ones."

"You're a dressmaker now, though, aren't you? Hardly what the child needs."

Wow, he was really on form with the insults, wasn't he, she thought. Dressmaker? Well, yes, she still made some of her signature designs but for the most part she outsourced the work now. She'd trained as a nanny when she'd left school, and had completed a full year intensive academic and practical experience program because her parents had been opposed to her trying to make a career following her artistic talent alone. But three years ago, when her last contract had finished, she'd realized it was time to follow her dream. That dream was now coming to fruition with her clothing label being distributed to high-end boutiques around the country and in various hot spots around the world. But Raoul didn't care about any of that.

"I've arranged cover for my business," she said, sending a silent prayer of thanks to her half sister, Tamsyn, for stepping into the breach. "Catherine's already hired me, Raoul."

"I'm unhiring you."

Alexis sighed. Bree's mom had said he might be difficult. She hadn't been kidding.

"Don't you think it's better that Ruby be cared for by someone who knew her mother, who knows her family, rather than by a total stranger?"

"I don't care."

His words struck at her heart but she knew them for a lie. The truth was he cared too much.

"Catherine is packing Ruby's things up now and bringing them over. She thought it best if she settled here from tonight rather than having me pick up Ruby in the morning."

Raoul's face visibly paled. "I said no, dammit! No to you as her nanny, and definitely no to either of you living here."

"Her surgery is scheduled for tomorrow afternoon. Ruby can't stay at her grandmother's house any longer. She needs to be home, with you."

Raoul pushed shaking fingers through hair cut close to his scalp—shorter than she'd ever seen it before. His hand dropped back down again and she watched as he gathered himself together, his fingers curling into tight fists as if he was holding on by a thread.

"Just keep her away from me."

Alexis blinked in shock. Catherine had said Raoul had little to do with his nine-month-old daughter aside from meeting the financial requirements of her care. But despite the warning, Alexis couldn't come to terms with what she'd been told. Ruby had been born out of love between two wonderful people who'd had the world at their feet when they'd married only two and a half years ago. She'd attended their wedding herself. Seen with her own eyes how much they'd adored one another and, to her shame, had been stricken with envy. That Raoul virtually ignored Ruby's existence was so terribly sad. Did he blame the little girl for her mother's death? Or could he just not bear the constant reminder of how he had lost the love he and Bree had shared?

Alexis forced herself to nod in response to his demand and started back up the unsealed lane from the winery toward the house—a large multiroomed masterpiece that sprawled across the top of the hill. Catherine had already given her a key along with a hefty supply of groceries and baby products. She'd need to put everything away before Catherine arrived with Ruby.

Ruby. A sharp pain lanced through her when she thought of the baby's cherubic face. A happy, healthy and contented child, she was obviously closely bonded with Bree's mom. To look at her, one would never guess that she had faced so much trouble in her short life.

After a slightly early arrival, exacerbated by a postnatal infection, Ruby had spent the first few weeks of her life in an incubator, crying for the mother she would never be able to meet. Catherine had shared with Alexis her theory that the pitiful cries, piled on top of his own grief, had been too much for Raoul to bear. He'd withdrawn from his newborn daughter, leaving her care to his mother-in-law. Catherine had been Ruby's sole caregiver ever since.

Transplanting her to her father's house and into the care of someone else would have its challenges. Getting Raoul to acknowledge and interact with his daughter would be the hardest—and the most necessary.

They needed each other, Alexis was certain of that. Even though she could do nothing else for Bree, she'd make sure that Raoul stepped up to his responsibilities to his late wife's memory and to the child she'd borne him.

She was here. He'd known that one day she'd come and he'd dreaded every second. Seeing her had cracked open the bubble of isolation he'd built for himself, leaving him feeling raw and exposed. He was unaccustomed to having to share this place with anyone but Bree—or, for the past year, Bree's memory.

Two years ago, returning with Bree after their marriage to his roots here in Akaroa, on the Banks Peninsula of New Zealand's South Island, had felt natural and right. He'd bought out his father's boutique vineyard operation, allowing his parents to finally fulfill their lifelong dream of traveling through the wine-growing districts of Europe and South America, and allowing himself to settle in to what he'd seen as an enjoyable new stage in his career.

At the time, it had been a fun and exciting change of pace. Raoul had gone as far as he could go as Nate Hunter-Jackson's second in charge at Jackson Importers up in Auckland. While he'd loved every minute of the challenges working in the wine purveyance and distribution network built up over two generations, his heart had always been locked in at the source of the wine.

After settling in following the wedding, Raoul had dedicated himself to the vines. Meanwhile, Bree had project managed the building of their new home, seeing to the finishing details even as Ruby's anticipated arrival had drawn near.

At the start of his marriage, what he did here, wrapped in the science of blending his boutique wines, had been an adventure, almost a game. His work had been filled with the same exuberant hopes for the future as his marriage.

Losing Bree had shaken the ground under his feet, and his work had gone from a pastime to an obsession. Life was filled with twists and turns that were beyond his abilities to predict, but this…this was something he could control. He was working with known quantities, with wines that had been made in the stainless-steel vats behind him from the very grapes grown on vines that snaked down the hillsides to the harbor—*terroir* that had become as much a part of him as breathing. Work was stable, steadying. And when he'd finished for the day and returned to the house, he could sink back into his memories and his mourning. He'd never shared this home with anyone but Bree—and now he shared it with her ghost.

Alexis's arrival changed all that. She was so vibrantly alive and in the moment that she made living in the past impossible. Even their brief conversation had been enough to make him feel self-consciously alert, keenly aware of the disheveled appearance he usually couldn't be bothered to notice.

And aware of *her* in a way that filled him with shame. He hadn't been the husband Bree had deserved, not entirely, not when—even though he'd kept it fully under wraps—he'd desired her best friend. Was it infidelity when a person only thought about another? He'd loved Bree, there'd been no doubt about that. Adored her, idolized her. Cherished her. But deep down inside, there'd been a primitive part of him that had craved Alexis Fabrini on a level so base he'd had to jam it down deep inside.

He'd been relieved when he'd heard Alexis had headed overseas—how, after her last contract as a nanny had neared completion, she'd changed career direction and had begun pouring herself into fashion design. Some of Alexis's designs still hung in Bree's closet. Bree had been so excited for her, albeit a little hurt and puzzled when Alexis let contact drop between them.

Living with Alexis would be hell. He gave a humorless laugh. What else was new? Just living was hell. Each day a torture. Each day a reminder that he'd failed in that most basic tenet of keeping his wife safe. Of ensuring her needs were put before his own.

He'd never made it a secret that he'd wanted a large family—and because he'd been so outspoken, so determined in his plans for the future she'd felt the need to keep a secret that would have made him change his mind. Given a choice between a family and Bree, he'd have chosen Bree every time. Yet she'd hidden the news about the aneurysm that killed her until it was too late, putting the baby's life ahead of her own.

Ruby. He could barely think about her without being reminded of failure yet again. Drowning in his own grief, he hadn't been able to bear the weak sound of her cries—or the bone-deep certainty that he would lose her, too. She'd been so ill at birth… It was better this way, he'd decided. To keep his distance and not risk the pain that would come if he got too used to having her in his life.

Raoul turned back to the table, to the wines he'd been sampling and assessing for what was his favorite part of wine production—the blending. He forced himself to settle back down in his chair, to study his notes and then to reach for another glass of wine.

Sour. He grimaced and took a sip of water, rinsing the bitter tang from his mouth before reaching for another glass. Again, sour. He threw himself against the back of his chair in disgust. He knew the flavor of the wine had little to do with his skills as a vintner and far more to do with his current state of mind. Whether he wanted to admit it or not, his working day was over—which left, what exactly? Time to go up to the house to reminisce about old times with Alexis?

His gut twisted at the very thought. Even so, he pushed himself upright and cleared away his work, neatly filing away his notes for tomorrow and rinsing out all the glasses, leaving them to drain on the rack before he started up the lane.

Alexis was in the kitchen when he got into the house. He could hear her moving around, opening and closing cupboard doors, humming in an off-key tone. It sounded so domestic and normal for a second he allowed himself to hope, to dream that it was Bree there in the kitchen.

But the second Alexis's curvy frame came into the doorway the illusion was shattered.

"I can see why Catherine sent me up here with all this food. You had hardly anything in the pantry at all, and the fridge just about echoes it's so empty. What on earth have you been living on? Thin air?"

He knew she was trying to be friendly but he armored himself against the attempt.

"I get by. I didn't ask you to come here and criticize how I live."

"No, you didn't," she said with a rueful twist of lush lips that were made for long, hot, hungry kisses.

Viciously he slammed a lid down on the thought. He wasn't going there. Ever.

"By the way," she continued blithely, "while I found Ruby's room easily enough, I'm not sure which room you wanted me in. I went into one of the spare rooms but it looked like your things were in there."

He hadn't been able to bear returning to the master bedroom, not with all its memories of Bree.

"Take the room nearest the nursery."

"But isn't that the master suite?"

"I don't use it, aside from storing a few clothes. I'll take the last of them out of there for you."

"Okay, do you need a hand? Maybe I could—"

"Look, I don't want you here, and I certainly don't need your help. Catherine's decided you should take care of Ruby, but that's all you're here to do. Let's just agree to stay out of one another's way and everything will be just fine."

He ground out the last word as if his life depended on it.

"Raoul—!"

"Don't," he said putting up a hand. "You're here now and apparently I can't do anything about that. But let me make one thing very clear. I don't want your sympathy, Alexis. I'm all sympathied out."

"I can see that," she said. Her voice was dry and calm but he could see the shadows in her dark chocolate-brown eyes and he knew he'd hurt her.

He closed his own eyes briefly and dragged in a leveling breath. He hadn't meant to be so harsh but it was his default setting these days. Living alone didn't make one the best conversationalist, that was for sure.

The sound of a car outside heralded the arrival of his mother-in-law and, from the shriek and gurgle of laughter that followed the sound of a car door opening, the baby. His blood ran cold. His chest tightened making it hard to breathe.

"I'm going for a shower," he said tightly, and left before Alexis could move to let Catherine and Ruby into the house.

He strode to his room and slammed the door behind him before moving to his bathroom and locking the door. He disrobed with a minimum of movement and stepped into the shower stall even as he turned on the faucets. The water, when it hit him, was chilling—painful—but that was nothing compared to the pain of the gaping hole inside him. Nothing at all.

He'd fought against this happening, having the baby here under the same roof, and he'd won the battle for so long. The nursery, so lovingly decorated by Bree, had never been used. He'd known, logically, that one day his defenses would be worn down, that he'd have to step up to his responsibilities as a father. He just never imagined those defenses would be stormed by the one woman in the whole world he'd hoped never to see again and yet still craved with a hunger he could never assuage.

Two

Alexis held little Ruby's weight against her, relishing the solid warmth of the child's small body and inhaling the special baby scent of her hair and skin. So far, so good, she thought as they watched Catherine drive away. The older woman had been torn, clearly reluctant to leave Ruby behind, but Alexis had hastened to assure her that she was doing the right thing, for them all, but most of all for herself. She was already nervous enough about her upcoming surgery, she didn't need the added worry of wondering how well Ruby would settle into her father's home.

A light breeze lifted a tuft of Ruby's fine auburn hair and brushed against Alexis's cheek, the touch as soft and delicate as fingertips tracing lightly across her skin. A sudden pang for Bree cut her to the quick. The realization that she would never see her friend again, never share a bottle of wine and silly laughter over happy remembrances. Never again squabble over who was the more handsome out of the Hemsworth brothers.

Her hold on the baby in her arms, the child her friend never got to see outside of a sonogram, tightened and Ruby squawked in protest.

"I'm sorry, precious girl," Alexis murmured into the baby's soft fuzz of hair.

She fought back the burn of tears that threatened to cascade down her face and made a silent vow. *I will look after your daughter, Bree, I promise. And I will love her and care for her and keep you alive in her heart forever.*

Stepping back indoors, Alexis noticed that Raoul was nowhere to be seen inside the house. A good thing perhaps? Alexis couldn't be certain. She popped Ruby on the floor with a few of the toys that Catherine had brought over with the baby and sat down with her. She seemed a placid enough child now, although Alexis knew from Ruby's grandmother that she'd been very ill and demanding as a newborn. Understandable, given her start in life, she rationalized as she watched the little girl reach for a multicolored teddy and pull it to her, cuddling it as she popped her thumb in her mouth. Her big blue eyes stared back solemnly at Alexis.

Somewhere in the house a door slammed shut and Ruby and Alexis both jumped. Alexis laughed softly.

"Goodness," she said rolling onto her belly on the floor and tickling the baby on one of her delightfully pudgy feet. "That was loud, wasn't it?"

She was rewarded with a shy smile that exposed four perfect pearl-like teeth and she felt her heart twist in response. While Ruby's coloring was exactly that of her mother's, her smile was all Raoul.

"You're going to be quite the heartbreaker, aren't you, young lady?"

The baby's chin began to wrinkle and her lower lip to quiver. Her thumb fell from her mouth and she let rip with a wail, her blue eyes filling with tears as she stared past Alexis.

"Oh, dear, was it something I said?"

Alexis pushed herself up into a sitting position and pulled the baby into her lap, rubbing her back in an attempt to soothe her but to no avail. A prickle of awareness up her spine made her realize they were no longer alone.

She swiveled her head and saw Raoul standing there behind them, frozen to the spot. His usually tan face was a sickly shade of gray.

"What's wrong with her? Why's she crying?" he demanded, his voice harsh and setting Ruby to cry even harder.

"Raoul, are you okay?" she asked, lithely getting to her feet and holding the baby against her.

His eyes were clamped on Ruby who buried her face into Alexis's chest and continued to cry.

"I'm fine," he said tightly, looking anything but. "Why's she crying like that?"

"I assume it's because she got a bit of a fright when you came into the room. Plus, this is all strange to her, isn't it? Being here, missing Catherine, having me around."

He nodded. "Please, can't you do something to calm her?"

Alexis gave him a rueful smile. "I'm doing my best," she said, jiggling Ruby gently. "Perhaps you could soften your tone a little?"

He made a dismissive gesture with one hand. "I'd prefer you keep the child confined to her room while I'm in the house."

"But this is her home. You are kidding me, right?" Alexis said incredulously.

His eyes dragged from Ruby's sobbing form to Alexis's face.

"No. I'm not."

He turned to walk out of the living room, but Alexis would have none of it.

"Stop right there," she said with as much authority as she could muster. "You act like Ruby is an unwanted stranger here. She's your daughter for goodness' sake."

Raoul turned around slowly. "It wasn't my wish for her to come here and her presence is disruptive. As her nanny, your role is to confine your skills and your opinions to her care and her care alone. Is that understood?"

Alexis didn't recognize the man in front of her. Sure, he mostly looked like the same Raoul Benoit she'd been introduced to shortly before he married her best friend, and he sounded the same. Her body certainly still had the same response to his presence, that unsettling thrill of awareness that buzzed along her nerve endings whenever she was near him. But the words… They weren't the words of a bereaved husband or a caring father. And he *did* care—whether he wanted to admit it or not. So why was he trying so hard to distance himself from Ruby?

"Is that understood?" he repeated. "Your charge is distressed. I suggest you do whatever it is that you need to do to calm her and do it quickly."

He tried to sound aloof but she could see the lines of strain around his eyes. It pulled at his heart to hear his little girl cry. She knew it as sure as she knew the reflection of her own face in the mirror each morning.

"Here, you take her for me and I'll go and get her dinner ready. It's time for her evening meal, anyway."

He took a rapid step back and looked as her as if she'd suggested he tip vinegar into a barrel of his finest wine.

"Are you telling me you're incapable of fulfilling your duties as a nanny?"

"No," she said as patiently as she could. "Of course not. I thought you might like to hold your daughter to distract her, while I prepare her something to eat before her bath."

"I don't pay you to hand the baby over to me, Alexis," he said bluntly before spinning around and leaving the room as silently as he'd entered it.

Ruby lifted her little head to peer around Alexis carefully, putting her thumb firmly back in her mouth when she was satisfied her father had departed.

"Well, that didn't go quite as well as I expected," Alexis said softly to the little girl. "I thought your grandmother might be exaggerating when she said that your daddy didn't have anything to do with you. Looks like we have our work cut out for us, hmm?"

She kissed the top of Ruby's head and, adjusting her a little higher on her hip, took her through to the kitchen. Grabbing a paper towel, she moistened it under the faucet and gently wiped tear tracks from two chubby little cheeks. Ruby clearly wasn't a fan of paper towels and Alexis made a mental note to search out the muslin squares she'd seen amongst the baby's things in the nursery. She popped Ruby into her high chair and gave her a plain cookie to chew on—who said you couldn't start dinner with dessert every now and again?—while she scanned Catherine's comprehensive notes on Ruby's diet and sleeping times. The baby was still napping twice in a day and, after a 250 ml bottle at bedtime, pretty much slept through the night except for when she was cutting a tooth.

It all looked very straightforward. Alexis sighed and looked at the little girl. How could Raoul not want to be a part of her care? The very idea was almost impossible to contemplate. If she hadn't heard him just a few moments ago she would have denied that he could possibly be so cold.

But was he really cold? There'd been something flickering in his hazel eyes that she hadn't quite been able to identify. Thinking back on it, could it have been fear? Could he be afraid of his own daughter?

Ruby chose that moment to wearily rub at her eyes with cookie-goop-covered hands, galvanizing Alexis back into action. If she was going to get a dinner inside the tot she needed to feed her now before she fell asleep in her high chair. After coaxing Ruby through her meal of reheated soft-cooked ravioli, which Catherine had thoughtfully made and supplied for tonight, she held Ruby carefully over the kitchen sink and turned on the cold tap, letting her clap her little hands in the stream as the water washed away the food residue.

"I think you're wearing about as much food as you've eaten." Alexis laughed as she used a clean tea towel to dry their hands and give Ruby's face a quick wipe before whisking her back through the house to the nursery.

After a bath and a new diaper, fresh pajamas, and a bottle, Ruby was down in her crib. Alexis rubbed her back for a little while, concerned she might not settle in what were obviously strange surroundings, but it seemed her earlier upset had worn Ruby out and she was asleep in no time. After Alexis checked to ensure the baby monitor was on, she clipped its partner to the loop of her jeans and left the room.

Outside in the hall she came to a halt. She really didn't know what to do next. Should she seek out Raoul and press him for more explanation over his behavior earlier, or simply carry on as if nothing had happened? She worried at her lower lip with her teeth. Until she'd seen him again today she would have done the former of the two—without question. But after that stilted, almost hostile, encounter, she was reluctant to muddy the waters between them any more than they already were.

She still needed to unpack her things, so she went into the master bedroom where she'd put her suitcase earlier on. The door to the walk-in wardrobe stood open and she gravitated toward it. One side was completely bare of anything but naked hangers, the other still filled with women's clothing. Her heart stuttered in her chest as she reached out and touched a few of the things hanging there, as a hint of Bree's favorite scent wafted out.

That awful sense of emptiness filled her again along with a renewed feeling of deep sympathy for the man who hadn't yet been able to bring himself to pack his dead wife's things away. She stepped out of the wardrobe and closed the door behind her, turning instead to the native rimu tallboy that stood proud against one wall. The drawers were empty, so she filled them with her things, then shoved her now-redundant case into the wardrobe without looking again at the silent memorial that still hung there.

A knock at her door make her start.

"Yes?" she called out.

The door opened and Raoul filled the frame. Instantly her senses sprang to life. Her body hummed with that almost electric responsiveness to his proximity—her eyes roaming over him, taking in the way his clothing hung just a little too loosely on his rangy frame. It was hard to believe he was the same man as before. But then again, he wasn't, was he? He'd been through hell and she needed to remember that as she tackled her new role. To perhaps be a little less judgmental.

For all the differences—from subtle to striking—in

his appearance and in his manner, there was no doubting the instant effect he had on her equilibrium. Even now she could feel her heart beat that little bit faster, her breathing become a little more shallow. She dug her fingernails into her palms in an attempt to distract herself from her reaction to him.

"I just wanted to make sure you'd settled in okay," he said stiffly, not quite meeting her eyes.

She nodded, unsure of what to say about Bree's things. Or even if she should say anything about them at all.

"The baby's quiet now. Is she all right?"

"Ruby's down for the night. Catherine tells me she usually goes through until about six-thirty, or seven, so as long as she isn't unsettled by sleeping somewhere unfamiliar, you shouldn't hear from her again until morning."

"How do you know she's okay? You're not with her right now."

Alexis tapped the monitor on her belt loop. "I have the monitor. As soon as she stirs I'll know, trust me."

"Hmm, are you sure it's working?"

"It looked pretty new when I removed it from the packaging and I put fresh batteries in this unit myself before Ruby arrived."

He flinched slightly and Alexis took a moment to realize why. Of course, he and Bree would have bought all the things in the nursery in readiness for when they brought their infant home for the first time. Bree was likely the last person to have touched that monitor before Alexis.

"They might be old. I'll get you new ones. Make sure you change them immediately."

Alexis fought the urge to salute at his command. Instead she merely inclined her head. He was showing concern, which was a good thing even if she wished it came with a less imperious tone.

"Is there anything else? I thought I might start getting our evening meal ready. Ruby obviously ate earlier but now I have time to put something together for us. Will you be joining me?"

"No." His response was emphatic. "I'll see to myself."

"It's no bother. I may as well cook for two adults as for one. I'll leave your meal warming in the oven."

His body sagged, as if he was giving up in this battle—perhaps choosing to shore up his strength for another time. "Thank you."

"If you change your mind about eating with me, feel free. It'd be nice to catch up. Or, if you'd rather, have breakfast with Ruby and me in the morning. It'd be good for her to spend more time with her dad, and good for you, too."

Raoul sighed and swiped one hand across his face. She saw his jaw clench before he spoke again.

"Look, I know you're determined to do what you think is the right thing, but you and the baby being here is a complication I can do without. Don't make it any harder for me than it already has to be."

"But—"

"No buts, Alexis. I mean it. If there had been any other alternative to this, believe me, I would have chosen it. Once Catherine is mobile again I expect things to return to normal."

"Normal? But this isn't normal, is it? Not by any stretch of the imagination," Alexis protested. "Bree wouldn't have wanted you to be so distant from your own flesh and blood."

He paled as if he'd been dealt a mortal blow. "Don't," he said brokenly, shaking his head and backing toward the door. "Don't throw that at me. You have no idea—"

He shook his head once more. "Just do what you were hired to do, Alexis. End of topic."

He was gone in an instant and Alexis wrapped her arms around herself in a vain attempt to provide some comfort for herself where there was none. So, it seemed she couldn't even mention her best friend without making Raoul run. That he'd loved her deeply was patently obvious. But how could that love not extend to their little girl?

Three

Raoul lay in bed unable to sleep any longer. It was time he rose anyway, time to escape to the winery before Alexis and Ruby took over the house. No longer was his home the quiet sanctuary contained by the boundaries of his property. No longer was coming to the house a peaceful pilgrimage to the past. No longer was it his safe place where he could be alone with his memories.

They'd been here a week—a hellishly long time, in his estimation—and since Alexis's and the baby's arrival he spent as little time as humanly possible in the house. And since he still wasn't ready to face the world at large, that meant he spent as much time as he could in the winery where he wasn't constantly being distracted by the presence of two very unsettling females.

Just yesterday he'd caught Alexis shifting things in the sitting room—raising the tide line, she'd called it—because Ruby was pulling herself up on the furniture and starting to walk around things, grabbing for whatever she could reach. While he understood the necessity of keeping Ruby safe, the idea of changing anything from the way Bree had left it was profoundly unsettling.

He yawned widely. Sleep had been as elusive last night as it had been since Alexis's accusation of his behavior being abnormal. Her words had stung. She had no idea what he went through every time he looked at Ruby. Every time he saw a miniature Bree seated before him. He'd almost managed to bring the shock of pain under control, but the echoing empty loss that came hard on its heels unraveled him in ways he didn't even want to begin to acknowledge.

And then there was the fear—an awful irrational beast that built up in his chest and threatened to consume him. What if Ruby got sick, or was hurt? What if he didn't know what to do, or didn't react fast enough? It was an almost unbearable sense of responsibility lessened only slightly by knowing Alexis was here shouldering the bulk of it. Raoul shoved aside his bedcovers and got out of bed, yanking his pajama bottoms up higher on his hips. Everything slid off him these days. It hadn't mattered when he was here alone but now, with his privacy totally invaded, he had to be a little more circumspect. Even locked in his antisocial bubble he could see that.

Suddenly his senses went on full alert, his skin awash with a chill of terror as he heard a muted thump come from the nursery followed by a sharp cry from the baby. For a second he was frozen, but another cry followed hard on the heels of the first, sending him flying down the hallway toward God only knew what disaster. His heart felt too big in his chest, its beat too rapid, and he fought to drag in a shuddering breath as he reached the doorway, almost too afraid to open the door and look inside.

Ruby's howls had increased several decibels. Where the hell was Alexis? The child's care was her job. Reluctantly, he turned the handle and pushed open the door. He winced as Ruby let out another earsplitting yell. Something had to be horribly wrong, he was sure. Fine tremors racked his body as he visually examined the red-faced infant standing up in her crib, howling her throat out.

His eyes flew over her, searching for some visible cause for her distress. She was so small—miniature everything from the tiny feet tipped with even tinier toes to the top of her auburn fuzzed head—all except for the sound bellowing from her lungs.

Clearly nothing wrong with those.

There was absolutely nothing he could see that could be responsible for her upset. Nothing external, anyway. Fear twisted in his stomach as he took a step into the room. It was always what you couldn't see that was the most dangerous.

One pudgy little hand gripped the top rail of the side of her crib, the other reached out helplessly…toward what? Looking around, he spotted a toy on the floor. From its position, he'd guess that it had been in the crib with her and she'd flung it across the room. And still she screamed.

Was that all this was about? A stupid toy?

He gingerly picked up the mangled black-and-white zebra and handed it to her, avoiding actual physical contact. The sobs ceased for a moment—but only a moment before she hurled it back to the floor, plonked herself down on her bottom on her mattress and began once more to howl.

"Oh, dear, so it's going to be one of those days, is it?" Alexis bustled past him and toward the crib.

"Where the hell have you been? She's been crying

for ages," Raoul demanded, pushing one hand through his hair.

"About a minute, actually, but yes, I agree, it feels like forever when she's upset."

She competently lifted Ruby from the crib and hugged her to her body. Raoul became instantly aware of how the child snuggled against Alexis's scantily clad form—in particular Alexis's full, unbound breasts that were barely covered by a faded singlet. She wore it over pajama shorts that, heaven help him, rode low on her softly curved hips and high on her tanned legs.

A surge of heat slowly rolled through his body, making his skin feel tight—uncomfortable with recognition of her lush femininity. But then he became aware of something else.

"What is that god-awful smell?"

"Probably the reason why she's awake earlier than normal. She needs a clean diaper and she's very fussy about that. It's good really, it'll make potty training so much easier later on. Some kids are absolutely oblivious."

Raoul backed out of the room. "Are you sure that's all? Maybe she ought to see the doctor and get checked out."

Alexis just laughed. The sound washed over him like a gentle caress—its touch too much, too intimate.

"I see nothing to laugh about. She might be sick," he said, his body rigid with anxiety.

"Oh, no. Nothing like that," Alexis replied, her back to him as she laid Ruby down on her change table.

With one hand gently on the baby's tummy, she reached for a packet of wipes, the movement making the already short hemline of her pajama shorts ride even higher and exposing the curve of one buttock. The warmth that had previously invaded his body now ignited to an instant inferno. He turned away from the scene before him, as much to hide his stirring erection as to avoid watching the diaper change.

He turned back a minute later, almost under complete control once more, as Alexis dropped the soiled packet into the diaper bin, one Raoul distinctly remembered Bree ordering in a flurry of nursery accessory buying the day they discovered she was pregnant. He didn't even remember when it had arrived or who had put it in here. He should probably have given it to Catherine but here it was, being used in a nursery he'd never imagined being used at all after Bree's death.

"Raoul? Are you okay?"

Alexis's voice interrupted his thoughts, dragging him back into the here and now as she always did.

"I'm fine," he asserted firmly, as if saying the words could actually make them true.

"Good, then please hold Ruby while I go and wash my hands."

Before he could protest, she'd thrust the baby against his chest. Instinctively he put out his arms, regretting the movement the instant his hands closed around the little girl's tiny form. His stomach lurched and he felt physically ill with fear. He'd never held her before. Ever. What if he did something wrong, or hurt her? What if she started crying again? He looked down into the blue eyes of his daughter, eyes that were so like her mother's. Her dark brown lashes were spiked together with tears and to his horror he saw her eyes begin to fill again, saw her lip begin to wobble. He couldn't do this, he really couldn't do this.

"Thanks, Raoul, I can take her back now if you like?"

Relief swamped him at Alexis's return and he passed the baby back to her with lightning speed. But the moment his arms were empty something weird happened.

It was as if he actually missed the slight weight in his arms, the feel of that little body up against his own, the sensation of the rapidly drawn breaths in her tiny chest, the warmth of her skin.

He took one step back, then another. No, he couldn't feel this way. He couldn't afford to love and lose another person the way he'd lost Bree. Ruby was still small, so much could go wrong. He forced himself to ignore the tug in his chest and the emptiness in his arms and dragged his gaze from the little girl now staring back at him, wide-eyed as she bent her head into Alexis's chest, the fingers of one hand twirling in Alexis's shoulder-length honey-blond hair.

"Are you absolutely certain she's all right?" he asked gruffly.

Alexis smiled. "Of course, she's fine, although she might be a bit cranky later this morning and need a longer nap than normal thanks to this early start today."

"Don't hesitate to take her to the doctor if you're worried."

"I won't, I promise."

Her voice softened and his eyes caught with hers. Was it pity he saw there reflected in their dark brown depths? He felt his defenses fly back up around him. He needed no one's pity. Not for anything. He was doing just fine by himself, thank you very much. And that was just the way he preferred it.

Except he wasn't by himself anymore, was he? He had Ruby and Alexis to contend with, and goodness only knew they both affected him on entirely different levels. Feeling overwhelmed he turned around and strode from the room, determined to keep as much distance between himself and them as possible.

* * *

Alexis watched him go, unable to stop herself from enjoying the view, finally letting out a sigh and turning away when he hitched up his pajama bottoms before they dipped any lower. He'd always been a beautiful man and it had almost hurt her eyes to see him nearly naked like that. His weight loss had only given his muscled strength more definition, particularly the long lean line that ran from his hip down under the waistband of his pants. Oh, yes, he still pinged every single one of her feminine receptors—big time.

She'd been glad for the distraction of settling Ruby or she might have done something stupid—like reach out and touch him. She might have followed that line to see what lay beneath it. To see whether she'd imagined his reaction to her own body before he'd so valiantly controlled it back into submission. Her mouth dried and her fingertips tingled at the thought. She closed her eyes briefly in an attempt to force the visual memory of him from her mind but it only served to imprint him even deeper.

No, acting on her ridiculous impulses would only complicate things beyond control. Her attraction to him was just as pointless as it had always been, and dwelling on it wouldn't do either one of them any good. She was here to do a job and she was doing it well—no matter how often he'd already managed to suggest otherwise in the short time she'd been here.

She'd taken a risk making him hold Ruby like that but it had given her the answer to a question she'd been asking herself all week. And just as she'd suspected, big, strong, successful Raoul Benoit was scared. Terrified, to be exact. Not so much of his own daughter—although, there was something of that, too—but *for* her.

Alexis hummed as she collected a few toys for Ruby

to play with while she took the baby to her room so she could get dressed for the day. As she did so, her mind turned over her discovery. It all began to make sense. His reluctance to be in the same room as Ruby, to hold her or to interact with her in any way. His near obsession with her safety. Obviously he'd felt she was secure in her grandmother's care, somewhere where he could ensure she was out of sight and out of mind. Someone else's problem.

But when she was close enough for him to hear her cries, all his fears took over. His instincts as a father had clearly propelled him into Ruby's room when she had woken this morning, but once there he had hardly any idea of what to do with them. She could help with that, could teach him—if he'd let her.

"Bree, it's going to be a hard road getting him back but I think we've made the first step," she said out loud to the photo of her friend that she'd put on the bedside table in her room.

Warmth bloomed in her chest and it was almost as if she felt her friend's approval slide through her before disappearing again. Dismissing the thought as being fanciful, Alexis quickly dressed for the day and scooped Ruby back up off the floor.

"C'mon, munchkin. Let's go find us some breakfast!"

She spun around, the movement making Ruby chuckle in delight. Yes, everything was going to be all right. She just had to keep believing it was possible.

Over the next few days Raoul remained pretty scarce, which served as a source of major frustration. Alexis wanted to gently include him in more of Ruby's routine here and there, but he always managed to duck away before she had a chance. On the bright side, the brief interaction Ruby had shared with her father seemed to have piqued her curiosity about the stern-faced man who hung around the fringes of her little world. Instead of crying every time she saw him she was more inclined to drop everything and barrel forward on all fours toward him if he so much as made a step into her periphery.

It was both highly amusing to see him realize that Ruby had fixated on him, and a bit sad, as well, that he distanced himself from her again so effectively afterward.

One step forward at a time, Alexis reminded herself. She and Ruby fell into an easy daily routine, helped in no small part by the fact that Catherine had enrolled the baby into a playgroup down in town where she happily interacted with other children her age and slightly older. It was good for both of them to get out of the house and interact with other people. Despite having been born a little early, Ruby was only marginally behind her peers when it came to developmental markers, Alexis observed.

One of the young mothers came over to Alexis and sat down beside her.

"Hi, I'm Laura," she said with a bright smile. "That's my little tyke, Jason, over there." She pointed to a little boy in denim jeans and brightly colored suspenders busily commando crawling toward the sandpit.

"Alexis, pleased to meet you," Alexis replied with a smile.

"Have you heard how Catherine is doing? We all have been wondering but didn't want to be a nuisance."

"The surgery went well. She's at her sister's home in Cashmere, recuperating. If you're heading into Christchurch at all, I'm sure she'd love it if you called by to visit."

"Oh, thanks, that's good to know."

Laura sat back and watched the kids playing for a

while. Alexis sensed she was trying to drum up the courage to say something but was perhaps figuring out the best way around it. Eventually, though, she seemed to come to a decision.

"We were surprised when we heard that Ruby was staying with her dad. Especially given..." Her voice trailed off and she looked uncomfortable. "Look, I don't want you to think I'm prying but is everything okay at the house? We were, most of us, friends with Bree during our pregnancies and our partners and Raoul all got along pretty well. We had our own little social group going. Aside from missing Bree, we really miss Raoul, too. All the guys have tried to reach out to him since Bree died, but he's just cut ties with everyone."

Alexis nodded. It was hard to come up with what to say, when it wasn't really her place to say anything.

"Things are going well at the house. We've settled in to a good routine," she hedged.

The fact that routine didn't include Ruby's father went unsaid. Raoul continued to spend the better part of most days in the winery. He'd made his displeasure clear on the few occasions when, at the beginning, Alexis and Ruby had walked down to bring him his lunch.

"Oh, oh, that's good," Laura said with a relieved smile. "Better than I expected to hear, anyway. You were friends with Bree, weren't you?"

"Since kindergarten," Alexis said, swallowing against the bitter taste of guilt that rose in her throat. "We went through school together near Blenheim and kind of drifted apart a bit when she went up to Auckland for university. We used to catch up whenever she was home, though, and stayed in touch until she married and I went overseas."

Even as she said the words, she was reminded again of

how she'd jumped on the opportunity to leave the country rather than remain and witness her friend's happiness. Shame shafted a spear through her chest, making her breath hitch and a sudden wash of tears spring to her eyes.

"We all miss her so much," Laura said, misunderstanding the reason behind Alexis's distress.

Laura reached for her hand and gave it a gentle squeeze. Alexis felt like a fraud accepting the other woman's sympathy. She hardly deserved it when she'd been the one to abandon Bree. She hadn't been here, hadn't even known what was going on, when her friend had needed her most—and all because she hadn't been able to keep her wretched hormones under control. She owed Bree a debt. It was why she was here now, and why she would stay as long as Ruby needed her, no matter what Raoul chose to throw at her.

Laura continued on. "Look, weather permitting, the playgroup is having a family lunch at the beach this Sunday afternoon. We're not planning to swim or anything, it's far too cold already this autumn, but there are barbecues and a playground and tables and it's so much easier to clean up afterward with the little ones. You and Ruby should come. And bring Raoul along, too, it'll do him good to mix with his mates again."

"I—I'm not sure. Can I confirm with you later on?"

It was one thing to accept an invitation for herself and Ruby, but quite another to do so for a man who'd clearly chosen to remove himself from his social circle.

"Sure," Laura said with an enthusiastic smile. She gave Alexis her cell number. "Just fire me a text if you're coming."

When Alexis got back home, Ruby was already asleep in her car seat. She carefully lifted the sleeping infant and transferred her into her crib, taking a moment to watch her. Her heart broke for the wee thing. No mother, barely a father, either. Alexis's hands gripped the side rail of the crib, her knuckles whitening. She had to try harder. Somehow, she had to get Raoul to open his life, to open his heart again. If she didn't she would have failed everyone, but most of all this precious wee scrap sleeping so innocently in front of her.

Four

Sunday dawned bright and clear. Raoul eyed the cloudless sky with a scowl. He'd been adamantly opposed to attending this thing today. Adamantly. Yet Alexis had barreled on as if he hadn't said no. In fact, when he thought about it, she hadn't so much *asked* him if he would go along, she pretty much *told* him he was going.

For a fleeting moment he considered disappearing to the winery, or even farther into his vineyards. Not that there'd be many places to hide there as the vines headed into their seasonal slumber, the leaves already turning and falling away. It was a shame it was still too early to start pruning. He could have lied and said that the work absolutely had to be done and right away, but he knew Alexis had grown up on a vineyard, too. She'd have known he wasn't telling the truth the instant he opened his mouth.

His stomach tied in knots. He really couldn't do this.

Couldn't face the well-meaning looks and the sympathetic phrases people trotted out—as if any of it would change the past. And he really didn't need to be within fifty meters of Alexis Fabrini for the better part of an afternoon.

Each day she was here he was reminded anew of how his body had reacted to her ever since the first time he'd seen her. About how his wife might now be dead and gone but his own needs and desires certainly weren't. After losing Bree, he'd believed that part of himself to be dormant to the point of extinction, until the second Alexis had walked into his winery. The discovery that all his body parts still worked just fine was a major, and often uncomfortable, inconvenience.

"Oh, good, you're ready!"

Alexis's ever-cheerful voice came from behind him. Instantly, every cell in his body leaped to aching life. Since that incident in the nursery the other day, he'd struggled to maintain a semblance of physical control. Even now the vision of her long legs and the curve of her pert bottom filled his mind. He slowly turned around.

Ruby was in Alexis's arms. Dressed in pink denim dungarees with a candy-striped long-sleeve knit shirt underneath and with a pale pink beret on her little head, she was the epitome of baby chic. She ducked her head into the curve of Alexis's neck, then shyly looked back at him, a tentative smile curving her rosebud mouth and exposing the tiny teeth she had in front.

His heart gave an uncomfortable tug. God, she was so beautiful, so like her mother. Ruby's smile widened and he felt his own mouth twist in response before he clamped it back into a straight line once more.

"Should we take your car or mine?" Alexis asked breezily.

His eyes whipped up to her face. She looked slightly smug, as if she'd just achieved some personal goal.

"I—I'm not sure if I'm going—I need to check something in the winery," he hedged. "How about you go ahead and I'll join you later in my own car if I have time."

Alexis's lips firmed and he saw the disappointment mixed with determination in her eyes. Eyes that reminded him of melted dark chocolate, complete with all the decadence and promise that brought with it.

"You're chickening out, aren't you?" she said, her voice flat. "You don't want to go."

Ruby picked up on her change of mood and gave a little whimper.

Chickening out? He instinctively bristled, programmed to instantly deny her accusation, but he had to admit she was right about him not wanting to go. If she insisted on putting it that way then sure, he was chickening out. Personally, he preferred to think of it as more of a strategic avoidance of a situation that would only bring him pain. Only a fool sought pain at every juncture, right?

"No, I don't."

"Fine," Alexis said with a sigh. "We'll go on our own. I just thought you were a better man than that."

"Better man? What do you mean?" he retorted, his pride pricked by her words.

"Well, I know you've been busily wallowing in your solitary world for at least nine months now, but you weren't the only person to lose Bree. I'm sorry to be this blunt, but you have to remember, all your friends lost her, too, and it was a double whammy for them when you shut them all out at the same time. I know they miss you and they're *your* friends, too, Raoul."

"I didn't..."

He let his voice trail off. He wanted to refute what

she'd said but he knew she told the truth. He had cut all ties deliberately. At the time, he hadn't wanted platitudes or sympathy or help, particularly from people who would advise him to "move on" or "embrace life again" when he had just wanted to be left alone with his memories and his regrets. And that hadn't changed.

Or had it? He missed the camaraderie of his mates—the beers and insults shared over a game of rugby, the discussion between fellow wine enthusiasts over one varietal trend or another. But he wasn't ready to get back out there, to reconnect with people...was he?

The idea was pretty terrifying. He'd been insular for so long now. Even if he could muster the energy to try, would his old friends even want to talk to him again? He had been outright rude on occasions. When he'd surfaced from abject grief he'd been filled with resentment instead, especially that their lives could go on unsullied while his had fallen into an abyss. And once he'd fallen, it had become easier to remain deep down inside the abyss rather than to claw his way back out and into the light.

Clearly Alexis had had enough of his excuses because she picked up the picnic bag she'd obviously packed earlier and headed to the door. He stood there, frozen to the spot as she blithely walked away.

"Wait!"

The sound was more of a croak than a word. She stopped in her tracks and half turned toward him.

"We'll take the Range Rover," he said, stepping forward and reaching to take the picnic bag from her.

The bag was heavy and made him realize just how strong she was. She'd already shouldered the baby's diaper bag as well, and had Ruby on her hip. It seemed to simply be Alexis's way. To do whatever needed to be done—to bear whatever burden had to be borne without resentment or complaint. He almost envied her the simplicity of that.

"Thanks, I'll transfer Ruby's seat over from mine."

"No, it's okay. There's a spare still in its box in the garage. I'll get that."

Alexis gave him a nod of acceptance and he was grateful she'd said nothing about his change of mind.

Twenty minutes later, as they approached the picnic area at the local beach, he felt his stomach clench into a knot and a cold wash of fear rushed through his veins. He started as Alexis laid her hand on his forearm.

"It'll be okay, Raoul, I promise. They won't bite. They're your friends, and they understand how hard this is for you."

Understand? He doubted it but he forced his thoughts away from Bree and to the here and now. To the vista before him, peppered with people he knew. People who knew him. And then, to the woman who sat beside him in the passenger's seat. The woman whose hand still rested warmly on his arm. A woman who'd put her own life and, he knew, her career on hold so she could look after Bree's daughter.

His gaze flicked to the rearview mirror. His daughter.

The sensation in his gut wound up another notch and he hissed out a breath.

"C'mon, let's get this over with."

He pushed open his door and turned away from Alexis, letting her hand drop. He stalked around to the back of his SUV and lifted the hatch, purposefully grabbing the diaper bag and the picnic bag out before lifting out the stroller. He tugged at the handles to try to unfold the thing but it remained solidly shut.

"I'll do that if you like," Alexis said, coming around the car with Ruby.

She pushed the baby at him, much like she'd done the other day. Stiffly, he accepted the child's weight into his arms. Ruby looked at him with solemn blue eyes and then reached up to pat him gently on the cheek. Alexis had the stroller up in two seconds flat and she put the diaper bag in the basket on the underside before placing the picnic bag in the seat.

"Shouldn't she go there?" Raoul asked.

"Nope, she's fine right where she is. Aren't you, precious?"

She reached out to tickle Ruby under her chin and was rewarded with a little chuckle. The delightful sound made Raoul's heart do a flip-flop in his chest and ignited an ember of warmth deep inside. He rapidly quashed the sensation. He couldn't afford to soften, it just laid you open to so much pain. He wasn't going there again. Not ever.

"No," he said emphatically, reaching for the picnic bag and putting it on the ground before buckling Ruby firmly into her stroller. "She's safer here," he said, once he was satisfied she was secure.

"She was fine with you, you know, Raoul."

"I know what you're trying to do, Alexis. It's not going to happen. You can't make me fit into the mold you want to squeeze me into."

Heat flashed in her eyes and her lips drew into a straight line. Something he'd noticed she did whenever she was annoyed with him—which was pretty darn often come to think of it.

"Is that what you think I'm trying to do? Squeeze you into a mold? For what it's worth, I'm not attempting to do any such thing. You're Ruby's father and it's about time you stepped up to your responsibilities." She softened her tone slightly as she continued. "Look, I know you miss

Bree, I know how much you loved her. But rejecting your child isn't going to bring Bree back. If anything it's only pushing her memory further away."

The permanent ache that resided deep within him grew stronger and he dragged in a breath.

"I'm dealing with this the only way I know how. The only way *I* can," he said quietly. "Just leave me be, okay?"

With that he picked up the picnic bag and walked toward the gathering group. This was hard enough as it was without fighting with Alexis every step of the way at the same time. Deep down he knew she had a point. Bree wouldn't have wanted this, wouldn't have been happy that he'd left Ruby with Catherine. After the amount of time the baby had spent in hospital, he was terrified to even hold her and it had seemed that Catherine needed her daughter's baby about as much as Ruby had needed a confident and loving touch. It had appeared to be the best choice for everyone for him to withdraw, to confine his contact with his daughter to financially providing for her care. After all, what did he know about babies? What if he did something wrong or missed some vital clue that could lead to illness or, even worse, death? Wasn't it better for him to take the time to mourn in his own way, safely alone where there was no one he could hurt—and no one who could hurt him?

Better or not, Alexis was dragging him out of the dark, and he wasn't happy about it. Her presence alone had been enough to spark a part of him to life he'd thought would be dead and gone forever. Basic human instinct, human need, had unfurled from where he'd locked it down, hard. She had a way about her—a warmth, a casual touch here and there—that had begun to thaw out the emotions he'd denied himself and that he knew he no longer deserved.

Emotions were messy things. They insidiously wrapped themselves around your mind and your heart and then when everything went to hell in a handbasket they squeezed so tight you could barely draw breath. He wasn't ready to risk that again. Not for anyone. The pain of loss was just too much. It was much easier to simply lock it all out, to prevent it happening.

He lifted a hand in greeting as one of the guys over by the barbecue area shouted a hello and began to walk toward him. Raoul steeled himself for what he anticipated would be an awkward reunion, but to his surprise he found himself relaxing under the onslaught of his friend's warm and simple greeting.

"Good to see you, mate," his friend Matt said, clapping his back in a man hug. "We've missed you."

Raoul murmured something appropriate in response and accepted the icy bottle of beer being thrust in his hand. Before long others joined them and, to his immense relief, no one mentioned Bree or his absence from their circle over the past nine months. He was just beginning to relax when one of the guys gestured over to where Alexis was sitting with the other women and the little ones.

"New nanny? Nice piece of work there, buddy," the guy said approvingly. His voice was full of innuendo as he continued. "Good around the house, is she?"

Raoul felt his hackles rise. Alexis *was* good around the house and great with Ruby, but he knew that wasn't what this guy was aiming at.

"Alexis is an old friend of Bree's. Ruby's lucky to have her. Besides, it's only temporary, until Catherine's back on her feet again."

His mention of Bree froze over the conversation as effectively as if he'd tipped a bucket of cold water over the guy.

"Hey man, my apologies, I didn't mean anything by it."

"That's fine, then," Raoul uttered tightly.

Anger still simmered beneath the surface for a while over the dismissive way the other man had talked about Alexis. She deserved more respect than that. While he might not necessarily have been warm or friendly toward her himself, he could certainly ensure she received the respect she deserved from others. He didn't stop for a minute to consider why that was so important to him and he missed the look exchanged between his friends behind his back as his gaze remained locked on his daughter's nanny.

Alexis felt a familiar prickle in between her shoulder blades as if she was under scrutiny. She turned and caught Raoul's gaze fastened firmly on her, a serious expression on his face. The moment their eyes met he turned his attention back to the group of men gathered around the barbecue where, by the smells of things, they were making a sacrificial offering of the meat as only a large group of guys could.

Despite the fact he was no longer looking at her, she still felt the impression of his gaze and a flush of heat stained her cheeks and chest in response. What had he been thinking to have such a somber visage? she wondered. Whatever it had been, he'd obviously pushed it to the back of his mind as he now appeared to be laughing at something someone else had said.

The sight of him laughing like that sent a thrill of joy all the way to her heart. He needed to laugh more often, deserved to. The way he'd hidden himself away, devoid of all company and support, had been wrong on so many levels she couldn't even begin to enumerate them. She knew everyone coped differently with grief, but he'd become a slave to his, and that hadn't done anyone any favors—not Raoul and certainly not Ruby.

She watched him a moment longer, relishing the warm sensation that coursed through her as she looked her fill. Laughter suited him. Happiness suited him. And somehow she had to make sure he had his fair share of both back in his world. He reached for another drink from the cooler, a can of soda this time, and she watched the play of muscles along his shoulders beneath the fine knit of his lightweight sweater.

Warmth soon became something more complicated as she felt her body react in a far more visceral way, her breathing quickening and a pull of desire working its way from her core to her extremities.

"He's easy on the eye, isn't he?" Laura's voice intruded from right next to her.

"What? Oh…um, yes." Alexis felt her cheeks flame in embarrassment at being caught out staring at the man who was essentially her boss.

"Don't worry," Laura said with a gentle smile. "Your secret's safe with me."

"Secret?"

Alexis deliberately played dumb, only to be on the receiving end of a gentle smile and a painfully understanding look.

"How long have you felt this way about him?"

Alexis sighed, the other woman's compassion breaking down any barrier she had thought to erect.

"A few years now," Alexis admitted, shocked that she'd given up her secret at the first sign of empathy from another person.

For so long she'd held the truth to her chest, fearful that anyone would find out how she felt and judge her for it. You didn't get attracted to your best friend's partner—it just wasn't done—and you certainly didn't act on it. That was a no-go area in every aspect.

It was terrifying to know that her secret was now out. Not even her parents had known how she felt about Raoul Benoit and, here, a virtual stranger had plucked it from her as easily as if it was a piece of lint on her sweater.

"You…you won't say anything, will you?" she hastened to add in an undertone.

"Of course not, Alexis. To be honest, I'm glad."

"Glad?" Alexis was confused.

"Maybe you're exactly what he needs now, hmm? To mourn someone is one thing, but he's been hiding away from *living* for far too long," Laura said, reaching out to give Alexis's hand a squeeze. "We all deserve a bit of happiness, right?"

"Right," Alexis agreed numbly.

Happiness. Could she bring that elusive ingredient back into Raoul's life? While her aim had been to reunite father and daughter, could he find room in his broken heart to consider love again?

She pushed the thought away. If he could accept Ruby into his life, she'd be satisfied. She had no right to hope for anything more.

Five

After everyone had eaten, the group of adults sat around watching their kids at play. Alexis kept her eye on Ruby as she crawled a couple of meters across the grass toward the playground where Laura and some of the other parents had taken their babies for a turn on the swings. The grass would be hell on those pink dungarees, she thought ruefully, but it was good for Ruby to be out in the fresh air and interacting with everyone else. It wouldn't be long before tiredness would set in—she was already overdue for her nap—but Alexis wanted to prolong the fun for as long as possible.

A cry of anguish from behind her dragged her attention off the little girl, distracting her for the moment it took to return a clearly much-loved piece of tatty muslin to its stroller-bound owner. She turned her eyes back to where Ruby had been, only to feel her stomach drop. She lurched to her feet, her eyes anxiously scanning the crowd for the little splotch of pink. Her feet were already moving, taking her over the grass and toward the playground. Ah, there she was. Relief flooded Alexis with the force of a tidal wave and she covered the short distance between them as quickly as she could.

Ruby sat on her little padded butt, chewing on something she'd picked up from the ground. A small stick by the looks of it, Alexis thought as she reached her.

"What's that she's got?"

Raoul appeared beside them to stand over his daughter, an expression of distaste on his face as he reached down and extricated the twig from Ruby's fingers. The baby voiced her disagreement with his action, loudly.

"I thought you were supposed to be watching her," he accused, holding the stick out for Alexis to see it.

"I was. I—"

"Not closely enough, it seems. God only knows what else she could have picked up and put in her mouth while you weren't looking."

"Raoul, you're overreacting. It's just a twig, and off a nontoxic plant at that. Babies learn by putting things in their mouths. Don't worry, she's fine."

"And if it had been a toxic plant? Or if she'd toppled over and the stick had gone into her throat? What then? Would she learn that you can die from something like that?"

There was a note of harsh censure to his voice that made her blood run cold in her veins. She should have kept a closer eye on Ruby, she knew that. It still hurt to hear Raoul speak that way to her. She reached down and gathered the little girl close to her, taking comfort from Ruby's closeness as she soothed the baby's cries, rubbing her back and automatically rocking gently from one foot to the other until she settled. Raoul threw the offending twig onto the ground with a sound of disgust.

"I knew this was a mistake. We're leaving now," he said, and turned on his heel to stride away before Alexis could answer.

"Are you okay?" Laura said as she came up beside Alexis. "I don't mean to pry but I couldn't help overhearing. Protective, much?"

"Yeah, he's right, though. I should have been keeping a closer eye on Ruby."

"He's paranoid about losing her, isn't he? I mean, we're all a bit off the scale when it comes to our own kids, but with him it's more, isn't it?"

Alexis sighed as she watched Raoul say goodbye to his buddies and then gather their picnic bag and Ruby's diaper bag together. His movements were short and jerky, a clear indication of his foul temper.

"Yeah, it's definitely more."

"He'll come around. Y'know, we all thought that maybe he didn't, or couldn't, love Ruby after Bree died. That maybe he blamed her somehow. But after seeing that, I think he possibly loves her too much—that he's afraid he'll lose her, too."

"I was thinking the same," Alexis agreed. "Hey, thanks for asking us along today. Sorry it kind of ended on a sour note."

"Don't worry about it. We're just glad you managed to talk him into coming. Maybe we can all get together again sometime soon."

Alexis gave her a thin smile and said her goodbyes to the others before joining Raoul over by the picnic table where he waited with ill-concealed impatience.

"We need to talk," he said as she drew nearer.

"When we get home," Alexis conceded.

Yes, they did need to talk, but she had the feeling that Raoul wasn't going to listen to her opinions no matter what she said. She flicked a glance at his stony face, lingering on the pain that reflected in his eyes. Pain that made her heart twist with longing to put things right for him. But she couldn't do it on her own. He had to meet her halfway.

As they drove back to his house she stared blindly out the side window doubting, for the first time since she'd come here, her decision to try and help out. She was in way over her head with this situation and she lacked the objectivity she needed to get through it.

How on earth could she be objective when all she wanted to do every time she saw him was to obliterate his grief with sensation, with her love?

Raoul turned the Range Rover into the driveway at home with a measure of relief. Ruby had fretted the entire journey home, making it seem a lot longer than the twenty-minute drive it really was. He was glad to have gotten her home, but the relief didn't compare to the fury that simmered through his body. Alexis had one job to do—look after Ruby. That was it. Except it wasn't.

Life was so much simpler before she came along. He'd relished his time alone. Life was lonely, yes, but predictable. Safe. Now, every day was a challenge and he rose each morning not knowing what he'd face. It used to be that he'd relish a challenge like that, but not anymore. Not when each challenge came with a new emotional twist that he'd thought he'd never feel again.

He pulled the SUV to a halt outside the house and got out, going around to the rear of the vehicle to extricate the bags and the stroller while Alexis took Ruby from her car seat.

"I'll just give her a bottle to calm her and get her settled for a sleep."

He responded with a curt nod. "I'll wait for you in the study."

While he waited he paced, and then he paced some more. He didn't know how to handle this, how to handle Alexis, but he knew he wanted her gone. Everything had blown up into larger-than-life proportions since her arrival, and he desperately wanted to fit everything back into its neat little boxes all over again—boxes he could keep closed or open at will.

It was nearly half an hour before he heard her quiet knock on his study door. She let herself in without awaiting his acknowledgment—a suitable simile to how she behaved with him on a daily basis, he realized with a rare flash of bleak humor.

"She was a bit difficult to settle, but she's out for the count now," Alexis said by way of explanation as she came in and crossed the room to take a seat.

As she walked, he couldn't help but notice that her jeans stretched tight across her hips, accentuating her very female curves. Curves that he had no business looking at, he reminded himself sternly. Except he couldn't quite bring himself to look away. Even after she sat down in the chair opposite his desk, he remained mesmerized by the fade pattern on the denim, by the all-too-perfect fit around her thighs.

Oblivious to the battle going on in his mind, Alexis blithely continued. "She was definitely overtired, after today, but I checked her gums and she's cutting more teeth, too, so that was probably part of the problem."

Raoul grunted something in response before taking the chair behind the desk. He needed the physical barrier between them. Scrambling to get his thoughts together, he drew in a deep breath.

"About today—" he started, only to be cut off by Alexis speaking over him, her words chasing one after the other in a rush.

"Look, I apologize. What happened was all my fault. I took my eyes off Ruby for a few seconds and she went out of my line of vision. I shouldn't have done it and it was wrong and I'm deeply sorry."

"Sorry isn't enough, Alexis. I don't think you're the right person for the job of caring for Ruby."

Raoul forced himself to look at a spot just past her, so he could pretend that he didn't see the flare of distress that suddenly crossed her features. A hank of her honey-blond hair had worked its way loose from her ponytail and she absently shoved it back behind one ear.

"Don't you think that's a bit of an overreaction?" she said, her voice shaking just a little.

"You're here to mind her. You didn't."

"Raoul, it's not like you weren't there along with several other adults who could see her."

She pushed up to her feet and leaned forward on the desk, the deep V-neck of her T-shirt gaping and affording him a breathtaking view of her breasts cupped in the palest pink lace. Flames of heat seared along his veins, taking the words he was about to utter and reducing them to ash in his mouth. He rapidly lifted his gaze to her face. Bad idea.

A flush of color stained her cheeks and her eyes shimmered with moisture making them look bigger and even more vulnerable than ever.

"Look, I admit I made a mistake," she said fervently, her voice even more wobbly now, "but no harm came of it and I promise you I will be far more vigilant from now on. She won't move an inch without me being on her shadow."

"I don't know," he said, shaking his head and fighting back the growing physical need to reach for her that rose inexorably from deep within him.

"She needs a nanny. If not me, then who else is there, Raoul? Catherine's not even two weeks out of surgery and she won't be home from her sister's for a couple of weeks yet. She couldn't possibly be capable of chasing and looking after an active child at that point—she'll barely be able to care for herself. Ruby could very well be walking by then, if the past few days are any indication. Who else can look after her? You?"

A cold dash of terror quelled the heat of his desire. There was no way he was assuming sole responsibility for Ruby. He simply couldn't. If Alexis, a trained nanny, could make a mistake like today, what hope did he have?

Alexis continued with her tirade. "I suppose you could always put her into day care but is that really what Bree would have wanted? Wasn't it always her wish to have her children raised at home? Can't you at least respect her wishes in that? You lock yourself up in this house as if you want to bury yourself in her memory, but don't you know how furious she'd be with you for pushing everyone away?"

"Enough!" he all but shouted back. "You've made your point. You have one more chance. But that's it, Alexis."

"What's the matter, Raoul?" she goaded. "You don't like to hear the truth?"

"Don't," he warned. "Don't mess with what you know nothing about."

"I know Bree would have hated to see you like this. So cold and closed down that you can't even show love or care to your own daughter!" Alexis persisted.

Raoul flew out of his chair and around the desk, grabbing her by her upper arms and swinging her around to face him.

"You think I don't feel? That I'm cold and don't care? Let me show you just how wrong you are."

Without thinking, he lowered his mouth to hers, his lips laying claim to hers with a sense of purpose that drove him to take and to plunder with little care for the consequences. She uttered a tiny moan, her arms coming up around his shoulders, her fingers pushing into his hair and holding him. Even now she sought to comfort him, it seemed.

But comfort was the last thing on his mind.

He softened his onslaught as he took the time to luxuriate in the soft plumpness of her lips, to taste the sweetly intoxicating flavor of her mouth and to—just for this moment—lose himself in sensation.

A shudder racked his body and he pulled her in closer to him, molding her body along the length of his own. Her hips tilted gently against the growing ridge of his erection, sending a spear of want through him that threatened to make his legs weaken beneath him.

His hands reached for her waist, for the hem of her shirt. He lifted the thin fabric, groaning against her as he felt the soft delicate heat of her skin. He stroked his hands upward until they came into contact with the rasp of her lacy bra. Beneath the lace her nipples jutted out, tight beads of flesh. He brushed his thumbs over them, once, twice. Oh, what he wouldn't give to take them, one by one, into his mouth right now. To tease her and taste her. To discover every last secret of this woman who'd remained a shadow in the back of his mind from the day he'd first met her.

The thought was as sobering now as it had been back

then. Reluctantly Raoul dragged his hands out from beneath her top and reached up to disengage her arms from around his neck. As he gently pushed her back his eyes met hers.

Desire reflected back at him, magnifying the demand that still surged and swelled inside him. Her lips were slightly swollen, glistening with temptation.

Raoul let her go and took a step back.

"Trust me, I feel," he said, his breath coming in heavy puffs. *"Too damn much."*

Six

Alexis stood in the study, watching Raoul's retreating form with a stunned expression on her face. What the hell had just happened? Well, okay, realistically she knew exactly what had just happened—but why?

One second they'd been arguing, the next… She raised a shaking hand to her lips, lips that still felt the searing heat of his possession. Her entire body pulsated with energy. Energy that begged for release. She slowly shook her head in disbelief. She'd always been attracted to him, she'd known that, but this…this reaction went way further than simple attraction. This went bone deep, soul deep. And it left her wanting so much more.

Physically, she'd always been incredibly drawn to Raoul—not only to his body and his mind, but to his heart. He'd been a fabulous husband to Bree and it was his devotion to her friend and their obvious love for one another that had made their happiness together all the more bittersweet for her to witness. Seeing how they'd felt about one another was a reminder to herself that she never wanted to settle for anything less. She wanted the kind of love that Raoul and Bree had had—the same kind of enduring love that her parents had enjoyed through multiple trials and tribulations in their marriage.

Most recently, all through her mother's rapidly advancing early-onset dementia, Alexis's dad had stuck by her—caring for her at home by himself, since Alexis had been overseas, until he was forced to see her admitted to hospital. Even then, he'd barely moved from her side until her death almost four months ago.

Alexis wanted that kind of devotion in a relationship. She was prepared to give it and she believed she deserved it in return. But none of the men she'd dated had ever shown that capacity for love. Then she'd met Raoul, the handsomest man she'd ever met *and* someone who loved so fully and deeply that it took her breath away. Was it any wonder she'd fallen for him in a matter of moments?

But what were his feelings toward her? After the blisteringly hot kiss, she knew attraction was part of it...but was that the extent of it for him? Was he capable of feeling anything more for her? She knew it was still early days for Raoul, that the pain of Bree's death was still a simmering thing lying on the surface of his every day.

She was caught between a rock and a hard place. Did she keep gently pushing him to expose the attraction she knew he felt for her any further? Or did she wait and see what happened next after today's kiss?

Bree would forever be a part of their lives. Ruby was full testimony to that, not to mention the fact that true love, like energy, could never be destroyed. But she also knew that love, *if* it existed between two people, could grow and become enriched in even the worst of situations. Her parents were the perfect example of that.

The question was, however, could Raoul Benoit give that to her? Would he ever take down the barriers he kept so firmly erected between them again?

Did she even have the right to ask him to?

Her first month caring for Ruby had passed in a blur of time, Alexis realized as she watched a fun educational DVD with Ruby, clapping hands with her and jiggling along with the music. She'd lifted Ruby to her feet and was holding her hands as the baby pumped her thighs in time to the beat. She couldn't help laughing at the happy energy the little girl exuded as she squealed and danced.

"Someone sounds happy. She's got her mother's sense of rhythm, I see."

Alexis turned to see Raoul standing in the doorway, a look on his face that was half quizzical and half humorous.

"Dad-dad-dad-dad!" Ruby shrieked as she saw her father.

Alexis bit her lip. Over the past few days the baby had gone from curiosity about Raoul, to grim determination to make him acknowledge her. Ruby plopped down onto her padded bottom and Alexis let her hands go, only to see the child pull herself up using the coffee table beside them and take at first one, then two, then more tentative steps toward her father.

"Oh, my God, she's walking. She's actually walking!" Alexis cried.

"Should she be doing that already?" Raoul said, his eyes fixed on his daughter's tiny form as it teetered toward him on the carpeted floor.

"Well, she's a little early at ten months, but she's been

showing signs of wanting to get onto her feet properly for a couple of weeks now. Oops, there she goes."

Ruby lost her balance but before she could hit the carpet, Raoul was right there. His large hands hooked under her tiny armpits and swung her up into an arc that made her release a gurgling laugh of sheer joy.

Alexis felt a pang in her chest at the sight. This was how it should have been all along. Father and daughter sharing special moments like this one.

"Dad-dad," Ruby said again, her little hand patting Raoul on the face.

"That's right, Ruby," Alexis said from her position on the floor. "That's your daddy. Good girl."

"She can't really understand I'm her father," Raoul said, putting Ruby back down on the floor.

He was forced to reluctantly hold her hands as she tugged herself up onto her feet again and continued to want to walk, this time with him bent over, holding her hands as she tottled toward Alexis.

"Why not?" Alexis asked, feeling her joy at seeing them together dim a little at his lack of pleasure in Ruby's behavior. "You are her father and she ought to know that, don't you think?"

"It would be no different if she called me Raoul. She only mimics what she hears you say," he said repressively.

Provoked, Alexis returned with, "I prefer to think she knows you are her dad. I think she deserves that, don't you? Or would you rather she grow up calling you Raoul? As if you were some stranger who just happened to live alongside her?"

He waited until Ruby was closer to Alexis before extricating his fingers from the baby's clutches. Beaming a toothy smile, Ruby continued to take steps unaided. Alexis opened her arms and Ruby walked straight into them.

"Look at you, you clever girl!" she laughed as she hugged the child and smothered her neck with kisses, eliciting yet more baby giggles. "I'm seriously going to have to keep my eye on you now, aren't I?"

She looked up and caught the expression in Raoul's eye. Was that longing she saw there? Did he wish he could express the same spontaneous love for his daughter that she did? Alexis gave Ruby another cuddle before setting her loose. Bit by bit she felt as if she was beginning to break through the shell he'd built around himself when it came to Ruby. The thought brought her to an idea that she wanted to suggest to Raoul.

Drawing on a liberal dose of courage, and buoyed by the fact that he'd stayed in the room rather than withdrawing again quickly as he was in the habit of doing, she launched into speech.

"Raoul, I've been thinking. Catherine is due home this weekend and I thought since it also ties in with Bree's birthday, the first time dealing with that date for both of you since she's gone, that it might be nice to have a bit of a get-together here—you know, invite a few of your friends, make it a potluck dinner kind of thing. I think it would be nice—partly to celebrate Catherine's recovery to date and partly to remember Bree."

"I don't need a gathering to remember her. It's not a good idea."

"I was afraid you'd say that," she said, dragging in another deep breath and refusing to be cowed by his rejection, "which is why I kind of went ahead and organized it anyway. Catherine was really eager to participate and she's just aching to see Ruby again, and Laura and Matt and the others were equally keen."

"You had no right to do that," Raoul said, a sharp edge to his voice that all but sliced through the air between them.

"Look, I know you're still struggling to get back to normal—"

"Normal? Normal died along with Bree. I don't think you quite understand just what that has meant to me."

His voice was quiet, yet filled with emotion and anger. Sensing the change in mood in the room, Ruby crawled onto Alexis's lap, turned her face into her chest and uttered a whine of protest.

"Which is exactly why we should honor her memory and have a get-together in remembrance of her. Catherine needs it, your friends need it. I truly believe you need it, too, and you'd agree with me if you could just let yourself believe that you don't have to face all your grief alone."

His hazel eyes narrowed as he stared down at her. The air between them thickened, filled with his unspoken words and met by her equally silent but no less adamant challenge.

"Fine," he uttered through clenched teeth. "But don't expect me to be involved."

"Just be there, it's all I ask."

"Sometimes, Alexis Fabrini, you ask too damn much."

He left the room, taking her heart with him. It was hard to feel a sense of victory when she knew how much this was hurting him.

"Dad-dad?" Ruby said, lifting her face away from Alexis and looking around the room.

"He's gone off again, poppet. But he'll be back. Bit by bit, he'll be back."

At least she sure hoped so.

Raoul looked around the gathering in his house. This was exactly the kind of thing Bree would have loved to have organized for her birthday. All their closest friends, her mother, some of his cousins who lived locally, Alexis...people he knew and should feel comfortable with. And yet, he felt like an outsider. A stranger in his own house. Sure, he went through the motions—made sure everyone had a drink, asked some opinions on his latest blend—but he felt as if he didn't belong. As if he was a mere onlooker, not a participant.

Conversations swirled around him, things he would normally have been a part of but as he overheard snippets from here and there he became increasingly aware of how life had continued for all of them. It seemed wrong to resent them for it, but he did—fiercely. The uninterrupted way their lives had moved on after Bree only made his empty world so much more hollow—the void in his heart echo that much more.

He looked to Catherine to see how she was coping. This had to be hard for her, too, but she appeared to be taking it all in her stride—not afraid to shed a tear or two over a shared memory or a hearty laugh at some reminiscence, and eager to hear everyone's news after her monthlong absence from the playgroup. She looked up and caught his gaze and he could see the concern reflected in her eyes—eyes that were very like Ruby's and reminded him so much of Bree.

And there it was again—the pain, the loss, the anger at having all that perfection torn away from him. Having choice removed from his hands. Losing Bree from his life, forever. Catherine pushed herself to her feet and, adeptly using one crutch, crossed the short distance between them. She laid one hand on his shoulder.

"She'd have loved this, wouldn't she? Alexis has done a great job."

"Everyone contributed," he said abruptly.

"But Alexis brought us all together. We needed that. It's been long overdue. I know I'm always going to miss her, it would be impossible not to, but I feel better today, y'know?"

He nodded because it seemed to be the response she expected, but inside he was screaming. No, he didn't know what the hell she was talking about. This was all too hard. He couldn't find it in him to allow himself to enjoy the company of everyone here today. He needed space, silence, solitude. The moment Catherine's attention was taken by one of the guests he slipped out the room and toward the front door. Once he had it open he walked through the entrance and kept going into the night—down the unsealed lane that led to the winery, past the winery and on down the hill until he could go no farther unless he wanted to swim the inky dark waters of the harbor.

He waited until the moon was high in the sky before he clambered back up the hill. The cold air had filtered through his clothing, his long-sleeved cotton shirt—fine in the centrally heated interior of the house—was totally unsuited to the outdoors. Initially he'd barely noticed it. Now, however, he was frozen through and through.

The outside lights were still on at the house when he got back but, he noted with relief, the large parking bay outside was devoid of cars. He slipped back inside and decided to go directly to his room. He had no wish to see Alexis and face her silent or, more likely, not-so-silent recriminations for ditching the party this evening. He just wanted to be alone. Couldn't anyone understand that?

"Raoul? Is that you?"

Alexis, dish towel still in hand, stepped out of the kitchen and into the hallway. He halted in his tracks—frozen like a possum in the headlights of an oncoming vehicle. She was the last person he wanted to face right now.

"Are you okay?"

He gave a bitter laugh. "Okay? No, Alexis, I'm not okay."

He turned to head to his room but heard her rapid footfall on the carpeted floor behind him. She put out a hand to arrest his progress.

"I'm sorry, Raoul. Maybe organizing today wasn't such a good idea," she said as she drew nearer.

He wheeled around. "You think?"

He could see his response stung her but he wasn't into mouthing platitudes so others could just blithely go on doing what they did without consideration for how it made anyone else feel.

"I told you that you asked too much," he growled.

"I know—now, at least. And I am sorry, Raoul. Everyone understood, though, especially today with it being Bree's birthday. It was bound to be hard. Even for me. Look, I know how you feel—"

"Do you?" he said incredulously. "Do you really? I don't think so. I don't think that for a minute you could *ever* understand how I feel so don't presume to try."

"You weren't the only one who lost her," she said, her voice small.

"She was my *wife!*" His voice shook, with fury and with something more that rolled and swirled inside him—filling his mind with a black emptiness that threatened to consume him. "She was my world," he whispered fiercely before striding the short distance to his room where he slammed the door solidly behind him, uncaring as to whether or not he disturbed Ruby.

He stood in the darkened room, hardly daring to breathe or move in case the angry monster that he could feel growing stronger inside him broke free. The monster that wanted to rail at the world for the unfairness that took Bree from him. The monster that was full of anger toward Bree herself, even though he could never openly express it, because she'd taken the choice of family or her away from him.

The monster that held the untold disgust he had with himself because, despite everything—the love he'd borne for Bree being paramount in his life—he still lusted for her friend, now more than ever before.

Seven

Alexis went through the motions of getting ready for bed but she was so wired right now she knew sleep would be impossible. Today had gone off well, if you discounted how it had left Raoul feeling. No one had seemed to mind when he'd cut and run from the gathering, not even Catherine who'd seemed to understand his need to be alone. The party had gone very pleasantly, even if she hadn't been able to enjoy it, too aware of Raoul's absence.

She'd not long thrown herself against the fine cotton sheets of her king-size bed and switched off her light when there was a gentle knock at the bedroom door. There was only one person that could be. She slid from the bed and walked quickly toward the door.

"Raoul?" she asked, as she turned the knob and opened the door wide.

His eyes flew across her, taking in her silk nightgown—one of her few indulgences from her time in Italy last year—and her bare feet in one sweep.

"I'm sorry, I shouldn't have disturbed you."

He went to walk away but she put out a hand to stop him.

"It's okay. Did you need me for something?"

He looked at her in the dark, and through the sheen of moonlight that filtered into her room she saw the glitter of his eyes. His face was pale, his whiskers a dark shadow on his cheeks and jaw. He'd never before looked so dangerous, or so appealing to her. She took an involuntary step back and saw the look of chagrin that crossed his face.

"I shouldn't have spoken to you like that."

"You're hurting. I—" She stopped herself before she could repeat her earlier words of understanding.

He'd been right. She couldn't possibly know or understand what he'd been through. Bree had been her friend for years, but the last two years of Bree's life she'd barely even spoken to her, battling with envy, then guilt, after Bree and Raoul had gotten together. Now, even though she desperately missed her friend, those bitter emotions were all still there. The envy that, even in death, her friend could command such unceasing love—and the guilt that she continued to not only want that for herself, but that she wanted it from the very same man.

She drew in a breath. "There's no need to apologize, Raoul. I should have been more sensitive to your needs."

"My needs? I don't even know what they are anymore. Sometimes I feel as if I don't know anything anymore."

She made a sound of sympathy and reached up to cup his face with one hand. "You've been through hell. You're still there. It's okay. I'll back off with the social stuff. You obviously need more time."

He lifted a hand to press against hers and she felt the heat of his palm on one side, the rasp of his unshaven jaw on the other. The mingled sensations sent a tingle of longing up her arm and she was appalled that even as the man was visibly struggling with a devastating loss, she couldn't hold her attraction back. That her body, having a recalcitrant mind of its own, was right now warming to his very presence. Her nipples were beading against the sheer fabric of her nightgown and she felt a long slow pull of hunger dragging from her core.

"Time is something I have too much of. Time to think. I don't want to think anymore, Alexis. For once, I just want to feel."

"Feel…?"

"Yes, feel. Something, anything other than the pain inside. I want the emptiness to go away."

He turned his head so that his lips were now pressing against her palm. If he'd seared her skin with a branding iron it couldn't have had a more overwhelming effect. She gasped at the jolt of electricity that shuddered through her hand and down her arm. When he bent his head to hers and his hot dry lips captured her own she felt her knees buckle beneath her. Momentarily she gave an inward groan at how clichéd her reaction was, but it was only seconds before awareness of clichés, or anything else other than this man and how he made her feel, fled from her consciousness.

All there was right now was scalding heat, flames of need licking up through her body as she clung to Raoul, as she anchored herself to his strength and poured all her years of forbidden longing into returning his kiss. When he lifted his mouth from hers she just stood there, dazed by the power of her feelings for him and by the emotion he aroused in her.

"Come with me, to my room," he rasped. "I can't do this in here."

She nodded, letting him draw her down the hallway and into his room. The bedroom door snicked closed behind them and he led her to his bed.

She tumbled into the sheets, Raoul following close behind. As the weight of his body settled against hers she flexed upward against him, pressing against the hard evidence of his arousal. He groaned against her throat, his unshaven jaw scraping softly against her skin, and she relished every sensation, every touch. It felt as if she'd put her whole life on hold for this very moment and she was going to savor every second of it.

Alexis fought open the buttons on Raoul's shirt, her fingertips eagerly skimming along the ridged muscles of his abdomen as she worked the garment away from his body and then off entirely. She wanted to touch every inch of him and then to taste every inch in turn. She trailed a gentle line down his neck and then skimmed over the strength of his shoulders before tracing the definition of his chest. Beneath her touch she felt him respond with tiny tremors, especially when she circled his nipples with the pad of her thumb then lifted her head to kiss him there.

He shifted, bearing his weight on one arm as he manacled her wrists with his free hand.

"But I want to touch you," she protested on a whispered breath.

"Too much," he said succinctly in reply before restraining her hands above her head.

She knew she could have pulled free at any time but there was something so decadently wonderful about being laid open to him like this. About giving him her trust, total and unquestioning.

He kissed along the line of her jaw, down her neck, making her squirm and arch her back, pushing herself upward, supplicant, toward him. And then, his mouth was at her breasts. Through the fine fabric of her nightgown she felt the warmth of his lips, his breath and then, oh, God, his tongue as he suckled on her.

His whole body shook with restraint as he lingered over each aching tip, sending shock waves of sensation tumbling over her and winding up the tension in her lower belly to near excruciating tautness. He let go of her hands to grab at the hem of her nighty and sweep it off her body, laying her bare to his scrutiny in the moonlit room.

A sense of unreality hit her, as if she was watching a black-and-white movie starring strangers coming together for the very first time. In a sense, that was exactly what was happening. Not for them a normal period of courtship. They'd been acquaintances, at best, when she'd run off overseas. Combatants since her return. For all that Alexis was falling in love with him, she barely knew him—not in all the ways that counted.

One thing she did know, though, was that in his time of need tonight, he'd turned *to* her rather than away. She would do whatever he wanted, give him whatever he needed of her, and along the way she'd receive a slice of what she had always wanted in return.

She moaned as Raoul continued his sensual onslaught on her body, his fingers and his tongue tracing a magical dance across the skin of her belly, and lower. When his tongue flicked across her center she all but jerked off the bed. It was as if every nerve in her body had congregated on that one point. It took bare seconds before she flew over the precipice and into the rolling swells of a climax so intense, so exquisite, that tears leaked from her eyes and down the sides of her face.

She was still riding the crest when she felt him shove his trousers off and move between her legs. With a guttural cry, he entered her still-spasming body. She felt herself stretch to accommodate his length, felt her inner muscles contract and squeeze against him, welcoming him into her heat, her heart. He thrust against her, deep and strong. She'd barely recovered from her first orgasm when she was in the throes of a second.

Through the rolling, intoxicating fog of pleasure she was aware of his body growing taut, of him surging into her once, twice more until with another cry he spent himself within her. He collapsed onto her, his body racked with paroxysms that mirrored her own. Alexis closed her arms around him, holding him to her, relishing the ragged sound of his breathing, the involuntary shudder of his hips against hers as he rode his climax to completion.

Raoul could barely breathe, much less think. He rolled off Alexis and sank into the mattress beside her as the perspiration on his body cooled. As the realization of what he'd just done slowly sank in.

Deep down he'd always known that sex with Alexis would be explosive. It was exactly why he'd stayed well away from her. Guilt slammed into him, chasing the buzz of physical satisfaction into oblivion. By doing what he'd just done, by seeking and taking pleasure, he'd just betrayed the one woman he'd pledged to remain faithful to.

Tears burned at the back of his eyes as recrimination filled him, making his mouth taste bitter, making each breath a painful necessity. He didn't deserve to seek respite. He certainly didn't deserve to find pleasure and most especially not in the arms of Alexis Fabrini.

He could feel her, lying silently beside him. Her breathing was still quick and shallow. The warmth of her body extended across the short distance between them, offering him succor. Support and comfort he didn't deserve.

He screwed his eyes shut tight. He was so wrong to have done this. He should have just stayed in his room, alone with the bottle of brandy and the snifter he'd taken from his study with the idea of finding oblivion in alcohol's potent depths.

Alexis reached across the sheets and took his hand in hers, squeezing silently. Even now she offered him reassurance. He felt the mattress shift slightly as she rolled onto her side to face him but he couldn't bring himself to open his eyes and meet her gaze.

He tensed, waiting for her to say something, but instead she reached out a hand and stroked his chest. The light circular movements of her hand soothed him, when he didn't want to be soothed. He wanted her to yell at him, to demand to know what he'd been thinking when he'd come to her room, when he'd all but dragged her back to his. When he'd given in to the clamoring demand of his body and taken her without thought, without care.

Without protection.

His heart hammered in his chest even as her hand worked its way lower, over his rib cage and to his abdomen. Despite the horrifying realization that had just dawned on him, his body continued to respond to her touch—to be soothed and ignited, both at the same time. His flesh begin to stir again, the thrum of desire beat through his veins.

"No!" he said abruptly, gripping her hand and halting it on its inexorable journey down his body. "We didn't use protection," he said grimly.

"It's okay," Alexis said. "I'm on the Pill."

He gave her a considering look. Was she telling the truth? She had no reason to lie. Through the gloom, she met his gaze full on and he saw enough there to relax just a little.

Alexis rose onto her knees, then straddled him, gently pulling her hand free from his grasp.

"So, I guess it's yes?" she whispered softly back to him. "Please, Raoul. Let me love you."

"This isn't love," he said bluntly, hating the fact he couldn't control his growing response to her.

He felt her flinch a little at his words and heard the sharply indrawn breath.

"Then let me enjoy you, let yourself enjoy me," she coaxed, bending her head to kiss him.

Her tongue swept along his lower lip before she sucked it between her teeth. He fought the rising tide of desire that continued to swell inside him—but made no effort to pull away. He could feel the heat of her core as she hovered over his belly, felt his penis twitch in response. Exactly when he surrendered to her will and became an active participant he wasn't entirely sure, but all of a sudden his hands were cupping her head and his fingers were tangled in the honeyed strands of her hair as he kissed her back with all the pent-up longing and despair that had tormented him these past ten months.

When she broke away he would have protested, but her small deft hands massaged and stroked him, gliding along his shoulders, down his chest, over his belly and finally, finally, reached his aching erection. He felt her fingers close around his length, felt her squeeze gently as she stroked him up and down. His hands fisted at his sides as he felt himself harden even more. When she shifted and bent to take him in her mouth he almost lost it right then and there. The slick moist texture of her lips and tongue against the smooth swollen head of his penis sent jolts of pleasure radiating through his body.

There was no room for any more thought, no room for right or wrong, there was only space for sensation and its inevitable, relentless buildup. With a final lave of her tongue Alexis released him from the hot cavern of her mouth and realigned her body so she was poised over him. He held his breath as her darkened silhouette slowly lowered over him, as he entered the silky hot wetness of her body.

She gave a moan of pure delight as she took him deep inside her, tilting her pelvis and rocking against him. He felt her inner muscles clench and hold him. Pressure built inside him until it became a demand he could no longer ignore.

His hands found her hips and he used the leverage to move beneath her as she set up a rhythm designed to send them both screaming into a molten mess of fulfillment. She grabbed at his wrists, pulling his hands free from her hips and guided them to the lush fullness of her breasts. He cupped and held them, his fingers massaging their softness until his fingertips caught tightly beaded nipples between them and squeezed.

"Oh, yes," she breathed, her hips grinding into him. She pressed her breasts more firmly into his touch, so much so that he bore most of her weight now on his arms. She was magnificent. Her hair in disarray around her head, her slender throat arched and her shoulders thrown back. His climax built inside him, demanding release, but he held back, gritting his teeth and fighting for control, and then he had no need to hold on a moment longer. A thin keening sound escaped Alexis's throat and he felt her entire body shudder. His shaft was gripped by a silken fist that squeezed and released until he, too, tipped over into heady addictive gratification.

Alexis slumped against him, and he drew her close,

her breasts now squashed against his chest, strands of her hair caught on his whiskered jaw. She shifted her legs to be more comfortable but they remained joined together and somehow it felt right. For now at least.

Refusing to question it a moment longer, Raoul allowed himself to drift into a slumber of sheer exhaustion, his arms still locked tight around her waist. Tomorrow would be soon enough to face the recriminations that would undoubtedly meet him in the mirror in the morning.

Eight

Alexis felt the cool sheets beside her and knew he'd gone, withdrawn from her again in every sense of the word. She'd hoped they'd stay together the whole night but she was realistic enough to know he had to be dealing with some serious personal demons about now.

She opened her eyes, searching for where he'd thrown her nightgown, understanding that it would probably be best if she returned to her room.

It was still semidark. A sound over by the floor-length window caught her attention. Raoul stood there, naked, framed in the window. His gaze was fixed on something in the distance, his body caressed by the silver hint of moonlight. She slipped from the bed and came up behind him. Her arms slid around his waist as she leaned against his back.

Still he didn't move, or acknowledge her presence. It was as if she was hugging a statue.

"Are you okay?" she asked softly, pressing a kiss between his shoulder blades.

She felt his body tense, then his rib cage expand as he drew in a breath.

"Yes…and no."

"Talk to me, Raoul," she coaxed. "I'm right here."

"What we did. It was wrong. I shouldn't have come to you last night."

"Raoul, I'm glad you did. We needed each other. What we took from one another, what we gave, we did that honestly. There's no reason for shame between us."

He remained silent for a while but she could still feel the conflict that coiled and strained inside him. Eventually he shook his head.

"I can't do this—"

He gestured futilely with one hand. Alexis loosened her arms and stepped back.

"It's okay," she said, even though she felt as if she might fracture apart.

It took all of her strength to hold her emotions together. Last night had been deeply special to her and, she'd hoped, special to Raoul, too. Apparently hoping that had been premature. So they were simply going to have to take this step by baby step. If she could give him his space now, perhaps it would allow him to realize that he deserved happiness, too.

"No, it's not okay. I have done nothing to earn your understanding. I've used you, Alexis, can't you see that? Don't you think you deserve better than that?"

She fought not to flinch at the harsh words. "Of course I do. We both do. But don't you think I got to use you, too? You're not alone in this, Raoul, no matter how isolated you feel, no matter how alone you try to be. I'm here…for you."

He faced her and she could see the scowl that twisted his handsome face into a mask of displeasure.

"Can't you even allow me to apologize for what I did?"

She shook her head vehemently. "You have nothing to apologize for. Nothing!" she repeated with even more emphasis than before. "Did you feel me try to push you away? Did I ask you to leave or did I turn my head away when you kissed me? No. I welcomed your touch, Raoul. I welcomed *you*. We all need help sometimes. Trouble is, you're too afraid to ask for it and if you do, you see it as some kind of weakness, something to be sorry about."

"I still shouldn't—"

"Oh, please." Alexis rolled her eyes. "Stop it. You were man enough to reach out to me last night. Just accept that I am woman enough to want to grasp hold of you, to be there for you. I don't do anything I don't want to, Raoul. Or anyone. So get over it."

Wrapping her bravado around her like a shield, Alexis walked away from him and found her nightgown on the floor. She dragged it on over her head and all but ran back to her room and into the en suite bathroom. She flipped on the shower and fought to take in a leveling breath as the water warmed. It was still early, at least another hour until sunrise and Ruby's usual time for waking, but there was little point in going back to bed. No way would she get any more sleep now. She stripped off her nightgown and stepped into the luxuriously tiled shower stall and closed her eyes against the stream of water, blindly reaching for the bar of soap she'd put there yesterday. Her eyes flew open when she encountered warm wet male instead.

Raoul's gaze was intense, his jaw a rigid line and his lips pressed firmly together as he stood there, water from the dual jets cascading over his hair and down his neck and shoulders.

He reached for the bar of soap and lathered it up in his hands before gently turning her around to face the shower wall. His hands were firm as he began to massage her shoulders with the scented foam, his thumbs working into knots she didn't know she had. He worked his way down the center of her spine, easing away any residual stiffness she had from her unaccustomed sleeping position during the night.

By the time his hands caressed her buttocks she was all but melting. Her breasts felt full and heavy, aching for his touch, her nipples ruched into tight nubs. She squeezed her thighs together to relieve some of the pressure that built at their apex but it only served to increase her hunger for more of his touch.

His hands left her for a minute, only to return, relathered and on a determined path around her body. She felt his erection pressing against her buttocks as he reached around her, cupping her breasts and gently massaging them. One hand began to track down her body, pressing her back against him. She widened her legs, felt him bend his knees and position himself at her aching center. She waited for his possession but he seemed comfortable just biding his time while his fingers teased and played with her, coaxing her flesh a little wider, grazing her clitoris with firm sweeps of his thumb.

Alexis's legs trembled as she felt her orgasm begin to build and build, the pressure almost too much to bear. When he finally slid inside her, he touched off something deep within. Something with more intensity, more complexity than anything she'd felt before.

She rose to the tips of her toes as Raoul drove into her body. She could feel the roughness of the hair on his legs against the backs of her thighs, the firmness of his belly against her buttocks. When he came, he came hard and so did she. Pleasure didn't just come in waves, it ricocheted through her again and again.

His head fell onto her shoulder and his arms wrapped around her until she didn't know who was supporting whom to stay upright anymore. Eventually their breathing slowed and Alexis felt strength return to her limbs. Hot water still pounded them both as Raoul withdrew from her. He slicked a hand with soap and gently washed then rinsed her clean. She was glad of the attention as, while she was regaining control of her limbs, her consciousness was still under question.

"Keep taking your pill," Raoul said in the shell of her ear, and then he was gone.

By the time she looked around, he'd swiped one of the towels from the heated rail and had left the bathroom. Steam filled the air, leaving her to almost wonder if she hadn't just dreamed the entire sequence of events. The racing of her heart, and the tendrils of satisfaction that still ebbed and flowed through her, confirmed it had been very, very real. She thought about what he'd said, as well as what she'd told him about being on the Pill.

Technically, she was, but since she'd been here she'd been less than fully careful about taking the contraceptive. In the past, she'd always been a stickler for taking her tablet on time, but with the adjustment to a whole new routine this past month she'd been a little lax. That was something that was going to have to change if they were going to continue with this…this…whatever it was. Clearly he had reached some personal decision about the two of them. One that involved their mutual pleasure, if nothing else.

She turned off the showerheads and stepped from the stall, drying her sensitized skin with a large bath sheet. Could she settle for that? The pursuit of physical release with none of the messy emotional stuff that usually came with it?

A while ago she'd have said a flat-out no. She had always wanted a relationship she could pledge herself to, fully and completely, and know that that pledge was returned. But Raoul had made it perfectly clear that he couldn't give her that. Could she settle for less than love from him?

A little aftershock of pleasure thrilled through her body again. Maybe she'd just have to give it a try and see what happened. At best, the ice around his heart may begin to thaw. At worst, well, she didn't even want to think about that just yet.

In the bedroom she grabbed her handbag and pulled her contraceptive strip from the side pocket. She'd missed three tablets in this cycle but not consecutively. Hopefully she'd still be safe. To avoid further memory lapses she added a new alarm to her cell phone, reminding her to take her pill each morning. To be doubly safe, she'd visit a pharmacy in town and consult with them about the morning-after pill, as well.

Sounds came through the baby monitor that Alexis kept on the bedside cabinet. Ruby was stirring. She quickly dressed and went through to the baby's room to start her working day—except somewhere along the line it had ceased to be work and was becoming something else instead. And as she lifted the little girl for a good-morning cuddle she realized that being needed was something she'd craved all her life.

Her parents had been sufficient to one another while she was growing up. And that was exactly as it should have been, she reminded herself as she changed and dressed Ruby. They'd always loved her, been there for her, but no one had ever truly needed her before. Not the way Ruby did now. Not the way she began to hope Raoul did, also.

A tiny flame of optimism flickered to life deep in her belly. This could work. They could become a family. She had to keep believing it was possible...because the alternative didn't even bear thinking about. Despite everything, despite her determination not to completely give her heart to anyone unless she was certain those feelings were returned, Alexis knew she was falling deeper and deeper into love with Raoul Benoit.

Only time would tell if he could feel the same way about her. She hoped against hope that he could, because if not, walking away from Raoul, walking away from Ruby, would be the hardest thing she'd ever had to do in her entire life.

She'd done something similar once before—distanced herself from him before she could let her feelings grow, knowing them to be futile when he loved Bree and was loved so passionately in return. But things were different now, so very painfully different, and it was going to be a difficult road ahead.

It had been a week and still he couldn't get her out of his mind. What on earth had possessed him to visit her room that night? Worse, what had made him take her back to his and then, in the morning, tell her in no uncertain terms to keep taking her pill? He'd had no right to any of that, a fact he'd reminded himself of constantly these past seven days as he'd forced himself to keep his distance. It hadn't stopped him wanting her, though, or remembering in excruciatingly vivid detail their night—and morning—together.

From his vantage point out in the garden he watched her sleeping in the window seat of the family room. She had a sketch pad on her lap and an array of colored pens spilled across the cushion she lay on. Her hair lay in a swathe across one cheek. Hair he knew was silky soft and carried a scent he found unique to her.

In sleep she looked peaceful, as if she no longer bore the weight of the world on her capable shoulders. His fingers tingled as he remembered how her skin had felt beneath them. How smooth and warm. She was so alive, so giving. Try as he might, he could not help but be pulled into her magnetic sphere.

She'd become a part of his every day in ways he had never imagined. Ways he never wanted or expected to imagine. But more, he now found himself wanting her to become a part of his nights, as well. Just one night with her had been nowhere near enough. He'd barely slept ever since for the memories of her in his arms, in his bed, crowding his thoughts. Replaying, time and again, the exquisite sensation of sliding into her body, feeling her welcoming heat, watching her shatter from the pleasure of his touch.

There'd been no recriminations from her. Not even when he'd treated her so bluntly these past few days. Ill-tempered and filled with mounting frustration, his fuse had been short and he hadn't been afraid to show it or to use it to push her away. She wasn't a fool, she'd read the signals. As a result, he'd noticed that she and Ruby had spent a lot of time away from the house and, dammit, he'd missed them—both of them.

As if Alexis sensed his observation of her, she stirred. A few of her pens slid off the cushion and onto the floor. They must have made some noise because she startled awake and moved to grab her pad from following in the same path. The sketch pad reminded him that she'd put her life on hold to come here.

He'd never have asked her to do that—to simply walk away from her growing business to look after a child who would have been fine with a different nanny, and a man who was perfectly capable of looking after himself. Things had been rolling along just fine here before her arrival—at least that's what he'd tried to convince himself. He knew, though, in all honesty, they hadn't.

What made someone do what she had done? he wondered. Simply shelve, at least for a little while, their own dreams and goals to help out someone else. Was it a lack of self-respect or belief? No, he knew she had self-respect, but she also had a big and giving heart. He'd seen it in the way she'd so quickly grown attached to Ruby.

He continued to watch as Alexis stood up and stretched, the movement pulling her long sleeved T-shirt upward, exposing the soft skin of her belly. In answer, his flesh stirred, reminding him that he'd been trapped in this awkward state of semiarousal this past week. He wanted her, but he didn't want the complicated hang-ups that came along with having her. And if he knew anything about Alexis Fabrini it was that she had a power of emotion stored up in that enticing body of hers. She deserved someone who could match her, physically and emotionally.

He had no space left in his heart for emotion.

He turned and pushed through the edges of the garden and strode out toward the winery. Somehow he had to find a release for all the pent-up energy having sex with Alexis had created. Somehow, he didn't think finishing labeling the wine bottles he was ready to put down would be enough.

Nine

Several hours later he was surprised at the sense of satisfaction he felt while recording the number of bottles of Pinot Noir he'd spent the better part of the day labeling. This wine was his best yet. While he was probably only looking at four hundred cases in total, he was sure that they would be integral in helping to establish his Benoit Wines label. If he could continue to ensure the same quality, and better, year after year, his reputation would be made.

The sound of the winery door creaking open surprised him and he looked up to see Alexis walking through the tasting room toward his small office. The late afternoon sun was weak, yet it still struggled through the windows as if determined to bathe her in shades of golden ocher. His body responded accordingly, again stirring to unwelcome life. His pulse beat just that bit faster, his gut clenched just that bit tighter.

She was alone, a fact that immediately put him on the offensive—the easiest way, he'd found, to cope with this unnerving awareness of her each time she was within a few meters of him.

"Where's Ruby?" he asked, his voice gruff.

"She's having a playdate with Jason over at Matt and Laura's. I'll pick her up in an hour."

"An hour?"

Raoul raised an eyebrow, his mind filling with all manner of things he could enjoy with Alexis in the space of sixty minutes. Just as quickly, he tamped those visions back where they belonged.

"Yes, the kids seem to get along in as much as they can socialize at this age. And, anyway, it's good for her to get out of the house. I said I'll do the same for Laura one day next week. I hope you don't mind. I'm sorry, I probably should have discussed it with you first."

Alexis seemed determined to justify herself to him. Was that what he'd reduced her to? Someone who constantly felt they had to make apology for their actions? He knew Matt and Laura well, he trusted them implicitly.

"If you think it's best for Ruby, it's fine. Did you want me for something?"

"I wanted to see if you're planning to have dinner with us tonight. If not, I'll put yours in the warmer."

"The warmer is fine."

She sighed, and the sound acted like a torch to touchpaper.

"What?" he demanded.

She shrugged. "Nothing."

"No, you sighed. There's something bothering you. What is it?"

"Well, if you must know, I'm sick of you avoiding me,

avoiding us. Is it because we slept together or is it something else I've done?"

He was about to refute her accusation but, in all honesty, he couldn't.

"I don't want you to get the wrong idea, that's all," he muttered.

"Wrong idea? Oh, like romance and candles?" Alexis laughed. It was a brittle sound that plucked at something deep inside him—made him feel unexpectedly ashamed for putting that sarcasm in her tone. She was the kind of woman who deserved both romance and candles—and more.

There was a cynical twist to her mouth as she continued. "Don't worry, Raoul. I know where I stand. I don't care so much for myself, but your withdrawal and your mood this week has been really bad for Ruby. Whether you like it or not, she's your daughter. When are you going to accept your responsibilities toward her?"

He bristled. "She's fed, isn't she? She's clothed and sheltered. What else does she want?"

"Love. *Your* love."

He got up from his chair and pushed a hand through his hair. "She doesn't need me. She has you, she has Catherine. I make sure she has what she needs, it's your job to provide it."

"It's not enough, Raoul."

"It has to be. That's all I have to offer her."

"I disagree."

"Really? You think you know me better than I know myself?"

"I think I know what you're capable of, and this iceman act isn't you. It isn't the real Raoul Benoit."

"Oh, and just who is?" he answered scathingly.

She stepped forward until she was directly in front

of him—so close he could feel the heat of her body. It was as if his own sought and craved it, as if deep down he longed for her warmth. He pushed the thought away. It would be a cold day in hell before he ever admitted to needing someone again. Alexis held his gaze as she lifted a hand and put it on his chest, over where his heart suddenly did a double beat at her touch.

"He's the man inside here. The one you won't let out. I don't know why you've felt the need to lock him away the way you have, but it's time to let him out. Don't you think he's done enough penance now? Don't you think you deserve to live your life?"

He pushed her hand away but the imprint of it had already seared through his clothes and into his skin. She had that effect on him. She could get beneath the layers and slide deep inside.

"Penance? You think that's what I'm doing?"

"Sure. What else would you call it? It's as if you're punishing yourself for something you had no control over. You didn't kill Bree. You weren't responsible for what happened to her."

He spun away from her, determined to make sure she wouldn't see the way that the anguish her words had wrought reflected on his face. She was wrong. So very wrong.

"Raoul?" she asked, putting a hand on his shoulder.

He shrugged her off. He didn't want her touch, her comfort.

"I *was* responsible," he said in a dark low voice. "My expectations killed Bree. I failed her."

"That's not true."

"If I hadn't been so determined to have a family, to fill the rooms of that house up the hill with our kids, she'd still be here today."

"You can't know that. Besides, that was her dream, too. In her letter she told me she was prepared to do anything, risk anything, to have a family with you. The aneurysm—"

"She died, Alexis, and it's all my fault!" he shouted, his words echoing around them.

Alexis looked at him in shock. He really truly blamed himself for Bree's death.

"It happened, Raoul. It wasn't something you or she could control or quantify. Not even the doctors could say if or when the aneurysm could bleed out."

"I know, it was a time bomb. But you know what the kicker is? I didn't even know it was there until it ruptured. She never told me about her condition or the risks to it from her pregnancy. She kept it a secret, hiding it away from me. If I'd have known, if I'd have had the slightest inkling that her health would be compromised by her pregnancy, I would have taken steps to make sure it never happened."

"But that would have been taking her choice to have a family away from her," Alexis protested. "She wanted your child."

"I wanted her."

His voice was bleak, so sad and empty and filled with loss. Alexis didn't know what to do. What he'd just told her explained so much—his withdrawal from society, his reluctance to have anything to do with Ruby. Which brought her full circle to why she'd come to talk to him today.

"You can't blame Ruby. She doesn't deserve that."

"I don't," he answered simply.

"How on earth can you expect me to believe you when

you can't even stay in a room with her for more than five minutes, let alone spend any time alone with her?"

Raoul rubbed a hand across his eyes and shook his head. "It's not what you think. I don't blame her. I just can't let myself love her."

His words struck her like an arrow through her heart. "How can you say that?" she gasped, shocked to her core.

"Because it's true. I can't love her, I won't love her. What if I lose her, too?"

"What if she lives to be a hundred years old?" Alexis countered.

"You don't understand, she was born prematurely, she was seriously ill for the first month of her life—"

"And she's overcome all that, she's a fighter. She's a strong, healthy growing girl and she needs her father—not some coward who's prepared to pay everyone to take over *his* obligations!"

Raoul stood up straighter at her accusation—anger flaring in his hazel eyes, making them seem more green than brown, standing out even more as his complexion paled. "You're calling me a coward?"

Alexis stood her ground. "If the cap fits." She shrugged with feigned nonchalance. Right now she was worried she may have stepped over the mark. But it was too late to back down. Besides, she wasn't about to break the momentum now that they were finally getting to the heart of his issues. "Let's face it, you can't even bring yourself to talk about what we shared last week, about our night together. Instead you've been snapping and snarling at me for days, when you haven't been avoiding me altogether. What's wrong, Raoul? Can't you admit that what we did, what we had together, was good? Do you not believe you even deserve even that?"

"No, I don't!" he shouted. "It's a betrayal."

"Of Bree? As hard as it is, as cruel as it is, she's dead, Raoul. You're living—although not as if you're alive. She wouldn't have wanted you to do this, to cut yourself away from everyone and everything that mattered to you both, especially the daughter you both wanted so badly."

"So what are you saying, that I should jump into bed with you at every opportunity, pretend I'm *alive?*"

"If that's what it takes," she said quietly.

He moved up to her, grabbing her upper arms in his strong hands. Even though he vibrated with anger, his hold was still gentle. She knew this was the real Raoul Benoit. This man with such passion in his eyes that even now, after her goading, she knew he wouldn't hurt her.

"And if I said to you that I want you now, what would you do?"

Alexis calmly looked at her watch and then back at him. "I'd say you have about forty minutes. Is that enough?"

"For now, maybe," he growled.

In the next breath he was kissing her and she thrilled to his touch. Their night together had only made her want more. His last words about taking her birth control had made her believe that he'd come to her again, but instead he'd been so aloof this week, so filled with latent anger. If releasing that anger was what it took to prize him out of his ice cave than that's what she'd do. She'd make him so mad he made love to her every single day. Anything to bring him, the real him, back again.

She shoved her hands under his sweater and scraped her nails across his belly. His skin reacted instantly, peppering with goose bumps. He backed her up until she felt the hard edge of his desk behind her thighs, and bent her backward onto its hard surface. Immediately, his hands were at the waistband of her jeans, tugging at the button and releasing the zipper. He yanked the denim down her legs and cupped her through her lace panties.

The instant he touched her she was on fire. Wet with longing and burning up for what would come next. His palm bore down on her clitoris, the firm pressure bringing her nerve endings to life. She tried to open her legs wider but was restricted by her jeans pooled at her ankles. Somehow, she toed off her shoes and kicked the offending garment away, spreading herself now for his invasion.

As he moved between her legs, she wasted no time unsnapping his jeans and pushing them down, her touch now hungry for the feel of him. She slid one hand under the waistband of his boxers, pushing the fabric away and freeing him, her fingers closing around the velvet coated steel of his erection. Already his tip was moist and he groaned against her as she firmed her grip on him, stroking him up and down, increasing and releasing her pressure as she did so.

Raoul slid a finger inside the leg of her panties and groaned again as he encountered her skin.

"So wet, so ready," he murmured before pulling her underwear down her legs and dropping them on the floor.

Then, his hands were back. He cupped her again, this time inserting a finger, then slowly withdrawing it, his thumb working the swollen nub of nerve endings at her core, stoking the intensity of the fire that burned so bright inside her.

With his other hand he pushed her sweatshirt up higher, exposing the plain cotton bra she'd worn today. For a second she wished she'd chosen something more beautiful, more enticing, but when he unsnapped the front clasp and lowered his mouth to her breast she went beyond caring.

His teeth grazed first one nipple, then the other. Her

skin was so sensitive to his ministrations she screamed softly, lost in the spirals of pleasure that radiated through her body.

More, she wanted more. She guided the blunt head of his penis to her opening and let go when he took over control, sliding his length within her so slowly she thought she might lose her mind. His thumb never stopped circling her clitoris and she knew she didn't have long before she'd come apart, but she wanted this to be about him, as well. About what they could share together.

She clenched her inner muscles and felt him shudder against her. Her hands coasted up his abdomen, stroking his chest and skimming his nipples before tracing back down again to his hips.

Raoul kissed a hot wet trail from her breasts to her throat, then along her jaw to her mouth, capturing her lips again with his caress. Subtly, he increased the pressure of his thumb and Alexis couldn't hold back another second. She gave herself over to the ever-increasing waves of pleasure that consumed her, that thrilled her to heights she'd never felt before with another man.

She clamped around him, again and again as her orgasm built in intensity until she lost awareness, was oblivious to the thrust of his hips and the ragged groan of completion that rent from his body as he climaxed inside her.

It could only have been minutes later, but it felt much longer, when Raoul stirred and withdrew from her.

"Stay there," he said, his breathing still ragged.

She didn't even want to open her eyes, she was so filled with the delicious lassitude that bound her in the aftermath. "I don't think I could move if I wanted to," she admitted, a note of wonder in her voice.

A rusty sound, almost like a laugh, came from where

Raoul was adjusting himself back into his clothing. He left the room and she heard the sound of running water from the small restroom off his office, then he was back with a warm, damp towel in his hands. He wiped her carefully, his touch sending off little shocks of sensation to remind her of what they'd just shared.

"You don't have to do that, I can take care of it," she protested, pushing herself up onto her elbows.

"All done already," he answered, leaving the room again.

She slid off the desk and reached for her panties, pulling them up legs that felt about as strong as overcooked spaghetti. But she felt compelled to move fast, to be dressed before he came back into the room.

His face was impossible to read when he returned and Alexis mentally braced herself, uncertain of what would come next.

"We need to talk," Raoul started, and he saw her pale before him, her eyes widen.

"Wasn't that what we were doing…before?"

He made a movement with his hand, brushing aside her words. "We need to discuss us."

"Us? What about us? Do you want to stop…?"

Her voice trailed away as if she couldn't quite find the words to define the exquisite pleasure they'd enjoyed together. But he had no such difficulty. It was what it was. Just sex. Period. It could never be anything else and she needed to know that.

"No. But I want to be clear going forward that it is only sex between us, Alexis. It will never be, and can never be, anything more than that. You want me to be alive. Fine, I'll be alive—with you—but it won't be anything more than this. I want us to be sexual partners, no strings attached. Can you accept that?"

He watched her carefully for her reaction. If she looked uncomfortable about this in any way, if the idea made her unhappy because she wanted more from a partner or because she secretly harbored feelings for him that she thought might be reciprocated, he hoped it would show on her expressive face. But for once she remained a closed book to him. A faint nod of her head the only acknowledgment of what he'd just said.

"Are you certain, Alexis? Because if you can't, we stop now. I don't want you to be under any illusion that we're going to fall in love and have a future. I'm never going down that road again. I did it once and I can't trust anyone that way again."

She caught her full lower lip between her teeth, the sheen in her eyes a telltale giveaway. A shaft of fear sliced through him. She wanted more. Of course she did. It was in her nature to love, to nurture. It was only natural she'd want the same in return. She was the kind of person who always put others first, the one others turned to when in need. But he didn't want all of that from her—couldn't accept it, couldn't give it to her in return.

"Can I have some time to think about it?"

"If you need time to think about it, you obviously have questions. If you have questions, or doubts, then we should probably forget the whole idea."

He could see her weighing his words. Before his eyes she changed. Her eyes cleared and the expression on her face hardened. She drew herself up to her full height and looked up at him. Then, to his surprise, she gave a brief nod and spoke.

"Yes, I accept."

"Yes?"

He barely dared to hope she was giving him the answer he desperately wanted to hear.

"Yes, I'll be your…" she hesitated just a barest moment "…your sexual partner."

"No strings attached."

The clarification was important. Vitally so.

"Agreed, no strings attached."

"And you'll keep taking your pill. I don't want there to be any mistakes. If you're not happy with that I'll take care of protection myself."

Maybe he should be using condoms as well anyway. You could never be too safe.

"I'm still taking my pill. I don't plan to stop, so don't worry. Is that everything you wanted to discuss?"

Hell, no, it wasn't.

"Just one more thing."

"And what might that be?"

"Our sleeping arrangements. I can't stay in your room."

"That's okay, I can sleep just as well in your bed—if you want me there all night, that is."

Did he? Of course he did. The idea alone had him hardening again.

"I do," he admitted, his voice roughening with mounting anticipation and desire.

She drew in a breath and then slowly released it. "Is that all?"

He nodded, suddenly unable to speak.

"Fine, I'll go and collect Ruby, then."

He watched her through the window as she left the winery and walked up the hill to the house, feeling as if something vital had changed between them and not for the better. But he didn't doubt that he'd made the right decision. He was just happy that she'd agreed. When he turned back to his work he didn't stop to question how right it had felt to hold her, or how desperately he needed to lose himself in her softness again. And again. All he wanted to think about was that, from tonight, he could.

Ten

No strings attached. God should have smote her for that lie. Her agreement had come back to haunt her virtually every day these past couple of weeks. There'd been strings attached to Raoul Benoit from the moment she first laid eyes on him—the very day Bree had excitedly introduced him as her fiancé. That instant attraction, that irresistible tug of physical awareness that happened every single time she saw him, only grew stronger.

He'd kick her out of here faster than she could imagine if he had any idea of how she felt about him. How each day, each hour, each second with him only made her love him more. She stayed with him every night. Falling deep into sleep after they made love, sometimes waking in the small hours to feel him reaching for her to make love all over again.

Last night, after he'd fallen asleep again, she'd committed a cardinal sin. She'd given in, against all her promises to herself to the contrary, and she'd whispered that she loved him. It had been a relief to get it out in the open, even if only for her ears alone.

She shifted her attention back to what she was doing and poured another jug of warm water over Ruby's head. Ruby squealed and splashed the bathwater vigorously, dragging Alexis's thoughts firmly into the present and her duties to her little charge. She laughed out loud at the child's sheer pleasure in bath time.

Strings, yeah, there were strings all right. Not least of which being the one that came from little Ruby and was now securely tied around Alexis's heart, as well.

It was impossible to refuse either of them anything but falling deeper in love with Raoul was starting to take a toll on her. Still, worrying about it wasn't going to solve anything. She just had to do what she did every day, and every night, and hope that the strength of her love could mend what was broken at Raoul's core.

She dragged a warmed towel from the rail and laid it on the floor before lifting a wriggling and squealing toddler from the bathwater. Now that Ruby was more confident walking, it was getting to be more and more of a challenge to keep her immobilized long enough to do simple things like dry her off and dress her. Since the baby had found her feet she'd been on the go all day every day. Of course, without the perception to realize what was risky and what wasn't, there'd been a few accidents—like the one at the coffee table in the main sitting room last week—which had left a small bruise on Ruby's ivory forehead.

Raoul had immediately removed the table and Alexis had been surprised when a local furniture maker had delivered a rounded edge oval one in its stead. Even though

Raoul tried not to care, it was obvious that he did, in spite of himself.

She patted Ruby dry, blowing raspberries on her tummy to make her giggle as she did so. As she righted herself, though, Alexis was assailed by a wave of dizziness. She put out a hand onto the edge of the bath to anchor herself. Ruby, not wasting a moment, rolled over and onto her knees, then gained her feet and headed straight for the door to the hallway as fast as she could go.

"Oh, no you don't, young lady!" Alexis called after the rapidly departing naked figure.

She shot to her feet, only to be hit by another dizzying wave. Black spots swam before her eyes and a roaring sound filled her ears. From what seemed like a great distance away, she heard Ruby's high-pitched squeal of delight. She forced herself to take a step, and then another. Her vision thankfully began to clear.

"I'm coming to get you," she called as she exited the bathroom just in time to see Raoul sweep the naked wriggling baby into his arms.

"Got a runaway, I see," he said, walking toward her and handing Ruby to her as soon as she was within distance.

"I just about need to tether her these days," Alexis said with a smile.

Raoul did a bit of a double take, looking at her more intently than a minute before.

"Are you okay?"

"I think I got up a little too quickly before. It left me a little dizzy but I'm fine now," she said, brushing off his concern.

"You look quite pale, are you sure you're all right?"

She nodded, and it was true. She was feeling fine now compared to earlier.

"Of course, I'm great. Really."

But there was a niggle there in the back of her mind, one she didn't want to consider right now if she could avoid it.

Later, after she'd settled Ruby for the night and had picked up the trail of toys that she had left through the house, she was surprised when Raoul sought her out. Usually he kept working in his study up until he was ready to retire for the night, often reading more about wine-making and blending techniques. He rarely joined her in the family room to watch television. But when they went to bed, it was a different story.

Usually, he came to find her wherever she was in the house and then took her by the hand back to his room. She cast a quick glance at the mantel clock above the family room fireplace. It was early, even for him.

"I've been thinking. It might be best if you sleep in your own room tonight," he said.

"Oh? Why?" *Sick of me already?* She clamped the words firmly behind her lips, not wanting them to possibly be heard in case they might be true.

"You need a decent night's rest and let's face it, I haven't exactly been letting you have one the past couple of weeks, have I?"

Disappointment crowded into her chest.

"It's okay. You haven't heard me complaining, have you?"

He gave her a crooked smile. One that made her heart lurch in that crazy way he always managed.

"No, I can't say I have but I'm worried about you. Get a good night, tonight, hmm? Situation normal again from tomorrow if you're feeling better."

He leaned forward and kissed her. Initially, his lips

were soft and undemanding but it was only a matter of seconds before their kiss deepened, before his mouth slanted across hers so he could kiss her more thoroughly. Heat snaked along her veins, priming her body in readiness for what usually came next. She looped her arms around his neck and gave back with everything she had in her.

She was so lost in the fog of desire that it came as a shock to realize that his hands had caught her at her wrists and were disentangling her so he could pull away.

"I'm fine, Raoul, honestly."

"Let me be the judge of that. One night. We can survive that, can't we? Now go. Get some sleep."

"Can't you just sleep next to me? We don't have to—"

He took a step back. "No, it doesn't work that way with us. You know that. No strings, remember?"

"Sure, I remember," she said, forcing a smile of acceptance to her face.

Just sex, she repeated in the back of her mind as she readied for bed. She continued repeating it for the next hour as she lay in the dark, staring at the ceiling, hoping against all hope that he missed having her in his bed just about as much as she missed being there.

The next morning Alexis felt a great deal more rested. Much as she hated to admit it, Raoul had apparently been right about the lack of sleep catching up to her. But then when she got Ruby out of her crib and was changing her diaper, the first wave of nausea hit her.

"Goodness," she said as she folded and bagged the offending diaper. "We might need to change your diet, young lady."

The second wave hit when she was preparing Ruby's breakfast cereal and stewed fruit—and with it came an overwhelming sense of dread. She was no idiot. She knew what her physical symptoms could mean. She hadn't been fully protected the first time she and Raoul had made love. Even though she'd made that trip to the local pharmacy and gotten the morning-after tablets, she'd been counseled that they were not always 100 percent effective.

"And ain't that the truth?" she muttered under her breath as she willed her stomach under control.

What had Raoul said, again, when he'd made his suggestion that they be sexual partners? He didn't want there to be any mistakes—yes, that was right. Well, it certainly looked as if she'd made a big one. But she needed to be sure. She already had plans to head out with Ruby today. Laura had suggested a playdate with little Jason again and Alexis had been looking forward to just having some time out alone in Akaroa, browsing the stores and stopping at one of the cafés for a triple-shot nonfat latte while browsing a tabloid magazine.

The thought of coffee completely turned her stomach. Alexis swallowed against the lump in her throat. Rather than indulging in her favorite vice, she knew exactly what she'd be doing at the local store instead—buying a pregnancy test kit.

Alexis stared at the indicator window on the stick. This wasn't how she'd imagined discovering she was going to become a mother—locked in the end cubicle of the public restrooms on the main street. Even though she'd known to the soles of her feet what the result would be, the strong positive that appeared was shockingly candid confirmation she really didn't need. One part of her was doing a crazy happy dance—shouting for joy that she was pregnant with Raoul's child. The rest of her quivered with anxiety.

The news that she was expecting his baby, after he'd

spelled it out perfectly clearly that pregnancy was an outcome to be avoided at all cost, would not be welcome.

She shoved the stick into its wrapper and back into the box—disposing of everything in the restroom trash can. Numb, she washed and dried her hands and walked outside, where everyone carried along on the pavement with their everyday lives, oblivious to the situation she now found herself in.

Alexis crossed the street to a park bench that sat on a grass berm, facing out to the harbor. Despite the cold day, she felt nothing. Not the sunshine on her face, nor the brisk wind that whipped along the shoreline, coaxing whitecaps on the water.

What on earth was she going to do?

She could only imagine Raoul's reaction. There was no room in his life, or his heart, for another baby. Hell, he fought against making room for the one he had.

But he was capable of love, Alexis knew that. She'd witnessed it for herself. He'd loved once and he could love again, she just knew it. His marriage to Bree had been happy, she'd seen that to her own cost. Somehow she had to convince him to take a risk on love again.

She understood that grief did strange things to a person—could blow normal emotions right out of proportion. She only had to look at her own family for proof of that.

Alexis's mother had had a first, unhappy marriage, and when she'd run away from it to marry for love, she'd been forced to leave her children behind. Years later, when her daughter from that marriage sought her out, Alexis's father had not reacted well. Her mother had been in the hospital by then, physically and mentally frail from the disease racking her body. Fear that seeing her long-lost daughter might upset her to the point of worsening her condition had made Lorenzo go so far as to enlist his business partner to actively steer her half sister, Tamsyn, away from discovering where their mother was. When Ellen Fabrini had died before Tamsyn could even see her again, Alexis had realized that nothing mattered more in this world than family. Nothing.

Maybe that was part of why she was so determined to break through the barriers with Raoul. To force him to learn to love again. To make him see how precious his daughter was—what a truly wonderful tribute she was to a marriage and a love that had sadly ended all too soon.

Unexpected tears sprang in her eyes. She blinked them furiously away. *Please don't let me become one of those overemotional wrecks with this pregnancy,* she silently begged. The last thing she needed was an exceptional change in her behavior that might tip Raoul off before she was ready to tell him her news.

An alarm on her phone chimed from the side pocket of her handbag, reminding her it was time to collect Ruby. She was no nearer to knowing what she needed to do about the baby she carried. Logically, there were steps to be taken. She needed to make an appointment with a local doctor, get her results confirmed, get checked out, etc. But, as to the rest—telling Raoul? She had no idea where to begin and, as much as it rankled to deliberately withhold the truth from him, she felt she had no other option right now. No other option at all.

She thought about the test kit in the restroom trash. Those things had a degree of inaccuracy, surely. She'd wait until she had official confirmation from the doctor. Then she'd decide what to do. Until then, everything would remain as it had been before.

Eleven

Raoul couldn't take his eyes off Alexis as she played with Ruby. The weather outside was miserable, cold and wet and blowing a gale. Alexis had lit the fire in the family room and put the guard around the fireplace. He'd wondered about the wisdom of the fire, even with the guard, but after watching Ruby he realized that she'd been schooled by Alexis to stay well clear of the hearth.

"Dad-dad!"

She'd spied him and ran toward him as fast as her little legs could carry her. He could hardly believe that an almost eleven-month-old baby could move so fast. Her hair was longer now and Alexis had tied it up into a little spout on the top of her head. Whoomph! Two little arms clamped around his legs as she came to a halt beneath him and gabbled off a rapid chain of baby babble.

"I think she's asking you to lift her up," Alexis said from her spot on the floor, her cheeks flushed with the heat of the fire.

"Asking, or telling me?" he said, bending down to unpeel her arms from his legs.

"Probably the latter." Alexis laughed. "Go on, pick her up."

"No, it's all right. I've got work to do."

"Oh, for goodness' sake! You won't drop her."

Alexis got to her feet and picked up Ruby and thrust her at him. Reflexively he took her. "Hold her! She's not made of glass. She's growing up before your very eyes, she's hale and hearty and everything's fine."

"Got out of the wrong side of the bed this morning, did we?" Raoul commented, awkwardly holding Ruby on his hip.

The baby reached for a pen he had in his shirt pocket and began playing with the clicker, eventually getting ink down his front. He extricated the pen from her increasingly deft fingers and waited for her to protest so he'd have an excuse to hand her back to Alexis. Instead, she lay her little head on his chest and gave a big sigh.

"You know exactly what side of the bed I got out of," Alexis responded, her voice softer now as she watched him and Ruby.

"She must be ready for a sleep," he said.

"No, I think she's happy to just sit with you for a bit. Why don't you read to her?"

"Read?"

"Yes. You know, pick up one of those paper things with the cardboard on the outside and words and pictures printed in the middle? I need to go and check on some washing in the dryer."

She was gone from the room before he could protest and he couldn't very well leave Ruby alone in here, especially not with the fire going. It felt weird, but he sat down at the end of the sofa and picked up one of the baby books Alexis kept stashed in a basket on the floor beside it. He adjusted Ruby on his lap and opened the book, starting to read from it. It's not like it was rocket science. The words were simplistic and thankfully few, and the pictures were bright and colorful. He'd just finished the book and closed it, ready to put it back on the stack when Ruby grabbed it off him and opened it again, her little fingers struggling a bit to turn the pages. Giving in, he started to read it for a second, and then a third time.

By the time Alexis came back into the room, a basket of folded washing on her hip, he was on to his fourth attempt. Ruby had settled back against his tummy, her little head growing heavy against him.

"Oh, look at that. She's out for the count," Alexis said softly.

"Must have bored her to sleep," he commented, thankful he could at least stop reciting the story line, now committed to memory, over again.

"Actually, no. She obviously feels very secure with you. At her age she can be a bit off with some people. A baby's stranger awareness is honed around this age. Some kids start even earlier. I think it's lovely that she knows she's okay with you."

Raoul felt outrageously proud but hastened to downplay the situation.

"It's just because she's used to being here now. That'll all change when she goes back to Catherine and you go back home."

"You're still sending her back to Catherine?" Alexis sounded shocked.

"Of course, that was the plan all along. Here, take her and put her to bed."

"Sure thing, boss."

There was something about the tone of Alexis's voice that set his teeth on edge.

"Alexis, just because I read her a story doesn't mean we're going to play happy family."

"No, of course not. That would take far more heart than you're prepared to admit to."

With that, she deftly scooped the sleeping baby off his lap and disappeared out the room. Her comment rankled. It shouldn't, but it did. He hadn't asked for her to leave him alone with Ruby and he certainly hadn't asked for her opinion about his plans for Ruby's long-term care. Yet why had he experienced that absurd sense of pride that the baby had settled with him, and why did his arms feel ridiculously empty now that she was gone?

It was almost ten weeks since Catherine's surgery. Ten weeks since Alexis had come to look after Ruby. Catherine was walking steadily on her own now and, with regular physiotherapy sessions, was regaining her strength and independence day by day. She'd asked Alexis if she could have Ruby to visit for a couple of hours and Alexis took the opportunity to make an appointment to visit the doctor and get official confirmation about her condition.

She'd done the math, by her reckoning she was just over six weeks pregnant, thankfully still far too early to show. Luckily, so far, her only symptoms were that she felt queasy every now and then only if she was overtired.

Even if her symptoms had been more drastic, it was unlikely anyone would have noticed. Raoul was still incredibly busy conducting his one-man band of business in the winery. Alexis was in two minds about it. Half of her was hugely relieved he spent so many hours out of her sphere right now, especially as she struggled to deal with the mental ramifications of her pregnancy. The other half, well, that just saw the time he wasn't there as missed opportunities to keep building up the tenuously fragile link that was starting to develop between Ruby and her father.

Still, she reminded herself, progress was progress, even if the steps were tiny.

What scared her most was, what on earth would happen when her pregnancy started to be more obvious? She and Raoul shared a bed, shared one another's bodies, every night. He knew her body so well, eventually he'd feel the changes that she had begun to notice herself. Already her breasts were more tender and responsive than before and, as she'd noticed when she'd fastened her bra this morning, they were already slightly fuller, too.

Somehow she had to find the courage to tell him before he picked up on the physical cues that she had no control over. Picking the right time was going to be the challenging part.

The visit to the doctor went smoothly. The doctor congratulated her on her pregnancy and she tried her hardest to show the appropriate enthusiasm. Even though she knew everything was okay, that she was strong and healthy and that the pregnancy should continue to develop normally, she still felt an underlying anxiety. While termination was out of the question, how on earth would she cope with all this?

She'd already put her working life on hold to be there for Ruby and yes, granted, she was paid for her role here, but that was nothing compared to what she could potentially earn as her fashion clientele continued to grow. Having Tamsyn keep things running smoothly in her absence was one thing, but would she be able to continue to expand her business if she was busy with a new baby, as well?

Making the decision to come here had come from a position of guilt—from the fact that she'd owed Bree's daughter the support and love she'd failed to give the child's mother. When she'd started to withdraw from Bree, after meeting Raoul, she'd felt her friend's confusion, the hint of hurt in the background of her initial emails.

The lengthy, handwritten letter Bree had sent her before she died had been full of apology for some slight she had imagined was the only reason that could have caused a wedge between herself and Alexis. Bree was sad that they'd drifted apart the way they had but she'd felt, of all the people she knew, that she could still turn to Alexis in her hour of need.

And Alexis hadn't been there.

She and Raoul both lived with their own sense of guilt, and it pulled at each of them constantly—drove them to make the choices they did, feel what they felt. Alexis could only hope that, with its source being a common link for them both, that somehow they could find a solution together for the future.

Catherine looked tired but happy when Alexis arrived at her house to collect Ruby.

"Did you get done everything you wanted?" she asked after she invited Alexis in for a cup of tea.

"I did, thank you."

Alexis looked at the woman who had been one of her own mother's best friends and who had packed up her whole life in Blenheim to move to Banks Peninsula when it had become clear that Ruby needed a full-time carer other than her father. Catherine smiled back.

"I'm glad. So, how's it all going? We've hardly had any chance to talk since I've been back home. How's Raoul doing?"

Alexis bowed her head and studied the fine china cup in her hands. "I didn't realize just how determined he was to keep his distance from Ruby. Sure, I've got him to hold her a few times but overall I'm not making much headway. He cares about her, I know he does, he just won't show it or even admit it to himself. He's so inflexible."

"Bree used to say that, too. I think that's why she never told anyone about the aneurysm. She knew he would have refused to have a family if he'd known, and she so wanted one with him."

"Have you told him that?" Alexis asked, lifting her head to meet Catherine's understanding gaze.

"Oh, I've told him several times but, as you say, he's inflexible with a good dose of intractable thrown into the bargain. Once he makes up his mind, it's made up. He still thinks he's responsible somehow. I believe he finds it easier to accept that than to think he had no control over what happened. He's not the kind of man who likes to relinquish control, is he? After all, while he won't care for Ruby himself, he makes sure she's cared for—and to his expectations. He's still superprotective, isn't he?"

Alexis's lips twisted into a rueful smile. "Yes, that he most definitely is."

"Bree was always the one thing he could never control. She would exasperate him something terrible at times." Catherine laughed. "It used to puzzle me that they managed to work everything out between them—two people so different. I don't think he'll ever forgive her for keeping that information from him, though. He's still angry at her. He's not going to heal or move forward until he can let that go. Oh, I know he *thinks* he's moving forward, especially with the development of his wines, but he's just going through the motions. His heart's not really in it."

Alexis pondered her visit with Catherine later that

night as she lay in bed, the book she'd planned to read lying open in her lap. The older woman's words about Raoul's anger and his need for forgiveness weighed heavily on her heart. She understood what Catherine had said because, she'd painfully realized, it applied to her, too. She'd never thought about it until now but she'd been angry with Bree for a long time. Angry that she'd met Raoul first, angry that she found her happiness with him.

It was petty and infantile but there it was. And she'd stupidly let those feelings get in the way of a long-standing friendship, one that had seen them through so many things together as they were growing up. So another part of her was angry with Bree for dying while things were still unsolved between them—for not giving Alexis a chance to come to peace with Bree's marriage and renew their friendship.

It occurred to her that while Raoul had to forgive Bree for not telling him the truth about her health, she in turn had to forgive herself for allowing her attraction to him to come between her and Bree, and for not moving past her issues before it was too late. Could she do that?

It wasn't as if she could appeal to Bree herself anymore for her forgiveness. Instead, she was doing all she could to care for Ruby, to try to ignite a relationship between father and daughter as she knew Bree would want. Was that enough?

She was still turning the idea over in her head as Raoul came into the bedroom.

"You look deep in thought," Raoul said. "Problem?"

"No, just thinking about things," she hedged.

She wished she had the strength to tell him about her feelings, even tell him about her pregnancy now—to pour out how she felt and to have him take her in his arms and tell her everything would be all right. It was a futile hope. He'd so effectively compartmentalized his life and locked his feelings away that she didn't dare expose her vulnerability to him.

She had to believe that he could love her back before she could declare her heart to him and, she realized, before she could tell him about their baby. Attraction was there—every night together was evidence of that—surely there had to be more to this for him than just a release of physical tension.

"What are you thinking about?" he asked as he began tugging his clothes off, distracting her with his movements.

"Just something Catherine said," she answered lightly.

"Oh." He paused in the act of pulling his sweater off and Alexis's eyes were immediately drawn to the ridged plane of his stomach. "Is she ready to take Ruby back?"

"Hardly!" Alexis remonstrated. A knot formed in her stomach. "Are you in such a hurry to get rid of me?"

He finished shucking off his clothes and slid into bed beside her. "No," he said, reaching over her to put her book on the bedside cabinet and pulling her into his arms. "Does this feel like I want to get rid of you?"

His erection pressed demandingly against her and her body answered in kind, hunger for him spreading throughout in a slow, delicious wave. She forced a laugh, pressing her fears and doubts to the back of her mind and grabbing the moment, and him, with both hands.

Their lovemaking was a feverish joining of bodies, as it so often was. As if each sought something from the other that only they could give. And yet, there was still that lingering sense of incompletion for Alexis as she searched for the emotional connection she so needed with the man in her arms.

That it remained a one-way street struck home now more than ever before.

Raoul fell asleep almost immediately afterward, but Alexis continued to stare at the ceiling in the darkened room, wondering just how much longer she could keep this up before she broke completely. She'd thought she had the strength to do this, to fight past his barricades, to wear them down and to fill his heart with her love. Had it all been nothing more than a pipe dream? It certainly felt like it.

Twelve

Raoul looked up from his breakfast to see Alexis coming down the hall. He was getting a late start on his day, something that he found himself doing more and more often recently. Sharing a little extra time with Alexis at this stage of the day was something he'd discovered he enjoyed. And he had to admit, watching Ruby's antics as she ate her breakfast had been known to bring a smile or two to his face.

Alexis came into the kitchen with Ruby, looking a little paler than usual—a worry mark scoring a line between her brows. He was so used to seeing her smile and being her relaxed and easygoing self that the sight of her like this rattled him. Raoul felt an unfamiliar tightness in his chest. Was she all right?

"Good morning," she said, popping Ruby in her high chair and doing up the harness that prevented her from climbing straight back out again. "I'm glad I caught you. I need to ask you a favor."

"A favor?" he asked, absently passing Ruby a small square of his toast, something that had become a part of their morning ritual.

Aside from wanting him to spend more time with Ruby, Alexis didn't usually ask him anything. He wondered what was on her mind. "What is it?" he asked, getting up from the table to rinse his dishes and put them in the dishwasher—and to position himself with his back to her, so she couldn't see the worry he was certain was written all over his face.

Alexis hesitated a little before speaking. "Look, I need to head out to an appointment this morning. I tried to see if Laura could have Ruby for me, or Catherine, but Catherine's got plans for today already and Laura's just texted me to say their household is down with a tummy bug so I can't leave her there. Can you have Ruby for a couple of hours for me?"

A couple of hours without Alexis in calling distance? Without even Catherine to call upon if anything should go wrong? Icy water ran in his veins.

He shook his head immediately. "No, I can't. I'm sending out samples of last year's vintage to restaurants around the country and I've got couriers coming and going all morning. I won't be able to keep an eye on Ruby, as well."

It was true, he justified to himself. The risks to Ruby if she was down in the winery with him were untold. A moment's inattention and she could get into serious mischief and his day was already too busy and structured to accommodate an active baby. Add to that the additional traffic that would be on the lane and the whole exercise would be a nightmare.

Contrition stung at the back of his mind as he saw Alexis accept the news. The frown on her forehead deepened.

"Okay, I'll just work around her, then," she said flatly.

"Can you change your appointment? What is it, anyway?"

She looked at him and for a moment he thought she looked scared. The urge to protect her from whatever the problem was filled him but was beaten back by the self-reproach he felt at not being willing to take Ruby for her.

She gave him a shaky smile, one that didn't quite reach her eyes. "No, don't worry, it's nothing important. I'll work something out. Are you heading down to the winery office now?"

"I'll be in my study here for a short while, then I'll go down to the winery."

She gave a little sigh. "I'll see you later on today, then."

"Yeah, sure. I should be all done by three."

He left the kitchen and started down the hall but his steps slowed before he reached the study. Something wasn't right. Alexis hadn't been herself for days now. Possibly even a couple of weeks. At least since the day she'd been to see Catherine with Ruby. He cast his mind back. She'd been worried then about something Catherine had said. Obviously it was still playing on her. He made a mental note to pursue it with her this afternoon.

From his study window he saw Alexis leave the house about a half hour later. She put Ruby in her car seat in the back of the car and buckled her in, just as she always did. Something wasn't right, though. Alexis moved more slowly than usual, more carefully. He continued watching as she went around the back of the car and put the diaper bag in the trunk before walking around to the driver's door.

Something definitely wasn't right. She leaned against the car, her hand to her stomach, then her legs collapsed beneath her.

He was out of his chair and flying toward the front door before he saw her hit the driveway. She was already stirring when he reached her side.

"Are you all right? What happened?" he demanded, his eyes roaming her pale features as her eyelids fluttered open.

"I need to see the doctor, Raoul. Can you take me, please?"

"I'll call an ambulance."

He had his cell phone out in his hand, his thumb already poised over the emergency call button. A wave of sick fear swamped him, making his hand shake, along with an awful sense of déjà vu. The last time he'd felt this scared, this totally helpless, was when Bree had gone into labor with Ruby.

Alexis's hand closed over his. "No, the medical center in town. They're expecting me—it's the appointment I told you about. Please, just take me there."

"Are you sure?"

"Please, let's just go."

He helped her up to her feet and shepherded her into the back of the car, with Ruby who was now beginning to fret.

"Not now, Ruby," he said sternly as he helped Alexis with her safety belt. "I need you to be good for me."

To his surprise, the baby stopped and popped her thumb in her mouth. Her big blue eyes stared straight at him. A tickle of relief that he wouldn't have to deal with a crying baby on top of his concern for Alexis flickered on the periphery of his mind.

"That's a good girl," he said absently before giving his sole attention to Alexis again. "Are you comfortable?"

"Enough for now," she answered weakly. "Can we go?"

He closed her door and then got into the driver's seat,

adjusting the rearview mirror so he could keep an eye on her in back. Her face was still pale and her big brown eyes met his in the mirror. She looked frightened and identifying that look on her constantly cheerful and indomitable face terrified him.

The drive to the clinic was short and Alexis was already struggling out of her seat even as he flew out of his to come and assist her. She waved him away.

"Let me go, I'll be all right getting in there. Just see to Ruby."

"She can wait, she's safe where she is for now. Let me see you insi—"

"No, Raoul!" Alexis's voice was sharp. "You can't just leave her in the car. I can manage for now."

Without waiting for him to reply she began walking slowly toward the entrance, disappearing between the front sliding doors as he fiddled with the baby car-seat buckle—cursing its efficacy until he had it loose—and lifted Ruby from her restraint. He ran with her to the building and straight to reception.

"Alexis Fabrini, where is she?" he demanded when he reached the counter.

The receptionist stared at him over the edge of her glasses. "And you are?"

"Raoul Benoit," he replied automatically.

"Are you her next of kin?"

Inwardly he groaned. He could see where this was going. They weren't going to let him see her, or tell him anything. "No, I'm not. I'm her employer. She has no family locally."

"Then I'll ask you to wait over there," the receptionist said firmly, gesturing to the bank of chairs lined up in the waiting area.

"I'd like to see her, be with her—"

"She's with the medical staff. I'm sure they'll call you if necessary," the woman placated. "There's nothing you can do right now but be patient."

There was a sympathetic look in her eyes as if she understood his frustration, but he didn't want her sympathy. He wanted Alexis. He wanted her well, not pale and trembling. Not sliding unconscious down the side of her car. That she hadn't hit her head when she'd fallen was sheer luck, but why had she passed out in the first place? She must have known something was wrong to have made the appointment in the first place—had she expected this to happen? And, if she'd had a medical appointment today, why hadn't she just been upfront and told him about it? They were lovers. They'd shared more with one another than most people. Knew each other intimately.

But sitting here, confused and worried, he was struck with how little he truly knew. He didn't know that she was unwell, or what she thought was wrong. Didn't know how long she'd been worried about whatever it was, or why she hadn't told him. And the more he thought about it, the more he realized how little of her thoughts she really shared with him. What were her hopes, her dreams for the future? Had he ever bothered to find out what they were? Had he ever taken the time to learn about *her?* What made her happiest, what made her sad? He knew for a fact that he made her angry with his reluctance to be a part of Ruby's life.

Ruby squirmed in his arms, wanting to be let down to play with a toy in the waiting area. He eyed it suspiciously. The wooden base looked clean enough but who was to say the roller coaster of colorful wooden beads was hygienic? Who knew what she'd catch if she played with it?

"I don't think so," he murmured to the little girl, holding her firmly on his lap.

Ruby squawked a protest.

"It's okay," the receptionist said blandly from behind her desk. "I disinfected all the toys at the end of clinic last night. She'll be fine."

Raoul still felt uncomfortable with the idea, but he nodded his acknowledgment and gingerly set Ruby on her feet. He followed her to the toy and sat on a chair beside it as the little girl squatted down and reached for the beads, picking them up and dropping them on the brightly colored wires that threaded through them.

"Here," Raoul said, getting down to her level. "I think you're supposed to do this."

He demonstrated with one bead, guiding it along a wire as Ruby watched. But she was having none of it. She quite happily continued to do what she was doing. With a sigh, Raoul sat back on his chair, his eyes flicking every now and then to the corridor where he assumed Alexis had been taken. The waiting was interminable—the minutes stretching out to ten, twenty, thirty, then forty. The long wait was getting to Ruby also, it seemed, as she worked her way from interest in the bead roller coaster to every other toy in the waiting room. Finally, she brought a book to Raoul, making it clear what she wanted him to do.

"Not now, Ruby. You read the book," he stated, but the baby continued to vocalize her demand.

Mindful of the risk of her cries disturbing the other people that were now coming into the waiting room, he lifted her onto his lap where, to his surprise, she settled quite happily and banged her hand on the book. He opened the cover and started to quietly read. When that book was done she squirmed back down and got another.

And so passed the next painfully slow ten minutes until Ruby began to fidget and fuss again. Feeling at a total loss, he stood up with her and started to walk back and forward, rubbing her gently on her back as he'd seen Alexis do so many times before. But it seemed he didn't have quite the knack he needed.

He looked again down the corridor where the examination rooms were. Which one was Alexis in? he wondered. Was she okay? What on earth could be wrong with her that they had to keep her so long?

Ruby's fussing worked up a notch. Raoul felt helpless. He had no idea what to do.

"Maybe she needs a bottle or a drink?" an elderly lady suggested from her perch on a seat near the door.

Raoul remembered the diaper bag that Alexis had put in the trunk of the car. "Good idea," he said with a grateful smile to the woman and headed out quickly to the car park.

He unzipped the bag with a bit of difficulty and spied Ruby's drink bottle inside. The baby nearly tipped out of his arms as she reached for it. He grabbed her and secured her with one arm before passing her the bottle. He watched with relief as she jammed it into her mouth and began to drink. Slinging the bag over his shoulder, he closed the trunk and went back into the waiting room.

Settled with Ruby in his lap again he kept an eye on the corridor. People came and went but there was still no sign of Alexis. Ruby began to grow heavier in his arms and he realized she was drifting off to sleep. He took the bottle from her weakening grip and popped it back in the bag and adjusted her slightly so she could lie more comfortably across his lap.

He looked at her face as she slept, a face that was so familiar to him it made his heart ache to see Bree reflected there. But there was more than Bree in her features. There was Ruby's own growing personality beginning to show, too. She felt so small in his hands, so precious. How on earth could he keep her safe for the whole of her life? How could he keep the bad things from happening to her, the disappointments, the setbacks?

The responsibility was crushing. How did people cope? How did they balance love with care and obligation? He'd thought he and Bree had had the perfect mix of devotion and trust, until he'd found out that she'd kept the truth about her health from him. They'd promised one another to love and honor each other, to care for one another in sickness and in health. But she hadn't honored his love for her when she'd withheld the risks of pregnancy from him. She hadn't given him—them—a chance to face the obstacles together.

The all-too-familiar mix of rage and defeat pummeled his gut. She'd left him with the child he'd so wanted, yet was now too scared to love. The sense of betrayal cut as deep today as it had when the medical team had rushed him from the delivery suite and when they'd eventually informed him of Bree's death, despite all their efforts to prevent it. She'd taken a risk to have Ruby and she'd paid for it with her life. And he was angry. So very angry.

He lifted his head and looked around the waiting room, reminding himself of where he was and why he was here. Again that infuriating and painfully familiar sense of helplessness seeped through him. Alexis was in a room in here somewhere and he had no idea why. He'd been shut out because he had chosen to shut her out of that part of his life, as well. If he'd tried to be more open with her, become a true lover to her, he'd be in there with her—holding her hand, supporting her. Being her partner.

The idea resounded through his mind. Was he even

ready to take that step with someone again? He examined his feelings for Alexis. Feelings he had tried to keep at bay, had tried to mask with desire and the purely physical side of being together. But he couldn't deny it any longer. Alexis meant more to him than a convenient bed partner—way more.

A sound from the corridor to the examination rooms caught his attention and he saw Alexis walking toward reception with a nurse at her side. He got to his feet, carefully so as not to disturb the sleeping child in his arms, and started toward her—catching the tail end of what the nurse was saying as he drew nearer.

"The doctor will refer you through to Christchurch's maternity services and you'll need to take it easy for the next few days until the bleeding subsides. Oh, and no sex until it's stopped completely." The nurse put a comforting hand on Alexis's arm. "Don't worry too much, the ultrasound didn't show up any abnormalities, but take care and don't hesitate to call us if you have any concerns."

"Thank you, nurse," Alexis said weakly, her face suddenly growing even more pale as she realized that Raoul was standing right there.

He looked at her in shock, bile rising in his throat as he played the words he'd heard over in his mind. Bleeding? Ultrasound? Maternity services? Just what the hell were they talking about?

Thirteen

Alexis took one look at Raoul's face and knew he'd overheard the nurse's instructions. This was the last way she would have wanted for him to find out. She wished it could have been different. Wished he hadn't had to bring her here at all, or wait for her, no doubt with questions piling up upon themselves as he did so.

When she'd woken this morning and discovered she was bleeding, her first reaction had been complete panic. She'd rung the clinic and made an urgent appointment, then tried to find someone to care for Ruby. When that hadn't worked out she knew she'd been pushing it to expect Raoul to look after the baby.

Fainting at the side of the car hadn't been her finest moment but it had achieved one thing right today, she realized as she flicked her gaze over the sleeping child in his arms. Raoul had clearly had to spend some quality time with his daughter.

"Can we go?" she asked quietly. She wasn't looking forward to the demands for an explanation that were certain to come once they were alone, but she needed to go home. She couldn't avoid telling Raoul any longer and she certainly wasn't about to do that here with the entire waiting room packed and all eyes now fixed on her and Raoul.

Tension rolled off Raoul in waves as he negotiated the road back to the house. Alexis tried to make herself as small as possible in the passenger seat and focused her gaze out the side window but in her periphery she could see him turn his head and glance at her every now and then, as if he expected the answers to all the questions that no doubt rolled around in his head to suddenly appear neatly scripted on her face. She was glad he didn't start questioning her in the car but she dreaded the moment that he would.

At the house, she went to lift Ruby from her car seat—the wee tot was still out for it—but Raoul pushed her gently aside.

"I'll take her, you go and lie down," he said gruffly, then competently lifted the baby from her seat and carried her down to her room.

Alexis did as he'd told her, going back to the master suite and suddenly feeling very shaky on her feet—though she wasn't particularly tired. Still, maybe if she could feign sleep, Raoul would leave her alone for a bit longer. She was out of luck. He was in the room in minutes.

"Tell me," he demanded as he came to stand beside the bed, looking down at her.

She shrank into the bedcovers, hating what she had to say but knowing it would be useless to try to stall or evade. There was no putting this off any longer, no matter how much it hurt. Even forming the words in her head felt all wrong, but verbalizing them—putting them out there for Raoul to hear—that was crucifying.

Alexis drew in a deep breath. "I had a threatened miscarriage."

She watched his face for his reaction, but could only discern a tightening of his jaw and the flick of a pulse at the base of his throat.

"Threatened miscarriage. What exactly does that mean?"

"I woke up this morning and noticed I was bleeding. The clinic told me to come straight in. They think it'll stop, that..." She dragged in another breath. "That the baby will be okay."

"Baby."

His voice was cold and flat, much like the empty expression in his eyes.

"Yes," she acknowledged in a whisper.

"And I'm assuming that I'm the father of this baby?"

"Yes," she said again, this time a little more firmly.

Raoul huffed out a breath and dragged a hand through his hair. "Tell me, Alexis. At what point were you going to let me know about this?"

"I...I don't know."

"What? Did you think you could hide it from me?"

"Not for long," she admitted, curling up onto her side.

He started to pace, back and forth, and when he stopped she knew what was coming.

"You lied to me when you said you were protected even though you knew how I felt about something like this happening. Why?"

"I thought I'd be okay, I'd only missed a couple of pills. I went to the pharmacy the next morning and got a morning-after prescription. I did everything I could to make sure this didn't happen."

"And yet it did."

"Yes, it did."

"I shouldn't have trusted you. I shouldn't have touched you. God, what are we going to do?"

"Well, if the bleeding stops as it's supposed to and everything settles down okay, we're going to become parents together," she said softly, trying to infuse her voice with enthusiasm and encouragement in the vain hope it might sink past his shock.

He looked at her in horror.

"*If* everything settles down? What are you saying—are you going to be okay?" he asked, his face suddenly pale.

"The doctor wants to refer me to maternity services in Christchurch to be certain. I need to wait for an appointment."

"No, no waiting. I'll get you in to see someone privately."

"I can't afford that, Raoul," she protested. "I don't have full cover on my medical insurance."

"I'll pay for it. I need to know what's going on." He diverted from his pacing path, seeming to head to the door—most likely to make the necessary calls to doctors right away.

"Raoul, please, believe me when I say I didn't want this to happen," she whispered before he could leave.

He closed his eyes and shook his head and she saw his throat move as he swallowed.

"Neither did I, Alexis. Neither did I. Try to get some rest. I'll see to Ruby when she wakes."

He took the mobile monitor that Alexis kept at her bedside and clipped it to his belt.

"But what about the couriers? I thought you had a busy day ahead."

"I do, but I'll just have to work around it, won't I?"

Tears of frustration pricked at the back of her eyes but she refused to let them go.

"Raoul," she said as he moved once more to leave the room. "I'm so sorry."

"Me, too."

She stared at the door as he closed it behind him, her heart aching for what she was putting him through. She'd seen the abject terror in his eyes this morning, followed later by shock when he'd overheard the nurse talking to her at the clinic.

Alexis pressed a hand to her lower belly, hoping against hope that everything would be all right. For all of them. This wasn't the way she'd wanted him to find out. She'd wanted to tell him, in her own time, her own way. But nature had decided otherwise. And now it was Raoul's turn to decide how to respond.

Raoul paced back and forth in the family room, bound to stay at the house by his promise to take care of Ruby and to let Alexis rest, which meant staying within range of the baby monitor. He fought his instinct to flee, to head deep into the vineyard and walk and walk until he could walk no more.

Dark clouds scudded across the sky, heavy with rain that began to fall in steady droplets, battering against the glass stacking doors that looked out over the garden. He leaned his forehead against the glass, welcoming the cold, the numbness. Anything was better than the horror that played through his mind right now.

Alexis. Pregnant.

He braced his hands against a door frame and stared blindly out into the drenched garden as the two words echoed over and over in his head.

This couldn't be happening. Not again. Hadn't life

dealt him a hard enough blow with Bree, now it had to throw this at him, too? This wasn't something he could come to terms with. And tied in with the fear he felt at her condition was a strong sense of betrayal—again. He'd trusted Alexis, believed she was telling the truth after that first time they'd been together. She'd never mentioned the slightest doubt that she was safely protected from pregnancy.

His eyes burned as the wind picked up, blasting cold rain directly at the surface of the glass doors. Still he didn't move. Couldn't. He was frozen to this spot as much as he was frozen inside. He'd begun to thaw, he'd felt it, noticed it bit by bit as Alexis had worked her way under his skin and into his heart. Had stopped fighting against it, had even begun to trust that maybe, just maybe, the time was right to live again.

He was a damn fool. Hadn't he learned his lesson the hard way? People who professed to love you were also prepared to lie to you, as well. Bree had. He hadn't thought that Alexis ever would. She was so honest, so open and giving. He'd heard Alexis say she loved him one night as he'd fallen asleep. He *knew* how she felt. It was there in her every word, her every touch. When they made love he could feel her giving him a piece of her every single time. Making him feel again, making him want more, even making him begin to dream.

But she'd lied, too. And now worse, she, too, was at risk. The baby possibly already threatening her life as well as its own.

He'd always wanted a big family. That wish continued to come back to haunt him. He fought back the scream that struggled to be released from deep inside of him, too afraid to let it go in case he couldn't stop howling once it started.

He couldn't do this again. He simply couldn't. He'd already lost one woman he'd loved—a woman he'd pledged to spend the rest of his life with. The pain of that loss had been crushing. Discovering she'd kept her life-threatening condition from him even more so.

He wasn't prepared to lose another.

Oh, my God, he thought, *I love her. I love Alexis.*

Hard on the realization came fear. With love came loss, he knew that to his cost. Already Alexis's pregnancy was putting her at risk. If the worst should happen and Bree's experience be repeated, he knew he wouldn't survive that again. He had to put away those feelings for good. He thought he had achieved that already but Alexis's steady and constant undermining of his stance with Ruby had undone that.

Her gentle ways, her care and support, all of it had left him wide-open to hurt all over again. He hadn't wanted to love her—hadn't even wanted to *want* her the way he did. Even now he felt the urge to race back to her room, to make sure she was okay, but he couldn't trust himself around her. Couldn't trust her.

He needed to pull himself together, to shore up his defenses all over again. Only this time he needed to make them impenetrable. Nothing and no one would get past them ever again.

Feeling stronger, more in control, Raoul dragged his cell phone from his pocket and thumbed through his contacts list. There it was, the number for Bree's obstetrician. He hit Dial before he could change his mind. For all that had happened to Bree, the guy was one of the best in the country and Alexis deserved that. And he himself needed to know exactly what they were dealing with.

A few minutes later, an appointment made—thanks to a cancellation—for in a couple of days' time, he shoved his phone back in his pocket. Until then he had to keep his mind busy and his heart firmly locked down back where it belonged, where nothing and no one could reach it.

"I don't see why you weren't prepared to let me wait until my appointment came through from the hospital," Alexis grumbled as he drove her to Christchurch two days later. "I've stopped bleeding anyway."

"Don't you want to know why you started bleeding in the first place?"

"Raoul, sometimes these things happen. There might not be a why, sometimes things simply *are*."

He shook his head, dissatisfied with her answer. "No, there's always a reason and always a solution. There has to be."

He heard Alexis sigh and out the corner of his eye he saw her turn her head and look out the side window.

"Are you feeling okay?" he asked, the same question he asked of her several times each day.

"I'm fine, a bit queasy but that's normal. Unless I'm driving I often get a bit of motion sickness."

"Do you want to drive?" he offered.

"No, it's okay, I'll be all right."

"Let me know if you need me to stop."

"Sure." She sighed again. "Do you think Ruby will be okay with Catherine? She was pretty upset when we left."

"She'll settle. Call Catherine if you're worried."

"No, I'm sure she'll settle, like you say."

They traveled the rest of the hour-and-a-quarter journey in silence. When they reached the specialist's rooms, Raoul parked the Range Rover, assailed again by the awful reminder that he'd been through this before. Maybe coming to the appointment with her wasn't such a great idea after all, he thought, his stomach tying in knots as they got out the car and he guided Alexis toward the building and through to reception.

Alexis gave her name to the receptionist and joined Raoul in the waiting room. He could feel her nervousness wash over him in waves. If theirs had been a normal relationship, he'd be holding her hand right now, infusing her with his strength and lending her his support. Instead, she perched on the chair next to him, as tightly wound as a bale of grapevine trellis wire.

"I'm okay, you can stop looking at me," she said through tightly clenched teeth. "I'm not about to break apart."

"That's good to know," he said, and leaned back into his chair, feigning nonchalance by picking up a discarded magazine off the chair next to him.

"Ms. Fabrini?" a man's voice called.

"That's me," she said, getting to her feet.

Raoul got to his feet as well and started to move forward with her.

"Hi, I'm Peter Taylor, nice to meet you," the doctor said to Alexis, extending his hand.

As he did so, he looked over her shoulder and spied Raoul standing there.

"Raoul, good to see you. How's Ruby doing?"

"She's growing and getting into everything."

The obstetrician looked from Alexis to Raoul.

Alexis spoke up in the awkward silence that sprang between them. "I'm Alexis, Ruby's nanny."

"I see. Well, would you like to come through with me? And Raoul?"

"No, just me," Alexis said firmly.

Raoul wanted to object, to shout he had every right to be there in that room with her, but he knew he had none. He'd made no commitment to Alexis and it was clear she didn't want him there, either. He lowered himself back down onto his chair, that sense of history repeating itself hitting him all over again.

So, he was to be kept in the dark, just like he'd been with Bree. With her, she'd managed to time her appointments for days when he'd be busy and unable to accompany her, except for when she had her scans. Thinking back on it now, she must have requested that all information about her aneurysm be kept from him because he knew now that they'd monitored it carefully throughout her pregnancy.

Waiting was hell. Not knowing what was going on was even worse. He couldn't just sit here. It was doing his head in. He went to the receptionist and told her to let Alexis know he'd be waiting outside for her, then turned and left the building.

It was cold and crisp today, the sun a distant beacon in a washed-out blue sky striated with wispy streaks of cirrus cloud. Raoul waited by his vehicle, and tried to tell himself he didn't care that Alexis had shut him out. He should embrace the fact, be glad she didn't want him to be a part of this. He could offer her nothing but a man broken by the past. A man now too afraid to trust. Look what had happened when he'd trusted her!

And if he kept telling himself these things, surely eventually he'd convince himself he believed them.

He uttered a sharp expletive under his breath and shoved his hands into his jacket pockets. Leaning against the side of the Range Rover he lifted his face to the sun and closed his eyes. If only he hadn't given in, if only he had kept his distance. If only she'd never come at all.

Life was full of "if onlys," so much so that a man could drive himself crazy worrying over them all. Things had been simpler before she came, there was no denying it. In this case, it came down to just a handful of questions. Could he go through this all again? Could he watch her grow full with child, *his* child, and wait again in fear for what might happen?

The answer was swift coming. No. He couldn't.

Yes, it was cowardly. Yes, it was stepping back from his obligations. But he'd been down this road already, and he wasn't strong enough to do this again. But, the question remained, could he let her go?

Fourteen

Alexis was in the kitchen making herself a cup of tea when she heard the front door open and close. Raoul was back. Her heart jumped in her chest and she wondered what he would say or do next. Since her consultation with the obstetrician they'd barely said more than two sentences to one another at a time.

She had yet to tell him everything about her examination—but she had good reasons for holding back. Raoul had withdrawn from her, wholly and completely. It wasn't just that she now slept alone back in the master suite, it was apparent in every way he interacted with her—or didn't interact, which was more to the point.

This pregnancy was a major step in her life, one she was willing to take on alone if necessary, and especially if she couldn't be certain that she had the wholehearted and loving support of a man at her side. Raoul, to be precise.

His heavy footsteps sounded in the hall and she felt the usual prickle of awareness between her shoulder blades that warned her he'd come into the kitchen and was staring at her. Slowly, she faced him.

"I'm going for a shower. Are you okay? Should you be up?"

He sounded like the Raoul Benoit she'd fallen in love with, yet different at the same time. She looked at his face, met the flat emptiness that now dwelled in his eyes. Her heart sank. Any hope she'd had of possibly turning him around on this situation between them sank right along with it.

"I'll be all right. As I've already told you, I'm just not supposed to do anything too strenuous. That's all."

He nodded. "Don't go lifting Ruby from her crib," he reminded her for the umpteenth time since Monday's race to the clinic. "I'll get her up when she wakes."

With that, he left her. He did that a lot lately. Made sure he was home around the times that Ruby went down for her sleeps and was back in time for when she roused. On the rare occasions he wasn't, she'd seen the censure in his eyes afterward when he returned to find she'd been lifting and carrying the baby, but she knew exactly what she was and wasn't capable of. Caring for Ruby was high on her to-do list, with all it entailed.

Behind her, the kettle switched itself off, the water boiled and ready to pour onto her tea bag, but still she didn't move. So, this was how it was going to be between them now. A cold politeness that ignored everything except the medical concerns involved in what was happening inside her body, the life they'd created together?

Part of her wanted to march on down the hallway behind him, to confront him, to force him to talk to her. Force him to acknowledge her and what they'd shared before he'd found out about her pregnancy—to find out if there had ever been more between them than just the convenient release of no-strings-attached sex. But that look in his eyes just now, it had chilled her. It had told her far more than words could ever say.

What they'd had, as little as it was—everything they'd shared when they'd shared each other—was over. Gone. Except for getting Ruby out of bed in the morning and putting her down for her sleeps, Raoul stayed well out of the way. The stresses and joys of pregnancy were entirely her own, with no one but herself to marvel over the life growing inside her—or worry over possible problems.

To her huge relief, all the signs of the threatened miscarriage had eased off, just as Dr. Taylor had said they should. Further, slightly obsessive reading on the subject told Alexis that a high percentage of women experienced what she had in their first trimester. Trying to convince herself what she'd been through was normal was easier said than done.

She felt fragile, adrift, and the massive chasm that had opened up between her and Raoul prevented her having anyone to share her fears with. This wasn't news she was ready to spring on her own family just yet—not when she still hoped against hope for Raoul's support, even for his love. Still, at least she had a visit from Catherine to look forward to today. When the older woman arrived, though, she clearly knew something was up.

As the two of them watched Ruby playing in the family room Catherine broached what was clearly bothering her.

"Alexis, did you know that Raoul has asked me to look for a new nanny for Ruby until I'm able to take her back full-time again?"

If the other woman had slapped her, Alexis couldn't have been more shocked.

"He wants me to leave?"

"He didn't say as much—well, not in as many words—but he requested that I make it clear in the advertising that it's a live-in position."

Alexis's head reeled. "He hasn't said anything to me. Not at all."

Catherine fidgeted in her chair. The corners of her mouth pulled into a small frown.

"He told me you were pregnant. Is it true?"

"Yes, it's true."

"How far along are you?"

"Nearly nine weeks now," Alexis answered with a small sigh.

"And you're okay?"

"Did he tell you about Monday? About taking me down to the clinic? And then to the obstetrician when we left Ruby with you on Wednesday morning?"

"No, but I guessed something had happened. He acted different again. Like he did after Bree died."

Catherine got up from her chair and joined Alexis on the couch. She put a comforting arm around her shoulders.

"Tell me," she commanded gently.

So Alexis did. She pushed aside her fears about how Catherine would react to what she had to say—after all, hadn't Alexis just been sleeping with Catherine's dead daughter's husband? It was a relief to off-load to someone, especially someone who had known her as long as Catherine had, someone who had been as much of a mother figure as her own had been. Catherine just listened, her arm tightening around Alexis from time to time, lending her more comfort, more silent strength.

When Alexis finished she realized her cheeks were wet. Catherine pressed a freshly laundered handkerchief into her hands.

"You poor dear," she said after Alexis had blown her nose and wiped her tears away. "You love him, don't you?"

Alexis nodded, then gathered the threads of her fraying thoughts together. "You—you're not mad at me?"

"Why would I be?" Catherine asked in astonishment.

"Because of Bree. Because it hasn't even been a year and here I was throwing myself at him."

Catherine laughed. "Oh, my dear girl. You? *Throw* yourself at Raoul? Hardly. Besides, he's not the kind of man a woman throws herself at without expecting to slide straight off that granite exterior of his." She patted Alexis on the leg. "Look, I love my son-in-law dearly and I know that he and Bree were ecstatically happy together when they weren't at complete loggerheads. We've all suffered for her loss. But I'm a realist. She *is* gone. As hard as that has been to bear we've all had to go on with living. Raoul…well, he's just been existing. When you came, something sparked to life in him again. You gave him something to fight against."

"Fight against? I don't understand."

"He'd shut himself down, put his feelings where no one could touch them. Not even Ruby. I still remember seeing him standing in the neonatal intensive-care unit, staring at her in her incubator. No emotion on his face, not even a flicker. I knew then that she would need help—they both would.

"Looking after Ruby helped me come to terms with losing Bree. It would have helped him, too, but with her being sick for that first month of her life, it only served to push him further away."

"I still can't understand how he did that," Alexis said, shaking her head.

She'd seen photos of Ruby in the NICU. They'd raised every protective instinct in her body. She'd wanted to reach right into the pictures and cuddle the precious baby back to health. How could Raoul not have felt the same way about his own daughter?

"He's a strong man with powerful emotions. Sometimes emotions like that can get to be too much, even for someone like Raoul," Catherine said. "Bree's father was like that, too. I'm sure she was drawn to that strength the same way I was with her father. But we had our troubles through the years, just as I know Bree had fights with Raoul, over the way that both men thought being strong meant shutting out anything that might make them vulnerable."

Ruby had stopped playing and had gotten to her feet and walked over to her grandmother who happily lifted her onto her lap.

"The sad thing is, he doesn't even realize what he's been missing out on. Or maybe he didn't, until you came along."

"Whatever good I might have done has been destroyed now," Alexis said ruefully.

"Maybe, maybe not. I think he needs a bit of time to come to terms with things."

"Well, if, as you say, he's looking for a new nanny, then my time is definitely running out."

Catherine gave Ruby a kiss and popped her back on the floor. "Don't give up, Alexis. If he's worth fighting for, then you have to fight."

She left soon after that, promising to call by again the next day. As Alexis and Ruby waved her off at the front door Alexis weighed Catherine's words in her mind. Could she do it? Could she fight for Raoul? Would he even let her?

* * *

He hated to admit it, but he missed being with Alexis. That said, he'd made up his mind. She had to go.

Obviously that left him with a problem. Catherine wasn't fit enough yet to take Ruby back on full-time so he had to find someone who would fill in for the short term.

In the meantime, he kept a surreptitious eye on Alexis. Watching like a hawk for telltale signs that she was overdoing things. He hated the thought of her leaving and yet he couldn't wait for her to be gone—for things to go back to the way they were before she arrived here. He tried to tell himself, over and over, that he'd be able to forget her, to put her from his heart and his mind. He only hoped it was true. He never even let himself think about the child—his child. *Their* child.

Raoul walked into the house and braced himself. Today he would tell her that she had to go as soon as he'd found a replacement. He wasn't looking forward to it. He went to his bathroom and turned on the shower, then stripped off his clothes and dived under the hot stinging spray. It had been cold out in the vineyard today where he'd begun cane pruning the vines. The work was slow but methodical and had unfortunately allowed him far too much time to think.

He closed his eyes and dropped his head to take the full brunt of the shower stream, blindly reaching for a bottle of shampoo. The instant he opened it he knew he'd taken the wrong one—his senses immediately filled with that fresh floral scent he always identified with Alexis. His body felt an unwelcome stirring of desire, his flesh growing semihard. He snapped the lid closed and threw the bottle to the bottom of the shower with a clatter.

She was everywhere. In his thoughts, in his dreams, in his bathroom. He finished his shower as quickly as possible. Determined to get facing her and telling her what he'd done over with as quickly and as painlessly as possible.

He could hear her in the kitchen with Ruby as he made his way down the hall and through the house. Could hear the love in her voice as she coaxed the little girl into eating her vegetables. It made something twist inside him, but he forged on.

"Hi," she said matter-of-factly as he entered the kitchen.

Ruby squealed her delight at seeing him, banging on her tray with a spoon. From the look of her, she'd been attempting to feed herself, and not very successfully if the mush all over her face and hair was anything to go by.

"I need to talk to you tonight. When's a good time?"

"What? You need to make an appointment to speak with me now?" Alexis's eyes looked bruised underneath, as if she was sleeping just as poorly as he was himself.

"I'd prefer to have your full attention. It's important," he said stiffly.

"If it's about hiring a new nanny, don't worry. Catherine already told me yesterday. So, have you found someone?"

She caught him on a back foot. "There have already been a few applicants."

"That's good," she replied, rinsing a muslin cloth at the kitchen sink and then coming over to wipe Ruby's face and hands before giving her a couple of slices of apple to occupy herself with. "I've been thinking, out of fairness to Ruby, it might be best if we have a two-week transitional period with both me and the new nanny here."

"You do?"

"It makes sense, don't you think? It wouldn't be good for the new nanny or Ruby if my leaving disrupted her too much. She's more aware of strangers now than she was when I arrived, less open to trust them."

"Right."

"Ruby's going to need you more, too."

"More?" God, he needed to stop with the monosyllabic replies.

"Of course, you'll be her touchstone. Her constant. She needs stability."

"She's going back to Catherine's soon."

"Yes, I know. Catherine said. Are you seriously going to do that? Send her back to her grandmother?"

"Of course. She can't stay here."

Alexis looked at him fair and square. "Why not?"

"Because it's not feasible, that's why not."

Saying the words caused a sharp hitch in his breathing. He'd mulled it over time and time again. As much as he was bonding with Ruby every day, he had to take a giant step back. It was the only way to stop the chance of being hurt.

"If she has a nanny, or even a rotation of nannies together with Catherine, I don't see why you have to turf her out of her home."

"I…"

The words he was going to say dried on his tongue. He'd been about to refute that it was Ruby's home but as he looked around him and saw the detritus that she spread about the place every day, he found he couldn't bring himself to utter the words. Nor could he honestly say he didn't want her here anymore. Sure, the idea of being solely responsible for her care still scared him witless, but for as long as she had a reliable nanny, or rotation of nannies as Alexis had suggested, then maybe it could work out.

He tried to think of what it would be like not to see

her cherubic face each morning or hear her chant "Dad-dad" as she did whenever she saw him. Even the mere thought of it made him feel empty, lost.

"Raoul?" Alexis prompted.

"I'll think about it. We'll have to see what the job applicants are like first."

She gave him a weak smile. "Well, that's progress, I guess."

Raoul continued to stand there, feeling at a loose end as she competently moved around the kitchen, putting the finishing touches to their evening meal and tending to Ruby.

"How are you doing…since Monday?" he asked awkwardly.

"Everything's settled down," she replied, keeping her back to him, but he saw her face reflected in the kitchen window and noticed how she hesitated over her task.

"When do you see the doctor again?"

"I had an appointment in four weeks' time but if I'm leaving then I think I'll see someone when I get home."

"I'll pay for your medical expenses, Alexis, and for the…baby, when it comes."

"I'll call you if I need help," she said, her words clipped.

"I mean it. I will stand up to my responsibilities toward him or her."

She made a sound somewhere between a laugh and a snort. "Except for the ones that really matter, right?"

He felt a flush of humiliation stain his cheeks. "I said it before, Alexis. You ask too much."

"Do I? When I, Ruby, everyone in your life, basically, is prepared to give you everything in return? Is it too much to ask you to love us, to care?"

His hands clenched into fists at his sides. He felt his

short fingernails biting into his palms and he relished the pain. It was the distraction he needed to remind himself not to reach out for her, to drag her to him and to show her exactly how much he felt for her. A fine tremor rippled through him.

"I've said what I wanted to say. Don't wait dinner for me. I'll eat later."

Alexis watched him leave the room. A view she seemed to have a whole lot of lately. She'd been an idiot to think she could win this tug of love with him. It had been destined for failure from the beginning. She deserved more than that, and so did he—so why on earth couldn't he see that? Why wouldn't he grab what he was offered with both hands and run with it?

It made her heart ache to think he'd chosen to remove himself from love, that he was so broken that he couldn't try again. No, it was more that he *wouldn't* try again. It was a conscious choice. She just couldn't understand why anyone would choose loneliness and solitude over love.

Over the next few days she watched as a handful of selected applicants arrived at the house for interviews with Raoul. Each time, he'd ask Alexis to bring Ruby in to the meetings to introduce her to her potential carer. Some introductions had gone okay, some not so much. When Raoul told her at the end of the week that he'd made a suitable appointment and that the woman would be starting the following Monday, Alexis's heart sank. Her time here now was limited. Soon, she'd have to leave and the very idea just broke her heart.

The only bright light in the darkness was planning Ruby's first birthday party next week. Catherine had suggested they hold the celebration at the play center since it was already designed to cater to a big group of small children and everyone who she would have been inviting went there anyway.

Raoul, though, was adamant he wouldn't go.

"No," he said emphatically when Alexis invited him.

"But it's Ruby's birthday," she implored.

"She won't know the difference."

Alexis rolled her eyes. "That's not the point."

"It's also the anniversary of Bree's death, have you stopped to think about that?"

"Of course I have," she argued back. It seemed they always ended up arguing these days and it was taking a toll. "But you can't punish Ruby for that for the rest of her life. Are you going to deny her a celebration every year because you lost Bree that day, too? Can't you grasp what you have for once, rejoice in it instead of holding on to what you've lost?"

"I said no. That's the end of it."

It was like talking to a brick wall. He'd distanced himself so effectively she had no idea of how to get through to him anymore.

The following two weeks passed in a blur. The new nanny, Jenny, was wonderfully competent. She'd just returned to the area after working for a family up in Wellington who had a job transfer to overseas. She hadn't wanted to go with them, preferring to stay in New Zealand, so the position with Ruby was perfect timing for her.

Alexis hadn't wanted to like the other woman and had, in what she recognized as a ridiculously petty way, resented how easily she'd taken over Ruby's care and how quickly Ruby seemed to bond with her. Each day Jenny took over more and more of Alexis's duties, and Catherine, too, agreed the other woman seemed to be working out really well.

With less time with Ruby herself, Alexis had more time to think about nursery preparations for when she got home, and even time to get back to her designs. She'd played a little with some sketches in the past couple of weeks, a few ideas for herself mostly, and her hands itched to see how the ideas would come to life in her preferred range of hand-dyed natural fabrics. She'd never imagined designing a maternity range of clothes before, especially not for the high-end fashion boutiques her work usually showcased in. Now she was getting excited about the idea.

Besides, she reminded herself, she'd need something to distract her once she left. This was going to be one of the hardest things she'd ever had to do. The second hardest was going to be telling her dad about her pregnancy. He'd be disappointed in her, she knew it, but the prospect of new life would help lift him from his grief and give them something they could look forward to together.

Alexis had toyed with the idea of phoning him with the news, or sending him an email, but she knew this was the kind of thing she'd have to tell him face-to-face. At least, she consoled herself, moving back to her father's home meant that she'd be nearer to Tamsyn, her half sister, and Tamsyn's husband, Finn, her father's business partner and the man who'd been like a big brother to her growing up. She could almost begin to tell herself she was looking forward to it.

"Wow, are those your sketches?" Jenny asked as she came into the kitchen where Alexis was working at the table. "You're good."

"Thanks. I'm thinking of expanding into maternity wear. These drawings are just ideas for now."

"So, you're a designer, not a nanny?"

"Both, really. I trained and worked as a nanny after

I finished school. The designing has come in the past few years and I spent most of the previous year, before I came here to help out Raoul, in Europe, traveling and looking for inspiration."

Help out Raoul. The words sounded so simple, so uncomplicated. Nothing at all like the tangled web of unhappiness and adversity it had turned into.

Jenny picked up one sheet and then another. "So is that why you're leaving? To get back to your work?"

Alexis looked up as Raoul entered the kitchen and helped himself to a coffee from the carafe on the warmer.

"We've imposed on her for long enough," Raoul said before she could say a word. "It's time she returned to her own life."

But this was the life she wanted. This life, with him, with Ruby. She could work from anywhere when it came to her designing, and goodness knew there was plenty of space here for her to establish a workroom. But he didn't want her, not like that, not as a partner, not as a piece of his heart. And that was where her dreams began and ended.

Clearly sensing the undercurrent that crackled between Raoul and Alexis, Jenny made a vague excuse about checking on some laundry and left, leaving the two of them staring at one another. Expelling a breath of frustration, Alexis gathered up her things and got up from the table.

"So have you warned the new girl off falling for the boss?" she said, determined to provoke Raoul in one way or another.

"Low blow, Alexis."

"I'm sorry. I shouldn't have insulted her like that. I'm sure Jenny has far more sense. She's very well trained, and she is good with Ruby."

"Yes, I think Ruby will be quite safe with her."

"Safe, Raoul? Safe? Is that all you can think about? What about loved? Don't you think that's equally as important in her life? Weren't you loved as a child, weren't your parents there for you every step of the way? Of course they were because that's what real parents are. They're the people who are always there for you—not the ones who just pass the buck on to someone else."

"That's rich, coming from a nanny. Without parents 'passing the buck' as you call it, nannies wouldn't even be needed."

She groaned, fed up to her back teeth with his bullheadedness. "At least every family I've worked for before has openly loved their children. Has included them in their lives when they haven't been tied to work."

"Enough!" He made a slashing movement with his hand as if he could just cut her off as effectively as he'd cut off his own feelings. "Stop pushing me, Alexis. Ruby has settled with Jenny, who has proven she's competent and knows what to do. Catherine is at hand if she needs any advice or help. You can leave today. I'll pay you through to the end of this month and you will hear from my lawyers regarding support for you and—"

"Today? You want me to leave today? But I still have another week."

Alexis sat down abruptly in one of the kitchen chairs, feeling as if all the breath had been knocked out of her. She looked at him, taking in his features and committing them to memory. The curl in his brown hair that had begun to grow overlong since she'd been here. The flecks of gold in his hazel eyes. The breadth of his shoulders and the lean strength of his body. All of it so achingly familiar, all of it so completely out of bounds. It was impossible to reconcile the lover who had filled her nights with pleasure with this cold shell of a man who stood before her, seemingly determined to never see her again.

"I don't need you anymore," Raoul said.

"And that's the trouble," she whispered. "You never did."

Fifteen

He didn't need her anymore. The words echoed round and round in her head as she pulled herself to her feet, gathered her drawings and staggered from the room. Alexis tried not to hear them when she returned to the master suite and began haphazardly throwing her clothing onto the bed as she picked the drawers of the tallboy clean. Tears streamed unchecked down her cheeks.

Alexis had thought the pain of saying goodbye to her mother had been hard enough, followed soon after by discovering Bree had gone, too. But this was something else entirely. This was raw and sharp and jagged and sliced at her insides with unrelenting strikes. He didn't need her, didn't want her, didn't love her. Each fact hurt as much as the other.

She went to the walk-in wardrobe to retrieve her case. As soon as she opened the door she felt a sense of Bree, as if she'd only stepped out for a minute and would be back any moment. The soft hint of her floral fragrance teased at Alexis's nostrils, reminding her of the kind of woman Bree had been. A woman so loved, so missed, that her husband wouldn't take a chance on love again. She couldn't compete with that. It was an impossible task. Her love simply hadn't been enough to bridge that breach.

"I failed, Bree," she said softly through her tears. "I thought I could do it, that with enough time, enough patience and enough love that I could bring him back, but I failed. I'm sorry, my friend. Sorry for everything, but especially sorry for letting my feelings for Raoul get between you and me."

In the distance she heard Ruby wake from her nap and Raoul's deep tones murmuring to her as he tended to the little girl.

"But he's doing more with Ruby, getting closer to her and learning how to be a father—at least I achieved that much, if nothing else."

Her voice cracked on the last words and she wheeled her case from the wardrobe and closed the door behind her. Closing it on so much more than a half-empty closet. Lifting the suitcase onto the bed, she shoved her things inside together with her toiletries, reaching every now and then for a tissue to wipe her face and blow her nose with.

She had to pull herself together, even if only long enough to say her goodbyes to Ruby. Whether Raoul would be there when she left was something else she'd have to face with her backbone straight and her shoulders squared. Part of her wanted to see him one last time, to draw this entire episode to a natural close, but there was another part of her that hoped he'd make himself scarce so she wouldn't have to face the pain of looking into his eyes and seeing nothing reflected back at her but relief that she was leaving.

Logically she knew they'd have to have some sort of ongoing contact, especially after the birth. He'd already made it clear he would financially support her. While that was probably the least she ought to be expecting from him, for her that was the lowest denominator in this complicated equation. She simply wanted him. All of him. Not just a no-strings lover.

She drew in a shuddering breath and then another until she felt as if she had herself under control. Taking a last look around the room, she pulled the suitcase off the bed and stood it up on its wheels. Could she do this? Could she really walk away from Raoul and Ruby and never look back?

Only time would tell.

Feeling as if her heart was breaking a little more with each step, she slung her handbag over her shoulder and, wheeling her suitcase behind her, left the room.

Jenny was in the hallway with Ruby in her arms. The instant Ruby saw Alexis she clamored to be let down and raced toward Alexis the instant her feet touched the ground. Alexis bent down and scooped the little girl in her arms, burying her face in Ruby's neck and inhaling that special, fresh, soft baby smell that was so precious. Three months, she'd cared for her, but it had only taken about three seconds to fall in love.

The pain in Alexis's chest sharpened as she whispered a goodbye to Ruby and handed her back to Jenny.

"Well, I'd better be off, then. If I've left anything behind, perhaps you could send it on to me? Catherine has my address."

"Don't worry, Raoul told me family matters have

drawn you away. Thanks for helping so much this past week. It's made taking over that much easier."

"I aim to please," Alexis answered with a bitter twist to her mouth. She looked around but couldn't see Raoul anywhere. "I thought I'd better say goodbye to Raoul, is he around?"

"Oh, he had to go down to the winery. Something about a truck coming to pick up some cases of wine, I think."

So, it was to be like that between them.

"I see," she said.

But she didn't see at all. Had their time together meant so little to him that he couldn't even give her the courtesy of a farewell face-to-face? She swallowed against the lump in her throat and grabbed at the handle of her suitcase.

"Well, I'd better be on my way, then. I've got quite a drive ahead of me."

She wasn't kidding. From Akaroa all the way to her home was going to take at least five and a half hours of solid driving. She only hoped she had the energy to cope with it.

Jenny followed her out to the car and helped her lift her case into the trunk.

"Thanks," Alexis managed through lips that felt numb.

In fact her whole body had taken on an emptiness that made her feel as if this wasn't really happening to her. It was better, at least, than the pain she'd felt a short while ago, she told herself. She slipped into the driver's seat and tried to summon a cheerful smile and a wave for Jenny and Ruby who stood on the driveway, waving goodbye.

Alexis drove on autopilot, the numbness that had mercifully invaded her body fading away as each kilometer flew under her tires. By the time she reached the outskirts of Christchurch she was crying again, great hiccupping sobs that made it impossible to see, let alone drive safely. She pulled over to the side of the road and grabbed her cell phone, calling the only person who had ever been there constantly for her all her life. The one person she'd been putting off calling.

"Daddy?" she said, through tears that threatened to close her throat. "I'm coming home."

"I'll bloody destroy him," Finn Gallagher growled malevolently. "No one treats my baby sister that way."

He and Tamsyn had met Lorenzo all set to drive down to Christchurch to collect Alexis. As he was so upset himself, they had worried that it wouldn't be safe for him to drive and had offered instead to fly to Christchurch to drive Alexis home themselves. Their timing meant they'd missed the only direct flight of the day but even with the detour to Wellington it was still faster than driving. Now they were ensconced in a hotel room having something to eat before they hit the road together.

"It's not all his fault, Finn. I went into it with my eyes wide-open," Alexis said as rationally as she could manage.

"Don't you dare condone his behavior. What he's done to you is unspeakably wrong," Finn replied, seething with suppressed fury.

"Finn, ask yourself this, how would you feel if it was you and Tamsyn, if she'd kept something from you that meant the difference between living the rest of your lives together or losing her forever? And then the next person you trusted also kept something from you?"

Tamsyn rose from where she'd been sitting and curved an arm around her husband's waist. "This isn't helping, Finn. Alexis needs our support, not your censure."

"I'm not angry at *her,*" he protested, but his wife's touch seemed to have a soothing effect on his temper. "I just can't stand to see Alexis hurt like this."

"I know," Tamsyn said gently. "Neither of us can. Our job is to be there for her as and when she needs us. She's a big girl and she's made her own choices."

"Yes, I have, and I'm strong enough to stand on my own two feet. Well, once I've got myself back together again, anyway," Alexis said ruefully, remembering only too well the wreck she'd been when Tamsyn and Finn had met her here in the hotel. "I'm so glad you came, thank you so much."

Her voice wobbled and her eyes filled with tears yet again. Instantly she felt the warmth of Tamsyn's arms close around her in a comforting hug.

"I'm s-sorry, I just can't seem to stop."

"Should we even travel tonight?" Finn asked. "Maybe it'd be better if we stayed the night and left in the morning."

"No, I want to go home. I need to."

"Sure you do," Tamsyn said, smoothing Alexis's hair from her face with a gentle hand. "And that's exactly what we'll do."

It was early evening when they finally got in Alexis's car to drive north. Exhausted, she lay down in the back and was soon asleep. By the time they arrived at her father's cottage it had been dark for hours. All the lights inside the cottage were blazing, their golden glow a flame of welcome. She sat up, rubbing at her bleary eyes, and was hit with a huge sense of relief when she saw her father's silhouette backlit by the veranda lights. Then, he was at her door and within seconds she was in his arms, listening to his voice murmuring endearments in his native Italian tongue.

Finally she was home, safe in her father's arms. As he led her into the house and to her bedroom, Tamsyn and Finn following with her suitcase, she wondered if Ruby would ever have the chance to feel that deep sense of security with Raoul.

Raoul flicked the collar of his jacket up and pulled his beanie down lower on his head. The weather had turned bitter cold. Or maybe it just seemed that way since Alexis had left four weeks, three days and two hours ago. He could count the minutes, too, but that had proven to be a fast track to Crazyville.

God, he missed her. It went beyond the physical. As much as he'd tried to ignore it and push her away, he missed what she'd come to mean to him. It had been difficult from the first to adjust to no longer sharing her bed after he found out about the pregnancy. He'd assumed that her permanent absence would make things more comfortable for him, ease the longing he felt for her touch. But the longing had become much worse, instead—now there was so much *more* of her to miss. Not just her body but her laugh, the sound of her voice. The warmth she brought to his life.

The house just didn't feel the same, didn't feel like a home. Ruby had become more irritable than she'd been under Alexis's care and he found himself watching over Jenny with the baby more and more often, hardly wanting to trust her with the child.

As a result, Ruby had begun to turn to him when he was in the house—complaining loudly if he didn't pay her the attention she obviously felt she was due. He felt the bond between him and his daughter growing stronger every day. And this time, he didn't try to fight it.

Somehow the little tyke had wrapped him right around

her little finger, and now she had a hold on his heart that terrified him and thrilled him in equal proportions. He found himself looking forward more and more to spending time with her each day, and to reading her bedtime stories at night—because one was never enough.

When she'd caught a cold from one of the other children at the play center, he'd been the one who'd sat up with her in a steam-filled bathroom at night as she'd coughed and spluttered herself back to sleep. He'd been the one to take her to the doctor every day until the doctor himself had told him—in the nicest way possible—that Ruby really, truly was going to be okay and to stop wasting their time.

He began to have a new appreciation for what Alexis had done in caring for her, and how she'd managed it all on her own. Realizing that had highlighted his own inadequacies as a father, and as a man. How he'd thought he could hide in his work and relegate his responsibilities to others—that it was enough to simply provide, but not to participate. How he'd made himself believe that if he stayed away, if he just threw enough money at a problem, that it would miraculously go away.

He'd been such a fool.

And that's what had led him here today, to Bree's final resting place. He laid the bunch of yellow roses, her favorite, at the base of her headstone and knelt beside her grave. The ground felt cold, so cold—as cold as his heart had been for far too long.

For quite a while he said nothing, remaining still, listening to the birds in the trees around him. He'd avoided coming here since the day they'd buried her. He'd told himself it didn't matter—that the Bree he'd known and loved had gone, she wasn't here anymore. But when he'd known he needed to talk to her, really talk, one last time, it had only been natural to do it here.

A cool wind worked its way around him, sliding under his collar and tickling around his ears. He shivered. He'd been compelled to come here—as if he couldn't move forward again until he'd done this. He took a deep breath and let it out slowly.

Any other time he'd have thought it verging on the ridiculous, needing to talk out loud to a headstone, but today nothing else had ever felt so right.

"Hi, Bree, it's me." He huffed a self-deprecatory laugh. As if it would be anyone else. "I know I should have been here more often, and probably brought Ruby, too, but I was so angry at you, Bree, so bloody mad I couldn't even think straight anymore."

Exasperation, fury, helplessness—they all flooded through him all over again. "What the hell were you thinking not telling me about the aneurysm? How could you have kept that from me? I wanted a family, but I wanted you more. Why couldn't you tell me about the risks?"

The cold air whipped around him more sharply and he pulled the collar of his jacket closed around his throat. He stayed like that for a while, not daring to speak for the emotion that built up inside him like a volcano about to blow. He closed his eyes and when he opened his mouth again, he talked instead about the first thing that came to mind. Ruby. Bit by bit, he felt the roiling emotions inside him begin to subside.

"Our daughter's beautiful, Bree. You would love her. She's just like you. From her hair to her eyes—all the way through to her ability to get her own way."

He felt a reluctant smile pull at his lips and he opened his eyes again. "Especially the latter," he added.

"I've let you both down, though. I've been so wrapped in my own anger at you, at the whole damn world, and in my fear of getting hurt again that I failed Ruby as a father. But you should know that she's fine. She's wonderful. Catherine's done a great job with her so far, and Alexis. Certainly a far better job than me.

"I felt so bad when Alexis arrived. She awakened something in me that I didn't want to feel again. That I'd *promised* myself I would never feel again." His voice trailed off as a thought occurred to him. "But you sent her to me, didn't you? And me, the fool that I am, I sent her away.

"She tried, Bree, she tried to break me out—to make me be myself again, to live my life again, but the anger and the fear held me back."

He dragged in another breath and let it go, noticing as he did so that his heart began to feel lighter. The darkness that had held him in its grip for so long was receding and with it came acceptance for Bree's decision. She'd been willing to risk everything for him and for the dreams they'd woven together, come what may. He'd thought he'd known love, understood it, but he'd known and understood nothing at all. Somewhere, he had to find the courage Bree had had. The courage to risk everything, to love absolutely, all over again.

"I'm sorry I never understood you well enough, Bree, and I'm sorry I've been so stupidly angry with you for all this time—especially because I let it rob so much of your love from me. Thank you for our daughter," he said roughly, bowing his head and closing his eyes. "Thank you for the all-too-few years you and I had together. I will always love you and you will always have a special piece of my heart."

He got to his feet again, his movements stiff, and

paused a moment to reflect on the woman his late wife had been before turning away from her grave and, he hoped, toward his future.

Sixteen

You're doing the right thing.

The memory of Catherine's words when he'd told her his plans was gently encouraging to Raoul as his car ate up the kilometers. Oh, of course he still had doubts. All he knew for sure was that he had to find out. There was something missing from his life. More particularly, someone. When he'd told Catherine he was going after Alexis, her first comment had been a simple "About time." But it was the hug she'd given him when he'd left Ruby with her this morning, on Jenny's day off, that had given him the most comfort. That and her words that he was doing what was right.

For so long he'd done the wrong thing, so long it had become habit, easier to slide into that than doing what he ought to have done all along. It didn't negate the seriousness of how he'd treated Alexis, or how he'd summarily dismissed her. He hadn't even had the courage to face her as she'd left, instead hiding in his work as he'd hidden from everything else this past year. Digging himself into things he could quantify and control, knowns versus unknowns.

But he was diving into the unknown now, in a headlong free fall. She was worth the risk.

As he left Christchurch and drove north, cruising through Kaiapoi and Rangiora and then further afield to Kaikoura he wondered what the hell he'd been thinking to send Alexis on this journey on her own. He hadn't been thinking, though, that was the problem. Certainly not about anyone but his selfish and self-centered self.

That was all going to change. If Alexis let him.

As he passed through Kaikoura he realized he had about an hour and a half to his destination. Logically he knew he should take a break but now that he was on the road, nearing Alexis with every revolution of his tires, he couldn't bring himself to stop.

He wondered how Ruby was doing. She'd been distraught when he'd left, almost moving him to tears over the way she'd kept reaching for him from her perch in Catherine's arms. He'd had to pull over after ten minutes on the road and call Catherine to make sure she was okay—which, of course, she was.

On the phone Catherine had assured him it was perfectly normal behavior for a one-year-old, in fact for any child who was attached to their parent, and that he should take heart from the fact that Ruby so obviously loved him. Even so, it had done little to alleviate the feelings of guilt he bore for putting his daughter through such a harrowing scene. It made him think about the things Alexis had said to him, about him needing to be a constant in Ruby's life. Well, she had that now, but he owed it to her to give her more. With any luck, after this journey, she'd have what she deserved. A father and a mother—and a brother or sister soon, too.

A weariness that can only come from long-distance driving pulled at his muscles as he drove slowly along the road Catherine had given him as Alexis's address. She'd warned him the driveway was hard to find and she hadn't been wrong; he was almost past the shrub-surrounded entrance before he realized it. Braking heavily, he turned off the road and into the driveway.

His heart began to hammer in his chest and nerves clutched at his stomach. Should he have called ahead? What if she refused to see him?

"A fine time to be thinking about this now," he said under his breath as he traveled up the lane and pulled to a halt outside a quaint turn-of-the-twentieth-century cottage. The skies opened as Raoul got out of the car, releasing a deluge of bone-chilling rain that forced him to run toward the wide covered veranda out front.

Even though he'd run, he was wet through when he got to the front door. He dragged a hand through his hair, skimming off the excess of water that threatened to drip in his eyes and down his face. He caught sight of his reflection in one of the front windows. Drowned rat. Not exactly the best foot to be putting forward when hoping to appeal to the woman you loved, he thought. Still, there was nothing else for it but to push forward.

He stepped up to the door and knocked. Inside, he heard steps coming toward him and he braced himself, both fearing seeing Alexis again and yet yearning for her so strongly that it was almost his undoing. His throat clogged with all the words he wanted to say but he was forced to swallow them back as the door swung open to reveal an older man with gray hair and the type of tan and deep lines on his face that spoke of a lifetime in the outdoors.

"What can I do for you?" the man asked in lightly accented English.

"I was wondering if Alexis was home," Raoul said awkwardly.

In all the ways he'd imagined this, he hadn't pictured seeing her father first. He felt about as nervous as he had as a teenager going to pick up his new girlfriend on their first date.

"I am her father, Lorenzo Fabrini," the man said, his dark eyes full of questions as they narrowed at him from under grizzled brows.

"Raoul Benoit," Raoul said, putting his hand out in greeting.

Alexis's father flatly ignored it and Raoul let his hand drop. His stomach clenched up another notch. This was not going well.

"So, now you come to see my daughter?"

"Mr. Fabrini, I apologize it's taken me this long, but yes. May I see her?"

The older man shook his head. "That is not up to me. If it were up to me you'd be back on the road and back to your miserable existence, where you belong."

He was right. Raoul's existence had been miserable—until Alexis had come along. And even then he'd been too trapped in his cycle of unhappiness to see how much better his life was with her in it.

"Please, sir, I beg of you. I know I was wrong, I know I hurt her badly—"

"Hurt her?" Anger flashed in Lorenzo's eyes. Eyes that reminded Raoul so much of Alexis. "You didn't just hurt her. You broke her. When she left here she was full of hope, full of purpose. When she returned she was empty, dead inside. Destroyed by you!"

He punctuated the air with his finger, making his point and with it, making Raoul awfully glad Lorenzo hadn't answered the door with a shotgun in his hand.

"I was wrong."

"Wrong! Pah! Wrong is denying your child your time and affection. Wrong is taking my daughter's love for you and belittling its worth. Wrong is using her for your own satisfaction and then sending her away when things got too hard. You call yourself a man?" Lorenzo muttered a curse in Italian. "I call you a worm. You're a disgrace."

"I know, you're not telling me anything I haven't learned already. I'm deeply ashamed of what I've done, of how I've hurt Alexis. Please, let me talk to her. Let me explain—"

"No, let me explain," Lorenzo interrupted, his finger once again pointing in Raoul's direction. "I am a humble man, a man who has worked hard all his life. I didn't finish school, I don't have all the fancy letters after my name that you all find so important these days. But I know what is important—that above all else, you honor life, you honor family, you honor love—and most of all, you honor the woman who brings them all into your life. You don't hide from her like a sniveling child."

"Sir, I respect how you feel, and I agree. I'm sorry for hurting her, truly sorry."

"Your apology is nothing to me and it is not my place to forgive you. It is Alexis you should apologize to."

"Please, then, let me see her. Let me talk to her."

"No."

Raoul felt his heart drop into his boots. "No? She won't see me?"

"No, she's not here—yet. If you are serious about making amends to my daughter you may wait here until she returns but you must promise me one thing."

"Anything, what is it?"

"That if she asks you to leave that you will go. Just go, and never bother her again."

The thought of never seeing Alexis again, never watching the way her face lit up when she was happy or never again seeing that fierce look of concentration in her eyes when she was working on her designs struck fear into Raoul. It was entirely possible that she would tell him to get lost. Hadn't he, essentially, done as much to her? Expected her to walk away, carrying his baby, and never look back? To be satisfied with some financial arrangement brokered by a pair of lawyers in separate parts of the country? If her state of mind was anything like her father's, she might tell him to do exactly that.

It was a risk he had to take.

"If that is what Alexis wants, then that is what I'll do."

Lorenzo nodded. "You may wait here," he said, gesturing to the sagging rattan chairs on the porch. "I will not have you here in our home, until I know she welcomes you also."

Without waiting for a response, Lorenzo closed the door in Raoul's face. It was no less than he deserved, Raoul thought as he lowered himself into one of the chairs. Despite being sheltered against the front of the house, the cushions still felt damp. Combined with his already cold, wet clothing, it proved to be an uncomfortable wait ahead. He didn't care. He'd do whatever it took to have his chance again with Alexis. And this time, if she was willing, he wouldn't mess up again.

Alexis drove carefully on the rain-slicked roads. At nearly sixteen weeks pregnant she was already finding it was getting uncomfortable to spend long periods in her car. Her tummy jiggled a little as a tiny occupant moved within her. She smiled. As exhausted as she felt after today's journey and meetings, those little movements still made her feel as if she was the luckiest woman in the world. Well, almost the luckiest.

She had a father who loved her and stood by her, no matter what. She had a half sister and foster brother who had pledged to support her in any way they could. She had new life growing inside her—a fact that never ceased to awe and amaze her. Her business was picking up again and, in reality, she lacked for nothing. Nothing except the love of the man she'd lost her heart to. Still, she consoled herself as she approached the driveway to her father's house, she had more than many others. Far, far more.

Through the rain, she caught a glimpse of the rear end of a vehicle standing near the front of the house. She was surprised to see her father had a visitor. He hadn't mentioned anything about expecting anyone when she'd phoned him to say she was on the road and heading home. As she drew nearer to the vehicle, though, recognition poured through her. The big black Range Rover was painfully familiar, especially with its VINTNR registration plate.

Her belly fluttered and she rested a hand on the movement. "It's okay," she murmured. "Looks like your daddy has come to pay a visit."

She gathered up her things and her collapsible umbrella and prepared to get out of the car. Before she could, however, her driver's door swung open and there he was. Alexis froze in her seat, halfway through the action of starting to put her umbrella up, torn between leaping from the car to demand an explanation for why he was there, and wanting to pull the car door closed and take a few extra minutes for herself.

"Let me take that," Raoul said, not bothering with the niceties of "hello" or "how are you."

He reached for her umbrella and held it above the driver's door, then extended a hand to help her out. She really had to get something a little less low-slung, she told herself as she was forced to accept his help to get out from behind the wheel. It wasn't as if her sedan was supersporty or anything but by the time she was full-term, getting out of here would require a crane.

"Thank you. How convenient that you were here. Just passing by, were you?" she asked as he shut the door behind her.

Her attempt at flippancy fell about as flat as her hair in this weather.

"No, I've been waiting for you," he answered as they half walked, half ran to the veranda where Raoul shook out the umbrella.

Standing in the shelter, her eyes drank in the sight of him. He was just as beautiful to her as he'd ever been and her heart did a little flip-flop of recognition. She ruthlessly quashed it. She'd had plenty of time to think in the past month and while she was inwardly overjoyed to see Raoul here, she was determined to hold firm to her decision to move forward with her life, without him. She wouldn't settle for half measures in anything anymore, especially now when there was not only herself to consider.

It didn't stop her concern when she saw him shiver and realized that he was soaking wet.

"Come inside," she said brusquely. "You need to get dried off."

"Thank you."

There was a strange note to his voice and she looked at him sharply, noting his attention was now very firmly on the bulge of her tummy.

"Have you been here long?" she asked as she wrestled her things to find her front door key.

"About an hour," he answered.

"Outside? You're soaking wet and must be freezing cold. Is my father not home?"

"Oh, yeah, he's home," Raoul said with a rueful smile.

"Oh," she said, suddenly flustered.

If he'd already talked to her father she had no doubt that there'd been more than a few terse words exchanged. Finally, thank goodness, she found her key and inserted it in the door.

"Hello? Dad? I'm home," she called as she pushed the door open and gestured for Raoul to follow her inside.

"So, you're letting him in?" her father asked as he came through from the kitchen into the sitting room of the compact cottage.

"He's traveled a long way, Dad, and it's pouring rain outside."

"I will give you your privacy," he said stiffly, his dark eyes fixed on Raoul as if in challenge. "But I will just be up the hill with Finn and Tamsyn. You will call me if you need me, yes?"

"Sure I will," Alexis answered, and crossed the room to give her father a hug. "Thank you," she whispered.

"Ti amo," he said, holding her close before releasing her. Then, with another silent glare at Raoul, he shrugged on a coat and stomped out the front door.

Silence grew uncomfortably around them. Finally, realizing she had to say or do something, Alexis put her things down on the coffee table between them.

"I'll get you something to dry off with."

"Thanks."

She was back in seconds, handing a towel to Raoul and stood there watching him as he toweled excess moisture off his hair. His shirt, however, was soaked through.

"You can't stay in that," she said. "Would you like a shirt of Dad's?"

"No, I'll be fine, I'll dry out soon. Besides, I don't think he'd—"

"Don't be silly, you'll catch your death that way. At least take your shirt off and let me put it through the dryer."

Raoul stepped up closer to her and took her by the hands. "Alexis, stop trying to find reasons not to talk to me."

"Is that what I'm doing?" she said, looking up into his hazel eyes and wondering exactly what it was that she read there.

Even now, after the way he'd summarily dismissed her, her pulse betrayed her by leaping at his touch. Some things, it seemed, would never change.

"Yes. Please, sit down. Let's talk."

"Sure, do you want a tea or coffee?"

"Sit," he commanded gently, and guided her to the sofa and sat down beside her. "I owe you an explanation and an apology."

Alexis fidgeted on the chair, unsure of what he expected of her. Did he think that just because he was about to say sorry that she'd forgive him everything? He was in for a sad surprise if that was the case.

"Go on," she urged him. "I'm listening."

She forced herself to calm down and pushed back into the seat, absently rubbing her belly. Raoul's eyes tracked from her face down to where her hand moved in slow, gentle circles.

"You're looking well," he said.

"You came here to tell me that?" she asked, her tone bordering on acerbic.

"No, what I came here to say is I am deeply sorry for the way I treated you. You deserved more."

"Raoul, I made my own choice when I accepted less," she pointed out.

"I know, but you, of all people—with your loving heart and your giving nature—you should never have been asked to settle for so little. I knew that and I took what you were prepared to give without thinking about the damage it might do. All I was concerned about was me. I just wanted… Hell, I don't even know what I really wanted. All I knew was that you offered me a light in the darkness, warmth in the cold. You made me feel again, but then I felt too much. I didn't know what to do, so I ended up pushing you away.

"I didn't want to be vulnerable again. When Bree died it hurt so much. It left me feeling so empty inside that every breath was agony. The idea of loving anyone again scared me into telling myself I *couldn't* love again—that I didn't deserve to."

"Everyone deserves love," Alexis said softly.

"I know that now." He drew in a shuddering breath. "For so long I was angry—felt so helpless. I hated having choice taken from me the way Bree did when she didn't tell me about her aneurysm. I'll never know whether, knowing the risks, she believed she'd get through Ruby's birth okay or whether she had some kind of premonition that she'd die and thought it would be worth it regardless, but either way she made choices that should have involved me and instead she shut me out. Doing that went against everything we'd promised one another, and if I couldn't trust her anymore, how could I trust anyone?"

Raoul leaned forward, his elbows on his knees and lifted one hand to his face, rubbing at his eyes.

"When Ruby was born I was too afraid to let myself love her. At first she was so ill that the doctors said her survival was touch and go, especially in the first few days. Even after she battled past that, I wouldn't let myself feel anything for her. She was so vulnerable, so dependent. I knew nothing about babies, nothing about being a father. We were supposed to have done all that together, Bree and me. The very idea of taking Ruby home and caring for her, alone, made me sick with fear."

"You would have had Catherine, your friends, your extended family," Alexis reminded him.

"I know that now, but I couldn't think rationally then. And there was something else, too." He made a sound of disgust. "I resented her. Can you believe it? I resented my tiny newborn daughter because her mother had chosen Ruby's life over her own. Rather than see her birth as a gift, I saw it only as a burden. So, instead of stepping up to my responsibilities I ignored them. I let Catherine take over Ruby's care, telling myself it was okay because I was grieving. But then it became easier to simply let things keep on going the way they always had. The more distance I had from Ruby, the closer she grew to her grandmother, the less I needed to worry that I might have to assume my obligations toward her as her father, any opportunities to fail her, hurt her or lose her."

"Ruby's lucky to have Catherine in her life," Alexis said, not minimizing in any way Raoul's desertion of his daughter. "She could have done worse."

"Yeah, she could have been forced to spend all of her first nine months with a father who saw her as a constant reminder of his failures as a husband and as a father. Every minute I spent with her, and Catherine would insist on bringing her around from time to time, she just forced me to remember that my big dreams for a family had taken her mother from us both. That, ultimately, I was responsible for everything that happened."

Alexis shook her head. "You're taking rather a lot on yourself. You weren't the only one involved here."

"It seemed like it at the time. Unreasonable, I know. Self-centered, definitely. I put myself in a loop where every day would be the same with work as my panacea, my catharsis. Even so, until you arrived, I was just going through the motions. Living only half a life."

"Until I arrived?"

"You made me remember what happened the first time I saw you, the way you made me feel. For months I'd imprisoned anything remotely like sensation. I thought I'd finally purged that from my existence, and then, there you were. A golden light just pulsing with warmth. And you wouldn't take no for an answer."

Alexis frowned, remembering their meeting when she arrived at the winery. "The first time you saw me…you mean back in April?"

"No, I mean the very first time. There were sparks between us the day that we met, when Bree introduced us. I know you felt them, too. It's why you pulled away from Bree, wasn't it?"

"Yes," she whispered.

Alexis closed her eyes in shame. He'd seen the way she'd felt about him even then? Did that mean Bree had seen it, too?

"I loved my wife, but for some reason I couldn't help but be attracted to you, too. When you came back, that all came rushing back with you. It left me not only hating that you'd roused emotions from deep inside of me again but also hating myself for what I saw as a betrayal of Bree."

His voice cracked on his words, making Alexis's heart squeeze in empathy. She searched in vain for the right words to say. Raoul turned to her, his face a tortured mask of pain.

"But I betrayed you, too. I betrayed your trust, your faith in me that I could be a better man and I betrayed your love. I'm so sorry, Alexis. More sorry than you could ever understand. You offered me a gift, a lifeline, and I threw it back in your face. I can see why you hesitated to tell me about our baby, but at the time I only saw it as history repeating itself, with you keeping a secret from me that involved me at its basest level."

"I would have told you, in my own time," she hastened to assure him.

"And, I'm ashamed to admit, I probably wouldn't have reacted any differently. I've been an absolute fool. I tried to ignore what you mean to me and I drove you away. Can you ever forgive me for that? Could you ever begin to want to give us another chance?"

Alexis drew in a deep breath. Could she?

"Raoul, you really hurt me. Making me leave you, leave Ruby—I…I don't know if I could put myself through that again. I could barely function for days afterward. I couldn't even drive any further than Christchurch the day you sent me away. I had to have help to get home. The first week I was back here I was like a zombie, barely functioning, barely speaking. It frightened the people who love me and it terrified me.

"I've only just started to put myself back together. To plan for the future. I know you said you'd always provide support for me before and after this pregnancy but I need to stand on my own two feet, too. There've been times recently when I needed to talk to you, needed to share something with you that's vitally important, but I've been too afraid because I couldn't be certain what your reaction would be. Will you hurt me again? Reject me? Reject what it is that I have to tell you?" She shook her head. "I just don't know and I don't know if I can trust you to be there."

Raoul felt his whole body quake at her words. All his old fears threatened to choke him. His throat seized and he couldn't find words to push past the obstruction. What was she saying? Was there some problem, some abnormality with the baby? Or with her—was she all right? Was the pregnancy putting her at risk, as it had with Bree? If she didn't tell him, how could he move heaven and earth to make things right for her? How could he keep her, and their baby, safe? Was he doomed to failure yet again?

Blood pounded in his ears and he fought to clear his mind from the daze of dread that had so quickly risen to consume him. He could do this. He was being given another chance, which was more than most people had in their lifetimes. He had to prove to Alexis he could be that man she needed, the man he believed that deep down, at the core of his heart, he still really was.

"I'm sorry I made you feel that way," he said, his voice sounding strained. "I want you to trust me. I want you to know you need never hide anything from me, ever again. I love you, Alexis, so much that it hurts to know that I've damaged what we started to have together, that I've risked your love and the right to be in your life and by your side. I will do whatever it takes, for as long as it takes, to be worthy of you. Please, give me another chance. Let me love you like you deserve to be loved.

Let me show you how much you mean to me, how much our baby means to me."

"Babies," Alexis said quietly.

His breath caught in his throat. Had he heard her right?

"Two of them, to be exact," she continued, her eyes watching him carefully, almost as if she expected him to get to his feet and run to the door and keep running.

He had to admit, she'd floored him. Panic threatened to overwhelm him. Pregnancy in itself carried risk, ergo a multiple pregnancy had to carry more. Could he do this? He reached beyond the panic and the shock at her words and let the idea play around in his mind.

Twins.

His heart swelled with hope and he reached for her hands, his own brushing against her swollen belly as he did so. His babies. A rush of pride and anticipation built up inside and he felt a smile spread widely across his face.

"Two of them," he repeated. "My God, are you okay? I thought you looked bigger than I'd expected but, wow, twins?"

"I'm doing fine. *We're* doing fine," she amended.

"How long have you known?"

"Since that first appointment with Dr. Taylor. His equipment was more accurate than that at the clinic."

He was stricken with remorse. He'd made her life so difficult, made the situation between them so uncomfortable that she hadn't felt able to reveal that news to him. News like that should have been a delight to be shared, not a burden to be borne alone.

"Alexis," he said, moving closer to her and drawing her into his arms. "I will spend the rest of my life making up to you and our children for what I've done if you'll only let me be a part of your future, yours and our babies'. You've taught me so much—how to be a real father to Ruby but most important, how to love again, to love you and Ruby *and* our unborn children. I owe you everything."

"You owe me nothing but your love, Raoul. I deserve that at the very least. Unencumbered and whole. Can you do that?"

Alexis drew back, searching his face for something he only hoped she could see.

"It's yours. Everything I am, everything I'm yet to be."

She didn't answer him immediately. Instead, she regarded him carefully for a few minutes. Time stretched out interminably.

"I'm not just answering for myself," she said eventually. "I'm answering for these children, too. They deserve unconditional love, no matter what happens now or in the future. I've loved you a long time, Raoul, at first from afar and then close up. I won't lie to you. All along it's hurt like hell and I'm only just beginning to recover. I'd all but come to terms with the fact that you would never be mine to love the way I wanted to love you. If I commit to you, I'm committing on behalf of the babies, as well. I need to be able to trust you, for all our sakes."

"I'm only human, I can't promise that I'll never let you down again someday in the future, Alexis. But I am prepared to pledge the rest of my days to being the best man I can be, the best husband, the best father."

"Husband?"

"I want to commit to you, Alexis. I want to wake up with you beside me every day for the rest of my life. I want to fight with you, I want to make up with you. I want to spend every minute of every day making sure you know I love you with everything I am and everything you've made me see I can be." He slid off the sofa and onto one knee in front of her. "Will you be my wife?

Will you come back to me, marry me and help me raise Ruby and our children together?"

"Oh, Raoul. I want that with all my heart. Yes. Yes, I will marry you and fight with you and make up with you and all those things. You're all I ever wanted from the first time I saw you. I never believed, in my wildest dreams, that we would have a chance together and I'm not going to let that go now. I love you, Raoul, so very, very much."

She slid down to her knees in front of him and wrapped her arms around him. As they drew close he was filled with unspeakable joy, as if things were right again in his world for the first time in a very long time.

"You won't regret it, Alexis. I promise. I will be a good and loving husband and father for as long as you'll have me."

"Forever will never be long enough," she whispered, lifting her face for his kiss and, as his lips touched hers, he knew she was right.

* * * * *

CHAPTER ONE

'AFTER WE VISIT THE DUCKS, there's got to be more knocking on doors for you and me, Ella. I know you'd probably rather be crawling around the furniture at home, but this is how it has to be for this morning.' Jessica Baker spoke the words to her daughter as she pushed the baby stroller over a rough patch of grass and let her glance rove around Randurra's memorial park.

Not that Ella could understand, but it made Jess feel better to speak out loud, to remind herself she did have a plan.

Ahead on the wide knoll beside the duck pond children were playing. A tall, dark-haired man watched them from beneath a gum tree. He was talking on his mobile phone.

Life went on whether people were trying not to shake in their boots or not. Jess didn't want to be someone who shook in her boots. She might wobble just a little here and there, but Jess was a single mother supporting her daughter. She couldn't afford to shake.

Any more than you can afford that enormous back bill of overdue rates and interest payable on the house.

Ten years' worth that Jess hadn't known existed, thanks to Ella's con artist father and the agreement he had made when he purchased Jess's small cottage, in exchange for Jess signing herself and Ella out of his life for ever.

Jess stiffened her spine and took one hand off the stroller to smooth it over her gold sleeveless top and down over the splash-dyed orange and black skirt. 'We'll be right, Ella. We'll sort this out somehow.'

In the stroller, Jess's daughter made a crowing noise. 'Du! Du!'

'Yes, indeed. We're going to see the ducks. You've earned that for being such a good girl this morning.'

Ella's vocabulary had a lot of 'Du' words in it, but in this case Jess was quite certain that her one-year-old knew exactly what she was talking about. Ella wanted to see the ducks before Jess finished her door-knocking and went home.

Jess's gaze moved ahead to the children. Two teen-aged boys wrestled each other on the grassy bank. A studious-looking girl of around ten had hold of a smaller girl's hand and was warning her not to go too close to the water. A third little girl had plonked down on the grass to pick blades of it. As a potential offering for the ducks?

'Let's go add our bread crusts to the offering, Ella.' Jess wasn't afraid of bunches of children. She looked after five regularly to bring in income. She'd had four more but that family had left Randurra at the start of December.

Jess had been trying since then to get more work. She was a qualified daycare mum. This morning when her financial situation had shifted from 'already un-comfortable' to 'downright scary' with the arrival of that notice about the overdue rates and interest, Jess had taken her efforts directly to the people of Randurra. She'd knocked on a lot of doors. She'd offered to do anything. It didn't have to be childcare so long as she could keep Ella with her.

Breathe, Jessica.

Jess and Ella were drawing closer to the duck pond area. The man had his gaze fixed on the children in that way that said 'father'. Were they tourists going somewhere for the long school summer holidays and had stopped here for a breather?

Jess's heart did a funny flip as the man turned his head and she caught a good look at his face. He appeared to be around thirty-six or thirty-seven. He was tall, with tanned skin and a firm jaw and thick, wavy, dark brown hair that just touched the collar of his white polo shirt. He had jeans on. Tan lace-ups on his feet. It was a warm day, but not killer hot as it had been in the few days straight after Christmas. Jess wanted to see his eyes.

No, she didn't.

All those children meant he must be married.

Jess wasn't looking for a man anyway. After the fiasco of Peter, Jess couldn't trust in that sort of relationship any more.

'No. You're a key client and the financials have been under my care for a long time. I want to be the one to do this work.' The man's voice was low, deep and utterly calm as he spoke into the phone.

But his posture had stiffened and as Jess drew closer she caught a glimpse of very genuine stress as his gaze roved over those five children before he asked for a little time to 'get things in place', and abruptly ended the call. In that one moment, he looked as Jess had felt this morning when she read the notice saying the house would be sold up if she didn't pay all the costs in thirty days or less.

The man looked out of his depth.

As though he was asking how he could fix this.

What had happened? Jess wondered.

She watched the man suck it all inside, paste on his previous expression and just stand there. But inside, his mind was racing, searching for those answers. Jess knew because Jess had done this.

'Can I help you somehow?' She spoke the words before she could stop herself, and made a gesture with her hand. The row of wooden bangles on her arm clanked. 'It's just that you were on the phone and you looked...'

She didn't want to say he'd looked panicked. Truly he looked far too strong to give in to outright panic.

Strong and appealing and manly.

All entirely irrelevant, Jessica Baker, and you're just as strong.

Occasional very justified bouts of the wobbles notwithstanding!

Jess cleared her throat. 'I'm a local. Did you need directions, or information about services or anything?' She might sound like an animated travel brochure now, but that was better than noticing the man as, well, *as a man.*

'Uh, hello. Thanks...' Deep hazel eyes fringed with thick black lashes searched her face, and then dropped to Ella where she sat in the stroller crowing in delight to see so many children playing near her.

He had beautiful eyes. Eyes that showed his age and maturity, and that made Jess's breath catch.

Did his eyes hold a hint of consciousness within them, too? Jess was twenty-two, a lot younger. She'd never noticed a man this age quite so much. She didn't really understand her reaction and…she wondered if she was correctly reading his.

He seemed to give himself a mental shake before he responded. 'That's kind of you. We just moved here so I don't have a good grip on everything about Randurra yet.' He extended his hand. 'Dan Frazier.'

Well, that was all about business so maybe Jess *had* imagined the other.

'Jess Baker. Jessica, really, but I prefer Jess. I moved here about fourteen months ago.' Just in time to settle into the cottage before she made the short trip to the local hospital to give birth to Ella. 'So I know pretty much everything there is to know about the town.'

She tried not to stutter over the words, because the touch of Dan's fingers closing around hers gave her the strangest feeling of…comfort. And made her too aware of him. She took a deep breath and lifted her hand to check that the green band in her hair was straight, its enormous bow sitting firmly. Did Dan Frazier think she was an airhead because of that bow? Jess wasn't. The clothing and accessories were part of keeping her head up, of showing her determination in her own way.

Life had thrown a major curve ball today, but she hadn't let that stomp her. She'd put on her bright clothes and had marched to the town council building. She'd done her best to calmly and rationally discuss the situation with that nasty man who'd delivered the overdue notice, Lang Fielder. It had been to no avail today but she wouldn't stop at one go!

And then she'd knocked on half the doors in Randurra,

looking for work. Jess still had the other half to knock on. She wasn't stomped yet.

'Da-a-ad.' A girlish voice came their way. 'Rob and Luke are going to fall into the water.'

'Are not.' A voice halfway to his father's deepness replied. 'We're just playing, Daisy.'

'Well, stop it. Don't you know there'll be approximately fifty thousand different kinds of germs in that pond?' The girl called Daisy pushed a pair of glasses up her nose in a knowing and disapproving way.

Jess stifled a smile.

'Maybe you can point me in the direction of childcare facilities in Randurra, if anywhere exists here that caters for a family group with this age range.' Dan's hand reached down to touch the silky hair of the youngest child, who'd come running to wrap her arms around his legs.

He met Jess's gaze again as he pushed his mobile phone into the breast pocket of his polo shirt. 'I thought I'd have time to check out various childminding possibilities. I didn't expect to need this kind of care more than rarely, anyway, but it appears the Frazier family's two-days-old sea change just ran into a typhoon.'

Randurra wasn't on the coast, of course. It was inland from Sydney. Apparently that phone call had produced a metaphoric typhoon that meant Dan Frazier needed urgent childcare for the whole family.

Could Jess be so lucky? 'I may be able to help you. What exactly do you need?'

'Oh, I don't need much.' He gave one short bark of laughter. 'Just the equivalent of Mary Poppins to fly down with her umbrella and volunteer to mind all my children while I travel to and from Sydney for the next few weeks, and for me to know they'll all be safe with her when she's a total stranger and I don't like leaving them with anyone.'

He frowned again. 'My sister used to cover the times when I had to work away from home, but I weaned right off needing that, and she's got her own life to focus on now.'

There was no mother in the picture? Was Dan a widower? Jess's mind boggled at the thought of him raising five children by himself. Peter hadn't even been prepared to be a part-time father to Ella from long distance.

Some other part of Jess that really should know better also insisted on pointing out Dan's single status.

A single status and almost twice your age, Jess!

'So you moved here, you didn't need childminding, and now something's exploded?' Better to ask about that. 'Is it to do with your work? Did it make a very big splat as it hit the wall?'

'That's a creative analogy.' He didn't smile, exactly, but the creases at the corners of his eyes did.

Dan went on. 'One of my clients needs to go through a potential change of ownership audit, and the prospective buyers want it done fast. I'm the company's accountant so I have to be on hand to help answer all the number-crunching questions, and supply the necessary information and explanations to go with it. This is a large key client for me, and they want this change of ownership. It's going to benefit the company tremendously and I need to hold on to their business, so I can't afford not to help.'

His gaze shifted over her hair and returned to her eyes. 'I moved the children here to get us all out of Sydney, into a decent-sized home that we could own ourselves. I thought I'd have all of January without having to think about work at all.'

'You can't blame yourself for the unforeseen.' She touched his arm briefly.

She only meant to express understanding and perhaps a little of the compassion that Mary Poppins might have extended when she finished folding her umbrella.

But it didn't end up feeling like only a touch. Dan's skin was warm and…manly. A tingle shot up Jess's arm.

Beneath her fingers, Dan's muscles locked as though he, too, had perhaps been startled by the contact. For a moment their gazes meshed and a consciousness passed between them.

Jess hadn't expected to feel such a strong connection. They had only just met. He was heaps older. She wasn't going there again with any man after the way Peter had hurt her. She withdrew her hand.

Over by the pond, one young Frazier after another fell still and silent.

Four sets of hazel eyes locked onto Jess, and baby Ella, and their father.

One whisper drifted to Jess on the summer breeze. 'Daddy's talking to a *girl*.'

Another. 'They're practically holding hands. He hasn't been near a girl since Mummy died.'

'Shut up, Rob. Shut up, Mary.' This came from the eldest boy. 'Whoever that is, Dad's not interested like that!' The boy sent a sharp stare Jess's way before he turned away, shoulders tensed beneath his T-shirt.

Jess felt put in her place, a woman far younger than this man and, indeed, why would Dan be interested?

You don't want *him to be interested, Jess.*

And perhaps the boy hadn't meant to sound so aggressive? He was probably used to dealing with all his younger siblings and occasionally got frustrated with them…

Had Dan heard those whispers? How long ago had he lost his wife? Had Jess misread his reaction when she touched him?

Had he wished she *hadn't* touched him? Or reacted… as Jess had reacted to him?

'Sorry about them. They're a little excitable thanks to the move.' Dan's neck had reddened slightly.

So he had heard. At least some of it.

'No need to apologise.' She ignored the neck. Well, other than the tanned, muscled appeal of it. Jess had to ignore that, too. Because widowed didn't necessarily mean emotionally available, even if the red was a result of consciousness of her, not simply embarrassment thanks to his children.

Not that it mattered to Jess one way or another, of course. Jess was very much *not* ready to jump into that particular pond again herself. She really needed this work and couldn't afford to let anything so foolish as a sudden attraction mess it up, if she could actually get Dan Frazier to employ her.

She *had* knocked on half Randurra's doors. She'd got nowhere. She had tried not to worry that she might get nowhere with the other half. Folks all seemed to have their childcare and other needs sorted out.

And perhaps Jess and Dan Frazier *could* help each other. 'Dan, I realise we've only just met and I haven't flown down with an umbrella like Mary Poppins. Actually, my brolly's black with pink polka dots and half the spokes are bent out of shape because I got it jammed under the seat of the car one day.' Jess drew a breath.

'But I'm a qualified, practising daycare mum.' An underemployed one at the moment. 'I care primarily for younger children but I am trained to take school-aged children as well.' If those opportunities came along. Jess spared a thought for the surly expression of Dan Frazier's eldest a moment ago, but if there were any problems she could win him over, surely? 'There aren't any official "Before and After School" style of care facilities in Randurra for school-aged children.'

Jess didn't want to tell Dan any more. She wanted to stick with 'I think I can help you', be Mary Poppins for him, Jess style, and they'd both benefit.

Instead, she drew a breath. 'There are two women older than me with grown-up children of their own who've recently become unemployed because the meatworks outside of town downsized. They haven't been in childcare professionally before but they're great women. I'm looking for more work, but I saw from the noticeboard at the supermarket that they're both looking for work in that line, too, or a combination of that and housekeeping. So you've got some choice and I too would be happy to help out with housekeeping duties.'

'If you have training with children... Are you saying you're available?' Dan's gaze seemed to travel over each feature on her face.

When his gaze rested briefly on her mouth, her lips wanted to soften. Instead, she forced a bright smile. He was probably just thinking she was way too young for the job. 'What exactly is it that you need for your children, Dan?'

He seemed to drag his gaze from her mouth and his brows drew together.

Dan Frazier *was* a little attracted to her. And from that look, he didn't want to be.

Well, there you were. Jess didn't want that, either. They were on the same page, even if she didn't know *his* reasons for that fact.

He was heaps older than her, a widower and father of five and a potential employer. Did he even have to have any other reasons? *Jess* didn't need any other reasons to stifle her consciousness of him out of existence than those she'd just listed. And that was *without* mentioning Peter.

'I need someone to watch the children up to five days a week at my home for somewhere between the next three to six weeks or so. It would help a lot if that person could also take care of laundry and meals and some other basic housekeeping.' Dan drew a breath. 'This work I have to do is going to mean long hours at home for a while for me. As well there'll be trips to Sydney maybe up to three days a week until it's sorted.' His hand rose to rub briefly at his breastbone before he dropped it back to his side.

In three to six weeks, working five days a week for Dan Frazier, Jess could really earn some money to help towards those repayment instalments. The money wouldn't pay the debt off but it might convince Councillor Fielder that Jess could *get* the money to keep making decent-sized instalments.

Surely if she made some regular payments the man would *have* to give her more time to pay the debt off? Ella's father should never have gone behind Jess's back in the first place, but that was typical of Peter Rosche.

And she could work from Dan's home. Of course she could.

'I'd like to help you.' Jess's fingers tightened around the handles of the stroller. 'I have some other children on Tuesdays and Saturdays, but I'd be willing to come to you the five other days, if you felt that could work for you. Ella would come with me, and I could give you a list of character referees.'

Not any family ones because Jess was alone in the world aside from Ella.

Her daughter started to fret in the stroller. 'Du, du, du-u-u!'

Jess leaned forward to unstrap her daughter and lift her out for a cuddle. 'Yes, sweetheart, we'll see the ducks now.'

Dan watched Jess cuddling Ella, and then he looked at his children and he lifted his youngest into his arms and started towards the duck pond. 'I could work around your Tuesdays and Saturdays.'

Dan told her how much he'd pay her per day. It was generous, even when he added, 'For that amount, I'd be asking you to remain there until I got home late some nights, but you and your daughter would have all your meals at my home.'

'It sounds very reasonable. I wouldn't mind doing that for you.' It sounded like a good way to save some money on her food bill, and Jess could drive the short distance back to her house at whatever time suited.

'Come and meet the children. That will be a good start, and…thank you. For approaching me and asking if I needed help.'

'You're welcome. It's nice to be able to help others.' Jess dropped a kiss onto Ella's head to hide the hope that wanted to force its way onto her face. Dan hadn't said he'd employ her yet.

But maybe he would. Maybe Jess would be able to help Dan while the money he paid her would help Jess.

Maybe Jess would be able to stop worrying, just a bit, and have enough money to stave off the wolves until she figured out something better for the longer term. Like tracking down Ella's father and making him take responsibility for setting her up for this fall?

Jess had tried to find Peter, just after Ella came along. He'd already disappeared by then.

Jess stuck her chin up. She could only try to sort things out, and she'd try with all her might. 'Righto, Dan. Take me to meet your children!'

CHAPTER TWO

'KIDS, THERE'S SOMEONE I'd like you all to meet.' Dan led Jess Baker to the duck pond where his children had been pretending not to watch him talking with Jess after Luke chipped them about their whispers.

The children were quite off the mark with their speculations. Jessica Baker was a great deal younger than him, not to mention those kinds of relationships should be kept out of the workplace.

Dan frowned. He simply wasn't interested in Jess. He might have noticed she was an attractive young woman, noticed her heart-shaped face, her slim straight nose, her honey-blond hair, those soft grey eyes, but he was not *attracted to her.*

And what mattered right now was that he needed to tell his brood that they'd be with a carer while he dealt with this business in Sydney. Deserting them when they'd only just arrived was the last thing Dan wanted to do, but he was going to have to do it.

Dan had a good business, but he was still a man with five children. He'd rented a house in Sydney and worked hard to save enough so they could buy their home out here, where things were cheaper and they could all enjoy a quieter lifestyle.

Jess Baker had told him her umbrella had bent bits, but something about the set of her chin suggested she might be a godsend, just the same.

'Luke, Rob, Daisy, Mary, this is Jess Baker.' Dan glanced at the child in the young woman's arms. He couldn't remember if Jess had said her daughter's name, yet he had no difficulty at all remembering the soft touch of Jess's fingers on his arm. He was…curious about her.

No. Dan wasn't curious. He was a father on his own with five children and eighteen years of memories of the one love of his life, and Jess was a very young woman and potential employee. Dan forced his gaze to Jess's daughter. 'And this is—'

'Ella.' Jess filled in the blank for him with a smile that transformed her face.

Rather than focus on that transformation, Dan gestured to the child in his arms. 'This is Annapolly. Her name's Pollyanna, but we started saying it the other way around and it stuck.'

Dan would simply push the confusing thoughts about Jess Baker away. And how could he think about reacting with awareness to this young woman anyway, when he hadn't done that about any woman at all for the last four years?

There'd been Rebecca for Dan since they were childhood sweethearts. They'd married, had the first four children. Partway through Rebecca's pregnancy with Annapolly, the doctors had discovered Rebecca had cancer. Rebecca had died a month after Annapolly's birth. Dan had just stopped with all that when he lost Rebecca.

'Hello.' Jess offered a uniform smile as her gaze shifted from one child to the next.

Rob responded with a curious, 'Hullo.'

'We saw you speaking with our father,' Daisy observed.

Mary asked hopefully, 'Are you gonna feed the ducks?'

'Yes.' Jess nodded. 'I am.'

Jess Baker was young, and she would come with her baby in tow, but Dan's instincts said Jess would be committed about the work. Those were the only instincts he needed to consider.

He pushed his thoughts into business mode. 'We'll have lunch at our new house. It's a big farm-style home on a ten-acre allotment on the northern edge of town.' To his children he added, 'I'll explain what's happened with my work and how Jess has offered to help us on the way back to the house.'

Throw Jess into the middle. Let Dan see how she managed among the stacks of half-unpacked boxes and the children.

'Straight after the ducks,' Jess agreed, and handed out pieces of bread.

Dan's younger children gathered around. Luke and Rob didn't. They'd fallen into a whispered conversation. No doubt they had questions. Dan would answer them when he had everyone in the van, and hopefully there wouldn't be too much of an explosion when he told them they'd be in childcare for a fair chunk of their holidays.

Maybe they'd accept Jess's care easily. Maybe this would be all right. Maybe Dan's sea change for the children wasn't about to turn into a premature disaster before they even had a chance to give it a go.

Maybe?

And maybe Dan *would* be able to shove aside the way he'd reacted to Jess. He certainly wouldn't let it happen again. Dan failed to notice that, in thinking that, he had admitted to himself there *was* a reaction in the first place.

'Jess, I wonder if you'd mind sorting out lunch while I see to things with Roy, here?'

The Internet technician had arrived in his van as Jess Baker drove up in her small, older-model hatchback.

Dan spoke the words as he, the children, Jess, and the Internet technician trooped into the house. Dan had taken his moment to explain the childcare need to his children on the drive back here.

To allow them to moan and groan and then to make it clear there was no choice.

Now all Dan could do was see if Jess could manage. He'd made it clear he expected cooperation from the children with that.

'Of course, Dan. That's what I'm here for.' Jess's gaze darted this way and that. The kitchen was farther into the house, to the left through the open-plan living room. Jess spotted it and asked, 'Do any of the children have food allergies?'

'No.' Dan was lucky in that respect.

'Great.' The bow atop Jess's soft hair bobbed as she nodded her head.

Her clothes were bright and cheerful, and there were enough wooden bangles making their way up her arm that she could use them to start a small fire if she needed to.

Something about the combination of puckish face, bright clothing and the determined set of Jess's chin told Dan she might have lived more life than her youthful age suggested.

Right now she stood straight as an arrow with her baby perched on her hip while she looked around at the chaos inside the house. At least she didn't turn and walk right out again.

Dan didn't want her to go. He wanted a chance to get to know her.

What you want is a chance for her to look after the family while you're dealing with this work situation.

And if he tried to get to know her he might as well be getting to know an alien species. Jess Baker was a whole generation away.

'If you'll come this way with me.' Dan gestured the technician forward.

As they walked away Dan heard Jess say to his two eldest, 'How are your muscles? Do you think you could push those boxes into a line so they block that half of the kitchen? That way Ella will be safe while I make lunch.'

'Looks like you and the little lady have some chaos happening here.' The technician flipped the comment Dan's way as they walked into the den.

'It's to be expected.' With another part of his mind Dan heard the first volley of questions from his curious younger offspring, and Jess's calm answers and the open and shut of cupboard doors as she looked inside. She wouldn't find much.

He had grossly overestimated how much unpacking

one man and five excited children could get through in an evening and the following day. Dan had taken them into town to the park hoping to calm them down so he could come back and finish the work. Or at least get halfway there with it. 'Things are under control. Let's get this Internet connection sorted out.'

Roy set to work. A few minutes later he turned to Dan. 'There you go. The problem was this component.' Roy showed Dan the small box. 'I've replaced it. You won't be charged for this. I'll just send this one back.'

With that issue sorted, and Dan therefore connected once again to his working world via his computer, he thanked the man and let him out of the side door. Dan quickly jumped on to check his emails. There was just enough room to sit with the boxes shoved aside and stacked up.

'Lunch is ready, Dan. There's enough for an extra person—' Jess broke off as she glanced into the den.

She'd looked quite serious at first. Dan would even have said there were worried shadows in the backs of her eyes. Had those been there when they first met? Had he been too busy thinking about his own problems to notice? Were they related to caring for his brood?

Somehow he didn't think so, though that could prove to be challenge enough for her.

As Dan asked himself these questions those shadows were overshadowed by a teasing grin.

'Has the technician left,' she quipped, 'or did the boxes eat him?'

'I'm fairly sure he left. You managed something for lunch for everyone already?' Dan dragged his gaze from her smile. It was generous, open, and, yes, there *were* shadows in the backs of her eyes now that Dan took notice.

Dan cleared his throat. 'Was it really that long?'

'Ten minutes.' Jess shrugged her shoulders. 'The children pitched in.'

Utilise the troops. If Jess could settle them down a bit, even for a while, Dan would be grateful.

Since when do you need someone else to help? You spent the last two years turning your business into a work-from-home affair so you could do it all yourself. This shift is the final step, to give the kids the rural setting you talked about with Rebecca.

Dan had occasionally had to call on his sister Adele to help him out, but mostly he had his clients trained to understand that he worked from home and that was that. And his sister was travelling right now, taking time for *her* life.

Well, Dan wasn't going to regret this move. It was for the children, but it was for Dan, too. Lately the city made him feel as if he couldn't breathe. And his largest client undergoing an intensive pre-purchase examination wasn't something Dan could have anticipated. He hadn't even known they were thinking about a change of ownership!

He'd be fine, though. He shouldn't need to ask Jess Baker for help for more than a month or so.

'Thanks, Jess.' Dan drew a breath that didn't do a whole lot to ease the tight feeling that had formed in the centre of his chest as he started thinking ahead to leaving the children to get through most of their holidays without the fun and outings he'd planned for them. 'I'm guessing the kids are all hungry. I admit I am, too.'

Did Jess Baker eat more than enough to keep a

sparrow going? She was small, slender. As she turned about the bright black-and-orange skirt swirled against legs that were tanned and sturdy.

Slender, but strong, then.

Dan lifted his gaze from her legs, and rapidly lifted it past other parts of her that seemed to catch his eye. 'I need to make those phone calls to your referees.'

More than that, he needed to stop noticing Jess in this way. He wanted Jess to work for him. And she was really young. And he…wasn't. And he didn't know a thing about her circumstances.

He had had his luck.

You haven't got over losing Rebecca.

He had, though. It happened four years ago. They'd all grieved and moved on. There'd been no choice. It was just that Dan knew he'd had more than his share. It would be impossible to love like that twice.

Meanwhile, there was Jess Baker, and… Dan stepped into the kitchen.

There was Jess's daughter playing with a set of plastic kitchen bowls in a makeshift playpen of packing boxes. There was Jess, handing out toasted cheese sandwiches and chocolate milkshakes.

Most of all there were five Frazier children seated around the dining table, looking…at least relatively cooperative.

'I cut up the apple pieces.' Daisy gestured to a bowl in the middle of the table. 'Jess said if she watched me, it would be okay.'

Rob grinned with a chocolate milk moustache. 'I made the milkshakes.'

'And Annapolly and Mary worked together to put the plastic plates on the table.' Jess smiled and ruffled both little girls' hair before she passed Dan a plate of cheese sandwiches and sat with one of her own. 'We thought maybe after lunch we could try to get the kitchen and bathrooms sorted out.'

Right.

Dan drew a breath. 'I'm sorry, kids, that I've had to change our plans and that I'll be travelling to Sydney a bit for the next while and working long hours.'

'Yeah, well, some of us are way too old for a babysitter.' Luke muttered the words half beneath his breath.

But Dan still heard them and frowned, because they'd been over this in the car.

As Dan opened his mouth to chide his son, Jess spoke.

'You're quite right, Luke. I'm hoping I'll be able to rely on you and Rob to guide me with some of what's needed for the younger ones.'

Luke raised his gaze and for a moment seemed to fight himself before he unbent enough to allow: 'We can do that. There'll be heaps of stuff you don't know about them.'

Jess gave the boy a gentle smile. 'And maybe if we all work hard to get along and help your father be able to focus on his work, he'll manage a small outing with you all here and there?'

'Exactly what I'm hoping.' It was what Dan had been thinking.

There was a silence for a minute, and then Luke said, 'It's not your fault that you have to do this, Dad. You work hard to look after all of us. We'll just have to do things around here until you can do some stuff with us.'

Jess searched Luke's face for a moment before her

gaze shifted to Dan. 'You must have been run off your feet since you got here, Dan. Probably everyone's feeling a bit out of sorts one way and another.'

Did she see the weariness that he'd been trying to hide from the kids for...Dan couldn't even remember how long?

'Yeah.' Dan cleared his throat. It had been hard to pack up their lives, to put the family photos away. He hadn't wanted to wrap up the pictures of Rebecca because he needed them in front of him and yet, since they arrived, that box had been the second last one Dan wanted to go anywhere near. The other held the urn of Rebecca's ashes.

Jess drew a deep breath and for a moment uncertainty flashed in the backs of her soft grey eyes. 'That is, if you're happy for me to continue, then I thought, as I said, we could do some unpacking after lunch.'

'I want to keep going.'

While the children finished their lunches, Jess showed Dan her written qualifications and gave him the phone numbers for her referees. 'Two are the mothers of the children I mind on Tuesdays and Saturdays.'

Today was Wednesday, so Jess had a couple of days before she would be with the other children again. 'The other referee is the woman who mentored me through training as a daycare mum.'

'Thanks, Jess.' Dan turned and headed for his den. 'I'll make sure I find time to make those calls this afternoon.'

The children pitched in to start sorting out rooms. Jess did her best to get everyone organised and help them all feel good about their achievements, and did well enough with the younger ones. Luke worked hard, but under his own steam and without a lot of communication. Jess would do what she could to draw the older boy out over time.

By mid-afternoon Jess's daughter had just woken up from her nap, Annapolly was parked in front of a children's programme on TV, and the rest of the children had gone outside with snacks to keep them going until dinner. Luke had placed himself in the role of supervisor out there.

'I hope you'll forgive me for disappearing and leaving you to it.' Dan had checked in with the family at intervals throughout the afternoon, but had taken the opportunity to work from his den as well. This financial examination was going to make its demands on his time.

He faced Jess across the kitchen table now and they both knew he had to give her his decision.

'I hope you were able to contact my referees.' Jess had tried to stay calm throughout the afternoon, but it hadn't been easy to beat back her worries about money.

'Your referees checked out fine.' Dan glanced about the now tidy kitchen. 'You've done wonders this afternoon.'

'Thank you. I welcome the chance to work hard.' Jess paused as her daughter crawled to her side. She picked her up and blew a raspberry kiss onto her neck.

Ella crowed and giggled.

Dan's gaze lingered on Jess's mouth before he quickly looked away, and Jess's heart skipped a beat. So much for controlling *that*. Apparently Dan could put paid to her efforts with a single glance.

Oh, why did she have to react to him like this? Be so conscious of him as a man when Jess had sworn off men and she'd meant it? Well, Dan didn't appear to want the attraction anyway so it would rapidly become moot, and that was *if* Dan kept Jess working for him.

'You're a natural mother, Jess. That much is very clear.' Dan hesitated, and then cleared his throat. 'Do you mind if I ask about other commitments? Will caring for my children interfere with other parts of your life?'

'There's just me and Ella, so there won't be interference from home with my work hours.' Jess drew a breath and slowly blew it out. Would he judge her for being a single mother?

'That's one less worry. I really need the help.' Dan straightened in his chair. 'Anything you can do towards housekeeping will also be appreciated.' He hesitated. 'I may be a little overprotective about checking in.'

Seeing that care in Dan touched a tender place down inside Jess because Ella's father had proved so different.

'I'd want a contact number for you at all times, too.' She made sure her expression—a professional one—reassured Dan that all of his concerns were acknowledged. 'Also a complete list of medical conditions or special needs of the children. And I'd want to be paid weekly either by cash or bank cheque.'

If Dan assumed Jess would need to access her pay without a waiting period, he'd only be assuming the truth.

They sat there for a minute, sizing each other up. Jess looked over his ruffled dark hair and the hint of beard on his jaw, the shadows under his eyes that suggested he hadn't got a lot of sleep just lately.

And she said softly around her consciousness of him,

'I'd like to help you, Dan, if you feel I've passed the tests.'

'I don't mean to make it seem like that.'

Jess shook her head. 'If you hadn't grilled me, I'd have worried whether you were taking enough care of your children.'

'You're young.' The words were low.

'You don't look that old, yourself, you know.' He looked seasoned and appealing. Jess shook her head to try to drive the thoughts out.

Dan glanced from his daughter watching the TV, to the children outside, to Ella in Jess's lap, to Jess. 'Will you stick around for the rest of the day? And then I'll need you here first thing tomorrow morning so I can get on the road to Sydney.' He threw his shoulders back as though to say now the decision was made he'd stick by it and make it work.

Relief flowed through Jess. 'Thank you for giving me this opportunity.' She got to her feet and bent her head over Ella's so Dan wouldn't see the depth of that relief in her eyes. 'Just let me pop home and get Ella's playpen, monitor and walker and a few other things.'

They'd be fine working together. And this consciousness of him would be extremely transitory.

Of course it would!

CHAPTER THREE

'WHY IS IT THAT PARENTS make up stories about where babies come from?' The question was earnest, as were all of Daisy Frazier's questions. Daisy went on. 'And why would anyone believe those stories?'

It was early evening, the following day. Jess and the children were outside on the veranda that swept around three sides of the rambling home. Dan had unpacked like an automaton all yesterday afternoon and probably well into the night after Jess left that evening. Jess and the children had helped, too, of course.

The house was halfway habitable now, thanks to those efforts, but it was still nice to get outside. Jess had sliced up wedges of watermelon and brought everyone out here. The boys were having a seed-spitting contest.

Ella and Annapolly were playing with dolls. Mary, Dan's quiet six-year-old, was sitting on the edge of the veranda watching her brothers and swinging her legs.

That left Jess and ten-year-old Daisy, who was gifted with an inquisitive mind.

'Do you see Annapolly and Ella, Daisy?'

Annapolly was explaining to Ella in her childish way all about how the dolls were going on a road trip to get to a new house where they'd live happily ever after with a frog that laid golden eggs. Ella listened with awed attention, even though she didn't understand.

'Yes.' Daisy's brow wrinkled and she pushed her glasses up her freckled nose. She had dark hair like her father. They all did. Daisy had the same considering expression, too. 'What about them?'

'They're happy in their make-believe world. They can enjoy their imaginations and make up whatever stories they want.'

Daisy pondered for a second. 'If that's why kids want to believe that babies come from under a cabbage, or the stork drops them, I suppose it's okay.' She sniffed. 'But it would make more sense if they had a pelican drop them. Then they could tell themselves that the baby could be kept warm and safe in the pouch in the pelican's beak until it got dropped off.'

'They could.' Jess stifled a smile over Daisy's pragmatic logic, and made a mental note to tell Dan this discussion with his daughter was coming, if it hadn't happened already.

Dan…

Despite his absence today, Jess had thought of him often. She'd asked herself how he was getting on in Sydney, had tried to remember whether he truly looked as handsome as she had thought on first meeting and again this morning when all of her awareness of him hadn't exactly been evaporated into oblivion.

Dan had phoned twice. Jess had assured him things were going well, and let whichever children had been hovering at the time have a quick chat to him. She'd at least attempted an attitude of professionalism on the surface.

After that second phone call Luke had tried to grill

her almost aggressively about her personal life, why she was by herself and a few other questions that could have become a problem if Jess had let them. Instead, she'd stated only that being the mother of Ella was the greatest joy of her life and firmly turned the conversation elsewhere.

'Time to go in, I think.'

Ella was getting sleepy. Annapolly and Mary were rubbing their eyes. Even the boys had lain back on the veranda floor after finishing their watermelon. And Jess had let her thoughts wander far enough. 'It's been a big day. Thanks for all trying hard today.'

There was the expected chorus from the younger ones of not wanting to go to bed but an hour later they were all in their rooms. It would be a while before some of them slept, Jess suspected, but she wouldn't be helping that if she hovered. She spent time doing chores and by then it was quite late and all the children were asleep. Well, she didn't know about Luke. His door was shut and she didn't feel she could intrude to check.

Jess curled up on the couch in the living room to rest until Dan got home.

She had five children and a baby to take care of tomorrow. The day after was Saturday and she had other children while their mothers worked at their Devonshire teas business.

Jess was an excellent daycare mum and trained to care for older children too. She would give that service to the very best of her ability; she would find her way forward with Dan Frazier's children. And when she got her first pay cheque she would go to the council and pay some money onto the overdue account there and talk to them about a more realistic payment plan. She didn't need to panic.

Things would be all right. And Dan would be back soon, and Jess *was* looking forward to seeing him. Just a little, and there was nothing wrong with that, provided she stuck to professional anticipation…

'Dan.' Jess spoke his name and sat up on the couch.

She'd been dozing when Dan unlocked the front door and stepped into the house.

'Hi. It's late. Sorry.' Dan's words were pitched low. He couldn't explain why they also emerged in a soft, deep tone. But coming home to find a woman sleeping, waiting for him, was something Dan hadn't done for years. Maybe the memory of that was what made him stop and take Jess in from the top of her head, with its messy cap of hair, to her bare feet with their high arches and purple painted toenails. It had to be memories, didn't it, even though Jess was nothing like Rebecca? He couldn't actually be truly attracted to Jess Baker.

'Was it very tiring, the trip into the city and the workload?' Jess's voice was soft and scratchy. Her cheeks had turned a gentle rose-pink as she met his gaze.

Because *she* was aware of *him?*

Rather arrogant to think such an appealing young woman would even notice you, Dan!

He took a step towards her. And then veered to the right to dump his briefcase on the couch because what would Dan do once he stood in front of Jess? Want to run his fingers through that fine, silky hair? Ask her to sit with him while he talked about his day? 'The financial examination process is very thorough. I won't mind not having to think about numbers until tomorrow.'

Dan needed to ask her about *her* work. How the children had fared today. He'd phoned in, but he wanted to hear more than those brief words. 'You'd ring me if there was a problem, not wait until I checked in?'

'Immediately.'

'I'll just look in on them. You don't mind? Then you can tell me how things went today overall. I don't want to hold you up from getting home.' He had to be businesslike about this.

'See them first, then I can give you a progress report.' Jess nodded. 'Ella's fast asleep in her travel cot. I can wait.'

Dan disappeared to the upper reaches of the house to check on his children.

In the living room, Jess watched his receding back until he disappeared from sight.

By the time Dan returned Jess had smoothed her hair. She didn't need to look like something that had been dragged backwards through a house, five children and a baby, she justified. She'd boiled the kettle and she tried to be very casual as she gestured, 'Would you like tea?'

That was suitably employee-like, wasn't it? And of course that was all Jess intended to be. Not that she'd been invited to be anything else. Not that she'd want to be invited.

Yes, you do.

No, you do not.

Dan smiled. 'At this point a good cup of tea would be worth crushing stones with my fingers for.'

Jess laughed, a low, startled sound that filled the kitchen and wiped Dan's face clean of the light-hearted expression that had accompanied his statement. In its place came the kind of tension that appeared in kitchens in the middle of the night when two people stood close together over a boiling kettle with nothing but silence around them. And a man's smile that had softened a girl's heart just a little more than she was ready for, so that she forgot to be careful and just enjoyed him for a moment.

Well, that kind of enjoying had to stop, didn't it?

'I'll make the tea, then.' Jess swung about to get cups down from the cupboard.

'I'll get the milk from the fridge.' He gestured, as though maybe they'd both forgotten where the appliance stood in splendour in the corner of the room beside the dishwasher.

They put together their teas and carried them into the living room. Dan sat in a recliner.

Jess sat on the couch. She had a view of Dan in half profile. How could he look so gorgeous from every conceivable direction?

It must be the distinguishing effect of his age, Jess. You know—the age that means he's a whole generation older than you are and therefore completely unsuitable to be interested in. And that's not even mentioning the fact that you are working for him.

And then there was Luke's attitude. Jess could imagine how well something between his father and the new carer would go down with Dan's eldest son.

Maybe the boy still missed his mother and couldn't deal with the thought of Dan finding someone else.

Jess's heart softened at that, for how could she blame Luke for his grief?

'Mary's quiet. I'm working to draw her out more.

Rob likes to talk but I told him I have big ears, I can fit it all in.'

'You don't.' Dan uttered the words and dropped his gaze to his tea. 'Have big ears.'

'Well, no.' Jess cleared her throat as Dan lifted his cup to his mouth. She didn't bring up Luke. Jess would rather try to win the boy over, give it some time and see how things went. Instead, she broached the other potentially awkward topic. 'Daisy asked about how babies are made.'

Dan's cup shifted in a slight, involuntary movement before he carefully put it down. 'I see. Perhaps you'd better tell me.'

'Well, she's an inquisitive girl. It goes with her kind of intelligence, I think?' No need to blush over something that was as simple as pelicans versus storks. 'It's just, if you haven't already given her that talk, I think it might be a good idea if you did it quite soon. I know she's only ten, but schools are fairly forward about those issues these days, and Daisy's very curious. Today it was why other children believe in the stork and cabbages. A week later it could be asking for an explanation about stem cell research or something equally tricky. I have a suspicion she might already know the, well, at least some of the mechanics about all that, so, you know—' Jess waved a hand '—maybe a father's perspective to help keep her comfortable as a child her age should be about the whole topic?'

Dan gave Jess one brief, trapped look. 'I can't ask you—'

To tell his daughter about it in a way that should come from a loving parent that Daisy trusted? Jess didn't want to even think about the topic while she was in the room with Dan and her heart was doing silly things in her chest.

But for Daisy…

'I could.' She bit her lip and rushed on. 'Talk to her, I mean.' The man was quivering in his boots at the thought of talking birds and bees with his daughter, not thinking about trying to investigate birds and bees with Jess.

Shut up, Jess. No, talk up. About Daisy. 'I could talk to her, but I really think this is something that needs to come from her dad.' She sought Dan's gaze and quickly looked away again. 'I think she might feel awkward talking with me about it.'

Jess drew a breath. 'Maybe once you've talked to her, you could get her a few books to read that explore related topics. Growing or waning numbers of children per family in various countries might be one area that could interest her. All sorts of things tie in with that. Politics, economics, religion.'

'Thanks.' Dan finally caught her gaze and held it. 'Aside from my daughter throwing you in the deep end, was everything else okay?'

'I think we all had a reasonable day, really.' Jess delved into another couple of issues with Dan, asked if he'd mind if she took them all into town tomorrow. It wasn't that far to walk and if they left early…

'That'd be fine provided you're comfortable the traffic won't be an issue if you're all on foot?'

He'd lived in a city.

Jess had, too, before she moved here. 'There's a pedestrian walk all the way from here into town. We'll stay on it, but traffic is always quite light anyway.'

He nodded. 'I'll be leaving for Sydney again early,

but I'll have the weekend at home. Thank you, Jess, for taking this on to help me.'

Dan wasn't comfortable with needing her help, and his care for his children shone through in every word he spoke. Jess…well, she found that attractive about him. Probably not surprising when she'd been hurt by a man who had not only wanted nothing to do with recognising his baby, but had insisted on writing an agreement to silence Jess on the topic for ever.

She'd signed. By then she'd realised how little Peter Rosche had truly ever cared about her and that she couldn't expose Ella to how much her father didn't want her. Dan loving his children to pieces, yes, Jess did find that appealing, but she needed to admire it from afar, not want to acknowledge it on any kind of personal level.

'Do you know how to drive a van the size of mine, Jess? I'll fit the baby seat back into it tonight, for Ella. I still have ours from when Annapolly needed it.' Dan's gaze shifted over her, perhaps to assess whether he thought she could manage the larger vehicle.

Perhaps because, like Jess, he struggled not to notice her? To be aware?

In your dreams, Jessica Baker.

'I haven't driven a van like yours, but I've driven a four-wheel-drive.' Peter had owned one, and let Jess drive it now and then.

'I took the van today, but I've a second car in the shed here that I got shifted down with us.' Dan shook his head. 'I should have thought of that before I went to Sydney. You need the van here in case you have to drive anywhere with the children. You don't have to walk if you don't want to.'

'Thanks. That sounds sensible.' Jess got to her feet. 'I'd better get Ella and head home.'

'Luke woke up when I checked on him. He said you let them have a watermelon-seed-spitting contest.'

Had the boy been accusatory about that? Jess paused a few steps away from the couch. 'Boys need to be a little bit gross, otherwise they don't know how to turn into men.'

Her eyes widened as she realised the way the words had come out. 'That is, I didn't mean it to sound as though men are gross. What I meant was—'

'Building strength by not having to act like girls all the time is important for the males of the race?' A smile twitched at the corners of his mouth.

This teasing style of grin was also a thing of beauty on Dan, Jess discovered, and she got caught in the headlights of it. Maybe that was because the smile reached all the way to the depths of his eyes even as it curved his lips in the most enticing way.

Home.

Now.

Before one more thought like that leaks from the one brain cell you have left, apparently, that's even trying to remain in control at the moment!

'I'll carry the baby for you.' Dan's smile had faded, too.

Jess nodded and forced her feet to take her forward, into the room where Ella slept, bum in the air, in the travel cot. Jess scooped her daughter up and set her into Dan's arms in a smooth motion. Their hands barely touched and yet it was a touch that Jess had secretly craved.

Ella snuggled her sleepy head into Dan's neck and softness came over his face.

Jess swallowed hard. She walked ahead of Dan out to her car, opened it up and took over to settle Ella into her car restraint. 'Thanks for carrying her. I'll see you in the morning, bright and early.' *Sleep well, Dan.*

'Goodnight, Jess.' Dan rubbed his hand across his jaw as though uncertain what to do with it.

Reach for her?

In your dreams, Jess.

Jess started the car's engine and was grateful that it was a small, economic one that went a long way on its tank of petrol.

'You'll be all right going home at this hour?' Dan frowned. 'I want you to text me from your mobile phone when you get home. That way I can store the number to check on you the next time, and I'll know you got there okay.'

'Thanks.' It was the silliest thing, but Jess had to turn her head away for a moment. She made a production of checking her blind spot and then she just rolled the car forward and drove away.

She had to do better at keeping her distance tomorrow, from Dan. Investing in his children was one thing. It was a part of the job, and that hadn't been completely easy so far. Luke had made sure of that.

Investing her feelings in Dan when he didn't want that and she couldn't afford to was a whole other matter.

'Not only can't afford it,' Jess muttered aloud as she turned the car into the cottage's driveway, 'I must not do such a thing. It's Jess and Ella and that's all. That's how it has to be.'

But Dan had been kind. Thoughtful. So much the

opposite of the treatment Jess had received at the hands of Ella's father.

How was Jess supposed to deal with it?

By realising he'd been kind and thoughtful from an *employer's perspective.* That was how!

CHAPTER FOUR

'AND MY BIRTHDAY's the eleventh of June.' Robert Frazier chattered beside Jess as she and all the children made their way back out of the council building in town the next morning.

They'd walked. It was a pleasant distance to the town centre from Dan's home; the morning was cool and fresh and the children had plenty of energy. Luke had wanted to stay home by himself but Jess had vetoed that.

At times Jess felt Luke was testing her. All she could do was try to be reasonable in return.

Jess had gained Luke's cooperation on this occasion and she had gone to the council to make her payment.

She just hadn't been able to get any better answers about the future of her home. She'd been given the run-around through three different people. She'd left Luke in charge while she did that, hoping the boy would soften if he realised she wasn't trying to treat him like a baby. Jess hadn't been able to tell whether her efforts with him had been successful or not.

Her efforts *hadn't* been particularly successful at the council. Well, she'd just have to go back when she only had Ella in tow and stick around until she got results.

'When we get home, Rob, we might make a chart of all the birthdays.'

Rob had already told Jess that Daisy's birthday was coming up. That was one to speak to Dan about when he got home later.

Jess shouldn't be viewing that discussion as the beginnings of a ritual, hoping for time with Dan regularly. 'Come on, kids. We'd better get back before the sun warms up too much and we don't feel like walking.'

After lunch Dan phoned and said he was coming home early and should see her mid-afternoon.

Jess got off the phone and found all the children in the living room.

'The laundry's all out on the line and I think I can get away with not doing too much else in the way of house cleaning for the day. Would anyone like to help make cookies?' Dan might like some home baking. Jess figured the kids wouldn't say no. While Luke and Rob opted to ride their bikes outside, she got the others involved and set to work.

Soon there were cookies cooling on trays and Jess had handed some out to each of the children. The boys had come in for their share and life wasn't bad. Luke wasn't glaring right now. Jess had a job to do that she was enjoying. The children had cookies, and she wasn't totally out of money yet.

'Annapolly's taking a bit of time to use the loo.' Jess frowned. The little girl had gone to the bathroom just a few short minutes ago, but even so. 'Luke, would you take everyone out on the veranda to eat the cookies, please? I'll be there in a minute. I just want to check on your sister.'

Luke frowned, but wordlessly herded the others

outside, and Jess turned her attention to seeking out Dan's youngest.

Independent loo visits for four-year-olds were important for feelings of pride and independence. Jess realised this and she didn't want to encroach on Annapolly's privacy. She didn't want to make unreasonable demands of Luke, either, and that was a whole other balancing act…

Jess strode towards the bathroom. Annapolly came out as Jess approached.

'There you are. I was wondering—' Jess broke off.

The little girl's face was red and there were tears running down her cheeks.

'Oh, Annapolly, what's the matter?' Jess hurried forward.

It was then that she spotted the wadded bits of white in Annapolly's nose. Annapolly drew a breath through her mouth, a prelude to screaming, Jess suspected, and possibly to choking because her nose was blocked. 'Did you shove tissue paper in there?'

What if she inhaled it and choked herself? How far in had she pushed the paper?

Annapolly nodded miserably.

Jess had to fix this. Now. She took Annapolly gently by the shoulder, whipped a tissue out of her own pocket, held it out and said firmly, 'Blow that nose out, Annapolly. A good big blow until you've got nothing left.'

Annapolly blew. There were more tears, but there was also lots and lots of tissue paper. As Annapolly let out the first cry Jess scooped the little girl into her arms. Had it all come out? Had she damaged her nasal passages? Brought on the risk of infection, bleeding in there?

Jess hurried to the front door of the house. 'Everyone to the van, please. Luke, will you take Annapolly while I get Ella and her stroller? We're going to the hospital.'

'What did you let happen to her?' Luke asked the question fiercely.

'She filled her nose with tissue paper and may have harmed her sinuses.' Jess hurried away to get her daughter. The boy didn't need to accuse Jess of anything. Jess was already accusing herself.

The other children asked questions as Jess drove the van towards the hospital. Jess explained, and felt even guiltier as they all fell silent.

'I want to phone Dad.' Luke bit the words out. 'He has a right to know about this.'

'I was about to ask you if you'd do that. He phoned earlier and said he was on his way home. It would be good if he could meet us at the hospital.' Jess dug her mobile phone out of her pocket and passed it to the boy.

Luke tried but after a few minutes he'd had no luck.

'Will you text him, please, Luke, and ask him to come to the hospital? He might be in a low reception area but he should be close to home by now.' Jess didn't have time to wait for the luxury of Dan's opinion, or Luke's approval. She had to get Annapolly checked now. 'At least we're almost there.'

'She's all right, though.' Rob said it as though he needed to believe it. 'We won't be leaving her there or anything.'

'No, we're not leaving her there.' Luke said this.

'She's coming home with us straight after, Rob. Don't be stupid.'

Jess might have chided the boy for the 'stupid' comment, but, if anything, Robert appeared reassured by his brother's harsh words, and Jess had enough to worry about right now so she left it alone.

The whole family fell silent as they stepped through the doors of the hospital's emergency entrance. Jess searched each face; saw their fear, Luke's fury and accusation. Behind his surly expression she saw Luke's fear, too.

Oh, Dan, what else have I added to your family's stress?

Why hadn't she just watched everyone more closely?

It was three minutes, Jessica, and you knew Annapolly had gone to use the loo. Filling her nose with tissue paper while she was there wasn't something you could have anticipated.

Maybe not, but it was Jess's job to anticipate, wasn't it?

Jess had Ella in the stroller. Luke had taken Annapolly into his arms. Jess eased the little girl from his hold and asked him to please watch his siblings while she spoke to the nurse. 'I may need to go into the examination room with her.'

'Dad had better get here soon.' With the brief words, Luke led the others to seats against the wall.

The lack of trust inherent in his statement didn't escape Jess.

'What have we here?' A friendly woman in her forties gestured Jess over.

Soon Annapolly was being examined. Her nose was declared to be sore, but the tissue paper was all out. No permanent harm had been done. The necessary germ-and-infection-repelling steps were taken. A few more tears were shed.

Jess could see the waiting room through the glass section of the doors and she saw when Dan arrived. There was a low-voiced conversation with Luke. The boy looked furious and was gesturing wildly. Dan also looked upset.

And the other children were all chattering at once.

They were probably telling Dan what a bad caregiver Jess had turned out to be, and they were right.

'You can go now, love.' The nurse looked at Annapolly. 'No more sticking things up your nose. Do you understand?'

'Yes.' Tears welled in Annapolly's eyes and she held her arms out to Jess.

Jess cuddled the little girl and would rather have liked to join in with the weepies, at least for a moment.

Instead, Jess thanked the nurse and took Annapolly, and Ella in the stroller, out to the waiting room where Dan was in the process of trying to break away from his children, no doubt so he could come and find out about his daughter.

'Dan. I'm so sorry.' Jess handed Annapolly over. The little girl was already reaching for him. 'The nurse says there's no permanent damage. The others have probably told you what happened.' Jess explained what the nurse had done.

Annapolly *was* going to be fine, but right now her nose hurt and that was Jess's fault. Dan would sack her for this, and Jess would deserve it because she'd let Annapolly get out of her sight and hurt herself.

'Let's all go home.' Dan's gaze went from the daughter

in his arms to the other children. 'Hospitals—' He didn't say more, just hustled everyone outside.

Jess drove the van back home while Dan drove in his other car, Annapolly, Luke and Rob with him.

Jess *never* lost track of a child when she looked after them at the cottage. She supervised *everything*. Well, she'd failed to do that at Dan's house, hadn't she?

When both vehicles stopped outside the house a few minutes later Daisy took Annapolly by the hand and said the little girl could come and lie on her bed with her and she'd read to her. Mary went with them.

Luke and Rob had still been talking to their father when the car pulled up. Rob disappeared outside to ride his pushbike and Luke cast a furious glance in Jess's direction before he turned back to his father. 'I don't like her. I don't want her here. She can't even take care of everybody and you seem to think the sun shines out of her, Dad. You don't even know her.'

He got on his bike and rode off to the far reaches of the property before Dan could do more than start to rebuke him.

That left Jess, Dan and Ella, who'd fallen asleep on the way back. Jess changed her and put her down to nap in the travel cot and went back to face Dan. There was nothing else for this but to take full responsibility and hope Dan could get over her negligence enough to trust another person with his children. She didn't know what to do about Luke. He would end this short association disliking Jess.

Well, Jess would just have to accept that, she supposed.

Dan was in the kitchen.

'You're eating cookies.' Jess blurted the words with a complete lack of comprehension.

'They're very good cookies. I don't get home baking like this very often and since my eldest just did his best to make sure I have a three-day heartburn, anyway, I think I deserve them.' Dan took another cookie and, with his other hand, poured two cups of tea. His mouth was still tight. 'Potato crisps are my usual addiction. I can go through packets of those in a day. I'm surprised the children left any cookies for me.'

'We'd only just got them all out of the oven when we had to leave for the hospital.' Jess glanced around her. She'd spotted empty crisp packets in Dan's den and thought it was the children. 'I didn't tidy up, just rushed out.'

'No, there tends to be a sense of panic.' He said it as though he knew. Dan handed her one of the cups of tea. 'Sit down, Jessica.'

Jess sat. She didn't think she could drink the tea, yet she found herself sipping the sweet brew and taking comfort from its warmth. But Dan. Why wasn't Dan yelling? Or very cold towards her? Something?

'You're going to sack me kindly but there's no way anyone is to blame but me.' That knowledge stabbed right through Jess's heart. 'I let Annapolly go to the bathroom and left it several minutes before I thought about the fact that she hadn't come back. You must have been worried when you got Luke's text message.'

'I don't know what's got into that boy—' Dan broke off, drew a tight breath and started over. 'I was worried.' His jaw tightened. 'And I admit, I did feel angry for a minute when I realised you were all at the hospital. I wanted to blame you for not watching them properly, for potentially risking harm to one of them.'

As Luke had blamed her. Well, in this case Luke had the right of it. Jess forced herself to sit straight and not lower her gaze. She deserved this. Every bit of chewing over that Dan needed to hand out. 'You have every right to be angry.'

'What I am is human, Jess.' Dan rubbed his hand over the back of his neck. 'I pushed my worry out into irrelevant anger for a brief moment. But the fact that Annapolly stuffed her nose with paper doesn't make you a negligent caregiver, no matter what my overactive mind might have tried to tell me to the contrary.'

Jess barely took in his words. 'I'm the one—'

'Who had to deal with the drama this time.' Dan shook his head. 'There's five of them, Jess. They range in age from four up to fifteen. It's a big house. No matter how good you are at your job there'll be times when more than one of them is where you can't see them. I do understand that. As their father, I *live that* on a daily basis. You can't tie them all to chairs in the kitchen all day. And I asked you to help out with housekeeping and other duties as well.'

'I guess so.' Jess frowned. 'Luke wanted to be left here by himself this morning and I wouldn't agree. I didn't think you'd want that.'

'No.' Dan put his tea down and leaned forward to face her across the kitchen table. His hazel eyes searched her grey ones. 'Annapolly is more than capable of using the bathroom on her own. You let her do that. She pushed tissue paper into her nostrils while she was in there. She came out in distress, you got her to blow it out and took her to the hospital to make sure there was nothing still lodged up there and to find out whether any serious damage had been done.'

He reached briefly to touch Jess's hand. 'I'm not sacking you, Jess. It was an accident, and Annapolly is okay. In the end that's what counts.'

He wasn't going to sack her. Dan wasn't furious. He'd had his bout of anger and that had been because of fear.

'Thank you.' Jess's words were husky with relief, and with consciousness of Dan's determination to be fair.

And of Dan himself…

And because that was so very unwise, she got to her feet.

Dan stood at the same time and Jess looked at him, overwhelmed for a moment. 'I'll work harder to keep a better watch on things in the future.'

Dan searched her face. 'You're all right about it now?'

No, she wasn't, but Jess *would* be all right. She would make that be so, somehow.

Maybe Dan read her confusion and uncertainty. Maybe he forgot for a moment that she wasn't one of his children in need of a comforting hug, because somehow his arms had opened and Jess was inside them with her nose pressed to his chest.

Jess was enveloped by the solid feel of him, of his broad shoulders making a protective curve while he drew her close to his body. There was tension in Dan's body. More when Jess wrapped her arms around him and hugged him back.

Maybe she shouldn't have done that, but she did, and their hug changed right at the end to something that wasn't entirely about comfort.

'I'll pack the rest of the cookies away into a tin.' Jess spoke the words with the length of the kitchen between them. She'd got herself out of Dan's arms and a distance away very quickly. She shouldn't have hugged him in the first place.

'Just as soon as I've checked on everyone.' She cleared her throat. 'Thanks, Dan, for your kindness and understanding. There won't be a repeat where you have to come to the hospital, because of something like this.'

Jess would make sure of it. He didn't need that. Jess wasn't so foolish that she couldn't imagine that Dan would have had to go to a hospital or more than one, when his wife died.

Jess didn't know what had been wrong with his wife or how she had died, but she'd seen how the children retreated into worried silence in Randurra's emergency department this afternoon. Some of Luke's anger had been about that, too, Jess suspected.

And she couldn't have stayed within that embrace. Not without risking Dan realising how it was impacting on her. They had a working relationship and needed to stick to it, for so many reasons! 'And I'd like to take the children back to the hospital very soon for a visit. We can take a gift to donate to the children's ward. It'll be a chance for the kids to see a brighter side of the hospital.'

Dan murmured an agreement. Jess hoped she could convince Luke to agree to this. She went to check on the girls, and then Dan's sons. Rob was fine. Luke was playing a computer game in his room, screeching a racing car around corners on the screen. Would that help him get out his aggression? Should Jess try to speak to him?

She knocked on his door and waited for his head to turn. 'Luke—'

'Dad told me you're staying.' He'd paused the game for the moment it took him to speak the words. 'Doesn't mean I have to like it.'

'No. It doesn't mean that.' Jess pushed back a sigh and left him to it.

When she came back, Ella was stirring in the travel cot and Jess got her up and took care of her needs and set about watching over everyone while she organised a meal. Everyone except Luke, who was still in his room.

Annapolly was okay. And Jess still had a job. She was more than grateful about that. Dealing with Dan's eldest was no doubt going to be even more difficult now, but Jess wasn't about to give up. She could see a good boy in there beneath Luke's aggression.

And the reason for his aggression, Jess? The fact that he didn't like the vibe he noticed between you and his father? What about the fact that vibe hasn't gone away?

In the end, it would be irrelevant and Jess had to hope that Luke would see that eventually. Whether Jess was aware of Dan as a man or not and even if Dan was aware of her as a woman, it wasn't something that could or should be pursued between them.

If Jess thought that Luke should allow his father to do whatever he wanted when it came to women, she was smart enough to know that she should not interfere.

Dan watched Jess settle his family in for the evening. She'd whipped up a meal for everyone while she kept a close eye on what all the children were doing, and kept her baby daughter happy, but he could see the tension was still within her.

Rebecca had looked just as devastated after the first trip to the hospital over a hurt child.

But Jess wasn't Rebecca, wasn't anything like Dan's late wife. Dan had hugged Jess because she'd looked as if she needed it, and he had rapidly realised the hug could easily have become more for him. He'd wanted so much to kiss her.

While Jess had broken out of his arms and distanced herself physically, Dan had worked to distance himself mentally. He wasn't happy to be attracted to Jess. Now wasn't the time for his libido to wake from hibernation and start giving him trouble. But it must only be physical awareness because his emotions were still with Rebecca. Well, no, of course they weren't, not in that way because Rebecca was gone and he'd grieved, but…

After the numbness and slogging through the days until the kids had got on their feet again, Dan now only wanted to focus on the children and his work. He *needed* to do that. He had nothing for anything else.

And Luke was being a complete pain about the whole topic, and that made Dan really uncomfortable. He hadn't thought about how his children might react if he wanted to start seeing a woman; it hadn't been something he'd expected to happen. It still grated to have Luke behaving so aggressively and taking a dislike to Jess when in Dan's opinion she didn't deserve it.

Yes, there'd been Annapolly's mishap, but Luke knew as well as anyone that accidents happened, and he'd started to be difficult before today's incident.

Well, Dan had told his son to pay Jess appropriate

respect, and when the dust of today's issues had settled a bit he would check to see if that was happening. There was no point taking it further, because Dan *wasn't* seeking anything but a working relationship with Jess.

As she got the children sorted out after dinner and ready for bed Dan turned his attention to work. Right at the moment he didn't have a whole lot of choice about that either!

'I'm leaving now, Dan.' Jess made the announcement from the doorway of his den. She looked ruffled and still uncertain of herself. She had Ella fast asleep in her arms. 'Thanks for fitting that baby restraint to the van before you left this morning. Oh, and I did want to bring up Daisy's birthday.'

'You're welcome.' He drew a breath. 'Daisy's birthday is next week.'

'Yes. I can make a cake, if you like.'

'That would be nice.' He cleared his throat. 'Her gifts are purchased, as are most of the birthday party supplies. What I can't provide is any extra children for the party. There hasn't been time yet or the opportunity to find any new friends for them here.'

Dan hesitated and then shook his head. 'That's not something I can do in the next few days, but a family party will still be fun for Daisy. I'll see you Sunday, then.' If he walked her to her car he'd do something irrational. Such as try to talk about things that were only going to make both of them feel awkward.

'I'll send a text to your mobile when I get home.'

'Goodnight, Jess.'

'Goodnight, Dan.' She walked away with Ella clasped in her arms. A slip of a girl who was the mother of a baby, but she was not the mother of any of Dan's babies.

So he would get some sleep and Jess would go home and get some sleep and look after her other children tomorrow. When she came back to Dan on Sunday she would have recovered from knowing that Annapolly hurt herself while under her care. Hopefully by then Luke would have a better attitude to life as well.

Dan went back to his workload at the computer and made sure his mobile phone was nearby so he would hear it when she sent her text message through to say she had arrived home safely.

He drew a packet of potato crisps from the stash in his drawer. He would make a list of what needed to be done for Daisy's birthday party, and when Jess came back on Sunday they would go through it and work it all out.

Dan and Jess, because that was what he was paying her to do.

And only that. Dan ate a few more crisps and wished he didn't feel so run-down as he tried to think about it all.

CHAPTER FIVE

DAYS PASSED. THE TRIPS to and from Sydney were tough. Long hours on the road, longer hours of hard work for his client company. Days at home without Jess's help meant working into the night to catch up time lost during the day. Dan pushed on. He didn't have a whole lot of other choice but he'd bought himself time for today.

His most academic child was eleven years old and Jess had worked miracles for the party. Dan glanced about the backyard. It wasn't an enormous crowd but it was one that was bringing Daisy happiness.

'Oh, Daisy, that's a really cool birthday present. I don't think I'd be allowed to have that for my birthday.' The comment came from a girl Daisy's age as his daughter unwrapped the birthday present Dan had bought for her.

The birthday group consisted of Daisy's brothers and sisters, Dan, Jess, Ella and three local girls who would be in the same school year as Daisy when she started at the public school a month from now.

Jess had found some potential playmates for Daisy.

'Dad lets me have things because he knows I'll be responsible with them.' Daisy spoke the words with a smile.

Dan returned that smile. 'Chemistry sets need to be used under careful supervision, but I think you'll enjoy it, Daisy.'

'You do well with her, Dan.' Jess made the comment from Dan's side. 'A chemistry set was a great idea for her.'

'Thanks.' Dan turned to look at Jess, and for once really *allowed* himself to look. Today she wore a floral print skirt teamed with a black sleeveless top, big wooden hoop earrings and a chunky wooden necklace. She looked young and vibrant and beautiful.

And Dan was pushing forty, a father of five growing children. What on earth did he imagine Jess might see in him when she could have any man of any age? She would probably only *want* a man much closer to her own age. Why even ask the question anyway?

Because you know you are attracted to her.

Well, he could just become unattracted. And right now Jess not only looked gorgeous, she also, behind her cheerfulness, seemed a little worried or…scared?

If that had anything to do with her work for him, Dan needed to know. Was Luke making things difficult for Jess still?

Jess lit the candles on the cake.

'You have to make a birthday wish before you blow out the candles, Daisy.' Another of the little girls made this suggestion as they all crowded closer. 'You can come to my house for my birthday, too. It's in March.'

'Thanks.' Excitement dawned in Daisy's eyes. 'I'd love to do that.'

Daisy blew out her candles. She even closed her eyes first.

The wheel of a baby walker butted against Dan's foot.

He glanced down and straight into a pair of soft grey eyes so like Jess's. Ella smiled up at him.

'Well done, Daisy,' Jess said.

Was Jess working very hard not to be aware of Dan, or was he imagining it? Dan needed to stop such thoughts whether they were right or not.

Jess went on. 'Time to dish up this cake and see if it turned out as well as I hoped.'

Jess had baked and decorated the cake last night. She was dedicated to her job. She handled the basics of the housekeeping with apparent ease, too, and that had taken a load off for Dan.

It had made him wonder if he could have a house-keeper on a permanent basis. He'd been busy saving to move the family, and he probably hadn't really wanted the interference anyway but with Jess…

Dan had enjoyed having her in the house. Especially on the days he'd worked from home.

Not good thoughts to have, Dan Frazier. She's the daycare mum who has also generously helped out with housekeeping and cooking, and that's all she should be to you.

'Would you like the treasure hunt now, Daisy? Excuse me.' Jess slipped past Dan to start supervising the activity. The hem of her skirt brushed against Dan's leg. Dan looked at a piece of bright fabric against his denim cut-offs and he breathed in and caught the scent of her perfume warmed against her skin and wanted…

'Ah, let me just give you some room.' Dan shifted back, and Jess's head dipped until all he could see was the fan of her lashes against her skin, and he knew Jess was just as aware of him as he was of her. If he kissed her, maybe he would be able to figure out why—

Dan's mind froze as the thought registered.

Jess moved away and the party went on around them, but from that point on Dan couldn't go anywhere near her without being conscious of her.

And from the way she kept avoiding his gaze, she was equally conscious of him.

Two hours later parents started arriving to collect their children, and soon after it was just Fraziers and Jess and Ella.

Dan turned to Daisy. 'Now that the party's over would you like to rest for a bit, or are you busting to get into your chemistry set?'

Daisy gave him a considering look. 'I'd like to read the books that came with it, first. And we don't want to start anything with that set while Mary and Annapolly are around. I think we'll need to use it after they've gone to bed at night, Dad.'

'Oh, clever work, Daisy.' Jess, who'd been tidying paper plates and plastic cups off the long trestle table, spoke softly beneath her breath so only Dan heard. 'Care for your sisters *and* negotiation for a later bedtime, all rolled into one.'

She turned quickly aside, but not before Dan saw the smile that crept to her face.

Dan cleared his throat. 'We'll discuss that later, Daisy.'

Daisy went off to read, and Mary and Annapolly played with leftover wrapping paper and pieces of ribbon. Jess warned them not to stick anything into their noses but Annapolly had learned that lesson.

Ella was still in her walker and Jess and Dan started in again on the mess.

Dan said abruptly, 'Daisy's eleven now, and I let Rob have an extra hour at that age.'

'Yes, of course. You know what you're doing, Dan.'

Jess pursed her lips and nodded soberly, while her eyes danced and the big wooden hoop earrings danced and that damned necklace sat between her breasts and kept drawing Dan's gaze.

'Thanks for finding some girls her own age to come to her party.' Dan all but growled the words, but he meant them, just the same.

'I knew one of them already and she was more than happy to bring two of her friends.' Jess's face softened. 'I'm glad they seemed to get along with Daisy.'

Dan shoved his hands in his pockets and glanced about the big yard at the party remnants. Even the tree cubby house was decorated in streamers. Jess had asked him to purchase them and then let the kids loose to make things festive.

'If you need to work, Dan, I can keep going here.' Jess glanced at the three little girls as she spoke. 'They're all content for the moment.'

She followed Dan's gaze to the tree house. 'This sure is a great home for children. I'd like to explore the rest of the property one day, though I guess they'd all need to be in the right mood.'

Dan could be in the right mood. In fact, Dan was in *too much* of a right mood at the moment. 'I'll help you clean up.' He couldn't just leave her with all of it, Dan justified.

They worked together to clear away the aftermath of the birthday party. Jess disappeared periodically to check on one or other of the children. She was being very vigilant in that respect and Dan suspected she still felt guilty over Annapolly's episode with the tissue paper.

Dan took out the trash and glanced up from the task and there was Jess on the veranda, lifting her daughter into her arms while she said something to Luke who'd been about to ride past her on his bicycle.

Dan's eldest gave Jess a sullen look and then cast one in his father's direction as well, and rode away. Luke needed to mend that attitude because Dan didn't want Jess leaving thanks to the boy being unreasonable.

I want to keep her working here so she's always around.

The thought pushed into Dan's mind, pushed past four years of defences and a lot of buried grief and just lobbed into his brain. Not his heart, though. This tightness that he had so often in his chest, that wasn't about Jess. That had started long before Dan met her. If there were other responses inside his chest right now that did relate to Jess, well, they were because she was working out so well for the kids.

'I just put Ella down for a nap. I think all the excitement today wore her out.'

Jess had joined him in the kitchen. He hadn't even realised he'd gone inside and had been standing there, staring into space. Thinking about the past and thinking about Jess.

'I don't know about your life. Except that you're raising your baby on your own, and you're proving to be good for my children.'

'I'm enjoying caring for them.' Jess bit her lip. 'Trying not to crowd them, but to keep a close enough eye on all of them at the same time. Trying to win Luke's trust. He's still angry over what happened to Annapolly, and…

well, I'm not sure what else is bothering him. I think the birthday party came off well, anyway.'

'It did, and Luke is just going to have to settle down.' Dan didn't want to think about the reasons for Luke's attitude. If Luke thought he had the right to decide Dan couldn't have a social life, he was wrong about that.

It wasn't the issue, here, but…

Dan pushed the thoughts away. 'Jess, will you tell me about your family? Where you grew up and what brought you here to Randurra?' Maybe if he understood Jess better, that would help him to guide Luke as well.

Or simply make it more difficult for you to keep your interest in her on a professional footing.

For a moment she was silent and then she drew a big breath and turned to search his eyes. 'I grew up in Wollongong, so not too far from Sydney, really. My parents died when I was small. I don't remember them. An older aunt raised me and she passed away during my last year of high school. I worked in a few casual jobs after high school until I decided to become a certified daycare mum.'

She hesitated before she went on. 'While I was expecting Ella, I came here to Randurra.'

A fierce expression came over her face. 'I'm going to make sure my daughter has security and love for as long as she needs it in life. That she's always got me and doesn't feel abandoned.'

As Jess had felt alone because of her loss of family?

Dan had been telling himself they had nothing in common but there was this…

Had she chosen to be a daycare mum as a means of trying to fill that lack of family in her life? 'Your vocation—'

'Is something that I truly enjoy. I adore children, and I know there are plenty of parents who want to work while their children are small, or need to. That's a personal choice. It's just, for myself, I'd prefer to keep Ella close by.'

Jess turned the conversation to Dan. 'What about you? You came here from Sydney, but what about your life before that? Do you have other family?'

'There's my sister and brother-in-law. Dad passed away ten years ago and Mum retired to Queensland. I see her about once a year.'

Jess nodded. 'And the children's mother…'

'Her name was Rebecca.' Dan drew a breath. It wasn't as though it was difficult to talk about her. He'd done so with the kids so many times.

Yet his chest still hurt, unexpectedly so when he looked into Jess's soft, understanding eyes. 'I loved her from when we were teenagers. We were together for eighteen years. She…got cancer while she was pregnant with Annapolly and the specialist team believed there'd be time to treat it but I lost her a month after the birth. That was four years ago.'

The moment Dan said it, he wondered if he should regret it. He didn't bare his soul to others, and the loss of Rebecca was something that was in his past now. He'd grieved and got on with his life, so why did it hurt so much to admit what Dan had known from the start? That Rebecca *had been* his chance at love and he… hadn't had enough time with her?

Jess didn't recoil. Instead, understanding and something that wasn't envy but perhaps longing flashed across her face before she quickly dropped her gaze. When she looked up again, her expression was guarded. 'I'm sorry for your loss, Dan. Thank you for telling me how she died. I don't think I mentioned that I took the children back to the hospital. We just dropped off a small gift to the children's ward. I think that was a good balancing experience for all of them.'

'Daisy told me about it.' Dan acknowledged her words with a dip of his chin, and wondered how his exploration into understanding Jess Baker had turned into an exposé of his own thoughts. 'What I really want to know is if you're okay, Jess? Sometimes I see worry in your eyes.'

She blinked, and blinked again and something in her face seemed to tighten before she threw back her shoulders and stuck out her chin. 'I'm okay, Dan. Of course I am.'

But Jess wasn't, not entirely. So what wasn't she telling him?

Dan pondered that question again the next day as he dug out the box of family photos and started to put some on the walls. The urn with Rebecca's ashes was still in its box.

The pictures felt somehow different. It must be the new house. And if Jess said she was fine, then he had to believe her. Didn't he?

Dan buried himself in his work. Over the following days he was able to scale down the amount of time he was spending in Sydney, but the hours were still long. When he felt tired he ate packets of crisps. He barely even thought about Jess being around all the time, or listened for her voice while he was working, or enjoyed checking in with her when he stepped out of his den to see how the children were getting along.

Right, Dan. That's exactly how it is.

Well, at least he seemed to have convinced Luke that he was only interested in how Jess cared for his family, and Jess seemed to be making progress whittling down the boy's defences.

Days went past with Jess feeling way too conscious of Dan. Why did it have to be like this when he had told her how much he'd loved his wife? Surely she had nothing left inside her when it came to trusting a man, and it was clear she could never compete with Dan's Rebecca, even if she wanted to.

'I think I'm confused.' Jess muttered the words at a pile of clothing as she shoved it into the machine in the laundry room.

Maybe she needed to believe that not every man was selfish and uncaring like Peter, Ella's father. Maybe that was all.

Oh, yes? And that fact alone made her pulse race every time she thought of Dan, or looked at him?

'Jess, I wanted to ask if you'd like—'

'Oh. Dan. I didn't realise you were there.'

He had his glasses on his nose, so he must have been working on the computer in his den. And he was so close. Jess could reach out and trace the grooves beside his mouth with her fingertips, or caress his ruffled dark hair.

And Dan could be totally resistant to all of the above, because she was his employee and not in his age bracket and he *had been* resistant to being aware of her, right from the start.

'Oh. Um…' *Think, Jessica. About something* other than *how delectable he looks.* 'What—what did you want to ask me, Dan?' Even saying his name sent a thrill through her.

They were in a house full of children. Anything else aside, no thrills were allowed!

Dan's gaze shifted over her face, the bright pink bandanna tied through her hair, down over the loose cream cheesecloth blouse and darker pink skirt and back up to linger on her lips before it finally came back to meet her eyes.

'We, ah, I've got a two-day gap where there won't be much happening with the situation in Sydney. I want to take the family to the beach.'

Right. Dan wanted to go away to the beach with the children. Jess would lose two days of being around him.

You'll lose two days' work. Remember you still haven't managed to get Lang Fielder to agree in writing to any extra time to make the repayments.

Jess had managed to see the man. He'd said she should go on making what payments she could out of her wages with that negotiation in mind. It wasn't enough of a reassurance.

Well, Jess didn't want Dan to see her fear. She had learned from being scammed and written out of his life by Peter Rosche that she had to stand by herself. For her sake and for Ella's sake, too. Jess *needed* to remember that. 'That sounds like a lot of fun. I'm sure they'll all enjoy it. When were you planning to go?'

'Tomorrow.' Dan said the word in a low, deep tone.

'Tomorrow.' Jess repeated the word on a breath before she remembered she needed to comprehend it, not merely say it. 'Right, well—'

'Would you be available to come with us? You and

Ella? I've picked days when you don't have to mind other children.' Dan backed out of the room as though he'd belatedly realised they were hovering in there, close, quiet, *together*.

Just as Jess had realised it.

He went on. 'You don't have to, but it'd make it easier for me. Two sets of adult eyes to watch them around the water.'

'For the children's sakes.' That was easy. *And* Jess could let herself be relieved about the pay as well. 'It's always better to have two adults with that many children and water involved.'

Jess had never taken Ella to the beach. But with Dan, she could go.

And spend two days of sun, surf and sand with a gorgeous man.

Oh, for heaven's sake. She'd just gone over this and they would be surrounded by children. There would be sand in shoes and hair and clothing, but there would certainly *not* be romance in the air.

'I'll be happy to make the trip with you, Dan.' Jess stuck her chin out. Way out. So far out that even she couldn't miss the fact that this was a statement about her work for Dan, not about wanting to laze on a beach with him.

Dan pushed his glasses up his nose, seemed to realise they were there, and whipped them off. 'I'm glad. I'll feel better about it.'

'I will too, Dan.' Maybe the couple of days away would help Jess think her way forward with the situation regarding her home.

If not, then she needed to start knocking on the other half of Randurra's doors, and hope that a great deal of lucrative work came to light as a result. Work she could do around her current two jobs.

And really, who needed sleep or rest, anyway, provided she could make sure Ella was happy, and keep getting more money to pay off the debt? As Dan preceded her, Jess made her way out of the laundry room. 'I'd better speak to everyone about packing for the trip.'

CHAPTER SIX

'EVERYONE READY FOR this trip to the beach?' Jess had supervised visits to the bathroom for the younger ones, and waited while various Fraziers ran around needing this item and that item that they simply couldn't leave behind for their trip.

She'd packed for herself and packed for Ella and checked what had been packed for the children.

Rob had wanted to bring half the house for playing with on the beach. He'd settled on two soccer balls, and a whole tube of tennis balls.

The girls wanted to collect seashells, so buckets for them.

And Jess had packed the spades because once they got there she assumed at least one of them would want to make a sandcastle.

Just as well it was a big van. Jess strapped Ella into her travel seat and waited while Fraziers piled in all around her daughter. Watched bouncy bodies and an abundance of energy until she saw for herself that everyone had seat belts fastened. Luke was the only sober one, and that didn't surprise Jess. She was doing what she could to befriend the boy, but he still treated her with suspicion and distrust half the time.

Then Luke dug Rob in the ribs with his elbow and challenged him to a race along the beach once they got there, Rob laughed and agreed and both boys smiled, and Jess really relaxed for the first time in ages.

Ella was kicking her legs and wiggling. Jess climbed in the front beside Dan, glanced at him and a big, silly grin spread across her face. She pushed her floppy hat off her head and let it dangle by its strings down her back. 'We're going to the beach.'

'Right after we stop in town for the things I know they'll all start asking for ten minutes up the road.' Dan's gaze took in the floppy hat, her face. He watched her strap herself in and his eyes came back up to briefly catch hers again.

How did he do that? Simply look at her and make her world shift? He probably meant absolutely nothing by it.

Jess took the hat completely off. 'Stopping is good. For what the children might want.'

Jess needed to stop fixating over Dan, and how good he looked in a navy polo shirt that set off the tan of his arms and khaki knee-length cut-offs that accentuated his thigh muscles.

'We'll have to be careful with sun block and staying off the beach during the worst hours of the day.' The words were primmer even than Mary Poppins could have been.

Jess didn't have a beach umbrella, but Dan had three tossed into the back of the van.

The younger children started chattering, asking their father questions and firing a few at Jess as well. Jess answered, and she drew a deep breath, which didn't help because Dan was wearing a really nice aftershave lotion.

'Jess?'

From the tone of Dan's voice, Jess suspected he might have asked her something already—and she'd been too busy daydreaming about sniffing his neck to hear it.

'I'm sorry, Dan. What did you say?' Jess glanced through the windshield and realised they'd come to a stop outside the town's supermarket. 'Oh. Shall I go in for the things? Do you have a list? Or did you want me to mind the children, or is everyone going?'

'We're all going,' Rob chimed in and then there were Frazier children bailing out of the van at the speed of light. 'We do this every trip. It's fun.'

Dan got Ella out of her seat and held her and they all trooped into the supermarket. The children proceeded to select one family-sized bag of crisps or sweets each, but first fell into discussion over what things they weren't having because didn't Mary remember getting sick eating those last year? And it wasn't a good idea for Rob to eat ones with yellow food dye because he got even more hyper than usual.

And then Luke seemed to realise that he was acting like a child, and took his bag of crisps, went to the checkout by himself, bought them and left the store.

Jess chewed her lip. 'Should I go after him, Dan?'

'Let him go.' Dan watched his son leave the store. 'He needs his space sometimes.'

Jess realised she had grown accustomed in this short time to the sense of family she received while caring for Dan's children. She didn't know how she'd been given the gift of becoming part of this, even if it was only for a few weeks or so.

She didn't want to lose her cottage and maybe have to leave Randurra to find different work, and not see Dan or his family again. There. She'd admitted both fears and what good had it done her? Jess was doing what she could about the cottage. And she didn't want these confused reactions and thoughts about Dan and her sense of family. Jess didn't *have* a sense of family except Ella, and that was everything to her.

'What would you like, Jess?' Dan gestured to the shelves. 'It's a family tradition to buy junk food for our road trips. Maybe not the best or healthiest tradition, but it's a treat, so choose something for you, and for Ella if there's something she can have.'

For a change from his usual savoury fare, Dan had a big tin of chewy-centred fruit-flavoured candies in his hand. Jess got mini ice-cream cones filled with marshmallow and topped with sprinkles for her baby daughter. 'Ella can go for an hour making a mess with one of those. Can I share your tin of candies, Dan?'

'Of course we can share.' He still had Ella in his arms, and his voice was deep. He looked tired and ruffled and as though he *still* hadn't had enough sleep.

Dan looked that way too often. Jess had been working hard to help him, but he was an automaton about getting through his work and everything going on with that firm in Sydney, about his children and stuff around the home as well. Jess suspected he'd been nothing but an automaton for a while now.

'I'll help you with them a lot, Dan. I'll make sure you get as much chance to rest over the next two days as is humanly possible.'

'You're generous, Jess. I—'

'Come on, Dad.' Rob bounced up and down on the balls of his feet. 'We're ready.'

'Jess, what sort of bathers do you have?' Mary came out of her shell to ask this, and to volunteer, 'Mine have pink, yellow and blue spots on them and they're really pretty. Annapolly has my old pair that I grew out of but she doesn't mind.'

'Um, well, I have a bikini.' Jess glanced at the several interested heads that had turned their way as this question was asked. Local women, doing their grocery shopping in the store, and already looking at Jess and Dan.

Jess didn't want to look at Dan, or to remember buying the bikini as her treat to herself after she got her figure back from having Ella. At the time, when she saw it on the sale rack and in her post-baby induced state, it had seemed like a good idea.

And then Jess had worn it carefully at home, in the secluded part of the backyard when she had Ella in the baby wader pool she'd also bought very cheaply. She had never let anyone else see her in it.

Well, it wasn't her fault if her curvy bits were a bit curvier these days than they had been. She coughed. 'I, um, I don't go swimming much.'

'What's it look like? What colour is it?' Mary asked the questions so innocently and she waited very earnestly for Jess to explain.

'Well, it's bright yellow with, um, with bumblebees on it. There are two parts to it and I usually wear a sarong over it. Do you know what a sarong is?' Jess wasn't about to miss the chance to interact with Dan's shyest child, but she would far rather describe a sarong than her bathers in any more detail.

She told herself Dan wasn't there with his ears on fire, and her bathers weren't that exciting.

She didn't mean *that* kind of exciting in any case.

Oh, Jess didn't know what the heck she meant and she'd been fine until it seemed as though the entire supermarket waited with bated breath for her answers about her swimming attire. Jess quickly explained about the sarong.

'Let's get these things bought so we can get back in the van.' She herded everyone to the checkout area. 'The sooner we get moving, the sooner we'll arrive at the beach.'

'Mary didn't mean any harm with her questions.' Dan spoke the words quietly into her ear as his children surged ahead to swarm into the van with their now purchased, and therefore consumable, goodies. A grin teased up one side of his mouth. 'And I'm sure you'll look lovely in yellow and bumblebees.'

He was in holiday mode. Dan's teasing was nothing but that, Jess assured herself. She tried very hard to believe it because she shouldn't hope for anything else.

She *didn't* hope for anything else. Did she?

'I know Mary was only curious.' Despite herself, Jess wondered if Dan *had* just flirted with her? Or simply teased her? Jess's gaze made its way inexorably to his face and discovered…he had done both! Well, that wasn't supposed to make Jess's heart feel all warm and mushy right along with a kick into overdrive of her pulse rate, but Dan was really attracted to her? Truly?

And why would that make you happy, Jess? It's bad enough that you've been noticing him. Do you really want to start thinking along those lines when you know how much your trust got shattered the last time you let yourself care for a man?

There were a dozen reasons why it would be smarter if Jess *didn't* care for this man!

Dan started the trip with some rock music. His children groaned but he ignored them. He had to have an occasional vice.

When he turned the music down twenty minutes later Jess glanced his way and gave a soft laugh. 'On the bright side, you're educating them by playing that song list.'

'How did you know I've used that justification?' He glanced at her, just once.

Her eyes were such a soft grey that it might be just as well he needed to concentrate on the road because the alternative was to get lost in those gentle depths. Those eyes were letting him in perhaps more than she realised right now.

Was he starting to care too much about Jessica Baker? He'd pushed this trip into being for his children, but he'd done it for Jess and Ella, too. He'd wanted them to be part of it, not simply because a second adult would be a good idea. Dan had wanted to do something for Jess that she might enjoy, give her something she might not otherwise have.

He wanted to see the worry disappear from the backs of her eyes, Dan realised. To see her completely relax even if only for a little while, as he managed to relax sometimes.

When was the last time you did that?

Dan could relax with Jess.

Again the thought crept up on him.

It was the last thing that should be in his mind

because why on earth would Jess want that? She was young and vibrant—young enough that like his children she probably thought his rock music was a piece of ancient history. It was disloyal to the memory of Rebecca anyway and Dan…still loved her?

Well, how did he answer that question? Of course he'd loved Rebecca. But he had also grieved for her and got over losing her because he had had no choice.

'Are we there yet?' Annapolly asked the question.

'No, Annapolly, we're not there yet.' Dan turned his attention to getting his family to their seaside destination.

And turned his thoughts away from the woman seated beside him in the front of the van. Away from noticing the way the air conditioning ruffled wisps of hair against her cheek. From the smell of a light, floral perfume blended with her skin.

Dan was not to be conscious of anything other than his responsibilities as a father and a family man and that was all. He wasn't avoiding dealing with any issues. He was simply being practical.

'That was a good kick, Rob. Well done.' Jess watched Dan's second eldest run up the beach to retrieve the soccer ball.

It was just after seven in the evening. There was a smattering of people on the beach, and a number of Fraziers all enjoying their visit to the seaside. Jess had to admit she was excited, too, if determined to keep very good watch over her crowd of charges.

The day had been beautiful and now they had a blue sky waning towards dusk, a soft, cooling sea breeze and the sun warm but not so baking hot that it would spoil their fun. There were miles of soft sandy beach with a ridge of shells tossed higher up. That augured well for collecting more of the same tomorrow morning. And the water itself. Oh, those rolling waves of endless blue water.

Jess let her gaze scan the scene again. Ella sat on a very large beach blanket beneath one of the umbrellas. She was quite content playing with a set of buckets that fitted inside each other and a plastic spade, which she banged on the buckets, chuckling gleefully as she did so.

Luke was in the water and his father was out there with him keeping a close eye, though the teen was a strong swimmer and a sensible one so far. Rob had taken his dip and got out to run up and down the beach. Mary and Annapolly had been given turns 'swimming' in the shallows with their dad before they came out to build a sandcastle.

Jess hadn't swum. Of course she'd love to, but she had a job to do. She was relieved that she wouldn't have to reveal the bumblebee bikini hidden away nicely beneath her sarong.

Dan was a good swimmer, too, though Jess had tried not to look too closely at him once he stripped off his shirt and the cut-offs and revealed a pair of board shorts.

'It's your turn to have a swim, Jess. Luke and I are going to take a rest. I'll watch Ella while you're in there.' Dan glanced at Ella in time to see her bang the spade on one of the buckets again and crow in delight at the resulting 'thwack' of sound. 'She seems content enough.'

Droplets of water trickled from Dan's wet hair, and

down the tanned muscles of his chest. His board shorts clung to his physique—

Well, Jess didn't need to be thinking about Dan's physique!

Dan's gaze came back to her. An edge of intensity appeared in his eyes that suggested he might have noticed her examination of him, or might be making one of his own across Jess's sun-kissed shoulders and down over her arms.

Dan's shoulders and upper arms were strong, the muscles defined and beautifully curved.

Looking away now.

And his tummy was really flat. And he was tanned and strong and, oh, she really wanted to touch all that wet, salty skin with her fingertips.

'I don't think I'll swim.' *I'd probably set the sea on fire from all the heat that just rushed into me thanks to those thoughts.* Not to mention the bumblebees and all the curves that were more curves than they used to be. 'I, well, I probably just won't.'

She didn't want to strip down to her bikini in front of—the children? Jess glanced down at her bright, multicoloured sarong, and then, despite herself, looked a little longingly at the water, and along the beach to where there were several women wearing bikinis far more revealing than her very ordinary one, even if it was bright and covered in bees.

'This trip…' Dan hesitated. 'I wanted to do something for the children, *and* for you and Ella. It's not much of a trip to the beach if you don't swim. I won't laugh at the bumblebees, I promise.'

Oh, that serious tone with the glints of mischief dancing in his eyes, all because Mary had asked those questions in the supermarket and Dan had been right there while Jess squirmed her way through the answers.

Luke had moved away, and Jess felt for a moment as though she and Dan were the only people on the beach, despite the children surrounding them.

Dan probably wouldn't even look at her anyway. He just wanted her to be able to enjoy herself, and she was being ridiculous.

'I'm a decent swimmer.' Jess made the decision that she would get in the water. If Dan could stand here dripping in board shorts, Jess could strip down to curvy bumblebees. 'I'll make sure I do the right thing out there. You'll have to watch all the children while I'm gone.'

As though Dan weren't more than aware of the necessity of keeping charge of his children. And Ella, of course. It went without saying. He'd just offered to do exactly that.

Jess was procrastinating. 'Right.' She dumped the sarong in one swift movement. She did not boggle at the thought of the bumblebees on her butt. She *certainly* didn't have that very old song about being afraid to get in the water flash through her brain.

If she didn't meet Dan's eyes then she wouldn't even know if he was looking or not.

'You have a perfect figure.' He said it in a half whisper. 'I suppose I knew, really, but I couldn't have imagined.' The words ended. Dan's hot gaze had travelled over her and Jess had seen it. He turned abruptly away and Jess tried to walk very naturally across the sand to the water.

She swam and pushed her thoughts away until there

was only swimming and the tug of the waves, and Dan and the children on the beach.

Dan hadn't really given her that intense look, she assured herself, forgetting that she wasn't thinking while she was out here.

Sure. Just as you didn't give Dan *an intense look.*

Jess forced her arms and legs to work for her, and rode the gentle waves, imagined bobbing like a cork. She kept the shore in her sights, but she let everything blur around the edges and she was successful eventually.

'Daddy, can I have a s'rong like Jess's? And why don't me and Daisy and Annapolly have 'kinis?' The question came from Mary as she sat down beside Dan where he'd come to play with Ella on her blanket.

Jess's daughter had noticed her mother's absence, but there were enough Fraziers to keep her distracted.

Dan was distracted. Mightily. The memory of Jess whipping off that sarong and dumping the colourful fabric onto the sand played through his mind over and over.

Not because of the sarong, but because of what it had revealed. Dan had never seen bumblebees look quite like that.

Jess was beautiful, curvy in all the right places, soft enough that he could imagine how nice it would feel to cuddle her—

'Dad?' Mary poked him in the ribs with one finger. 'Did you hear me?'

'You and your sisters have those bathing suits because they look good on you.' Dan dragged his gaze away from the sight of Jess out there enjoying her time in the water.

His voice dropped about an octave as he went on. 'Jess has her suit because it looks good on her, too.'

'She shouldn't dress like that when she's supposed to be working for us, looking after everyone.' Luke's words came from behind Dan with low anger. 'She's just trying to make you interested in her, and all you do is look at her all the time. I hate her and I wish you'd never hired her!'

'What's got into you, Luke?' Dan turned and stared into his son's set, angry face.

Luke's glance shifted beyond him. 'I mean every word of it and don't tell me to apologise, Dad, because I won't. On top of everything, you're treating her like she's part of the family. She's not. She's just the babysitter and not even a good one because she let Annapolly hurt herself.'

'Apologise, Luke.' Dan started to his feet.

Luke was faster. He shook his head and stalked away across the beach.

Dan didn't need to turn to know that Jess was standing there, but he looked anyway, and caught her determined, forced smile as she reached for her sarong and pulled it over the bumblebees. 'Don't force him, Dan. He won't mean it anyway, if you do that.'

Had Dan allowed the sight of her to short-circuit his sensible brain functions?

And Jess's eyes had clouded over with desire when she'd seen his bare chest… How did he feel about that?

Should he only worry about Luke's behaviour and ignore the rest of this? Dan was usually controlled and focused. Right now he didn't know which urge to cater to first. He wanted to chase after Luke and demand an explanation and apology, which would no doubt end in an argument because right now his son wasn't in the frame of mind to be reasonable and Dan didn't exactly feel like being tolerant either.

Or should he try to sort this out with Jess? 'I can't allow him to speak that way.'

'No, but you can give him time to cool off a bit just now.' Jess stuck her chin out. 'Thanks, anyway, for the swim, and if you think I've dressed inappropriately—'

'I don't think that.' Dan frowned. 'And Luke was having a go at me as much as at you.' As each word emerged Dan wanted to become angrier, and he battled to push back the feeling. Something told him once he asked himself just *why* he felt so resentful of Luke's attitude, he would have to deal with a whole bunch of questions he wasn't sure he was ready to confront.

'Well, it was nice to swim. I haven't had a swim in the sea for years.' Jess drew a deep breath and seemed to come to a decision. 'If you feel it would be best to replace me, Dan, with someone Luke can get along better with—'

'That won't be necessary.' Dan appreciated her making the offer, but he wasn't going to let her go. 'I don't want to lose you, Jess.'

To lose her help, he'd meant.

But was that all he'd meant?

Dan glanced her way. Luke's outburst notwithstanding, Dan *was* becoming more and more attracted to Jess. Even in the face of the conflict with Luke, Dan wanted to get to the end of the day and all the children in bed. And why did he want that?

So he could find a private nook and kiss Jess stupid? Dan acknowledged he would like to do exactly that. Did he really think it would resolve anything? It would just complicate things even more.

'I'm glad you enjoyed the water.' He felt not quite certain of his ground. When Dan worked he *was* completely certain of his ground. He was good at his job and he did it well, and he powered through it with a great deal of focus while he still managed to watch the children besides. Yet right now Dan felt as though there were other parts of him that hadn't been living.

He shouldn't be feeling like this. In the end he'd made the choice to be content, so why did Luke's attitude bother him so much? Because there was something more to it than Luke needing to mind his manners around Jess, though that was very important.

'I think we'd better pack up and head back to the beach house.' Dan got to his feet and started gathering paraphernalia together. Perhaps once there, all of these feelings would settle down.

He felt weird when he lifted the beach umbrella out of the sand. Dan brushed the feeling aside and got on with rounding up the children. They'd go back to the beach house, maybe buy fish and chips on the way from a local shop, eat, and he expected the children would fall asleep quite quickly because it *had* been a long day. The thought of a nice salty meal of fresh seafood did appeal. It might halfway reward him for the talk he was going to have to have with his son.

'Mum used to make great sandcastles when we went to the beach.' Rob's words were directed to Jess.

Luke had yet again stalked ahead of the family to the van.

'What sort of castles do you remember, Rob?' Jess

ruffled the boy's hair before she bent to pick up her daughter from the blanket.

It was the first time Dan had heard any of his children mention Rebecca to their caregiver. But that wasn't the reason the words sliced right through Dan.

He hadn't thought once about Rebecca while they were at the beach. For the first day since he lost her, Dan hadn't had a thought in his head about the mother of his children. All those thoughts had been directed at Jess, to being so conscious of her.

Luke's anger had been towards Jess, and Dan, but had it really been about this? Had Luke somehow seen that his father was drifting from those memories and Luke felt resentful and lost as a result? Dan felt lost as he asked this question because he didn't know. He hadn't wanted to forget. He couldn't forget.

Rob started to explain the intricate sandcastles he remembered building with his mother. Dan added his few words here and there because the children would have felt it was strange if he didn't. He got everyone packed into the van. And guilt ate at him because his heart had been given to Rebecca and there was nothing left, so why did he think it was okay to want Jessica Baker?

To think about things with her that had been part of his marriage? Not only physical closeness, but friendship and getting to know a woman and wanting to be part of *her* life, to understand her better.

Dan set the van in motion.

He had no answers. All he had were questions that he didn't want to know about and a son he had to deal with when he got him to himself for a moment!

CHAPTER SEVEN

'THEY'RE ALL DOWN FOR the count finally.' Jess made the announcement as she joined Dan on the front porch of the compact beach house. It was almost midnight. The younger children had been overtired and excitable.

Dan had taken Luke away in the van straight after dinner and they'd both come back looking like thunderclouds. Actually Luke had seemed on the verge of tears, a fact Jess had noted and made sure she drew the attention of the other children away from him, and kept it away. She didn't want him to feel the sting of embarrassment. Her heart ached for the boy and she wished she could find some way to help him, or at least help him to know that she meant him no harm.

And yet her feelings towards Dan hadn't changed. Jess couldn't shut them down because of Luke. They were there. Tonight Jess needed to comfort Dan, and be comforted by him, as much as she needed to try to reach out to his son. This tangle of feelings wasn't easy.

'Thanks, Jess. It was a busy and long enough day.' Dan was seated on the only piece of furniture out here, which happened to be a swing seat. He bent down and retrieved two glasses of white wine from the floor beside it, and held one out to her.

Jess sat, and took the wine from him with a surprised and grateful sigh. 'Where did you find this?'

'It was in the fridge, part of the service for renting this seaside cottage.' Dan smiled. 'Tonight I think we've both earned a glass.'

'I won't argue.' Jess sipped the wine and closed her eyes and let the fruity tang of it slide across her tongue.

Dan set the swing into gentle motion, and she leaned back and let the sound of the ocean, the sea breeze, the taste of the wine all touch her senses.

And Dan, Jess? Is he touching your senses too?

Oh, she was super aware of him seated beside her. Their thighs were almost brushing. Dan had his wineglass in one hand. His other arm was draped across the back of the seat. If she leaned back a little more she would practically *be* in his arms.

Jess wanted to be, that was the trouble. She wanted to be in Dan's embrace more than anything and she couldn't let herself want that. There were so many reasons. She was Dan's employee. Her home was under threat. She needed her job with Dan for as long as he wanted to keep her on, to get money to pay off the debt on her cottage. Dan had only just spoken to Luke to try to get him into a better place about Jess's presence as the caregiver. Jess was younger. Dan was older. He was her employer.

There were other reasons why Jess couldn't trust—

'I hope today didn't exhaust you too much, Jess.' Dan's low words came to her through the quiet of the night.

Came on a breath and she turned her head. Light spilled from the lounge room inside. She'd walked out through the sliding doors to join Dan on the porch. The light illuminated just enough for Jess to see the strong planes of Dan's face and to want to trace each one of them with her fingertips.

Her worries blurred as she stared into his eyes. Her sensible reasons for resisting the way he made her feel faded too.

'It didn't exhaust me. But what about you, Dan? I don't think you managed much rest for yourself today.' In fact, Jess thought Dan might have overdone it a bit today, because he'd looked quite used up when they left the beach, and again after playing in the yard with Rob for a while tonight.

He'd looked upset, too, when Rob mentioned building sandcastles with...Rebecca, Dan's late wife. She'd been a beautiful brunette with soft brown eyes and a smile that Dan must see in his daughters every day. Jess had pored over the framed photos with the younger children back at the Fraziers' house.

And the talk with Luke couldn't have been easy for Dan, either.

'A good sleep tonight will sort me out.' Dan shifted slightly, slowed the movement of the swing seat down to the gentlest motion. As he did so his thigh shifted against Jess's. She had a skirt on with a T-shirt top. Dan was wearing another of his polo shirts and denim shorts. Yet even through the layers of skirt and shorts, Jess's skin warmed, sensitised to that brush of his body against her.

'What do you have planned for the kids tomorrow—?'

'I hope the children don't wake at dawn tomorrow—'

Jess drew a tight breath.

Dan stopped.

Their eyes met and held, and Dan made a sound that was half yielding, half resistant, and Jess's breath stopped in her throat.

'Jess.' Dan spoke her name with all the suppressed desire that Jess felt.

She should say no, should get up, walk away, think about her position here and all those reasons, but Jess didn't. She couldn't do it because she did desire Dan. She was attracted to him and in the back of her mind she had asked herself a hundred times—

When Dan lowered his head, she lifted her lips and met him. His foot came to rest on the floor and the tiny motion of the swing seat stopped.

Dan's lips closed over Jess's and his arms came around her. Her arms rose to his chest and one locked about the back of his neck. Jess had dreamed about Dan's neck. The strong column of it; how the muscles would feel beneath her hand. She hadn't known that he would feel so warm. That she would feel such tensile strength in him, or that his kiss would feel like this. She told herself it was safe. The children were asleep. She and Dan could do this and it wasn't hurting anything.

Dan's firm lips softened, and brought her the taste of wine that was also in her mouth. Jess's wineglass was long gone, somewhere on the floor. She didn't even remember finishing the drink or putting it down. She wanted to blame the abandonment of her thoughts on that wine but she couldn't.

The bubbles floating inside her were not from the small amount of alcohol. These were Dan-inspired bubbles and Jess didn't want them to ever stop. All her careful thoughts and self-protection frayed away, unravelled as Dan's lips consumed hers, took her mouth with desire and a need that matched her need.

Jess melted into him. That was what Dan felt as he kissed her, as their lips meshed together and he experienced all the sensations of holding her, kissing her, feeling her body soften against his and her arm creep about his neck so she could hold him closer, draw more from their kiss.

His heart pounded. Every sense and sensation was focused on the woman in his arms, the taste of her soft lips. Dan had asked himself how Jess could truly be attracted to him, what she could see in a man his age. There was Luke, being difficult, and Dan's own confused feelings.

And there was this—him kissing her and her kissing him in a way that not only assuaged curiosity and awareness but invoked tenderness, the kind of tenderness he would have given and exchanged only with Rebecca…

What was he doing?

What kind of risk was he taking when he had nothing inside him to give, nothing that hadn't already been given, handed over to the woman he had loved with all his heart? What was he doing seeking this with Jess when his eldest son was inside, angry and upset because he thought Dan was crossing a line with an employee that he shouldn't cross?

Luke had thrown that at Dan along with a lot of deeper accusations about Dan not honouring his mother, and Dan…hadn't been able to argue because Luke was right about Jess's position as an employee, and in the end, though Dan didn't want his son trying to dictate to him about his personal life, Luke's accusations about the rest of it only matched Dan's own thoughts too.

Dan's hands came up to Jess's shoulders. He eased his lips from hers and set distance between them. Dan on this side of the swing seat. Jess on that side. And he prayed to whatever god might be listening that he hadn't just hurt her and that he hadn't just hurt himself. This *wasn't* right.

It couldn't be.

Regret washed through him. For doing something that was wrong and disloyal. He couldn't remember how it had felt to kiss Rebecca. The memory wouldn't come, was pushed down beneath the sensation of kissing his children's daycare mum. Dan had always been able to remember.

Yet this kiss had felt special, exceptional, but was he talking himself into these thoughts because he craved closeness? Because Jess was attractive and working in proximity with him and so it was almost easy to let himself—?

'It's the holiday setting.' A trace of panic laced Jess's tone. She blinked as though to try to dispel the lingering effects of what they had just shared. 'The sea and how late it is and sitting out here. It didn't mean anything. We just didn't think—'

But they had thought, hadn't they? Dan had known that Jess would join him out here and he'd waited and in some part of him he'd known he would kiss her, even despite the upheaval with his son and all the reasons it would have been smarter not to do it.

Jess had done her final round inside the house and checked on her daughter and she'd known, too. Dan felt certain that she had. But could she be more truly invested in this than he was?

Jess was young, a single mother and working for him. Why put her in a position where she might feel vulnerable, whether she'd been prepared to step into that place with him for a moment or not?

She was obviously having second thoughts about it now.

Just as he was. 'I had no right to do that, Jess, and yet a part of me wanted it to happen.' He hated to admit it but he couldn't make it sound as though Jess had been the one to try to make it happen. They'd both drifted towards this and in the quiet of the night with all the children tucked away… 'That was even more wrong because I know I can't—'

'I know.' Jess hushed him with the low words. 'I know, Dan.' She got up from the seat. Her face was tight, filled with tense emotion. Uncertainty and resolve at war with each other. Shadows. Unease. And still the impact of his kisses was there for him to see upon her swollen lips and in the blurred confusion in her soft grey eyes.

Desire whispered again, and Dan frowned it down.

'It's late.' The need to get away filled her words. 'And I think the children probably will be up early in the morning. I need to be up too, to be on duty the moment they wake and to do my best to start trying to win Luke's trust again after—after him opening up about his feelings today.'

She didn't say more and Dan pushed down his own mixed feelings on that topic for examination later.

Jess simply went on. 'So I'll say goodnight now and hope that you sleep well and get really good rest. I worry about you getting too tired sometimes.'

She went inside. Dan picked up the wineglasses, and dumped them in the kitchen, and made sure all the doors were locked. He would do as Jess suggested and sleep, and when he woke tomorrow he'd remember what it had been like to kiss Rebecca.

There would be no Dan and Jess, because Dan and Jess didn't exist. Not in any way other than employer and employee. He might be tempted, he might need to draw some lines in the sand with his son so Luke respected Dan's right to have needs, but none of that changed the fact that his relationship with his much younger childcare provider needed to remain firmly fixed in business.

Dan took himself off to bed.

Jess leaned against the closed door of the room she was sharing with Ella. She'd shut herself in there and listened as Dan went about the house checking that everything was locked up and secure. Checking that his children, and, by association because they were here, Jess and Ella, were safe before he went to bed.

Dan had kissed her. Jess's insides were still shaking from the impact of that kiss. She didn't want to think about it, was afraid if she did she might discover thoughts and reactions and emotions inside herself she couldn't let herself find.

He'd pushed her away, had regretted the kiss probably before it was even over. Jess had seen in Dan's eyes the conviction that she would be too much trouble to be worth it. Some of that would be about Luke's attitude, about her working for him…

People found ways, though, when things mattered enough, didn't they?

You don't want *Dan to find a way, Jess.*

Jess didn't have what she would need to invest emotionally. She had her life to live and she needed to rely on herself, be the best mother possible to Ella and the best daycare mum she could be, but with the exception of the love she gave to her daughter, Jess needed to do those things while keeping the deepest parts of herself locked away where they would stay safe and not suffer any further blows of rejection.

What could Dan Frazier do but reject Jess? He'd done it just now, hadn't he?

Jess pushed away from the door and went to the single bed beside her daughter's cot. Jess's clothes were there in a zipper bag. She got out her pyjamas, put them on, crawled under the sheet and prayed for sleep and for tomorrow to have erased every memory of Dan's mouth over hers, his arms snug about her, and most of all to have erased the feeling of security and rightness that Jess had felt in his embrace.

There was no such security to be found. Dan didn't have it to give.

'Eating outside at a picnic table is fun. I'm glad we thought of it.' Daisy didn't hesitate to take credit for the idea of eating their breakfast out of doors, though in fact it had been Dan's suggestion because he'd wanted to allow Jess to sleep in a little if she could.

It was not because he didn't feel ready to face her after that kiss. Dan glanced in Luke's direction. Was it because of the uneasy state of matters between him and his son? It was, in part. It was also because Dan hadn't been able to get the kiss out of his mind.

'Do we have any more orange juice, Dad?' Rob asked

the question after lifting the two-litre bottle on the table and discovering it was empty.

'You keep going on your breakfast, Rob. I'll get more juice from the fridge.' Dan left the children. It was bad that, because of Luke, he almost felt relieved to walk away. He was going to have to try to sort things out better than this, but what should he say? Butt out of my personal life? It's none of your business? It wasn't that simple.

Dan stepped into the kitchen, and heard a sound from the room Jess and Ella were sharing. The door had been closed when he got up this morning but he noted now that it was halfway open.

Had Annapolly taken a peek in there? She was a horror for helping herself to doors that weren't locked. Dan hesitated for a moment and then decided to go shut it. It was six in the morning. Let Jess sleep in while she could. Ella, too.

Let a little more time pass before Dan had to confront what happened last night? The awareness *was* mostly due to proximity, wasn't it? And to his senses waking up after a four-year slumber in a way Dan hadn't realised was going to sneak up on him?

He stepped quietly to the door of the room and reached to pull it closed.

He paused as he took in the sight inside. A baby in a cot, covers kicked off lying on her tummy with her nappy-padded bum in the air. A smile twitched at the corners of Dan's mouth despite himself.

Then his gaze shifted to the bed beside that cot and his smile faded because there was Jess in a set of very short floral baby-doll pyjamas with frilly bits all over and a lot of bare skin. She, too, had kicked off her covers and was sound asleep on her tummy.

And yes, Dan was still attracted and it had only taken that glimpse of her to make it clear. But there was more than that. There was tightness in Dan's chest because… he wanted to step into the room, climb into the bed, pull the sheet up over both of them and cuddle up with her. He wanted that, and it wasn't only about physical awareness. It was about a kind of closeness that Dan feared might mean he didn't only *want* her, but some part of him thought that he needed her?

'Du!' A wriggle of sound came from the cot.

By the time Dan looked, Ella was on her back, grinning up at him.

'Do you want to get up, Ella?' Dan whispered and shifted to the side of the cot. The little one wriggled, rolled and pulled herself up to her feet using the cot's railings for support.

Dan picked her up, grabbed a disposable nappy and the bits and pieces he'd need to sort her out, and took her into the girls' room. Two minutes later he had a dry cooing baby in his arms. He got Rob's juice from the fridge and took Ella outside to join the others.

The children fussed over Ella. She was a beautiful baby. Dan had forgotten what it was like to have such a little one. Ella was wide awake but still a bit cuddly. She laid her head in the crook of his neck and watched his rowdy family from the safety of his arms. And Dan… wished that all of life could be so simple. Just provide a pair of arms and that would be enough.

Luke had the seat to Dan's right. Ella reached out her arms to him and gurgled.

'I think she wants you to hold her, Luke.' Dan caught

his son's eye just as Ella wiggled even more, waving her arms for Luke to take her.

'I don't know why she likes me so much.' Luke half grumbled the words, but he took Ella and his expression was soft as he sat her on his knees.

Dan looked at his eldest, who was so close to being a man now, and wondered where the years had gone, and hoped that he and Luke wouldn't remain at loggerheads. He didn't want that. Deep down, Dan didn't think Luke wanted that, either.

And Dan thought about Jess asleep in bed inside and how he'd felt when he saw her there. Maybe what he felt was lonely, and Jess was around and he'd kissed her so of course he'd want to kiss her again…

Dan poured himself some cereal, added a generous portion of milk, and started a conversation with the children about what they'd be doing today before they got in the van to go back home.

Probably when Jess woke, Dan would look at her and wonder what all his fuss had been about anyway.

'You let me sleep in.' Jess spoke the words in a shocked tone as she joined Dan at the outdoor breakfast table. She'd woken to the sound of Ella crowing somewhere outside and had realised Dan must have got her daughter up and left Jess to sleep.

Jess had never started a day without taking care of Ella. And the thought of Dan coming into the room, seeing her sleeping…

What if she'd been flat on her back snoring? She'd woken on her side, curled up in a ball, but Jess knew she wriggled around before she actually woke up. Ella did the same thing.

'You're dressed.' Dan spoke the words with an edge of relief. A second later his ears turned red at the tips. He glanced at his children, then turned back to Jess and all but shoved a box of breakfast cereal her way as she took a seat at the table. 'You were asleep. I went to shut the door. I think Annapolly was the culprit though I couldn't say for sure. Ella was awake but I couldn't see the sense in waking you.'

With these statements made, Dan poured a glass of juice for himself and drank half of it in one gulp.

There hadn't been time from waking to joining everyone at the table for Jess to think about anything other than the shock of waking without her daughter in the room, and knowing she should be on duty and Dan had left her to sleep. She'd thrown on the first clothes she found and rushed outside. She hadn't even combed her hair, and now Jess became aware of so many things all at once.

Her less-than-properly-groomed state. Dan looking fresh and attractive and far more capable of satisfying her than any bowl of cereal.

Luke holding her daughter, and Ella patting his face with complete contentment. Jess had a theory about that. Children and animals—they knew a kind heart when they found one. That gave Jess hope that she *would* be able to get things in a better place with Luke over time.

If you stop showing any interest in his father!

Jess had realised that kissing Dan had been a mistake. All she'd done was expose herself to Dan backing away afterwards. But this morning Jess was having trouble accepting that assessment. What was wrong with her? Did she want to line up to be rejected when she couldn't stack up to what Dan had already had in his life? When Dan wasn't prepared to stand up for her? Not really? If he cared enough he would address the issue with his son and make it clear to Luke that he had the right to pursue a relationship.

Hadn't she had enough second-rate treatment from Ella's father?

Jess didn't want to be negative. She had Ella. She had a job and she would have a home. Jess just needed to sort that out properly with Lang Fielder one day very soon. She didn't need anything more.

Jess pushed out every thought aside from her work, this work right now. And she worked. She made sure the children had the best time possible when they all went back to the beach. She gave two hundred per cent to trying to win Luke over. She assisted Dan at every turn and she did it without responding to him as a man, at all.

This was the way it needed to be. Jess and Dan, working as a team to give his children the best short holiday experience possible, and for Jess to give the best care for them, overall.

Jess reminded herself of these thoughts as the family made their way back to Dan's sprawling home late that day after touring two museums on the way home, and stopping for various adventures including afternoon tea at a truck stop.

'You can go, Jess. You must be as exhausted as I am.' Dan seemed to have to dig for the smile he offered.

'Thanks for taking me and Ella along for the trip.' Jess made a point of saying goodnight to each of the children before she lifted her sleeping daughter into her arms.

It didn't matter if Luke didn't respond. He *was* softening. Jess could sense it.

And you don't think that's simply because he told his father to stay away from you and he's getting the impression Dan obeyed?

What a tangle it was!

Dan brought her luggage to the car for her, and Jess finished her thanks loudly enough that if any of the children were inclined, they would hear every word. 'It was a treat I doubt I'd have been able to give Ella any time soon and I appreciate it for that reason.'

'And I appreciated having help while we were there.' Dan's eyes were cloudy with a combination of exhaustion and banked-down longing when Jess straightened from strapping Ella into her car restraint.

A moment later he blinked and that impression was gone. Had Jess imagined it? Or was Dan still struggling, after all, to set aside those feelings?

Oh, Jess, don't hope for that to be the case!

Jess couldn't let herself think about consciousness. *Dan* didn't want to think about it. Dan…didn't want Jess. This was clear, and Jess needed to keep it clear within herself. 'Goodnight, Dan. I'll be here day after tomorrow as usual.' She would be here for as long as he could offer her work.

And in the end that was that, wasn't it? Jess needed to keep trying to find other, ongoing work, too, and most of all she needed to forget all about any feelings towards this man who was a temporary employer and nothing else.

CHAPTER EIGHT

'JESS.' DAN'S DEEP voice said her name with concern. A moment later he had hold of her shoulder. 'What's wrong?'

'I'm fine, Dan. There's nothing wrong.' Jess blinked furiously and forced a smile, determined to make Dan believe it.

Dan had come upon her in the hallway outside the room that held Ella's travel cot. Her grumpy baby had finally given in to sleep after being fractious all morning. Had Dan noticed that Jess had been struggling to do her job properly with the rest of the children because of Ella's mood?

If Ella's in a mood, it's more than likely because she's picked up on her mother's anxiety.

'I'm sorry, Dan. I hope Ella's grizzling didn't disturb your work in the den.' When Ella had finally given in and fallen asleep, Jess hadn't been able to hold back that anxiety any longer. She'd leaned against the wall outside Ella's room and panic had washed over her. She hadn't expected Dan to come along and find her there.

'If she's sick or you need anything—' Dan didn't seem to be aware that his fingers were gently rubbing at Jess's shoulders.

Jess wanted to lean her head forward onto his chest, take what comfort she could. For a split second she even considered pretending that Ella's grizzling had been anything more than reacting to Jess's mood, but it hadn't been. 'Ella's fine. She'll sleep now and have forgotten her grumpiness when she wakes.'

'Okay. If you're sure.' Dan dropped his hands but his gaze didn't leave her face.

'I need to check on the girls, Dan.' Jess didn't. Not really. They were content playing tea parties on the veranda. Dan's sons were riding their pushbikes around the front part of the ten-acre allotment, where Jess could still look out periodically and keep an eye on them.

If anything, at the moment, Luke seemed to be cold towards his father rather than Jess. Not that there was a whole lot of comfort in that.

'The girls are happy enough. I can see Rob and Luke out there on their bikes and they're fine for the moment, too.' Dan blew out a breath. 'There's something troubling you, enough that you looked devastated just now. I'm sorry if I caught you while your guard was down, but I wish you'd tell me, Jess. If it was Luke—'

'No, Luke had his say at the beach. I'm sure if you feel there's a need to encourage Luke to change his attitude about your personal life, you'll address that topic with him.' Did Jess sound snippy saying that?

You have a right to your opinion about it. Dan made it pretty clear he wasn't prepared to go into battle with his son over any involvement he might want with you.

But that was just it. Dan *didn't* want to be involved with Jess. How many times would she have to remind herself of that fact before it truly sank in?

And Dan wasn't a horrid man. He was just one who

had kissed her, and then decided that hadn't been a smart idea. Jess had agreed with him, so why was she going on about it now? She didn't *want* Dan and Luke to battle because of her.

'Jess.' Dan's voice softened again. 'I know there have been some tough patches. I've added to some of those for you and…I regret that. But won't you tell me what's wrong now?'

Jess looked into Dan's eyes and there was something in there of the day *she* had asked *him* if she could help him. A fellow feeling, at least. A measure of care.

'I'm going to lose my home. Ella's father didn't turn out to be a very nice person.' Jess hadn't understood that until it was too late, and maybe she should have held back from admitting it to Dan, but he'd once said that he wanted to know more about her life.

This was a major part of her history, but Dan had said that to her as her employer, at the start, not…as anything else. 'He didn't want a baby, and he didn't want me. After I told him Ella was on the way, he wanted me to sign an agreement that I would never name him as her father or ask him for any support and that Ella and I would get out of his life and stay out.'

Jess had been hurt and she needed to remember that pain and be careful not to let it happen again.

Somewhere along the line with Dan, she'd lost some of her focus.

A frown formed between Dan's brows. He took her by the elbow then, and ushered them both into the kitchen where he turned her to face him. 'If he fathered your baby, Jess, he owed you support. Financial maintenance at the least, throughout Ella's childhood.'

'I know.' And Jess did know. And she knew that Dan

would never have behaved as Peter Rosche had done. She wasn't trying to judge Dan by Peter's standards, or lack of them.

Jess just didn't want to get hurt any more. She pushed a sigh out between her lips. 'In theory, that's how it works but he'd made it so clear he didn't want anything to do with either of us. I thought he'd only be a horrid influence in Ella's life anyway.

'I signed his agreement and I thought I'd been smart because I bargained to have him buy the little cottage here for me so I'd have a safe place to raise Ella.'

Jess had pointed the cottage out to Dan when they came back from their trip to the beach, so he knew it was small, nothing special, though it was on a decent-sized block surrounded by three other cottage properties, all with an elevated view.

'What happened?'

'He bought the cottage and didn't tell me that he'd done a deal with the local council regarding ten years' worth of overdue rates on it.' Jess felt naive for letting that happen. 'Lang Fielder, the councillor, claims that he's been sending notices that the overdue rates and interest had to be paid, but those went to some address invented by Ella's father. It got to the point where Lang delivered a final notice to the property itself. That's when I found out about it.'

Dan nodded. 'That notice was delivered directly to you?'

'Yes. A couple of weeks ago.' Jess swallowed down on a mix of anxiety and frustration. She didn't want to let the anxiety win, but it really was getting the upper hand at the moment. 'The cottage isn't worth much, Dan. You've seen it. It's right on the edge of town. The shaded outdoor areas help for my daycare, but the cottage itself is quite small and very basic. Over one third of its value is owed to the council in back rates and accumulated interest. Ella's father has disappeared, and I've been given to the end of the month to pay all of it in full or they'll sell the property to get the money.'

The frown between Dan's eyes deepened. 'Have you spoken to a solicitor? You can't lose your home. That's not fair.'

No. It wasn't fair, but in Jess's experience not all of life always was. 'I got two letters in the mail yesterday while I was minding my other children. One was from the local solicitor I approached, to say they can't get legal aid funding to help me. I can't pay them normal rates, so that's the end of that. The other letter was from Lang Fielder at the council, formally declining my request to make ongoing payments off what's owed. He says because it's got as far as it has, the council is exercising its right to recoup the money by selling the property. Market value is irrelevant so long as it sells for enough to get their money back. And apparently the council already knows of an interested buyer.'

'I'll help you. There's got to be more—'

'It's not your responsibility, Dan.' Jess shook her head. She appreciated Dan's care, perhaps even more because it came purely from a temporary employer's perspective now.

That knowledge shouldn't have stung, but it did, a little.

Dan half turned away to get cups down and put on the kettle. He efficiently got tea making sorted before he faced her again. 'Jess, you got me out of a tight spot by offering to help me. I have a solicitor who's handled heaps of stuff for me. Let me ask him to look at your situation. If there's something that can be done, he'll be able to tell us.'

He held up a hand. 'And before you say anything about money, he won't charge me for this. He took over a smaller practice last year that had belonged to his uncle. The financials were in a mess and I sorted that out for him as a favour. He told me if I ever needed one back to let him know, so…let me call that favour in on your behalf.'

'You're not making that up to try to save my pride?' Because Jess simply wouldn't be able to tolerate that. Not at all. She searched his face.

He shook his head. 'It may not change anything, Jess, but you need to know where you stand legally. How about if I try to ring the guy now and you can speak with him and explain the situation?'

Dan took her silence as agreement, and made his way to the den. And that was fine because Jess needed help. She just hadn't expected to have it handed to her free of charge thanks to Dan's generosity, right when she was doing her best to feel resentful towards Dan for…

For what, Jessica? For not standing up to his son and pushing for the right to have a relationship with you, when you already knew deep down it would be dangerous to pursue such a relationship because you've been hurt before, and it would have been stupid to enter into anything like that when you work together as well?

Even with Luke's attitude aside, there were still plenty of valid reasons why Jess should have stayed away from letting herself desire Dan, and vice versa.

'Jess, I have the solicitor on the phone. His name is Jonathan Porerri.' Dan spoke from the doorway of his den. 'Just tell him what you told me. I've given him fax and email information and we've organised things so he's retained to assist you with this situation.'

Right. Jess's tummy knotted up, but she'd explained the situation to Dan. If that hadn't killed her she could explain it again to a stranger on the other end of a phone line. At least at the end of it she would come out with a better idea of where she stood, and therefore what her next movements needed to be, and how quickly she needed to make them. She had to take this opportunity to get some advice and be grateful for it.

Dan watched Jess step inside his den. He moved out of the room and closed the door behind him. How much trouble was she in? What kind of rat would treat her that way? Make her sign herself and her baby out of his life and in the process of doing that, set her up so he knew she wouldn't have a roof over her head a year later?

Instincts inside Dan were roaring. He wanted to find this man and make him take responsibility for his actions, for leaving Jess in a position where she was worrying about having a home.

Oh, yes? And you've treated her perfectly the entire time she's worked for you?

Dan hadn't, but that was complicated, and he certainly hadn't set out to harm Jess deliberately in any way. He would never try to do that.

'I've finished the call.' Jess stepped back into the kitchen several minutes later.

She was pale, but seemed very composed. *Too* composed? Dan opened his mouth to ask—he wasn't sure what.

But Jess met his gaze and spoke before he could. 'Thank you, Dan, for giving me the opportunity to pick your solicitor's brains about my situation. He's asked me to fax him some information that I need to get from the cottage. Would you mind if I collected that now? Ella's asleep.'

'Of course.' What Dan wanted most was to take her into his arms and comfort her. And that confused him. He believed, and he truly meant it, that it wasn't right to have any interest in Jess Baker aside from being her employer.

You're dodging issues, Dan. Luke's attitude is right up there with the best of those issues. Why do you think he feels so opposed to you experiencing any interest in Jess? He believes you should only ever have feelings for his late mother, and...

What if Dan wanted to have feelings elsewhere?

Before he could think about that, Jess nodded and started for the door. 'I'll be back soon.'

Jess drove the short distance to her cottage. How much longer would she have it? Did she have to lose it? What work could she get to support her and Ella when all she knew was how to be a daycare mum?

Jess parked her little car beside her equally unpretentious cottage and forced a controlled expression to her face before she stepped out.

'Just get the paperwork. Ella's asleep back at Dan's. You don't have time to waste.' Jess got a small locked box and took out her copy of the agreement she'd signed with Peter Rosche and what paperwork he'd given her in relation to ownership of the cottage. There was nothing in it to say there were back rates owing, as Jess had checked at least ten times since Lang Fielder delivered that notice to her doorstep.

As she drove back towards Dan's house she passed Lang driving out towards her home looking smug. Well, if he'd been looking to speak with her he could just miss out. She'd rather hear back from this solicitor and then see what needed to be done.

'Oh, good, I can hear Ella starting to stir.' Jess spoke in the most determinedly cheerful tone she could muster as she stepped out of Dan's den ten minutes later. She'd faxed all the information to the solicitor and he'd told her he would speak with her by phone later in the day or tomorrow, to let her know his thoughts after reading everything. 'Thanks, Dan, for the use of your fax—and for the use of your solicitor.'

Jess started towards the room that held Ella's travel cot. 'Are we taking the children to the town fair? I know the boys were hoping they could go this afternoon.'

Once the words were out, Jess replayed them in her head and heat climbed into her cheeks because how could she just do that? Just assume it would be 'Jess and Dan' taking the children to the fair? As though they were all one big family and Jess had the right to make such sweeping suggestions.

No, she hadn't thought that, but Dan might be too busy. 'That is, *I* would be more than happy to take them.' And she would be, but there was another side to it. 'I'm just a bit concerned that it'll be like the beach. I can imagine they'd have more fun if we didn't all have to stay together in one tight pack, but if I was on my own I wouldn't want them running rampant all over the fairground.' Not to mention if Luke decided to show his stubborn streak and go off on his own. 'But can you spare the time, Dan?'

'We'll all go. I'll make up the time later if I have to.

We'll only be there a few hours.' Dan started towards the outside of the house. 'I'll go round up the boys. I suspect by the time I convince Rob he has to change into clean clothes before we leave, you'll have the girls sorted out.'

So they went to the town fair.

Jess came across the sons of a family she knew and introduced the boys to Rob and Luke. They got into conversation during the cow show.

'Actually those ones are bulls.' Jess said this to Mary, who'd made the observation that the cow part of the fair wasn't all that interesting.

'Why don't you come to our place one day soon?' One of the boys made this invitation to Luke and Rob. 'We've got heaps of cool computer games and other things.'

Rob's eyes lit up. 'Can we, Dad?'

'If the parents would like to give a call to confirm it's okay, yes.'

Dan handed over a business card with his mobile number on it. They went their separate ways then.

Jess walked at Dan's side pushing Ella in the stroller, and refused to think about the picture of a family that they must all make. They weren't a family. They were two very separate families, but, more even than that, Jess was the employee. That put her in a whole different league.

'We're going on that one, Dad.' Rob pointed to a ride that gave Jess vertigo just trying to look at it. 'It's got to be the best one here.'

Jess took the girls to various sideshow stalls, and showed them through the big hall filled with craft items and baked goods before they went in search of Dan and his sons again.

'Dad, will you take me on that ride? Please? I want to go on it, but not by myself.' Mary asked the question of her father while Rob and Luke made their way forward in a queue for another more adventurous ride.

The ride Mary had indicated was a beginner's ride with completely enclosed cage seats that turned similarly to a merry-go-round.

'I'll go on it with you, Mary.' Daisy made this offer. 'Annapolly would probably like that one as well.'

Annapolly was indeed keen. In the end all three girls lined up for the ride with their father. Jess smiled at the picture of Dan's strong imposing back as he waited for the ride with his three daughters.

'Let's watch Luke and Rob have their fun while we wait, Ella.' Jess pushed the stroller to a vantage point and watched Luke and Rob get into one of the cross-barred seats. Moments later the ride had begun and they were climbing high into the sky as the speed of the ride picked up.

Two rotations later there was a sickening, grinding sound. The ride operator shouted, and the ride came to a jarring stop with occupants of a lot of the cages shrieking in shock.

'Oh my God.' Luke and Rob were stuck right at the top of the ride. Dan's boys were *not safe* up there. They weren't in a full locking cage. There was nothing but a cross bar keeping them secure while they dangled there.

Ella had fallen asleep in the stroller. Dan was stuck on the other ride with his daughters.

Jess caught the eye of a local woman nearby. 'Mrs

O'Donnell, would you please watch my daughter? My charges are stuck up there.'

The kindly middle-aged woman took charge of Ella's stroller, and Jess rushed to the base of the ride. She yelled up: 'I'm here, Luke and Rob. Don't move!'

'I don't like this, Jess.' Rob's voice quavered. 'It's all shaking.'

Jess didn't like it either, and she caught sight of the ride manager who seemed to be doing nothing but wringing his hands while another man ineffectively prodded at the gear mechanism of the ride. Jess searched both boys' faces before she yelled out again.

'Luke's there with you, Rob. He's not going to let anything happen to either of you, are you, Luke?'

She held her breath as she waited for Luke's answer, and her heart softened with gratitude as he told his brother fiercely that he'd hold on to him all day up there if need be.

'We're not going to fall, Rob. All we have to do is be sensible, and hang on tight if things start banging about again.'

Luke's words were stern. In that moment Jess saw more of Dan in the boy than she ever had. And she saw what he was holding back, too, holding back his own concerns, and the knowledge that despite his assurances to Rob they *weren't* safe.

Jess strode to the ride manager. 'What's happened here? Those are my charges at the top of the ride.'

'It's nothing. Please step aside.' The manager cast a trapped look her way. 'We'll have this fixed in a moment.'

The other man shook his head. 'I really think we need to call in a crane to get them all off the ride. I don't like how this break looks here.' He pointed to what Jess had already seen, a sheared-off piece of metal, a bunch of cogs out of alignment.

A potential serious accident waiting to happen?

'Call for a crane, now.' Jess's words were harsh, low.

There were other people beginning to gather around as they realised the ride wasn't merely temporarily paused for some reason.

The manager glared at Jess before the other man said in a low tone, 'It'll be bad if any of them panic or try to climb down, Jack. Call for the crane.'

Jess stood close by until she'd heard the call go through. Once it had she spoke to Luke and Rob again, told them their dad would be here very soon. Dan's ride had been stopped as well and he was coming over. 'A crane's on the way to get you all down.'

Once she'd told the boys this, Jess pulled out her own mobile phone and called the police. She briefly explained what had happened and asked them to attend.

Things moved quickly after that. The crane and the police arrived. Dan and the girls joined Jess, and she quickly explained the situation and took charge of the girls while Dan called out to his sons. Jess retrieved her sleeping daughter from Mrs O'Donnell, thanked her, and rejoined Dan.

'Oh, I don't want to watch this.' But Jess did watch, and prayed and held on to Dan's arm until Rob and Luke were safely transferred from the top of the ride to the crane, and from there to ground level.

'You're all right?' Dan pulled them both aside and listened as Rob spilled out how scary it had been.

'Luke was great with him, Dan.' Jess spoke quietly.

'He kept Rob calm, reassured him up there until you could get here from the other ride.'

'Thanks, Luke.' Dan hugged both sons before he released them. 'I need to speak with the ride manager, and then the police. This shouldn't have happened and I want to know why it did.'

It was Luke who held on to his father's arm. 'Dad—Jess was the one who made them get a crane in, and called the police on them.'

'Thanks.' Dan met Jess's gaze briefly before he strode to where the police were questioning the ride manager and his assistant.

'Dad's gonna kick heads.' Rob said it with a hint of ghoulish glee.

'I'm so relieved you're all right, Rob.' Jess spoke from the depths of her heart, but she also caught Luke's gaze and smiled before she could stop herself, and Luke… almost smiled before he looked away.

Dan did what he had to do and then came back to join them. 'I've had quite enough of this place. The police have my number. Let's go home.'

CHAPTER NINE

'DAD'S REALLY STRESSED about what happened with that ride.' Daisy made this observation to Jess later. 'He's been on the phone in his den with the police and stuff like that half the afternoon. If he's not taking phone calls, he's checking on Luke and Rob. They're all right though, aren't they, Jess?'

'Yes, Daisy. They're okay.' Jess thought in truth that the boys were probably more resilient about the whole thing than the adults had been. They'd had a fright. In the end nothing terrible had come of it and they'd got over it. Rob had already been on the phone bragging to the new friends he and Luke had met at the fair about the excitement of being stuck up there.

But Dan had to deal with getting to the bottom of what had gone wrong, and why, and work with the police and others to ensure responsibility was taken for the incident, and that there wouldn't be a repeat. Meanwhile, Jess needed to feed everyone and get the children into bed, at least the younger ones, because that was *her* job. 'I must put something on for dinner. I confess I've been a bit distracted, too. It was a little frightening while they were stuck up there.'

'You should give us all pizza.' Daisy glanced outside to where Luke and Rob were sitting on the veranda.

The boys were talking, rather than riding their bikes. Maybe they'd had enough excitement for one day, too.

Daisy went on. 'Dad usually treats everyone if we've had a rough day. He won't want to eat until later, though.' She added with calm unconcern for exposing her father's finer feelings, 'His guts get in a total knot over stuff like this.'

They did end up treating the children with pizza. Jess said she might 'like to eat a bit later if that would suit Dan' and he readily agreed and disappeared back into his den to try to catch up on his Sydney-related workload while Jess got everyone sorted for bed.

Luke, for once, left his door open while Jess took care of the smaller children. When they were all in their rooms, she hesitated for a moment and then briefly poked her head in. 'You're all right, Luke? No after effects from that drama earlier today?'

'Yeah, I'm okay.' He seemed a bit at a loss.

A sound came through the baby monitor in Jess's pocket. 'I'd better go check on that. I guess Ella's going to take more than one tucking in tonight to get her to sleep.'

Jess checked on her daughter, settled her and then took care of some laundry and cleared up the bathrooms and kitchen before she finally went in search of Dan. She met him as he was returning from checking on the children.

'They're all asleep.' He shoved a hand through his hair.

It was already ruffled from, Jess assumed, several such treatments. She tried not to think about being the one to do the ruffling. 'You look fed up, and justifiably so. What have the police had to say about the problem with the ride?'

'There will definitely be a hefty fine for the owners and a probable suspension of licence. The problem appears to have resulted from negligence rather than any tolerable wear and tear or other issues.'

'Then I hope they receive the harshest fine and punishment possible.' Jess drew a breath. 'Shall I order us some pizza now, Dan?'

'Actually I got on the phone before I checked on the kids. It should be here soon. Can we eat it on a desert island where there's nothing at all to bug us or cause concern? You know, I really could do with just a couple of hours where I could totally relax.' As the words left his mouth, Dan frowned. 'And so could you. I'm sorry. With what happened to Luke and Rob on that ride I forgot you were waiting on a call from my solicitor today.'

'It's okay.' That news hadn't come, and it could wait another day. 'I think we've had enough to contend with for today.'

Jess was trying so hard, but she *was* still aware of Dan as a man. Remembrance of the kiss they'd shared hovered constantly on the edge of her thoughts, lifting that awareness to a higher level, making her long for more even though she knew how foolish it was to do that.

Why had she let Dan kiss her when she knew it could only end in hurt for her because he didn't have anything in his heart?

'I don't know of any nearby desert islands.' Jess tried

for a light smile. 'When Daisy wants to escape she goes into the tree house.'

Just as the doorbell rang Dan gave Jess a considering look.

He strode to the door and opened up, and came back a moment later with the pizza. 'Why not? There's a bottle of sparkling grape juice in the fridge. We'll eat pizza and drink that and get away from the day for a bit.'

When Jess simply looked at him, he added, 'You have the baby monitor, and you know once my lot fall asleep nothing short of a fire-alarm situation would wake them so we won't be worrying about them.'

And it would get them both out of the house, and potentially give Dan's 'guts' a chance to settle down. 'I've never eaten a meal in a tree house.'

When they climbed up there, Jess drew a breath. 'Here we are, then.'

'Yes. Looks like Daisy's had a tea party or something up here.' Dan's glance roved the room and he fell silent.

Jess's gaze followed Dan's to a picnic blanket spread across the floor. Scatter cushions to lean on. Flowers from the garden picked with girlish hands and stuffed into a plastic tumbler. They were already wilted.

'How—' She couldn't very well say romantic though that was the word that sprang to mind. 'How lovely the view is through the cut-away window. You can see heaps of stars.'

Jess pretended an extreme rate of interest in those stars while Dan set down the boxes of pizza in complete silence. After a moment she heard the fizz as he opened the bottle of sparkling grape juice and the sound as he poured it into the plastic tumblers they'd brought out and she knew she had to turn around.

Dan's ears were red again. And Jess felt as though she were on a date, which was quite ridiculous. Yet they were here, secluded, nothing but each other's company and a house full of children not at all far away, but they might as well have been miles away.

'We don't have to do this, Dan—'

'At least it's quiet out here—' He broke off and handed her one of the cups.

It wasn't real wine, but all Jess could think about was being kissed anyway.

Reclining back on those scatter cushions and being kissed by Dan. 'It's—it's good that it's quiet. For the peace of it, I mean.' That was what she *should* mean.

She took the sparkling juice and sat, and she would just have to stop thinking about this being a romantic setting. It was a children's tree cubby house. How *could* that even be romantic?

Jess reached for the first pizza box. 'Well, I'm certainly hungry. How about you?'

'It does smell good.' Dan reached for a slice of pizza.

Their hands brushed.

Not a big deal, Jess.

They ate in silence for a minute or two.

'How are things progressing with your Sydney client?' Jess hadn't asked for a few days, but prior to the fiasco at the fair today Dan had been working from home more.

In the back of her mind where all the tensions and concerns about the future lurked, a part of Jess hadn't wanted to ask in case Dan had almost resolved things and wouldn't need her for much longer. She wasn't ready to face yet another worry over finances. She wasn't ready to leave...Dan.

Dan finished his slice of pizza and selected another before offering the box to her. 'I think my clients are close to being fully assessed now. A purchase offer shouldn't be too far away.'

'You won't need my help for much longer, then.' Jess forced herself to smile. She would be fine. She and Ella had made it this far and they would go on making it whether Jess lost this work, whether she also lost their cottage or not. Of course they would be fine.

'For at least another month, Jess, if you can do it.' Dan drew a breath. 'I'll cope without you if you can't commit for that long. I don't want to get in the way of other plans you might need to make, but if you *can* stick at it for another month it'll give me time to wrap up this problem, get the kids started at school, and hopefully for things to start to settle down. I've really appreciated all your help, including the things you've done in terms of housekeeping.'

'I hope I can find enough work in Randurra to stay here, Dan. That's what I'll be aiming for. Actually I'd like to ask for half of tomorrow off to do some more door knocking if that's all right?'

He agreed straight away, and Jess went on.

'I'll stay on with you another month if at all possible.' It was Jess's turn to draw a breath before she went on. 'I don't feel comfortable asking you for help finding out my rights regarding the cottage.'

'You're independent. I understand that.' His glance drifted over the chunky wooden necklace that matched the bangles on her arm, and down to the cleft between her breasts before he looked away. 'But it was easy for me to get that help for you, and I wanted to.'

'Thank you, Dan. I do appreciate it.' Jess's skin warmed as though Dan had touched her, and she became aware very suddenly that the only sounds around them were of night insects and the occasional hoot of an owl somewhere in the distance. They were very alone out here, whether there were children sleeping in the house or not. They were alone and Jess didn't think she was the only one aware of it…

'That was a nice break.' Jess gathered the used plates together and piled them on top of the pizza boxes and hoped she didn't sound as desperate to escape her thoughts as she was. 'I'll take these in and get Ella and head home.'

'Leave it.' Dan stilled her movements by the simple expedient of laying his hand over hers. 'It can stay here until morning but you're right. It's time to go in.'

They couldn't stay out here and drift as they had done. If they did, the drifting *would* end in kisses. The truth of that was in Dan's eyes, and she didn't want him to reject her twice.

So they went inside and Jess got Ella and put her in the car, drove home and sent Dan a text message that they'd arrived safe and sound. She put Ella to bed and climbed into her own bed and while she waited for sleep to come she did what she could to toughen her resolve.

She *had* let herself care too much about Dan, and she'd pushed back her concerns about losing her home and tried not to think about them because she didn't want to face the choices she might have to make to survive. Moving out of Randurra. Getting work outside the childcare industry that would separate her from Ella.

Jess had to knock on more doors, and see what work she could find. She had to get ready for whatever Dan's solicitor might tell her, have her plans already in train to deal with whatever life threw down.

And she had to push aside any feelings she might think she had towards Dan that were not about work.

Jess could do it all alone. She *had been* standing alone. And she would go on standing alone. For herself, and for Ella. That was all. Her determination had nothing to do with pushing people away to keep herself safe.

Jess was the one who'd been pushed away by Peter Rosche, and in the end Dan was doing that to her, too. He wanted her as a daycare mum, but he did not want her for herself.

Well, Jess did not need him in that way.

She didn't!

CHAPTER TEN

THE NEXT DAY DAWNED clear and sunny with a gentle breeze taking the edge off the heat. In the afternoon Dan suggested a walk to the dam on the property to try to catch yabbies for a bit of fun.

'Daddy, Daddy, I've got one. What do I do?' Mary yelled the words as her line of string went tight in the muddy water.

The children were spread out around one side of the dam with bits of sausage tied to pieces of string, and the string tied to sticks planted in the mud at the edge of the water. Rob and Luke had managed to resist throwing dried mud clods into the water. They'd thrown them up the bank instead.

As mini excursions went, Jess thought this one was rather inventive, and Dan had seemed happy to forfeit the time in his office to spend it with the children, instead.

Dan went to Mary's side and put his hand over hers. He had an old plastic colander from the kitchen to use as a net. 'We just pull the string in gently like this until we can see the yabby in the shallow water. He's a lot like a crab except long and thinner. He'll hold on to the meat with his pincers. Once we have him close, we'll scoop him up.'

They pulled. They saw the yabby. They scooped and all had a good look at him.

'Sausage works pretty well to catch them with, Dad.' Daisy sounded surprised. 'But you said that smelly older meat would work even better?'

'Yes. I'm fairly sure.'

Jess leaned close to Dan's ear to whisper, 'You're an expert now that you've been on the Internet to find out all about it.'

'Totally.' Dan turned his head and his lips came close to brushing her cheek.

Dan's eyes darkened and his gaze dropped to her lips before he quickly turned his attention to releasing the yabby so they could all watch it back itself into the water and disappear. He missed the furious look that Luke cast their way, but Jess didn't, and she wished she could explain to Luke—

What? That there was nothing between her and Dan? When all Dan needed to do was come anywhere near her and she all but melted, and she couldn't seem to do a thing about it no matter how hard she tried!

Jess moved away from Dan and she took care to keep her distance for the next hour that they stayed, catching and releasing yabbies. Rob wanted to keep them and cook some but Dan said no.

'I'm not sure if they'd be safe to eat,' he said, 'and I don't think I'd be all that keen to cook them anyway. But we'll have a campfire tonight, Rob. I checked the weather report and we can do it in a safe spot in the backyard.'

Ella had fallen asleep in the stroller under the shade of a gumtree.

Jess helped gather everything up and they all made their way back to the house. Rob and Luke got in a bit of a spat with each other over something Jess didn't hear, shoving and pushing. Dan broke them up and looked frustrated but seemed to push all his feelings inside. Where did the tension go when he did that?

Mary asked a question and Ella started to wake up in the stroller, and then they were back at the house and Jess didn't get time to try to figure anything else out.

They cleaned up, and got ready for their outdoor supervised campfire in the backyard. Dan had asked Jess to help him, and it was her job to do whatever he needed whether there were tensions in the air, or not.

'Grubs are fun.' Rob twisted another piece of dough around his stick, closed it over the end and held it out to the fire's flames. 'I'm going to pour even more golden syrup into this one when it's cooked.'

'You're already covered in the stuff.' Luke made this observation while he prepared another grub stick for himself.

'Why are they called grubs?' Daisy wanted to know.

'Because they look like witchetty grubs that can be eaten as bush tucker.' Jess hadn't needed to look on the Internet to know that one. The grubs had been her idea.

'I never thought Dad would let us eat things cooked on sticks.' Rob turned his stick over the flames again. 'Even if it is just dough, it tastes really good.'

'Yeah, well, he hasn't got any scruples when it comes

to some people and what they want to do.' Luke muttered the words beneath his breath, but Jess heard them, and a glance at Dan's face showed that he had, too.

'Go to your room, Luke. That was completely uncalled for. You're done here for the night.' Dan spoke the words quietly.

Luke stared at his father for a moment before he threw his stick into the fire and stormed inside.

Rob threw a glance at his father. 'I didn't mean to get him in trouble.'

'Leave it, Rob. It's nothing to do with you.'

The family event went on, but all the pleasure had gone out of it for Jess. The campfire dwindled. One by one the children made their way inside to wash and get into bed and then it was just Jess and Dan as he dumped sand over the coals.

'I'll get my sleeping girl and head home, Dan.' She tried to find something neutral to say. 'It's good that you were able to spare the time from your work for this afternoon and evening. You'll have another busy day in your office or in Sydney tomorrow.'

Something in his face made Jess pause.

'The audit is finished. I can spend the remainder of the school holidays at home and do what I can to get the kids in a good place about starting their classes.'

'Well, that's great.' Dan had asked for a month more from Jess, but with the pressure removed things would be different for him. 'You'll be okay now, Dan. You'll get on with things and the children will really settle in here.'

'That sounded rather like a goodbye.' His gaze searched her face.

'You won't need my help any more.' That was the

thing. 'I can't let you keep paying me to work here when that's the case.'

'I want to keep you working for me, Jess.'

'I'll be okay. The regular children will be back with me as of Saturday and I have new ones starting then as well.'

'That's good, Jess. But I do still want you here.' Dan drew a breath. 'Sometimes trying to balance everything is, well, it's hard. The ongoing work I mentioned before, help with housekeeping and even watching Annapolly a couple of days once the others are back in school is something I think I'd really like.'

'I'll help you, Dan.' If he still needed her. 'Of course I will for as long as you want me.'

Jess couldn't say otherwise anyway. She didn't have the luxury of that choice.

Dan blew out a deep breath. 'Good. That's really good.' He didn't want to let Jess know just how relieved he felt. Dan wasn't sure he wanted to think about the level of relief himself. For tonight all he was prepared to consider was that he still needed her help.

He was thinking of his children, making sure things were in a good place for them. Helping Jess in the process, and helping himself because what he'd admitted to her was true.

And Luke, Dan? Are you thinking of Luke when you make this decision?

Luke would just have to respect Dan's choice. Dan hadn't been in to see his son after sending him inside. He would check on him before he turned in, but if Luke was still awake he didn't expect to make any progress trying to talk to him.

You're avoiding even trying to do that because you

don't want to have to confront what Luke is feeling. He's jealous that you want to express interest in someone other than his mother. He doesn't want you replacing Rebecca with…Jess.

Dan didn't want to pursue that path at all. That was what Luke didn't seem to understand. Dan had fought his attraction to Jess and he was still fighting it.

'Goodnight, Jess.' He tried not to sound distant but simply professional. He wasn't sure whether or not he succeeded.

'Goodnight, Dan. I guess I'll see you in the morning.' She got to her feet and quickly left him.

CHAPTER ELEVEN

'I'M SORRY.' JESS drew a shaken breath. 'I'm just really shocked. I can't believe this.'

But the proof stood in front of her. A man and a woman in their mid-fifties who'd climbed from their car outside Jess's cottage just as she waved off the last of her charges and started to turn to go back inside.

It was Saturday. Jess had Ella in her arms, and as the woman looked from Jess to her baby daughter moisture pooled in her eyes and a hopeful smile came over her face.

'We're sorry to spring ourselves on you this way.' The man also seemed shaken, but he offered Jess a very sincere glance before he went on. 'There's a bit to talk about, if you'd be willing. Once we learned you were supposed to be here, we decided to drive out from Sydney. We weren't even sure if we'd be able to find you or if it was all real.'

They'd introduced themselves as Dalia and George Rosche. They were Peter's parents, if what they were saying was true, and they'd hired a private investigator to track him down. They hadn't succeeded, but the investigator had found out about the cottage Peter purchased for Jess, and had learned that a young woman lived there with her baby daughter.

'What made you think—?' Jess hesitated, uncertain how to put it.

'That we might find a grandchild here?' Dalia blinked. 'Peter got drunk at our house a year ago. He'd brought another man with him, some friend. We heard him tell the man that, well, that he was a father but he'd made sure he'd never have to be responsible for it. Ever since then we've been asking ourselves how we could find you.'

The words about her son had been harsh, but behind them Jess could sense shame, and…hope to know her granddaughter?

Jess laid her hand on the older woman's arm. 'You're not responsible for Peter's actions, Mrs Rosche. I think perhaps we should go inside.'

She made tea for the couple. George Rosche looked a lot like Peter, but the similarities appeared to finish on the surface.

George started the conversation. 'We realise you don't owe us anything, Jessica. Is it okay to call you that?'

'Of course.' Jess set Ella down and let her crawl around the floor.

'And you must call us Dalia and George,' Peter's father went on. 'We're hoping that, despite Peter's behaviour towards you, you might allow us to play a part as grandparents in your daughter's life.'

'I—I don't know what to say.' Jess didn't know how to deal with the knot of surprise and hope that had tightened into a fist in the middle of her chest. She drew a breath and whispered, 'Do you really want to?'

They talked for three hours. It was an emotional three hours for Jess, for the grandparents, but not for Ella, who played happily about the cottage and didn't realise she was the centre of some very focused and hopeful attention from this older couple.

Jess changed her daughter while George and Dalia took a moment to speak quietly in the kitchen. When she came back she drew another deep breath and handed Ella into Dalia's arms. The older woman held the little girl while silent tears ran down her face.

George had his moment, too, his large hands holding Ella awkwardly before he noisily cleared his throat and handed her back to Jess.

'I think you really mean what you've been saying.' Jess sought Dalia's eyes. 'I hope you'll forgive my doubts, but Peter—'

'Was not at all kind to you.' It was George who completed the sentence. 'Our son bought this cottage for you, but he made an agreement about back rates on it with the local council.'

'I signed an agreement to stay out of Peter's life in return for him buying me this cottage.' Jess could see no harm in admitting it.

'And he double-crossed you by hiding those back rates.' Dalia closed her eyes briefly before she turned to her husband. 'We have to make this right, George. We can't allow this young woman to be treated like that by our son.'

They offered to pay off the back rates debt.

'I can't let you do that. It's not your responsibility.'

'We can talk about that later.' George cleared his throat. 'We've probably taken up enough of your time for today but we appreciate meeting you and our granddaughter.'

'It has been a bit of a surprise.' But Jess didn't want to lose these people. They were grandparents who wanted to know Ella. Jess had to give that a chance.

'Are you staying overnight in the area?' she ventured.

'We have a room booked at the motel in the centre of town.' Dalia got to her feet. 'Come, George. We've worn the poor girl to a frazzle and our granddaughter is getting sleepy.' She turned to Jess. 'Would you allow us to come again tomorrow? You'll need time to think about all of this but we truly would like to get to know you, and have a chance to contribute at least a little to our granddaughter's life if you'll let us.'

Jess agreed to a second visit and explained that it would have to be quite early, as she had to work elsewhere the next day. And she did need time to think as well. They exchanged mobile phone numbers, and the older couple went on their way. Jess tucked Ella into her cot, and, once her daughter was asleep, turned in herself.

She couldn't let these people pay off her debt. That would just be wrong. But to have them as part of Ella's life, loving grandparents who wanted to know their granddaughter? That would be so wonderful for Ella.

A little prickle of loneliness stabbed at Jess's heart. Because this would be great for her daughter, but *Jess* wasn't any relation to George and Dalia. And of course that didn't matter. She had a chance to have something special for Ella. That was what counted.

So go to sleep, Jess Baker. Tomorrow you have grandparents visiting your daughter again.

* * *

'It's Aunt Adele and Uncle Clive!' Rob shouted and a troop of Frazier children raced off the veranda to meet the car.

Jess was just arriving, too.

Dan hadn't exactly been waiting on the veranda for Jess's arrival. He'd been supervising the children, he told himself.

'Hey, Dan. We thought we'd surprise you.' Adele called the words as she climbed out of the car.

The children swarmed around her and Clive, all talking at once, even Luke.

'I thought you were both still travelling.' With one part of him, Dan watched Jess getting Ella out of the car as he smiled at the visitors. 'It's great to see you, though.'

Adele explained that they'd finished their trip a little early. Her hand covered her tummy for a moment before Clive took over the conversation.

'We had the time so we decided to drive down, Dan.' Clive's glance shifted to Jess and her daughter.

'Come meet my sister and brother-in-law, Jess.' Dan walked to Jess's side. 'Adele, Clive, this is Jess Baker. Jess has been providing childcare and housekeeping for me while I handled a work crisis that blew up in Sydney.'

'Oh.' Adele took Jess's hand and shook firmly while Clive nodded and smiled. Adele glanced back to Dan. 'How did that happen? You were supposed to be able to take things easy while you got settled in.'

Dan explained and they all went inside. Adele had brought small treats for the children, and handed those out before she and her husband settled with Dan and Jess in the kitchen for cups of tea.

Jess made the drinks and would have left them to it. 'I can watch the children while you all catch up.'

'Stay.' Adele smiled. 'It would be nice to get to know you.'

At first Dan thought Jess might seem a bit overwhelmed because of the sudden arrival of his relatives, but there seemed to be something deeper disturbing her, as though she'd already had some kind of shock.

Well, she's worried about losing her cottage. That's enough to make anyone shocked.

Dan had been thinking about that. He wanted to help. There had to be some way that they could work something out.

Just what are you asking yourself, Dan?

'Dan? I asked whether you'd allow it?' Adele's prompting made Dan replay the part of the conversation that hadn't fully registered because he'd allowed his thoughts to wander.

'You want to take the children overnight to Sydney?' He blinked.

'It would be nice to spoil them a little, and it would give you a break.' Adele's face softened as she half turned her head to glance behind her into the living room. 'I don't want to lose being part of their lives now that you've moved and don't need my occasional help with childcare.'

She glanced again at Jess before she turned back to her brother. 'And I'm glad you've finally got help with some of the care and housekeeping. It's way too much for someone who's working full time as well.'

'Can we go, Dad? Please, please, please?' Mary had

heard the invitation and come into the kitchen. In moments, four other Fraziers had added their hopes to the mix.

Dan agreed. A flurry of packing followed and it seemed before he could blink Adele had piled them all into Dan's van. She left her car behind to be collected when they brought the children back.

Dan and Jess stood on the veranda in a sudden silence broken only by the sound of Ella crawling to Jess and making a little bewildered sound as if to ask, 'What was all that about?'

'It's all right, Ella. They've just gone for a visit with their aunt and uncle.' Jess picked up the little girl and stroked her hand over Ella's soft wispy hair. 'You keep getting shocked by strange people turning up, don't you?'

While Dan drew a breath to ask what she meant, Jess turned her head and spoke to him.

'With your family gone for two days, did you still want me, Dan?'

More with each passing day.

'Yes.' He cleared his throat and cast about for an excuse—*for the things he'd been holding off doing because it was too hard with heaps of children.* 'Any chance you'd like to help me with some light yard work this morning? And maybe get ahead with some baking this afternoon while I flatten all the moving boxes and arrange to have them taken away for recycling? I hadn't realised Adele might miss the children like that.'

Jess smiled and bounced Ella in her arms. 'I liked her, Dan. She seemed a really good sort. Your brother-in-law, too.'

She rolled her sleeves up, then. Metaphorically at

least. She slathered Ella in sun block, put a big hat on her and placed her in the playpen in the shade, and they set to work while the sun was still low in the sky.

CHAPTER TWELVE

'ELLA'S DOWN FOR THE COUNT. She napped earlier, but apparently watching people carrying boxes is exhausting work for a one-year-old.' Jess made the observation as she stepped into the living room. 'I'll try to get a bit more work done, Dan, before I go home—'

'Leave it for tonight.' Dan glanced up from where he'd been pressing buttons on the TV remote to change channels. 'In fact, would you like to watch some television with me?'

Jess hesitated and then, when she glanced at the screen, said, 'Is that show what I think it is?'

He'd found an old comedy show that Jess loved. Dan gestured to the seat beside him on the couch. 'Come and watch it. We've worked hard enough today to earn it.'

They had, Jess justified, and plopped down beside him. She refused to think about the wisdom or otherwise of what she was doing.

One comedy show led to another, and then to a discussion about ones they liked best, and Dan dug through the family's DVD collection. They selected two movies. For the second one, Jess brought cocoa and cookies and somehow they ended up sitting closer. She could feel Dan's shoulder and arm against her side.

There were a dozen reasons why she should go home. Her response to Dan's nearness was top of the list but she couldn't make herself get up, or say the words. And the longer she stayed there, the more aware of Dan she became, and the more she sensed that he was equally aware of her.

Yet Dan had pushed her away, and he hadn't wanted the complication. Oh, Jess didn't know what to make of her feelings, or of what she thought she might sense in him.

At about the halfway point of the story, Dan glanced her way and she turned her head. He clicked off the television and tossed the remote down. 'What are we going to do, Jess? I thought I was making it up, that it couldn't be all that it is, that I couldn't…want you as much as I do, but it just doesn't go away, does it?'

'No.' His words to her had been so sincere. Jess might have held her own need at bay if it hadn't been for that. She might have held away from him. 'It doesn't go away.'

He kissed her then, and Jess wound her arms around his neck and kissed him back. She wanted him. She had done for ages, since they first met really, and she was tired of fighting her feelings, tired of holding back when all she wanted and needed was to be in his arms. In some ways she needed that even more because of Luke's resistance to her presence in his father's life.

Dan raised his lips from hers. 'You work for me, Jess, and you're so much younger. I don't want to make you feel—'

Don't do it, Jessica. Don't invest yourself emotionally, and don't let this end up where it wants to end physically. It won't mean the same thing to him.

'I want this, Dan.' Jess spoke firmly. 'I want to be in your arms tonight while it's just us. It doesn't have to be more than that. Just…tonight.'

Jess pushed aside her concerns and told herself to see it as a gift.

Dan stroked her hair away from her face with his hand and his gaze sought hers. There *were* emotions in his eyes. Questions, concerns, need and an edge of uncertainty. He too seemed to push it all aside. He drew a deep breath and their kisses deepened.

Jess melted into his arms in a tangle of emotions that she wouldn't face. Not now. Not yet. Her hands touched his chest through the cloth of his shirt. His muscles were firm beneath her fingertips. He smelled of blunted aftershave and sunshine and Dan. She closed her eyes and didn't even notice that the sweetness of his kisses had pushed through the walls she'd shored up around her heart.

'Jess.' Dan rose from the couch where he'd been kissing her. He needed to take her to his bed and take what they'd begun to its fulfilment and after that…

After that it would be over. Jess had said it. "Just tonight." She knew what she wanted, and for tonight, while his children weren't here, what harm were they doing?

Dan pushed his own thoughts down. He only wanted to focus on the moment. If he was avoiding issues, that was one more thing he didn't want to acknowledge.

He threw back the cover on his bed and Jess stood at the edge of it. He took her hands and lifted them to his chest. She pushed his shirt over his head and her nails scraped lightly over his skin. Need rushed through Dan in a tight wave.

His hands shook as he removed Jess's sleeveless top. A knot tightened inside him but Jess looked into his eyes, and her gaze was soft and welcoming.

Jess pushed her skirt down over her hips, and Dan removed the rest of their clothes slowly, touching every part of her as it was revealed. He drew her down on the bed and took her into his arms…

'Dan. Please.' Jess's hands clasped his shoulders and she acknowledged her need for his hold and his touch and his possession.

His eyes were soft and filled with desire, blurred with passion held in check. Jess wanted him to give all of that to her, and, if she was fooling herself that she would still hold that gift tomorrow, she couldn't care. She needed this. The chance to give herself to him and have him give himself to her. She needed it more than she wanted to acknowledge.

So she didn't. She just opened her arms to him, and when he led them to their zenith Jess looked into his eyes and those walls built around her heart didn't hold together as well as they should. She had a suspicion that she might have let Dan find his way further into all those parts of herself that she'd needed to protect after Peter than she'd meant to.

'Stay, Jess.' His hands soothed her, stroked across her body even as he pushed out a breath and a well of tension that had perhaps been in both of them, washed away on their tide of fulfilment. Lethargy followed for Jess.

She tucked her head against his chest and his arms came around her. Dan eased into sleep and she lay there and closed her eyes. She didn't want to think because there had been too much thinking about too many things in her life and she had not found any answers. Now she had hope with Ella's grandparents and she would survive at whatever home she found to live in.

Would she go on working for Dan? Was it best to do that, or to walk away after what had happened tonight?

How *could* she walk away when he was helping her to afford to live by the income his employment provided?

She should have thought of that before she made love with him! But Jess couldn't regret it. She pressed her face to his chest and she didn't regret any of it.

'Good morning. I woke up because of Ella so I thought I'd get started early on breakfast and then I've written a shopping list. If you'll give me the card, I'll take Ella with me to the supermarket. You'll need to be well supplied for when the children get back, and your sister and brother-in-law might decide to stay as well.'

Jess put a cup of tea in front of Dan and pushed the breakfast cereal and milk his way. She bent to pick Ella up off the floor, sat down with her and started to spoon baby cereal into her mouth.

Jess's head was bent over the task and she was going determinedly about her business, but her hand shook as she fed her daughter.

'Jess.' Dan didn't know what to say to her. He was shocked by how he had felt when they made love. Dan had told himself it was just about sex. He was attracted to her. It had been a long time. He'd...justified it in that way. But it hadn't felt like just sex. He didn't know what he had felt.

'Du—du-u-u!' Ella wriggled on Jess's lap and Jess set her down on the floor.

She still didn't meet Dan's gaze. What could he say to her? How did he reassure her that what happened—? Dan didn't even know what he wanted to say. What they'd shared had stunned him, but it had been…ill advised. And Dan felt guilt, and didn't want to have to confront that feeling.

'Du—Da-a-a—'

Dan glanced down in just enough time to see Ella pull herself up on the leg of the chair Jess was sitting on. She reached out first one hand towards him and then the other.

Ella tottered forward.

Jess gasped and held her breath.

Dan shot his hands out. 'Come on, Ella. Look what you're doing. You're walking. All by yourself.'

Ella got three and a half steps in before she seemed to realise that she was on her feet, and started to wonder how she was doing it. Dan caught her up just as her legs wobbled, and praised her for her amazing efforts.

'Did you see that, Jess? She walked.' Even in the face of this morning's concerns, Dan couldn't help but grin.

'I've been waiting for this moment.' Jess's words were filled with pride, and then her voice turned husky as Dan passed Ella to her and she cuddled her daughter close. 'What a good girl you are, Ella.'

Ella gave a baby laugh and cuddled back, but Jess still had the strangest look on her face. It had come the moment she saw Ella walking to Dan.

Dan looked at her with her daughter in her arms, and he thought about Ella walking to him and all the memories of all of his children, and he wondered what it would be like to have a child…with Jess?

The thought so startled him that he fell silent. Did he *want* to have a child with Jess? That would mean that he wanted—

Dan's mobile phone rang. The caller was Adele. 'Hello, Adele. How are you? How are the children? Is everything okay?'

He sounded quite normal, Dan thought. Not like a man asking himself questions that he'd believed were answered four years ago.

'Yes, we're all fine. Just letting you know we'll be back today at about five.' Adele cleared her throat. 'And that we, sort of, well, shopped a little.'

'No problem.' Dan could feel his ears turning red, as though some part of him felt that his sister would know that Jess was here holding her daughter, and that Dan had made love to Jess last night.

Well, now it was today and they had their lives to get on with. They weren't going to cross those boundaries again. They'd both agreed about that so Dan didn't have to psychoanalyse *or* regret.

'I'll see you later, Dan.' Adele's tone was a little questioning, but she ended the call without saying more.

He set the phone down. Of course Adele would wonder. He hadn't asked to speak to any of the children or what they'd been buying or any of the things he'd normally have done.

'I—I should get busy with some housekeeping, Dan. It's too early to go to the shops.' Jess heard the tentative edge to her tone as she addressed him, and forced her chin up. She couldn't fall apart. Not now. Not because of last night. Not because Ella had walked to Dan and

Jess's heart, those walls around her heart, had taken one final big shake and crashed down.

Ella had reached out to him with total trust and taken her first steps to him.

Jess had reached out to him last night and taken a step with him too. She'd thought she had it under control, but she hadn't. Because when she watched Ella walk to Dan, it hit Jess just why *she* had felt so deeply about what they had shared last night. Why she had needed it and longed for it so much.

She'd fallen in love with him! All the way in, heart, soul, the whole lot. She hadn't realised she was doing it and now she had and she had to *undo* it! She couldn't love Dan. Not like that. He wouldn't give back in the same way and she'd end up so hurt.

Been there, done that, and Peter Rosche had turned out not to even be the man Jess had thought she'd fallen for.

Dan was Dan. Jess had no doubt that he was exactly who he was. Her complete lack of doubt was what should concern her most of all. Dan was a man who'd loved and lost and would never love again. Eighteen years with his Rebecca. How *could* he ever move past that amount of history with a woman he had loved utterly?

'I apologise, Jess.' Dan's low words weren't really unexpected.

They still hurt, and wasn't that silly? But Jess didn't want to hear him apologise. She wanted him to refuse to say sorry for any aspect of last night, to want to keep her and find some means to take their relationship forward…

'There's no need to say anything.' There was no need

for Jess to think such thoughts, either. It wasn't going to happen. Not in a million billion years.

'I think there is.' His mouth tightened. 'You work for me. I shouldn't have put you in a position that could make you uncomfortable with me afterwards, could risk that. I don't want to lose you as the carer for the children. Even when they're back in school I want at least two days a week—'

'What happened was a joint decision.' Jess had walked into it, eyes open. She'd made up her mind what she wanted. But her *heart* hadn't realised what it was letting itself in for.

Dan was worried that she'd feel too uncomfortable to stay with him—and he wanted her to stay on more permanently! A frown came to her brows as Jess started to think what that would be like, now. She loved Dan. She was *in love with* Dan.

And he *liked* her. He wanted her to help him with housework and the children. He didn't want her for herself.

It was still work, and Jess cared about his children, even the difficult Luke.

Jess drew herself up. 'This job matters to me. I like knowing that I'm helping you. If you're happy to carry on, I don't see why we can't.'

He blew out a breath and his face for a moment reflected relief.

Because he was trying to back away from what happened last night, Jessica, and without losing you for his children. Don't read anything more than that into it.

Dan might even have been concerned how she would react to a perceived breach of their employer/employee relationship, but it had been a joint choice.

Jess excused herself then. There was nothing more to be said. She'd fallen in love in a totally unsuitable way with a man who didn't love her back and never would.

With Ella scooped into her arms, Jess took her daughter away to change her nappy, and then immersed herself in taking care of laundry and house cleaning and shopping.

They ate sandwiches for lunch and Jess baked, and then put on a casserole so there'd be food for when Dan's children got back. Mid-afternoon she excused herself and went home.

Jess hadn't told Dan about her visits from Peter's parents but it could wait. There hadn't exactly been the right moment.

CHAPTER THIRTEEN

'JESS. IT'S...DAN.'

'Dan. What's the matter?' Jess had been sound asleep when her mobile phone started to ring. She'd leapt from bed and grabbed it, hoping the sound wouldn't wake Ella. It was still dark outside. The bedside clock said five a.m. Why would Dan call at this hour?

'I—don't feel right. One eye blurry. Face feels funny.' He drew a sharp breath. 'Called—to go to hospital.'

'Oh my God. Dan!' Jess snatched up the skirt she'd had on last night and pulled it on with the phone to her ear. 'You've called an ambulance?'

'Yes. Need you to come.'

A sick knot lodged itself deep inside Jess. 'I'm coming. I'll grab Ella and be right there, Dan.'

Jess disconnected and threw on the rest of her clothes, shoved her feet into sandals, snatched up Ella and the carry bag she always kept with her, and rushed to the car.

What was happening to Dan? He'd been struggling to speak. The symptoms sounded like a heart attack, didn't they, or a stroke? Either one was really bad!

She was at Dan's minutes later, in time to see Luke walk beside the officers as they loaded a gurney into the back of the ambulance. Dan was on that gurney. Jess drew up as close as she could, got Ella out and into her stroller in record time—her daughter was still more than halfway asleep—and hurried over. Her stomach lurched for Dan even as she worried how Luke would respond to her.

'Jess. I don't know what to do!' Luke blurted out the words without leaving his father's side. Tears formed in his eyes and he blinked them back fiercely.

'Stand back and let us load him, son.' The first ambulance officer caught Jess's gaze as he and the other man got Dan loaded into the back of the vehicle. 'Are you his partner?'

'Yes.' She was Dan's *working* partner and she loved him. That was enough as far as Jess was concerned. She wrapped her arm around Luke's shoulders and held on tight to the boy, and hoped he wouldn't get upset about that lie. 'Tell me what's wrong with him.'

'He'll be properly diagnosed at the hospital.'

'But you must have some idea.' Jess tried not to sound as worried as she felt. Beneath her hand, Luke's shoulders locked with tension.

'It's presenting as some form of stroke.'

'That's serious.' Luke made a choked sound, quickly stifled.

'We're going to take care of this, Luke. Your father's going to be all right.' Jess spoke almost sternly, but oh, she was terrified.

'Jess.' Dan said her name.

Jess's heart leapt into her throat as she curled her fingers around Dan's and held on. 'I'm here, Dan.' The words were choked. 'You need to get to the hospital.'

Worried eyes sought hers. 'Take care—?'

'I will, Dan. I'll take care of everything.' Of course she would.

Jess turned to the nearest ambulance officer. 'Please!' She didn't know what she was begging for, only the taste of fear in her mouth. Nothing could happen to him!

Dan relaxed back onto the gurney. He caught his son's gaze with his eyes, and a moment later Luke had his arms around his father. Luke dry sobbed, once, and then the ambulance was on its way.

'We should have gone with him,' Luke said in a strangled tone as Jess hurried him inside. 'We could have woken everyone up.'

Jess struggled to think. 'I have to organise babysitting.' She needed to be at the hospital, to do whatever she could, ensure Dan got the best care. Anything! Jess snatched up the phone.

In what felt like an hour but was less than half that time, Jess had organised babysitting and was on the way to the hospital.

'Thanks—thanks for letting me come with you.' The words came uncertainly from Luke's mouth as Jess screeched her car to a halt in the closest visitor parking space at the hospital. She flung her door open and half jogged with Luke to the entrance.

'He's going to need you, Luke.' It was all she could manage for the worried boy. *Jess* was worried. Sick with it.

If anything bad happened to Dan… If she lost…

'You're scared, too.' Luke cleared his throat.

'Yes, Luke, I am.' Jess couldn't tell him she was even more scared because she'd fallen in love with his father.

In Luke's mind that part of his father belonged to his mother and always would. Jess couldn't fight that out with Luke. Not now.

Maybe Luke, too, was too upset to think about it because he didn't say anything, just stuck to her side as she rushed to the front desk. 'Dan Frazier. He came in by ambulance.'

'Are you the partner?'

Jess glanced at Luke. 'Yes.'

'He's being cared for. You can take a seat for the moment.'

Jess and Luke sat. 'I wanted them to be open with me about his condition, Luke.'

'I know.'

It was a tense wait before they were allowed to slip in to see Dan briefly. He had a nurse watching him and he was in the intensive care unit.

There were monitors hooked up to him; his face was pale.

'Jess. Lukey.'

He couldn't be talking if he was really in trouble, could he?

'Dad.' Luke's breath rushed out of him. 'It took forever for them to let us in.'

There was so much else that Luke wasn't saying. Jess knew it because each and every fear was inside her, too. Was he all right? What had been happening while they were closed out there? Was Dan going to be all right?

The nurse told them they couldn't stay long.

Jess went straight to the side of the bed and took

Dan's hand. Luke hovered behind her until she reached with her other hand and drew him forward.

The affection in Dan's eyes made that action immediately worth it. 'Sorry. Worrying…everyone.'

'What happened, Dad?' Luke asked in a hushed tone.

'Wasn't too bad…Luke. Had…' He glanced at the nurse.

'Dan's had what we call a transient ischaemic attack.' The nurse held Jess's glance. 'This is sometimes referred to in lay terms as a mini stroke. Although it was quite scary, there aren't usually any lasting effects from this kind of attack. We just want to do our tests and make sure we take all the steps we can to ensure we don't have a bigger repeat.' She smiled at her patient. 'Don't we, Dan?'

'Yes.' A fierce expression came over his face. 'Going to get better.'

Luke swallowed and nodded. 'Of course you are, Dad.' His voice quavered before he added, 'You're not allowed to do anything else.' It was as close as the boy could come to asking Dan not to die.

Dan's glance moved between Jess and Luke. He looked worried.

Jess was worried.

Luke was worried.

And they had to pull together for Dan right now.

'Luke's been a great support, Dan.' Jess let her glance catch the boy's eyes before she looked back to Dan. 'And I organised babysitting before we got here.'

Jess had got one lady to look after Dan's children and Ella, and the other to care for her day-care children until further notice.

The nurse stepped forward. 'I'm going to have to ask you to leave now.' She looked at Jess. 'You can come back to check on him this evening. He needs to rest.'

'We have to go, Dan.' Jess didn't want to leave his side.

Dan nodded and caught his son's gaze again. 'Be fine, Luke.' His expression as he turned away showed he didn't believe this and Jess's heart lurched again.

Dan *had* to be fine!

The nurse ushered them out with kind efficiency whether they wanted to go or not.

When Jess got out into the reception area, she went straight to the desk. 'The nurse has explained a little of Dan's condition but I would really like to speak with the doctor as well, and if anything else happens I want to be notified immediately.'

'Of course.' The receptionist took details from Jess and gestured behind them. 'Take a seat. Doctor will be out to see you as soon as he can manage.'

They sat. They waited again. Should she send Luke away while she learned all of what had happened to Dan? 'It might be better if you leave me to speak with the doctor, Luke.'

'Please. Let me stay with you. If anything's— I'd rather...'

'All right, Luke.' One glance at his set face and Jess put the idea of shielding him out of her mind. She might not feel that Luke was old enough or mature enough to have to deal with something like this, particularly after losing his mother as he had, but it was happening anyway and keeping him in the dark about any of it wasn't going to help him.

Finally the doctor came out and addressed Jess. 'You're the partner?'

'Yes. Jessica Baker.' Jess gestured to Luke. 'This is Dan's eldest son.'

'Right. Well, the nurse has explained that we believe Dan's had a transient ischaemic attack.'

'And that Dad won't have lasting symptoms from it,' Luke put in.

'That's usually correct though there can be permanent damage to the brain, but in the case of your father we're not concerned that there'll be anything nasty.' The man drew a breath before he went on. 'For now we've run some tests and will be conducting some further tests to determine what caused the TIA. He'll also be seen by a neurologist, and once we know where we're up to we'll be putting Dan on a plan to do everything we can to ensure that this remains an isolated, one-off incident.'

But that wasn't something that could be guaranteed? 'If it happened again—?'

'It would most likely be a more serious event than this one.' The doctor went on to delve into various things that could cause a TIA. 'Dan's already let us know that he's probably getting too much salt in his diet, and not exercising enough. We'll see what else turns up as the result of our tests and what the neurologist thinks when he sees him.'

Until that moment, Jess hadn't fully let the seriousness of Dan's situation sink in. 'He's not old, he's healthy, even if he does eat too many packets of crisps and things.' The words blurted from her, but even as she said them her thoughts turned to what he'd been through in the past four years.

To him working so hard to get his family in a position where he could move them out of the city. Working mostly from home so he could care for the children full-time by himself, be fully responsible for them.

Had Dan even realised how much pressure he'd been putting on himself all the time? How much had he pushed down inside himself while he tried to be Superman to his family? Had that contributed?

'Why don't you go home, get some rest and give us a call this afternoon?' The doctor laid a hand briefly on Jess's arm. 'The best thing for our patient now is to rest, and I'm guessing that knowing things are under control at home will help with that. He was worried about you, and about his children.'

'I'll take care of everyone!' Tears tried to sting the backs of Jess's eyes at the thought of Dan worrying even for a minute about her in the middle of this.

She thanked the doctor and she and Luke made the trip back home.

'Jess—I'm…sorry for being…for not being nice to you.' Luke's low words stopped her before she could get out of the car when they arrived. 'It's just that Dad…'

'I know, Luke.'

'But you really care about him, don't you?' Luke swallowed hard. 'That way, I mean.'

'Yes.' Jess couldn't see the point of trying to hide something that Luke had recognised long ago. 'I do. But he doesn't—'

He didn't care about her in the same way. She couldn't choke the words out.

And she wasn't sure if Luke heard her, because the others had rushed outside all asking questions at once.

Jess helped Luke answer those questions, and counted

the hours until she could go back to the hospital and see Dan again. She needed to see for herself that he truly was going to be okay.

The day dragged. Finally Jess was able to go back to the hospital. She took sleepwear for Dan, toiletries and anything else she felt he might use once he was allowed out of the intensive care unit.

The intimacy of packing for him didn't escape her, but now wasn't the time to dwell on those feelings. Jess needed to feel she was doing something for him.

'Is he truly doing okay?' Jess asked the duty nurse as she entered the intensive care unit. 'I phoned several times today and they said there hadn't been any more problems, but—'

'He's as well as we can hope.' This was a different nurse. She was brisk and not inclined to enter into any kind of dialogue. 'You can have five minutes with the patient and then you'll have to leave.' She turned her back to attend to one of the other patients.

Jess moved to Dan's bedside. His eyes were closed and his face looked drawn and pale. Her heart stumbled with fear and longing to tell him how much she loved him, to beg him to stick around, to not let anything happen that would take him from her, but she didn't have the right to those words with Dan. She didn't have the right to any of it.

'Jess. You're here.' Did his voice hold a hint of tenderness?

She searched his eyes. The face that she had come to know and love as she'd cared for his children.

That was what would be on Dan's mind. His babies, not his baby*sitter.*

'I'm here, Dan.' She clasped his hand because didn't

they say that contact was healing? Jess pushed aside the thought that she was looking for healing for her own fears, too. 'The children are fine. They've been worried about you but I got a good sitter for as long as it's needed, and another one for my other day-care children. It's all taken care of.' Her voice turned husky as she pushed the rest of the words out. 'All you have to do is...get better.'

And not die on her. That was Jess's deepest fear. Luke's, too. The knowledge of that was what had pulled them together today, but it was a temporary fix. It didn't mean Luke would truly accept Jess, and Dan wasn't about to ask him to anyway.

'The doctors say I was lucky this time.' His fingers curled around hers. 'I'm worried about the children, Jess. Adele and Clive...love them, but they have their own lives. The kids already lost their mother. They need me.'

The raw honesty of Dan's words, of his fears for his family, wrapped around Jess's tender heart and squeezed. She forced her emotion back, couldn't let it out. Not now. She had to be strong for him. So that he could go on being strong for himself. 'You're going to recover, Dan. The doctors will tell you what you need to do to avoid—'

'A worse episode?' He swallowed. 'They've made it quite clear that's what I could expect if it happened a second time.'

She had known that, but it still struck fear even deeper into her heart to hear him say it. 'Dan. Please... stay well, get better and...stay well.'

For his children. He probably thought she meant for

the children and Jess did, but even deeper inside she meant for her. Would he please stay well for her?

Her fingers tightened around his hand, and his tightened too. Jess let herself lean forward then and wrapped her arms carefully around his shoulders. A sob tried to break free and she bit it back but for a moment she clung to him and every fear and uncertainty in her own life and now in his combined together into a deep well inside her. Dan's life was the only thing that would help her. Dan living, day in and day out, well and healthy and not under threat of being lost to her for ever.

Oh, Jess understood the fears of his children only too well, because they were deep inside her too.

The nurse bustled over to take Dan's readings, and told Jess she had to go. Jess got one last look at his face, murmured his name and the promise that she would be back in the morning.

'Have—have a good night, Dan. I'll see you in the morning.' She needed to hear the words, even if she spoke them aloud herself. She *would* see Dan in the morning.

And Jess did, and visited him again that afternoon, and by the afternoon of the next day he'd been transferred to a normal ward and was able to have a visit from his children though they had to take turns going in two at a time.

Dan was starting to look better. But his concerns about the future remained in the backs of his eyes, and remained deep within Jess as well.

She heard from Dan's solicitor that she had no grounds to fight the situation with her cottage.

On the fifth day the doctor let Dan go home. Two days later Jess got a notice that her cottage would be auctioned one month from that day. She'd handed over care of her other day-charges to one of those two older women who'd helped out during Dan's hospitalisation.

At least she had a month to take care of Dan and to figure out what to do about accommodation for her and Ella. She'd heard from Ella's grandparents again, but hadn't been able to give them much more than a quick hello on the phone as she'd explained that her employer was sick in the hospital, though she did let them know that the auction date for the cottage had been set.

While Jess's heart ached constantly for Dan, for reassurance that he couldn't give her, to find some way to *make it* that he never got sick again, she focused on him and the children, and seeing to their needs. She slept at the house and expected everyone to understand, and they seemed to. Even Luke appeared grateful for her constant presence, and Jess was very careful, after her initial raw, unguarded fear for Dan, to try to be as professional as possible in front of all the children.

The next evening when the children were all in bed, Dan asked her to come out on the veranda with him. It reminded Jess of another night, of her first kiss with him on a swing seat. Jess had memories, too, of making love with Dan in his bed in his room here in the house. But she couldn't afford to torture herself with those memories.

She had a lot of needs when it came to him, but, for now, she could only do all she could to help with his recovery.

Dan watched expressions chase themselves across her face and gave thanks that he'd escaped this time with what was commonly called a mini stroke. The functional difficulties it had caused were gone. He was on doctor's orders about reducing salt in his diet, going for a walk every day, and there was a medication he had to take for a while until they felt it was safe for him to stop using it.

'I got off lightly this time.' He'd ended up facing his mortality anyway, and he needed to talk to Jess about it. Dan had done nothing but think of what could have happened if it had been worse. What if it had maimed him for life? Made it impossible for him to work? Or killed him? That was the one that worried Dan the most.

'You did get off lightly, Dan.' She drew a shaky breath.

As he searched her face beneath the veranda light where they stood side by side at the railing, Dan saw the stress and strain that Jess had been through since he called her on the phone that morning stamped across her face. 'I'm sorry it was hard on you, too, and I appreciate everything you did to look after the family.'

'Adele and Clive would have been here in a minute if you'd let them.' Jess turned to search his face. 'Your sister loves you and the children very much.'

'I know it.' He blew out a breath. 'She's in the early stages of pregnancy. They weren't planning to have any children, and she's a little older than is probably optimal. She's going to need to look after herself and—'

'Avoid stress? That's what I want you to do, too, Dan.' But she nodded to show she agreed with him.

'Jess, I'm going to do everything I can to try to make sure this isn't repeated, but I can't guarantee it.'

'I don't want that to happen to you again.' Her distress was real, and deep.

Dan's heart clenched. 'If something happens to me—'

'It won't! And I'll stay, Dan. I'll help for as long as

you want.' Jess sucked up a breath. 'I don't need to find other work until…you don't need me any more.'

Her generosity humbled him. Her willingness to make her life work around his so she could help him… Well, Dan had a request that would be asking her to do even more of that. 'I want to ask you something, to put a suggestion to you that I hope might be of benefit to both of us in the end.'

Dan had thought and thought about it until he made the decision to ask her. He needed this reassurance if Jess could be prepared to give it. Needed it so he could know his children would be secure. That need had been all consuming for Dan since he suffered the TIA.

'What is it that you want to ask, Dan?' Jess frowned.

'I need to know my children will be in a secure situation if anything does happen to me.' When she would have protested again, he held up his hand. 'I'm not looking for that to happen. I want to live a long, healthy life and if I get to have any say in it that's exactly what's going to happen. But I can't control fate. This mini stroke made that abundantly clear to me. I want to get my children into the most secure position that I can, and I've come to realise that relying only on myself to care for them and be there for them has been rather arrogant of me. I've assumed things that I can't control.'

'Life is like that.' Jess's mouth tightened. 'There have been things in my life, too, that I haven't been able to control. They've just happened whether I felt ready for them or not.'

'Luke told me you got notice that your cottage is going to auction a month from now.' He said it gently because he knew that had to have cut Jess deeply.

Her shoulders tightened. 'I wasn't going to trouble you by telling you about that.'

'I wish you had.' He laid his hand over hers where it rested on the veranda railing. 'It's not fair for you to be dealing with the fallout of my visit to hospital, and trying to keep all your own worries away from me.'

And that brought Dan to the rest of what he wanted to say to her. Behind them he heard the faintest rustle of sound—a breeze picking up along the veranda?

Somehow it felt right to be holding Jess's hand as he said these words. Dan didn't love her but there were other things he could offer and maybe those would be enough?

'You need a home and security, Jess, and I need security for my children so I can stop worrying about them ending up without a parent.' His words were low, quiet, but spoken with conviction just the same. 'You and I—there's an attraction between us and I like to think there's at least some affection, too.'

Jess listened to Dan struggling through each word and her heart lodged very firmly in her throat because what was he saying? 'I don't understand, Dan.' She didn't. All she could comprehend was his hand over hers, how much she loved him, the need to keep him safe and the knowledge that Dan was right and she couldn't guarantee anything. Jess hated that fact.

'Will you marry me, Jess?' Dan's words were stronger as he asked the question, but then they quietened again. 'Help me to feel that I've made my children as secure as possible, and ensure security for you and Ella at the same time?' He turned her hand into his and searched her eyes, and his words became even quieter. 'I would do everything possible to be a good husband to you. I'd hope for a normal relationship between us. I realise there's not love, but—'

'What are you doing, Dad? You can't marry her! I don't want her in our lives like that. She's *not Mum!*' The words burst out from behind them.

Jess gasped and turned.

Dan turned, too.

But Luke had already disappeared back into the house with only the thunder of his feet as he ran up the stairs echoing behind him.

'I'll talk to him, Jess. The two of you were getting on so much better, I thought—'

That it had all been fixed? That Luke had calmed down and now wouldn't mind if Dan wanted to ask such a thing of Jess?

He was asking her to provide added security for his children, but to Luke that must sound as though Dan were trying to replace his mother. But Dan was very far from according Jess the place of a beloved wife in his heart.

'What you want is a practical arrangement.' Jess forced the words out. She made herself hold his gaze and not let him see for one moment how much his offer had built her hopes and devastated her, all at once. 'It's a big thing to ask and there *is* Luke to consider. He obviously feels passionately about this issue, maybe enough that you'll never get him to change his mind about me. I—I'll need time to think, and you will need to speak to him, Dan, and explain...that you don't...love me. That it's not about that.'

The words crushed her, but she forced them out anyway.

'I know you need time, Jess, and I will speak to Luke.'

Dan drew a breath. 'It is a big issue for all concerned but it is an arrangement I believe could be helpful to all of us.'

It was bigger than Dan could know, because Jess loved him. All that he'd said was true, but there was one key thing that he didn't understand. While he would be trying to be a good husband and feeling affection for her, Jess would be madly and deeply in love with him.

That wasn't an even situation, and Jess didn't know if she could take it on. Security for her and Ella, yes, that was a factor that mattered to her and she appreciated Dan was trying to offer something that would benefit everyone. How could she say no when he needed this to feel safe, and to make sure his children were safe?

Jess loved all of them, prickly Luke included, though obviously she loved Dan very differently.

Heart, soul, mind, body and spirit.

The words pushed through her, came from deep inside her. And suddenly she couldn't stand here any longer, looking into his eyes and…loving him with everything she had. 'I—I need to go to bed, Dan. I'll think, and you might change your mind once you speak to Luke—'

'It won't happen, Jess.'

Because there was no comparison to Rebecca, and Dan would help his son understand that?

Jess whirled away before he could see the emotions on her face. She got to her bedroom, closed the door, and then and only then did she allow all of what she was feeling to come.

Jess was being offered what her heart most desired, a future with Dan, but without the love. With Ella's father, she might have made a huge mistake in trusting him, but at least in the beginning she had truly believed she loved him. That love hadn't been returned in the same measure, any more than Dan's would be.

Dan should be asking Jess to marry him because he loved her. She had a right to expect that. But it was still true that it would solve problems for both of them.

And just to confuse things for her further, Jess now had Ella's grandparents, who wanted to be part of her daughter's life.

Which was truly wonderful.

It was, but where did this all leave Jess?

CHAPTER FOURTEEN

'AND SO YOU SEE, DEAR, Lang Fielder was planning the whole time to get your property off you cheaply. He intended to knock it down along with the three others he already owns in this area and have enough money to pay for the mansion he wants to build on the site.' George Rosche was again seated in Jess's kitchen in the cottage. 'All it took was for him to move into that position at the council and get control of the situation with the notices about the back rates on your home.'

Dalia sat beside George.

Ella was tottering about the kitchen showing off her new walking skills to both grandparents.

And Jess was sitting like a stunned fish, trying to comprehend what had just been said to her.

George and Dalia had phoned and asked her to see them urgently. Dan was well enough for Jess to decide to meet them here at her cottage. Maybe while she was absent Dan would take the chance to speak to Luke about asking Jess to marry him.

'Jess, the man had no right to let that situation go for the length of time that he did and not inform you of what was happening. He had his own agenda from the start.' Dalia's fury on Jess's behalf warmed her heart.

Dalia glanced at her husband and said in a rush, 'Well, it made us cross and I do hope you understand, dear. We're Ella's grandparents and it's clear to us that you're a very special girl. You shouldn't have been treated the way you were by our son.'

'Just tell her,' George put in.

Dalia drew a breath. 'We paid off the back rates and interest so that nasty man couldn't go ahead with his plans. The auction is cancelled. The cottage is yours now fair and square.'

'We could easily afford it, so don't worry about that.' George nodded. 'But you should still bring this man's actions to the attention of council's management. He should be sacked for such underhanded dealings. We'll be more than happy to help you with that, if you want.' He made a hurrumph of sound. 'It will serve the man right, too.'

'The times that I went to the council and had to practically beg to see him, and he encouraged me to pay what I could off the debt knowing that he planned to buy the cottage out from under me for practically nothing.' Jess spoke the words in shock and anger. 'I will speak to management at the council.'

She searched both their faces before she added almost uncertainly, 'If you really wouldn't mind, the added support while I do that—'

'We would like to help you.' George said it quietly but his expression was completely sincere.

Jess almost didn't know how to respond to their supportiveness. She was used to standing alone, to having no choice but to make her own way, her own decisions. What would it be like if she married Dan? Would he be planning for them to support one another in that way? Could Jess live with that, a gift of support but no love?

She needed to figure out the answer.

But first she had to deal with this. And as that thought came Jess fully comprehended what the couple had done. 'George, Dalia, thank you for what you've done for me.' They'd been so generous! 'I—I'll need to pay that money back to you. It's yours and in the end you don't owe me anything.'

'We know that's how you feel about us, dear.' Dalia leaned forward to pat Jess's hand where it rested on the table. 'But you were struggling, and that situation wasn't right. It wasn't a difficult thing for us. Please, just accept it? There are no strings attached of any kind. We don't want you to feel pressured, even to let us be part of Ella's and your life, though we would really love that. Peter is our only child and, well, we never thought there'd be a grandchild or a lovely young woman who is her mother.'

They talked for a while longer. And Jess did accept the gift, but more importantly made it very clear that she welcomed their involvement in Ella's life and always would. She swallowed. 'Family isn't something that I've had much of for myself and if Ella can have that with you, and a little for me too, well, I want it.'

With that decided, George asked if it might not be best to go to the council now and confront the issue of Lang Fielder's behaviour.

Jess drew a deep breath and nodded. This had to be done and the sooner the better. They took separate cars and made their way there. When the clerk tried to refuse to allow them to see the manager, Jess threw her shoulders back. 'We're not leaving until this is done.'

They were ushered into the manager's office. Jess drew a deep breath and explained the situation. The manager was clearly shocked and blustered somewhat. Jess stuck her chin out. 'I want you to call Lang Fielder in here. Ask him what he was planning to do and how he intended to go about it.'

The manager took the time to access council records before he called the other man in. Once he did, he spread out the evidence before him and looked at Lang. 'I thought I knew you, Fielder, but clearly I didn't. If this is the kind of illegal activity you can carry on in your place of work, I want no part of you. Your position here is terminated, effective immediately.'

'You can't do that. I'll file a complaint—'

'And while you're doing that, I'll be investigating every other matter that you've handled since you started work here.' The manager stared Lang down. 'You should hope there won't be formal charges either from the council or from Miss Baker.'

Lang glared back, and after a long moment he stalked to the office door and yanked it open. 'You haven't heard the end of this.'

It was an empty threat and the manager said as much once he closed the door behind Lang and phoned through to staff to let them know the situation so they could see Lang safely off the premises.

The manager shook his head, apologised again to Jess, and after some further discussion in which he assured her the issue would be fully dealt with they were ushered out.

'Thank you.' As they stood outside Jess impulsively hugged the older couple.

George and Dalia said their goodbyes and left. Jess put Ella into the car and drove to Dan's.

She now truly owned her cottage and it couldn't be taken from her. There was security in that, and kindness from Ella's grandparents. More than that, they wanted to be part of Ella's life and they wanted to be part of *Jess's* life, too.

'Family, Ella,' Jess murmured quietly. 'We've been given some family who—really want us.'

The last words were a little choked, and Jess quickly cleared her throat. Dan had also asked her to be part of his family. She needed to give him her answer. Why couldn't she just go to him and say yes? Wasn't that in everyone's best interests?

The situation has changed now that you own the cottage outright.

But Dan's need to make his children secure hadn't changed, and his wish to make Jess his wife hadn't changed. She would have the chance to love him, even if he didn't love her back…

'Time to go inside, Ella. We at least need to find out whether Dan's spoken with Luke, and how that went.'

'Jess. I hope you had enough time with Ella's grandparents.' Dan searched Jess's face.

He wasn't sure what had happened but whatever it was, he would try to help. He was waiting for her answer to his proposal. He hadn't found that waiting period easy but he respected her need to think. He hadn't even known that Ella's grandparents wanted to start a relationship so they could get to know their grandchild until Jess asked him for some time off this morning.

'Dan, did you speak with Luke?'

There was something in Jess's tone that made him immediately tense.

'I did.' Dan had spoken to his son, explained that he wasn't trying to replace Rebecca in any of their lives.

Luke had cried a little. Dan wished he'd realised what was buried within his son. 'I didn't know he'd held on to a lot of the pain from the loss of his mother. He… let some of it out with me, and I think over time he'll continue that process.'

'That's good, Dan.' Jess was happy to know that he had got to the bottom of Luke's pain and that his son looked as though he could start to go forward now.

'He won't stand in the way, Jess, if we…'

If they married. If they tried to become firm friends who would help one another through life and with the various children.

Jess nodded.

'I need to tell you about Ella's grandparents.' She sought for the right words and in the end just told him, as concisely as she could, what had happened about the cottage and Lang Fielder's dismissal from the council. 'I own my cottage now, fair and square. George and Dalia have been very generous. Most of all, even more than the money, I value that they cared enough to help me, and to help me get justice for the way Lang Fielder tricked me and tried to cheat me.'

Dan listened to Jess's words. There was hurt hiding underneath her anger over Councillor Fielder's behaviour. He could see that and as he looked into her eyes and felt all her pain as though it were his own Dan realised there were things he'd been holding back from letting himself acknowledge. He'd spoken to Luke and said all the words that he'd felt were the right ones, but even then he hadn't realised…

'My money worries are over, Dan.' Jess said it as though the fact was only beginning to sink in for her. At her feet, Ella started to grizzle, and Jess picked her up and cuddled her and the little girl tucked her head into her mother's neck.

Jess went on. 'The cottage is secure thanks to Ella's grandparents, the parents of Peter Rosche. Too bad if Peter made me sign something saying I'd never tell his name. He broke his end of the bargain and his parents came and found me and asked to be part of Ella's life and wanted me as well anyway!'

'That's really special news, Jess.' He meant that.

'I would never have let George and Dalia pay off the money owed to the council if I'd known what they planned to do.' She chewed her lip.

Ella decided she'd had enough cuddles and wriggled. Jess set her down and she went straight to play with a set of large blocks on the floor.

'But they did it anyway.' They probably felt guilty for the way their son had treated her. Not their fault, but Dan would have been the same. 'It sounds as though they really needed to do that for you, Jess, as much as it was a help to you.'

And he couldn't help asking himself how this would impact on her answer to him.

She didn't need him now. Not the way she had before Ella's grandparents came along.

But he…needed her.

His heart squeezed. For a moment he felt panicked, wondered if he was about to repeat the mini stroke.

But it hadn't felt like this.

And as he took a breath he realised *why* his heart had just felt as though someone had locked a fist around it. He didn't want to lose Jess. He wanted her to agree to be his wife. For his children, for security. But most of all Dan wanted that for himself. It was the one part of it that he had failed to see.

He'd…fallen in love with Jess.

Dan hadn't believed he could ever do that again. He'd thought all of his love had been for Rebecca. He had fallen for Jess differently, but just as deeply as he'd loved his wife. No wonder he hadn't known exactly how to explain things to Luke. Dan hadn't understood his own feelings.

'Dan, I have to give you my answer. I don't want you to have to wait any longer.'

At her words, he sought her gaze and realised he could have made a complete mess of all of this. He'd asked her to marry him for worthy reasons, but those reasons hadn't allowed for how Jess might feel emotionally about him, for the fact that he loved her and needed to know if she could love him in return.

Could he convince Jess to love him in the way that he loved her? Could he help her to trust him, even though Peter Rosche had hurt her? Even though Dan was older? And though he'd been so slow to recognise his feelings prior to making that proposal? Could Dan help his children to accept that he loved Jess and needed her to be in his life?

Dan needed to speak to his children and he needed to do his proposal to Jess over, and this time do it properly. He realised that, as well as Luke needing to adjust, and maybe the others too, though he knew they all had a lot of affection for Jess already, *he* had to fully let go of Rebecca. He should have done it a long time ago. He needed to take this final step.

'Jess, would you let me speak to you about that tonight? After the children have gone to bed?' He wanted to take the time to give her something special for when he asked those words a second time.

Rob and Daisy started squabbling outside on the veranda and Jess got up to go and investigate. 'I guess that would be a better time.'

As she went about her work in the home Dan went into his den and picked up the phone so he could start making his plans for the night.

'You and the children were quiet when you got back after your walk.' Jess tried to keep the nervous edge out of her tone.

Dan had taken the children for a walk on the property a few hours ago. He'd had something in a carry bag with him, and a shovel. They'd been gone quite a while. When they got back, they had all seemed subdued, surprised, emotional somehow…

And then Mary had hesitated, run forward and hugged Jess around the knees and skittered off again. Daisy had tipped her head on the side and looked at Jess and then at Ella and she'd seemed somehow to make a decision. She'd given a nod of her head and taken Annapolly by the hand and they'd gone inside.

Rob had looked at Jess, too, and then looked away as though embarrassed and she thought he might have had evidence of earlier tears on his face.

And Luke…

One glance at Luke's face had told her the boy had been through something deeply emotional. If Dan had spoken to them all about marrying her and this was the reaction—

But then Luke had wrapped his arms around his father's middle and hugged him hard and let out a deep sigh as though a weight had lifted from his shoulders and then he, too, had gone inside.

Now it was just Jess and Dan and it was evening. Ella was sleeping in the travel cot. Dan had asked Jess to go home and change into something pretty and meet him back here. He was getting the other caregiver in to stay with the children, and he and Jess were going…out, but some place quite close.

Jess was mystified, a little uneasy, trying not to wonder just what Dan was up to and why she would need to wear a nice dress to discuss the future. Dan had already made what he wanted from her quite clear. Did he need to call it all off because his children hadn't been able to accept the idea?

But she dressed in her pretty dress, and Dan—Dan wore black dress trousers and shoes and a crisp pale green shirt.

Jess glanced at her yellow sundress with the big red and orange flowers splashed all over it. 'I hope I'm dressed appropriately for the occasion.' The dress had a square neckline and flared about her knees. She'd teamed it with her row of wooden bangles and the chunky wooden necklace and just a little understated make-up.

'You look perfect for where we're going.' Dan crooked his elbow and gave a half smile.

If Jess hadn't known him so well she might have missed the edge of tension beneath that smile. But she did know him, and she did see it. She linked her hand through his arm and he…led her to the tree cubby house!

'Shall we, Jess? It seems to be the right place for this discussion.'

Somehow they were at the top of the ladder and inside the space, and oh—

'It's beautiful.' The whole place was decorated with bouquets of flowers—store-bought ones that must have cost him a fortune! There was a picnic blanket on the floor again, scatter cushions to lean on. A bucket with… wine in it? Two beautiful fluted glasses and a platter of colourful fruit pieces.

Her heart started to pump hard. What was he doing?

Dan took her hand and led her to the picnic blanket. 'Shall we sit, Jess?'

His hand shook slightly as he poured the wine and handed her one of the flutes.

'You didn't have to do this.' She chose a grape from the platter and popped it into her mouth. The sweet taste blended with the taste of wine on her tongue. 'I know that what you offered, well, that it isn't all about romance really or…feelings, and I'd already made up my mind to tell you…but of course if the children—'

'I'm hoping that I might be able to start all that over, Jess.' He set down his wineglass. He'd barely taken a sip.

All she knew was that she loved him and she was prepared to take the risk of marrying him and hope that his affection for her would be enough. She couldn't think of living life without seeing him. If this gave her the opportunity to be with him then Jess wanted to take that chance. And it *seemed* as though he wasn't trying to tell her that he'd changed his mind after speaking with his children. 'You're not withdrawing—?'

If he did she would find a way to handle it. She would. Jess didn't know how, but she was strong. She'd do it if she had to.

'I asked you to marry me primarily to give security to my children, and to you.' He took her hand in his again and his fingers gently stroked over hers.

'I know, and even without me needing that help any more, what you asked for the children was very valid.' Jess drew a breath. 'I care about them, Dan. They've all found their way into my heart.'

Being with Dan would give Jess and Ella a sense of family, too, something Jess had never expected to have. She'd gained grandparents for Ella, and all this. She was determined to appreciate it. 'Ella will have siblings to love and grow up with. I really value that.'

'And I value you, Jess.' He drew a breath. 'You're generous and giving and kind. I love your beautiful clothes and accessories that are so much a part of who you are. I love that you're so determined about life and how cheerful you are even when things are tough.'

'I'm not always cheerful.' She had her moments, and she remembered one such, just after she'd found out about the auction on the cottage. 'Well, you've seen that.'

'I've seen a lot of different parts of you, Jess.' His fingers curled around hers and his voice deepened. 'I took the children today and we went to that big old tree down at the end of the property.'

'So you could talk to them about the possibility of marrying me?'

'Yes. And we took Rebecca's ashes and buried them beneath the tree.'

'Oh, Dan.' Emotion clogged her throat. 'That can't have been easy.'

'It was something that we all needed, I think.' He smiled and there was only peace on his face as he went on. 'I hadn't totally let go, Jess. I'd been holding on to how much I'd loved Rebecca so that I wouldn't have to face the risk of fully living my life again. I told myself, because the children had grieved and I'd helped them and time had passed, that I'd done all I had to as well, but that wasn't true.'

'You've done a wonderful job with the children, Dan.' Her fingers squeezed right back around his. 'And you're not to blame for loving your wife so much that you knew you could never love again like that. I understand.'

Dan drew closer to her until they were both leaning back on the cushions and his shoulder was brushing hers. Their hands were still intertwined. 'I thought that was what I knew, but, Jess…I did fall in love again. I fell deeply, but I hadn't realised what was happening until I made a proposal for good reasons, but not for the *right* reasons, and Luke carried on about it and you said you'd work out your answer.

'When you came in this morning and told me that Ella's paternal grandparents had paid off the money owed on your cottage, I knew you didn't *need* me for security.' His mouth softened. 'It was then that I realised *I needed you* for myself, because I was in love with you. I hoped that I hadn't messed everything up by asking you to marry me for those other reasons.'

'Oh, Dan.' Could she believe what she was hearing? Her heart had hoped so desperately for Dan to love her but she hadn't expected it. 'But there *is* Luke. I don't want to hurt him, Dan.'

'And I…love you for that.' Dan drew a breath. 'Luke saw feelings in me towards you that I hadn't recognised myself for what they were. Today I admitted everything to him and we talked openly about the loss of his mother, all of it. I think Luke will really be able to fully heal now, and he does understand that I care for you because you're you. It's no reflection on that past relationship.'

Dan's gaze held hers and his expression became very serious. 'I learned that I can love deeply, twice over, Jess. I was worried for the security of my children. That stopped me from recognising and accepting what I was feeling towards you. I can't guarantee anything in life, but I want the chance to love you with all my heart. I hope for you and I to have very long lives together.'

'I was going to say yes, Dan.' She admitted it as love spread through her heart, too, set free finally by his words. 'I fell in love with you the night that we made love. I *realised it* the next morning when Ella walked to you. When you asked me to marry you I wasn't sure what I should say. I wanted to be with you, but I was afraid that it might hurt too much to love you and not be loved in the same way in return. I…went through that with Peter.'

'You would have said yes for the children's sakes.'

'For all of us, really, but only if you'd been able to assure me you felt confident we could get Luke into a better frame of mind about it all.' Jess could understand why people would make choices to keep their children safe. 'I love that about you, Dan. I've admired your commitment to your family from the first day we met.'

'I fell in love with all of you.' He ran his fingers over

the bangles on her arm until they clanked together. 'The way you came to me and offered help even in the face of your own problems. Your care of the children. Your love for your daughter.'

'I'm hopeful that I can build a good relationship with Ella's grandparents.'

'I think you're already well on the way to that, and, if you give me the chance, I'll support it every step of the way.' Dan blew out a breath and then searched her face. 'Will you marry me, Jess? Because I love you and need you in my life?'

'I love you and need you too. You have my whole heart.' Oh, how good it felt to say those words. She was finally able to open all of her heart and give it to this man, and know that it would be safe with him. 'Yes, I will marry you. I will love you, and love your children, and spend the rest of my life enjoying every aspect of all of you.'

'Thank you.' He kissed her then, a deep, reverent kiss that held all of his love, and allowed Jess to give all of her love back to him.

When they finally drew apart, Dan's expression sobered. 'I can't guarantee—with what happened with that mini stroke—'

'I know.' Jess understood the concerns only too well. She would carry them buried in the back of her heart probably for a long time. 'You're doing all the right things to look after yourself and put yourself in the best place to avoid a repeat of that.'

It was all Jess could ask. All that Dan could ask of life, as well. 'You're right, Dan. There are things that happen that we can't control. I will hope and pray for your health and the chance to love you long into the future.' And then she smiled. 'And I'll control your salt intake whether you like it or not. No more stashes of salty snacks for you.'

'I know. I'll behave.' His laugh was rich and full of promise. He wrapped his arms around her while he was still chuckling. She felt the vibrations of his humour as he held her, and she smiled too.

'I'd like to stay out here and make love to you, Jess.' He said it with longing in his tone, but also with a degree of resignation.

'But there are a bunch of children and a fill-in caregiver waiting inside for the outcome of this meeting?'

'Yes. I suspect that's how it's going to be.'

She got to her feet and held out her hand to him. 'It won't always be easy or smooth sailing, but I am excited about the future. Let's go inside and tell them the news.'

It hit her then, really, that she was about to become stepmother to five children and a hint of panic surfaced. 'Will they be okay with this? In the end, at least?'

He got to his feet and brought her hand to his lips. 'Like me, they know they are getting the joy and pleasure of being able to love a second time. I think even Luke will come to appreciate that deeply in the end.'

His words brought moisture to her eyes, but she blinked and let her joy come through. 'This is the start of the rest of all our lives together.'

'Marry me soon, Jessica.' Dan's voice softened with love and need. 'A wedding right here beside the house, with all the children as attendants. We'll make a beautiful setting for it. Ella and Daisy and Mary and Annapolly can wear pretty dresses and garlands of silk flowers. We'll make Rob and Luke dress in tuxedos. I want to see you in a beautiful bridal gown as I exchange rings with you.'

'Then we'll do all of that, Dan.' She whispered the words. 'I will marry you very soon right here.'

He swept her into his arms and kissed her again, and then led her out of the tree house and back inside so they could share their good news…